DARREN SHAN

THE LAKE OF SOULS

THE SAGA OF DARREN SHAN
BOOK 10

For:

Bas — you steer my vaparetto!

OBE's

(Order of the Bloody Entrails) to:
Nate — the Sheffield Shanster Seer!

Banshee Babes:
Zoë Clarke & Gillie Russell

Global Grotesques:
the Christopher Little Clan

DARREN SHAN

VAMPIRE DESTINY TRILOGY

THE SAGA OF DARREN SHAN

THE LAKE OF SOULS
LORD OF THE SHADOWS
SONS OF DESTINY

HarperCollins *Children's Books*

Hunt for Darren Shan on the web at
www.darrenshan.com

The Lake of Souls first published in Great Britain by HarperCollins *Children's Books* 2003
Lord of the Shadows first published in Great Britain by HarperCollins *Children's Books* 2004
Sons of Destiny first published in Great Britain by HarperCollins *Children's Books* 2004

First published in this three-in-one edition by Collins 2005

HarperCollins *Children's Books* is a division of HarperCollins*Publishers* Ltd,
77-85 Fulham Palace Road, Hammersmith,
London W6 8JB

The HarperCollins *Children's Books* website address is:
www.harpercollinschildrensbooks.co.uk

4

Text copyright © Darren Shan 2003, 2004

The author asserts the moral right to
be identified as the author of the work.

ISBN 0 00 717959 6

Printed and bound in England by
Clays Ltd, St Ives plc

VAMPIRE DESTINY TRILOGY

THE SAGA OF DARREN SHAN

THE SAGA OF DARREN SHAN

PROLOGUE

DEATH WAS on the cards that day, but would it be ours or the panther's?

Black panthers are really leopards. If you look closely, you can see faint spots blended into their fur. But trust me — unless it's in a zoo, you don't ever want to be that close to a panther! They're one of nature's greatest killers. They move silently and speedily. In a one-on-one fight they'll almost always come out on top. You can't outrun them, since they're faster than you, and you can't out-climb them, because they can climb too. The best thing is to stay out of their way completely, unless you're an experienced big game hunter and have come packing a rifle.

Harkat and I had never hunted a panther before, and our best weapons were a few stone knives and a long, round-ended stick that served as a club. Yet there we were, on the edge of a pit which we'd dug the day before, watching a deer we'd captured and were using as bait, waiting for a panther.

We'd been there for hours, hidden in a bush, clutching our humble weapons close to our sides, when I spotted something long and black through the cover of the surrounding trees. A whiskered nose stuck out from around a tree and sniffed the air testingly — the panther. I nudged Harkat gently and we watched it, holding our breath, stiff with fright. After a few seconds the panther turned and padded away, back into the gloom of the jungle.

Harkat and I discussed the panther's retreat in whispers. I thought the panther had sensed a trap and wouldn't return. Harkat disagreed. He said it would come back. If we withdrew further, it might advance fully the next time. So we wriggled backwards, not stopping until we were almost at the end of the long stretch of bush. From here we could only vaguely see the deer.

A couple of hours passed. We said nothing. I was about to break the silence and suggest we were wasting our time, when I heard a large animal moving. The deer was jumping around wildly. There was a throaty growl. It came from the far side of the pit. That was great — if the panther attacked the deer from there, it might fall straight into our trap and be killed in the pit. Then we wouldn't have to fight it at all!

I heard twigs snap as the panther crept up on the deer. Then there was a loud snapping sound as a heavy body crashed through the covering over the pit and landed heavily on the stakes we'd set in the bottom. There was a ferocious howl, followed by silence.

Harkat slowly got to his feet and stared over the bush at the pit. I stood and stared with him. We glanced at each other. I said uncertainly, "It worked."

"You sound like you didn't … expect it to," Harkat grinned.

"I didn't," I laughed, and started towards the pit.

"Careful," Harkat warned. "It could still be alive."

Stepping in front of me, he moved off to the left and signalled for me to go right. Raising my knife, I circled away from Harkat, then we slowly closed on the pit from opposite directions.

Harkat was a few steps ahead of me, so he saw into the pit first. He stopped, confused. A couple of seconds later, I saw why. A body lay impaled on the stakes, blood dripping from its many puncture wounds. But it wasn't the body of a panther — it was a red baboon.

"I don't understand," I said. "That was a panther's growl, not a monkey's."

"But how did…" Harkat stopped and gasped. "The monkey's throat! It's been ripped open! The panther must—"

He got no further. There was a blur of movement in the upper branches of the tree closest to me. Whirling, I caught a very brief glimpse of a long, thick, pure black object flying through the air with outstretched claws and gaping jaws — then the panther was upon me, roaring triumphantly.

Death was on the cards that day.

CHAPTER ONE

Six months earlier.

THE WALK up the tunnels, coming off the back of our battle with the vampaneze, was slow and exhausting. We left Mr Crepsley's charred bones in the pit where he'd fallen. I'd meant to bury him, but I hadn't the heart for it. Steve's revelation — that he was the Lord of the Vampaneze — had floored me, and now nothing seemed to matter. My closest friend had been killed. My world had been torn asunder. I didn't care whether I lived or died.

Harkat and Debbie walked beside me, Vancha and Alice Burgess slightly in front. Debbie used to be my girlfriend, but now she was a grown woman, whereas I was stuck in the body of a teenager — the curse of being a half-vampire who only aged one year for every five that passed. Alice was a police chief inspector. Vancha had kidnapped her when we'd been surrounded by police. She and Debbie had taken part in the fight with the vampaneze. They'd both fought well. A shame it had been for nothing.

We'd told Alice and Debbie all about the War of the Scars. Vampires exist, but not the murderous monsters of myth. We don't kill when we feed. But other night creatures do — the vampaneze. They broke away from the vampires six hundred years ago. They always drain their victims dry. Their skin has turned purple over the centuries, and their eyes and fingernails are red.

For a long time there'd been peace between the two clans. That ended when the Lord of the Vampaneze emerged. This vampaneze leader was destined to lead them into war against the vampires and destroy us. But if we found and killed him before he became a full-vampaneze, the war would go our way instead.

Only three vampires could hunt for the Vampaneze Lord (according to a powerful meddler called Desmond Tiny, who could see into the future). Two were Vampire Princes, Vancha March and me. The other had been Mr Crepsley, the vampire who'd blooded me and been like a father to me. He'd faced the person we thought was the Vampaneze Lord earlier that night and killed him. But then Steve sent Mr Crepsley tumbling to his death in a pit of flame-tipped stakes — shortly before he let me know that the person Mr Crepsley killed was an impostor, and that Steve himself was the Vampaneze Lord.

It didn't seem possible that Mr Crepsley was dead. I kept expecting a tap on my shoulder, and the tall orange-haired vampire to be standing behind me when I turned, grinning wickedly, his long facial scar glinting as he held up a torch, asking where we thought we were going without him. But the tap never came. It couldn't. Mr Crepsley was dead. He'd never come back.

Part of me wanted to go mad with rage, seize a sword and storm off after Steve. I wanted to track him down and drive a stake through his rotten excuse for a heart. But Mr Crepsley had warned me not to devote myself to revenge. He said it would warp and destroy me if I gave in to it. I knew in my soul that there was unfinished business between Steve and me, that our paths would cross again. But for the time being I pushed him from my thoughts and mourned for Mr Crepsley.

Except I couldn't really mourn. Tears wouldn't come. As much as I wanted to howl and sob with grief, my eyes remained dry and steely. Inside, I was a broken, weeping wreck, but on the outside I was cold, calm and collected, as though I hadn't been affected by the vampire's death.

Ahead, Vancha and Alice came to a halt. The Prince looked back, his wide eyes red from crying. He looked pitiful in his animal skins, with his filthy bare feet and wild hair, like an overgrown, lost child. "We're almost at the surface," he croaked. "It's still day. Will we wait here for dark? If we're spotted..."

"Don't care," I mumbled.

"I don't want to stay here," Debbie sobbed. "These tunnels are cruel."

"And I have to inform my people that I'm alive," Alice said, then frowned and picked dried blood flecks from her pale white hair. "Though I don't know how I'm going to explain it to them!"

"Tell the truth," Vancha grunted.

The Chief Inspector grimaced. "Hardly! I'll have to think up some—" She stopped. A figure had appeared out of the darkness ahead of us, blocking the path.

Cursing, Vancha ripped loose a shuriken — throwing stars he kept strapped in belts around his chest — and prepared to launch it.

"Peace, Vancha," the stranger said, raising a hand. "I am here to help, not harm."

Vancha lowered his shuriken and muttered in disbelief, *"Evanna?"*

The woman ahead of us clicked her fingers and a torch flared into life overhead, revealing the ugly witch we'd travelled with earlier in the year, while we were searching for the Lord of the Vampaneze. She hadn't changed. Short thick muscles, long untidy hair, pointed ears, a tiny nose, one brown eye and one green (the colours kept shifting from left to right), hairy body, long sharp nails and yellow ropes tied tight around her body instead of clothes.

"What are you doing ... here?" Harkat asked, his large green eyes filled with suspicion — Evanna was a neutral in the War of the Scars, but could help or hinder those on either side, depending on her mood.

"I came to bid Larten's spirit farewell," the witch said. She was smiling.

"You don't look too cut up about it," I remarked without emotion.

She shrugged. "I foresaw his death many decades ago. I did my crying for him then."

"You knew he'd die?" Vancha growled.

"I wasn't certain, but I guessed he would perish," she said.

"Then you could have stopped it!"

"No," Evanna said. "Those with the ability to sense the currents of the future are forbidden to interfere. To save Larten, I'd have had to abandon the rules I live by, and if that happened, all chaos would break loose."

The witch stretched out a hand, and even though she was many metres away from Vancha, her fingers cupped his chin tenderly. "I was fond of Larten," she said softly. "I hoped I was wrong. But I couldn't take it upon myself to spare him. His fate wasn't mine to decide."

"Then whose was it?" Vancha snapped.

"His own," Evanna replied steadily. "*He* chose to hunt for the Lord of the Vampaneze, to enter the tunnels, to fight on the platform. He could have walked away from his responsibilities — but he chose not to."

Vancha glared at the witch a moment longer, then lowered his gaze. I saw fresh tears splash in the dust at his feet. "My apologies, Lady," he muttered. "I don't blame you. I'm just so fired up with hatred…"

"I know," the witch said, then studied the rest of us. "You must come with me. I have things to tell you, and I'd rather talk on the outside — the air here is rank with treachery and death. Will you spare me a few hours of your time?" She glanced at Alice Burgess. "I promise I won't keep you long."

Alice sniffed. "I guess a few hours can't make much of a difference."

Evanna looked at Harkat, Debbie, Vancha and me. We shared a glance, then nodded and followed the witch up the last stretch of the tunnels, leaving the darkness and the dead behind.

Evanna gave Vancha a thick deer hide to drape over his head and shoulders, to block out the rays of the sun. Trailing after the witch, we moved quickly through the streets. Evanna must have cast a spell to hide us, because people didn't notice us, despite our blood-stained faces and clothes. We ended up outside the city, in a small forest, where Evanna had prepared a camp amidst the trees. At her offer, we sat and tucked into the berries, roots and water she'd set out for us.

We ate silently. I found myself studying the witch, wondering why she was here — if she'd really come to say goodbye to Mr Crepsley, she'd have gone down to where his body lay in the pit. Evanna was Mr Tiny's daughter. He had created her by mixing the blood of a vampire with that of a wolf. Vampires and vampaneze were barren — we couldn't have children — but Evanna was supposed to be able to bear a child by a male of either clan. When we met her shortly after setting out to hunt the Vampaneze Lord, she'd confirmed Mr Tiny's prophecy — that we'd have four chances to kill the Lord — and added the warning that if we failed, two of us would die.

Vancha finished eating first, sat back and burped. "Speak," he snapped — he wasn't in the mood for formalities.

"You're wondering how many chances you've used up,"

Evanna said directly. "The answer is — three. The first was when you fought the vampaneze in the glade and let their Lord escape. The second, when you discovered Steve Leonard was a half-vampaneze and took him hostage — although you had several opportunities to kill him, they count as one. The third chance was when Larten faced him on the platform above the pit of stakes."

"That means we still have a shot at him!" Vancha hissed excitedly.

"Yes," Evanna said. "Once more the hunters will face the Vampaneze Lord, and on that occasion the future will be decided. But that confrontation will not come in the near future. Steve Leonard has withdrawn to plot anew. For now, you may relax."

The witch turned to me and her expression softened. "It might not lighten your load," she said kindly, "but Larten's soul has flown to Paradise. He died nobly and earned the reward of the righteous. He is at rest."

"I'd rather he was here," I said miserably, gazing at the leaves of an overhanging tree, waiting for tears which still wouldn't come.

"What about the rest of the vampaneze?" Alice asked. "Are any of them still in my city?"

Evanna shook her head. "All have fled."

"Will they return?" Alice asked, and by the glint in her eyes I saw she was half hoping they would, so she could settle a few scores.

"No." Evanna smiled. "But I think it's safe to say that you will run into them again."

"I'd better," Alice growled, and I knew she was thinking of Morgan James, an officer of hers who'd joined the vampets. They were human allies of the vampaneze, who shaved their heads, daubed blood around their eyes, sported V tattoos above their ears, and dressed in brown uniforms.

"Is the nightmare over then?" Debbie asked, wiping her dark cheeks clean. The teacher had fought like a tigress in the tunnels, but the events of the night had caught up with her and she was shivering helplessly.

"For you — for now," Evanna answered cryptically.

"What does that mean?" Debbie frowned.

"You and the Chief Inspector can choose to distance yourselves from the War of the Scars," Evanna said. "You can return to your ordinary lives and pretend this never happened. If you do, the vampaneze won't come after you again."

"Of course we'll return to our lives," Alice said. "What else can we do? We're not vampires. We don't have any further part to play in their war."

"Perhaps," Evanna said. "Or perhaps you'll think differently when you've had time to reconsider. You'll return to the city — you need time to reflect, and you have affairs to put in order — but whether or not you'll choose to stay..." Evanna's eyes flicked over Vancha, Harkat and me. "And where do you three wish to go?"

"I'm continuing after that monster, Leonard," Vancha said immediately.

"You may if you wish," Evanna shrugged, "but you'll be wasting your time and energy. Moreover, you will jeopardize your position. Although you are fated to confront him again, it's not written in stone — by pursuing him now, you might miss the final destined showdown."

Vancha cursed bitterly, then asked Evanna where she suggested he should go.

"Vampire Mountain," she said. "Your clan should be told about the Vampaneze Lord. They must not kill him themselves — that rule still applies — but they can scout for him and point you in the right direction."

Vancha nodded slowly. "I'll call a temporary end to the fighting and set everyone searching for him. I'll flit for Vampire Mountain as soon as night falls. Darren — are you and Harkat coming?"

I looked at my fellow Prince, then down at the hard brown earth of the forest floor. "No," I said softly. "I've had all I can take of vampires and vampaneze. I know I'm a Prince and have duties to attend to. But I feel like my head's about to explode. Mr Crepsley meant more to me than anything else. I need to get away from it all, maybe for a while — maybe for ever."

"It's a dangerous time to cut yourself off from those who care for you," Vancha said quietly.

"I can't help that," I sighed.

Vancha was troubled by my choice, but he accepted it. "I don't approve — a Prince should put the needs of his people before his own — but I understand. I'll explain it to the others. Nobody will trouble you." He cocked an eyebrow at Harkat. "I suppose you'll be going with him?"

Harkat lowered the mask from his mouth (air was poisonous to the grey-skinned Little People) and smiled thinly. "Of course." Mr Tiny had resurrected Harkat from the dead. Harkat didn't know who he used to be, but he believed he could find out by sticking with me.

"Where will you go?" Vancha asked. "I can find you using the Stone of Blood, but it'll be easier if I have a rough idea of where you're heading."

"I don't know," I said. "I'll just pick a direction and…" I stopped as a picture flashed through my thoughts, of circus vans, snake-boys and hammocks. "The Cirque Du Freak," I decided. "It's the nearest place outside Vampire Mountain that I can call home."

"A good choice," Evanna said, and by the way her lips lifted at the edges, I realized the witch had known all along that I'd choose to return to the Cirque.

We went our separate ways as the sun was setting, even though we hadn't slept and were ready to drop with exhaustion. Vancha departed first, on his long trek to Vampire Mountain. He said little when leaving, but hugged me hard and hissed in my ear, "Be brave!"

"You too," I whispered back.

"We'll kill Leonard next time," he vowed.

"Aye," I grinned weakly.

He turned and ran, hitting flitting speed seconds later, vanishing into the gloom of the dusk.

Debbie and Alice left next, to return to the city. Debbie asked me to stay with her, but I couldn't, not as things stood. I needed to be by myself for a while. She wept and clutched me close. "Will you come back later?" she asked.

"I'll try," I croaked.

"If he doesn't," Evanna said, "you can always go looking for him." She handed a folded-up piece of paper to Alice Burgess. "Hold on to that. Keep it closed. When the two of you decide upon your course, open it."

The Chief Inspector asked no questions, just tucked the paper away and waited for Debbie to join her. Debbie looked at me pleadingly. She wanted me to go with her – or ask her to come with me – but there was a huge ball of grief sitting cold and hard in my gut. I couldn't think of anything else right now.

"Take care," I said, turning aside and breaking eye contact.

"You too," she croaked, then sobbed loudly and stumbled away. With a quick "Goodbye", Alice hurried after her, and the two women slipped through the trees, back to the city, supporting one another as they went.

That left just me, Harkat and Evanna.

"Any idea where the Cirque's playing?" the witch asked. We shook our heads. "Then it's lucky that I do and am going there," she smiled. Standing between us, she looped her arms around my left arm and Harkat's right, and led us through the forest, away from the city and its underground caverns of death, back to where my voyage into the night first started — the Cirque Du Freak.

CHAPTER TWO

ALEXANDER RIBS was sleeping in a large tyre hanging from a tree. He always slept curled up — it kept his body supple and made it easier for him to twist and contort when he was performing. Normally he kept the tyre on a special stand in his caravan, but occasionally he'd drag it outside and sleep in the open. It was a cold night for sleeping outdoors — the middle of a wintry November — but he had a thick, fur-lined body-bag to keep the chill out.

As Alexander snored musically a young boy crept towards him, a cockroach in his right hand, with the intention of dropping it into Alexander's mouth. Behind him, his older brother and younger sister looked on with impish glee, urging him forward with harsh hand gestures whenever he paused nervously.

As the boy neared the tyre and held up the cockroach, his mother — always alert to mischief — stuck her head out of a nearby tent, ripped her left ear off and threw it at him. It spun through the air like a boomerang and knocked the cockroach from the boy's pudgy fingers. Yelping, he raced back to his brother and sister, while Alexander slept on, unaware of his narrow escape.

"Urcha!" Merla snapped, catching her ear as it circled back, then reattaching it to her head. "If I catch you bothering Alexander again, I'll lock you in with the Wolf Man until morning!"

"Shancus made me do it!" Urcha whined, receiving a dig in the ribs from his older brother.

"I don't doubt he put you up to it," Merla growled, "but you're old enough to know better. Don't do it again. Shancus!" she added. The snake-boy looked at his mother innocently. "If Urcha or Lilia get into trouble tonight, I'll hold you responsible."

"I didn't do anything!" Shancus shouted. "They're always—"

"Enough!" Merla cut him short. She started towards her children, then saw me sitting in the shadow of the tree next to the one Alexander Ribs was hanging from. Her expression softened. "Hello, Darren," she said. "What are you doing?"

"Looking for cockroaches," I said, managing a short smile. Merla and her husband, Evra Von — a snake-man and one of my oldest friends — had been very kind to me since I'd arrived a couple of weeks earlier. Though I found it hard to respond to their kindness in my miserable mood, I made as much of an effort as I could.

"It's cold," Merla noted. "Shall I fetch you a blanket?"

I shook my head. "It takes more than a slight frost to chill a half-vampire."

"Well, would you mind keeping an eye on these three as long as you're outside?" she asked. "Evra's snake is moulting. If you can keep the kids out of the way, it'd be a real help."

"No problem," I said, rising and dusting myself down as she went back inside the tent. I walked over to the three Von children. They gazed up at me uncertainly. I'd been unusually solemn since returning to the Cirque Du Freak, and they weren't quite sure what to make of me. "What would you like to do?" I asked.

"Cockroach!" Lilia squealed. She was only three years old, but looked five or six because of her rough, coloured scales. Like Shancus, Lilia was half-human, half-snake. Urcha was an ordinary human, though he wished he could be like the other two, and sometimes glued painted scraps of tinfoil to his body, driving his mother wild with exasperation.

"No more cockroaches," I said. "Anything else?"

"Show us how you drink blood," Urcha said, and Shancus hissed at him angrily.

"What's wrong?" I asked Shancus, who'd been named in my honour.

"He's not supposed to say that," Shancus said, slicking back his yellow-green hair. "Mum told us not to say anything about vampires — it might upset you."

I smiled. "Mums worry about silly things. Don't worry — you can say whatever you like. I don't mind."

"Can you show us how you drink then?" Urcha asked again.

"Sure," I said, then spread my arms, pulled a scary face, and made a deep groaning noise. The children shrieked with delight and ran away. I plodded after them, threatening to rip their stomachs open and drink all their blood.

Although I was able to put on a merry display for the kids, inside I felt as empty as ever. I still hadn't come to terms with Mr Crepsley's death. I was sleeping very little, no more than an hour or two most nights, and I'd lost my appetite. I hadn't drunk blood since leaving the city. Nor had I washed, changed out of my clothes, cut my nails — they grew quicker than a human's — or cried. I felt hollow and lost, and nothing in the world seemed worthwhile.

When I'd arrived at the Cirque, Mr Tall had spent the day locked in his trailer with Evanna. They emerged late that night and Evanna took off without a word. Mr Tall checked that Harkat and I were OK, then set us up with a tent, hammocks and anything else we required. Since then he'd spent a lot of time talking with me, recounting tales of Mr Crepsley and what the pair of them had got up to in the past. He kept asking me to chip in with my own recollections, but I could only smile faintly and shake my head. I found it impossible to mention the dead vampire's name without my stomach tightening and my head pulsing with pain.

I hadn't said much to Harkat lately. He wanted to discuss our friend's death but I couldn't talk about it, and kept turning him away, which upset him. I was being selfish, but I couldn't help it. My sorrow was all consuming and endless, cutting me off from those who cared and wished to help.

Ahead, the Von children stopped, grabbed twigs and pebbles, and threw them at me. I stooped to grab a stick, but as I did, my thoughts flashed back to that underground cavern and Mr Crepsley's face as he let go of Steve and crashed upon the fiery stakes. Sighing mournfully, I sat down in the middle of the clearing, taking no notice as the Vons covered me with moss and dirt and prodded me curiously. They thought this was part of the game. I hadn't the heart to tell them otherwise, so I just sat still until they grew bored and wandered away. Then I remained there, filthy and alone, as the night darkened and grew colder around me.

As another week dragged by, I withdrew further and further inside myself. I no longer answered people when they asked a question, only grunted like an animal. Harkat had tried talking me out of my mood three days earlier, but I swore at him and told him to leave me alone. He lost his temper and took a swipe at me. I could have ducked out of the way of his chunky grey fist, but I let him knock me to the ground. When he bent to help me up, I swatted his hand away. He hadn't spoken to me since.

Life went on as usual around me. The Cirque folk were excited. Truska – a lady who could grow a beard at will, then suck the hairs back into her face – had returned after an absence of several months. A big party was held after that night's performance to celebrate her return. There was much cheering and singing. I didn't attend. I sat by myself at the edge of camp, stony-faced and dry-eyed, thinking — as usual — about Mr Crepsley.

Late in the night, there was a tap on my shoulder. Glancing up, I saw Truska, smiling, holding out a slice of cake. "I know you feeling low, but I'm thinking you might like this," she said. Truska was still learning to speak English and often mangled her words.

"Thanks, but I'm not hungry," I said. "Good to see you again. How have you been?" Truska didn't answer. She stared at me a moment — then thrust the slice of cake into my face! "What the hell!" I roared, leaping to my feet.

"That what you get for being big moody-guts," Truska laughed. "I know you sad, Darren, but you can't sit round like grumpy bear all time."

"You don't know anything about it," I snapped. "You don't know what I'm feeling. Nobody does!"

She looked at me archly. "You think you the only one to lose somebody close? I had husband and daughter. They get killed by evil fishermen."

I blinked stupidly. "I'm sorry. I didn't know."

"Nobody here does." She sat beside me, brushed her long hair out of her eyes and gazed up at the sky. "That why I left home and joined with Cirque Du Freak. I hurted terrible inside and had to get away. My daughter was less than two years old when she die."

I wanted to say something but my throat felt as though there was a rope tied tight around it.

"The death of somebody you love is the second worst thing in world," Truska said softly. "Worst thing is letting it hurt you so much that you die too — inside. Larten's dead and I am sad for him, but if you go on as you are being, I will be sadder for you, because you will be dead too, even though your body lives."

"I can't help it," I sighed. "He was like a father to me, but I didn't cry when he died. I still haven't. I can't."

Truska studied me silently, then nodded. "It hard to live with sadness if you can't get it out with tears. Don't worry — you'll cry in end. Maybe you feel better when you do." Standing, she offered me a hand. "You is dirty and smelly. Let me help clean you up. It might help."

"I doubt it," I said, but followed her into the tent that Mr Tall had prepared for her. I wiped the traces of cake from around my face, undressed and wrapped a towel around myself while Truska filled a tub with hot water and layered it with scented oils. She left me to get in. I felt foolish stepping into the sweet-smelling water, but it was wonderful once I lay down. I stayed there for almost an hour.

Truska came in when I'd stepped out of the tub and dried myself. She'd taken my dirty clothes, so I had to keep a towel wrapped around my middle. She made me sit in a low chair and set about my nails with a pair of scissors and a file. I told her they wouldn't be any good — vampires have extra-tough nails — but she smiled and clipped the top of the nail off my right big toe. "These super-sharp scissors.

I know all about vampire nails — I sometimes cut Vancha's!"

When Truska was done with my nails, she trimmed my hair, then shaved me and finished off with a quick massage. When she stopped, I stood and asked where my clothes were. "Fire," she smirked. "They was rotten. I chucked them away."

"So what do you suggest I wear?" I grumbled.

"I have surprise," she said. Going to a wardrobe, she plucked forth brightly coloured clothes and draped them across the foot of her bed. I instantly recognized the bright green shirt, purple trousers and blue-gold jacket — the pirate costume I used to wear when I lived at the Cirque Du Freak.

"You kept them," I muttered, smiling foolishly.

"I told you last time you was here that I have them and would fix them so you can wear again, remember?"

It seemed like years since we'd stopped at the Cirque shortly before our first encounter with the Lord of the Vampaneze. Now that I cast my mind back, I recalled Truska promising to adjust my old costume when she had a chance.

"I wait outside," Truska said. "Put them on and call when you ready."

I took a long time getting into the clothes. It felt weird to be pulling them on after all these years. The last time I'd worn them, I'd been a boy, still coming to terms with being a half-vampire, unaware of how hard and unforgiving the world could be. Back then I thought the clothes looked cool, and I loved wearing them. Now they looked childish and silly to me, but since Truska had gone to the trouble of preparing them, I figured I'd better put them on to please her.

I called her when I was ready. She smiled as she entered, then went to a different wardrobe and came back with a brown hat adorned with a long feather. "I not have shoes your size," she said. "We get some later."

Pulling on the hat, I tilted it at an angle and smiled self-consciously at Truska. "How do I look?"

"See for yourself," she replied, and led me to a full-length mirror.

My breath caught in my throat as I came face to face with my reflection. It may have been a trick of the dim light, but in the fresh clothes and hat, with my clean-shaven face, I looked very young, like when Truska first kitted me out in this costume.

"What you think?" Truska asked.

"I look like a child," I whispered.

"That is partly the mirror," she chuckled. "It is made to take off a few years — very kind to women!"

Removing the hat, I ruffled my hair and squinted at myself. I looked older when I squinted — lines sprang up around my eyes, a reminder of the sleepless nights I'd endured since Mr Crepsley's death. "Thanks," I said, turning away from the mirror.

Truska put a firm hand on my head and swivelled me back towards my reflection. "You not finished," she said.

"What do you mean?" I asked. "I've seen all there is to see."

"No," she said. "You haven't." Leaning forward, she tapped the mirror. "Look at your eyes. Look deep in them, and don't turn away until you see."

"See what?" I asked, but she didn't answer. Frowning, I gazed into my eyes, reflected in the mirror, searching for anything strange. They looked the same as ever, a little sadder than usual, but...

I stopped, realizing what Truska wanted me to see. My eyes didn't just look sad — they were completely empty of life and hope. Even Mr Crepsley's eyes, as he died, hadn't looked that lost. I knew now what Truska meant when she said the living could be dead too.

"Larten not want this," she murmured in my ear as I stared at the hollow eyes in the mirror. "He love life. He want you to love it too. What would he say if he saw this alive-but-dead gaze that will get worse if you not stop?"

"He ... he..." I gulped deeply.

"Empty is no good," Truska said. "You must fill eyes, if not with joy, then with sadness and pain. Even hate is better than empty."

"Mr Crepsley told me I wasn't to waste my life on hate," I said promptly, and realized this was the first time I'd mentioned his name since arriving at the Cirque Du Freak. "Mr Crepsley," I said again, slowly, and the eyes in the mirror wrinkled. "Mr Crepsley," I sighed. "Larten. My friend." My eyelids were trembling now, and tears gathered at the edges. "He's dead," I moaned, turning to face Truska. "Mr Crepsley's dead!"

31

With that, I threw myself into her embrace, locked my arms around her waist, and wailed, finally finding the tears to express my grief. I wept long and hard, and the sun had risen on a new morning before I cried myself out and slid to the floor, where Truska slipped a pillow under my head and hummed a strange, sad tune as I closed my eyes and slept.

CHAPTER THREE

It was a cold but dry March — star-filled nights, frost-white dawns and sharp blue days. The Cirque Du Freak was performing in a large town situated close to a waterfall. We'd been there four nights already, and it would be another week before we moved on — lots of tourists were coming to our shows, as well as the residents of the town. It was a busy, profitable time.

In the months after I first cried in Truska's tent, I'd wept a lot for Mr Crepsley. It had been horrible — the slightest reminder of him could set me off — but necessary. Gradually the tearful bursts had lessened, as I came to terms with my loss and learnt to live with it.

I was lucky. I had lots of friends who helped. Truska, Mr Tall, Hans Hands, Cormac Limbs, Evra and Merla all talked me through the hard times, discussing Mr Crepsley with me, gently guiding me back to normality. Once I'd patched things up with Harkat and apologized for the way I'd treated him, I relied on the Little Person more than anyone else. We sat up many nights together, remembering Mr Crepsley, reminding each other of his personal quirks, things he'd said, expressions he'd favoured.

Now, months later, the tables had turned and *I* was doing the comforting. Harkat's nightmares had returned. He'd been suffering from agonizing dreams when we left Vampire Mountain at the start of our quest, dreams of wastelands, stake-filled pits and dragons. Mr Tiny said the dreams would worsen unless Harkat went with him to find out who he'd been before he died, but Harkat chose to accompany me instead on my hunt for the Vampaneze Lord.

Later, Evanna helped me stop his nightmares. But the witch said it was only a temporary solution. When the dreams resumed, Harkat would have to find out the truth about himself or be driven insane.

For the last month Harkat had been tormented every time he slept. He stayed awake as long as he could – Little People didn't need much sleep – but whenever he dozed off, the nightmares washed over him and he'd thrash and scream in his sleep. It had reached the stage where he had to be tied down when he slept — otherwise he stumbled through the camp, hitting out at imaginary monsters, causing damage to anything he encountered.

After five days and nights, he'd fallen asleep at the end of our latest show. I'd tied him down in his hammock, using strong ropes to strap his arms by his sides, and sat beside him while he tossed and moaned, wiping green beads of sweat from his forehead, away from his lidless eyes.

Finally, early in the morning, after hours of shrieking and straining, the cries stopped, his eyes cleared and he smiled weakly. "You can untie me ... now. All done for tonight."

"That was a long one," I muttered, undoing the knots.

"That's the trouble with putting ... sleep off so long," Harkat sighed, swinging out of his hammock. "I postpone the nightmares for a while, but I ... sleep longer."

"Maybe you should try hypnosis again," I suggested. We'd done everything we could think of to ease Harkat's pain, asking all the performers and crew in the Cirque if they knew of a cure for nightmares. Mr Tall had tried hypnotizing him, Truska had sung to him while he slept, Rhamus Twobellies had rubbed a foul-smelling ointment over his head — all to no avail.

"No good," Harkat smiled tiredly. "Only one person can help — Mr Tiny. If he returns and shows me how to ... find out who I was, the dreams ... will hopefully stop. Otherwise..." He shook his squat, grey, neckless head.

After washing off the sweat in a barrel of cold water, Harkat accompanied me to Mr Tall's van, to learn our schedule for the day. We'd been doing a variety of odd jobs since hooking up with the Cirque, putting up tents, fixing broken seats and equipment, cooking and washing.

Mr Tall had asked me if I'd like to perform in the shows, as his assistant. I told him I didn't want to — it would have felt too weird being on stage without Mr Crepsley.

When we reported for duty, Mr Tall was standing in the doorway of his van, beaming broadly, his little black teeth shining dully in the early morning light. "I heard you roaring last night," he said to Harkat.

"Sorry," Harkat said.

"Don't be. I mention it only to explain why I didn't come to you straightaway with the news — I thought it best to let you sleep."

"What news?" I asked warily. In my experience, unexpected news was more often bad than good.

"You have visitors," Mr Tall chuckled. "They arrived late last night, and have been waiting impatiently." He stepped aside and waved us in.

Harkat and I shared an uncertain glance, then entered cautiously. Neither of us carried a weapon — there seemed to be no need while we travelled with the Cirque Du Freak — but we bunched our hands into fists, ready to lash out if we didn't like the look of our "visitors". Once we saw the pair sitting on the couch, our fingers relaxed and we bounded forward, excited.

"Debbie!" I yelled. "Alice! What are you doing here?"

Debbie Hemlock and Chief Inspector Alice Burgess rose to hug us. They were simply dressed in trousers and jumpers. Debbie had cut her hair since I last saw her. It was short and tightly curled. I didn't think it suited her, but I said nothing about it.

"How are you?" Debbie asked once I'd released her. She was studying my eyes quietly, checking me out.

"Better," I smiled. "It's been rough but I'm over the worst — touch wood."

"Thanks to his friends," Harkat noted wryly.

"What about you?" I asked the women. "Did the vampaneze return? How did you explain things to your bosses and friends?" Then, "What are you doing here?" I asked again, perplexed.

Debbie and Alice laughed at my confusion, then sat down and explained all that had happened since we parted in the forest outside the city. Rather than make a genuine report to her superiors, Alice claimed to have been unconscious the entire time since being kidnapped by Vancha March. It was a simple story, easy to stick to, and nobody had cause to disbelieve her.

Debbie faced rougher questioning — when the vampaneze told the police we were holding Steve Leonard, they also mentioned Debbie's name. She'd protested her innocence, said she only knew me as a student, and knew nothing at all about Steve. With Alice's support, Debbie's story was finally accepted and she was released. She'd been shadowed for a few weeks, but eventually the police left her to get on with her life.

The officials knew nothing of the battle that had taken place in the tunnels, or of the vampaneze, vampets and vampires who'd been busy in their city. As far as they were concerned, a group of killers — Steve Leonard, Larten Crepsley, Darren Shan, Vancha March and Harkat Mulds — were responsible for the murders. One escaped during their arrest. The others broke out of prison later and fled. Our descriptions had been circulated near and far, but we were no longer the problem of the city, and the people there didn't much care whether we'd been humans or vampires — they were just glad to be rid of us.

When a suitable period had passed, and interest in them dropped, Alice met Debbie and the pair discussed their bizarre brush with the world of vampires. Debbie had quit her job at Mahler's — she couldn't face work — and Alice was thinking about handing in her resignation too.

"It seemed pointless," she said quietly, running her fingers through her short white hair. "I joined the force to protect people. When I saw how mysterious and deadly the world really is, I no longer felt useful. I couldn't return to ordinary life."

Over a number of weeks, the women talked about what they'd experienced in the tunnels, and what to do with their lives. They both agreed that they couldn't go back to the way they'd been, but they didn't know how to reshape their futures. Then, one night, after a lot of drinking and talking, Debbie said something that would change their lives completely and give them a new, purposeful direction.

"I was worrying about the vampets," Debbie told us. "They seem more vicious than the vampaneze. Their masters have morals of a kind, but the vampets are just thugs. If the vampaneze win the war, it doesn't seem likely that the vampets will want to stop fighting."

"I agreed," Alice said. "I've seen their kind before. Once they develop a taste for battle, they never lose it. But without vampires to attack, they'll have to look elsewhere for prey."

"Humanity," Debbie said quietly. "They'll turn on humans if they get rid of all the vampires. They'll keep recruiting, growing all the time, finding weak, greedy people and offering them power. With the vampaneze behind them, I think they might pose a real threat to the world in the years to come."

"But we didn't think the vampires would worry about that," Alice said. "The vampaneze are the real threat to the vampire clan. The vampets are just a nuisance as far as vampires are concerned."

"That's when I said we needed to fight fire with fire." Debbie's face was stern, unusually so. "This is *our* problem. I said we needed to recruit humans to fight the vampets, now, before they grow too strong. I was speaking generally when I used 'our' and 'we', but as soon as I said it, I realized it wasn't general — it was personal."

"Victims wait for others to fight on their behalf," Alice said roughly. "Those who don't want to be victims fight for themselves."

By the time the sun rose, the pair had drawn up a plan to travel to Vampire Mountain, elicit the approval of the Princes, and build an army of humans to counter the threat of the vampets. Vampires and vampaneze don't use guns or bows and arrows — they make a vow when blooded never to avail of such weapons — but vampets aren't bound by such laws. Alice and Debbie's army wouldn't be bound by those laws either. With the help of the vampires they could track the vampets, then engage them on equal, vicious terms.

"We'd almost finished packing before the glaring flaw hit us," Debbie laughed. "We didn't know where Vampire Mountain was!"

That's when Alice recalled the piece of paper Evanna had given her. Returning to her apartment, where she'd stored it, she unfolded it and discovered directions to where the Cirque Du Freak was currently playing — here by the waterfall.

"But Evanna gave you that paper months ago!" I exclaimed. "How did she know where the Cirque would be?"

Alice shrugged. "I've tried not to think about that one. I'm just about OK with the notion of vampires, but witches who can foresee the future ... that's a step too far. I prefer to believe she checked with the guy who runs this place before she met us."

"Though that doesn't explain how she knew when we'd read the message," Debbie added with a wink.

"I suppose this means we're meant to ... guide you to Vampire Mountain," Harkat mused.

"Looks like it," Alice said. "Unless you've other plans?"

Harkat looked at me. I'd made it very clear when Mr Crepsley died that I didn't want anything to do with vampires for a while. This call was mine.

"I'm not keen on going back," I sighed. "It's still too soon. But for something this important, I guess I don't have much of a choice. As well as showing you the way, maybe I can act as the middle man between you and the Generals."

"We were thinking along those lines," Debbie smiled, leaning over to squeeze my hands. "We're not sure what the vampires will think of two human women turning up with an offer to build an army to help them. We know little of their ways or customs. We need someone to fill us in."

"I'm not sure the Princes will ... accept your proposal," Harkat said. "Vampires have always fought their ... own battles. I think they'll want to do the same now, even ... if the odds are stacked against them."

"If they do, we'll fight the vampets without them," Alice snorted. "But they'd be fools to disregard us, and from what I've seen, vampires aren't foolish."

"It makes sense," I said. "Send humans to fight the vampets and leave the clan free to focus on the vampaneze."

"Since when did vampires do things ... because they made sense?" Harkat chuckled. "But it's worth a try. I'll come with you."

"Oh no you won't," someone chortled behind us. Turning, startled, we saw that we'd been joined in the van by a third, uninvited guest, a short man with a savage leer. He was instantly recognizable and immediately unwelcome — *Mr Tiny!*

CHAPTER FOUR

THE CREATOR of the Little People was dressed in his customary yellow suit and green Wellington boots. He eyed us though thick glasses and twirled a heart-shaped watch between the fingers of his left hand. He was small and pudgy, with pure white hair and a cruel, mocking smile.

"Hello boys," he greeted Harkat and me. "And *hello!* beautiful ladies." He winked rakishly at Debbie and Alice. Debbie smiled, but the ex-Chief Inspector was wary. Mr Tiny took a seat and removed a boot to empty dirt out of it. I saw the strange, six webbed toes I'd glimpsed once before. "I see you survived your run-in with Master Leonard," he drawled, putting the boot back on.

"No thanks to you," I sniffed angrily. "You knew Steve was the Lord of the Vampaneze. You could have told us."

"And spoilt the surprise?" Mr Tiny laughed. "I wouldn't have missed that fatal confrontation in the Cavern of Retribution for anything. I haven't enjoyed myself so much in years. The tension was unbearable, even though I guessed the outcome."

"You weren't in the cavern," I challenged him. "And you didn't *guess* the outcome — you *knew* how it would end!"

Mr Tiny yawned insolently. "I might not have been there physically," he said, "but I was there in spirit. As for knowing the final outcome — I didn't. I suspected Larten would fail, but I wasn't sure. He *could* have won.

"Anyhow," he said, clapping sharply. "That's in the past. We've other fish to fry." Looking at Harkat, he spun his watch so that it caught the light shining in the window of the van and reflected it into Harkat's round green eyes. "Been sleeping well, Master Mulds?"

Harkat stared straight back at his master and said blankly, "You know only too damn ... well that I haven't."

Mr Tiny tucked his watch away without taking his eyes off Harkat. "Time to find out who you used to be," he murmured. Harkat stiffened.

"Why now?" I asked.

"His nightmares have intensified. He must come with me and search for his true identity, or stay, go mad — and perish."

"Why can't you just tell him?" I prodded.

"Doesn't work that way," Mr Tiny said.

"Will I be gone long?" Harkat asked quietly.

"Oh yes," came the answer. "For ever, if things don't go well. It's not a case of simply finding out who you were and returning. The road is long and dangerous, and even if you struggle along to the end, there's no guarantee you'll make it back. But it's a road you must tread — unless you'd rather go loopy and die." Mr Tiny let out a fake sigh. "Poor Harkat — trapped between the devil and the deep blue sea."

"You're all heart," Harkat grumbled, then faced me with a look of disgust. "Looks like this is where … we part company."

"I could come with you—" I began, but he cut me short with a wave of a rough grey hand.

"Forget it," he said. "You have to lead Debbie and … Alice to Vampire Mountain. Not just to guide them, but to … protect them — it's a hard trek."

"We could wait until you returned," Debbie said.

"No," Harkat sighed. "There's no telling how long … I'll be gone."

I gazed helplessly at Harkat. He was my best friend, and I hated the thought of leaving him. But I loved Debbie and didn't want to abandon her.

"Actually," Mr Tiny purred, stroking the top of his heart-shaped watch, "I think young Shan *should* accompany you — assuming you value your life."

"What do you mean?" Harkat barked sharply.

Mr Tiny studied his fingernails and spoke with a deceptively light tone. "If Darren accompanies you, your chances of survival are fair. Alone, it's practically certain you'll fail."

My eyes narrowed hatefully. Mr Tiny had set Mr Crepsley and me on the trail of the Vampaneze Lord, knowing it was a journey bound to end in death. Now he wished to launch me on another.

"Darren's not coming," Harkat said as I opened my mouth to lay into Mr Tiny. "He has problems of his own ... with the vampaneze. This is my quest, not his."

"Of course, dear boy," Mr Tiny simpered. "I fully understand, and if he chooses to go with the beautiful ladies, I won't say anything to stop him. But it would be terribly wrong of me not to let him know in advance the awful–"

"Stop!" Harkat snapped. "Darren goes with Debbie and ... Alice. End of story."

"Harkat," I muttered uncertainly, "maybe we should–"

"No," he stopped me. "Your loyalty lies with the vampires. It's time you returned to the fold. I'll be OK on my own." And he turned away and wouldn't say anything more about it.

We broke camp before midday. Debbie and Alice had come well equipped, with ropes, thick jumpers, climbing boots, strong torches, lighters and matches, guns, knives, you name it! As a half-vampire, I didn't require any special tools. All I packed in my rucksack was a good strong knife and a change of clothes. I was wearing jeans, a shirt and a light jumper. Although Truska had gone to a lot of trouble restoring my pirate costume, I didn't feel comfortable in it — it was a child's outfit. I'd picked up more normal gear over the last few months. Truska didn't mind — she said she'd give the costume to Shancus or Urcha when they were older.

I didn't wear my shoes. The trek to Vampire Mountain was a solemn tradition among vampires. No shoes or climbing gear were allowed. Normally you weren't allowed to flit either.

In recent years, because of the War of the Scars, that rule had been relaxed. But the others still stood. Debbie and Alice thought I was crazy! It's hard for humans to understand the world of the creatures of the night.

One other thing I did take was my diary. I'd thought the diary lost for ever — it had been left behind in the city, along with the rest of my personal belongings — and was astonished when Alice produced it with a flourish.

"Where'd you get it?" I gasped, fingering the soft, crinkled cover of one of the several notepads that made up the diary.

"It was part of the evidence my officers collected after you were arrested. I sneaked it out before I quit the force."

"Did you read it?" I asked.

"No, but others did." She smiled. "They dismissed it as the fictional work of a lunatic."

I looked for Harkat before we left, but he was locked away in Mr Tall's van with Mr Tiny. Mr Tall came to the door when I knocked and said the Little Person was not receiving visitors. I called out "Goodbye" but there was no reply.

I felt lousy as we cleared the camp, having said farewell to Evra, Merla and my other friends. But Harkat had been firm about his wishes, and I knew it made more sense to go to Vampire Mountain and take my rightful place in the Hall of Princes again.

Debbie was delighted to have me back, and held on tight to my hand, telling me how excited she was — and a bit scared — to be heading for Vampire Mountain. She pumped me for information — what did vampires wear, did they sleep in coffins, could they turn into bats — but I was too distracted to answer in any great detail.

We'd walked two or three kilometres when I drew to a sudden halt. I was thinking about the times Harkat had saved my life — when he'd rescued me from the jaws of a savage bear, when he'd jumped into a pit during my Trials of Initiation and killed a wild boar as it was about to gouge me to death, the way he'd fought beside me, swinging his axe with speed and skill, when we'd taken on the vampaneze.

"Darren?" Debbie asked, gazing into my eyes, worried. "What's wrong?"

"He's got to go back," Alice answered for me. I stared at her and she smiled. "You can't ignore the obligations of friendship. Harkat needs you more than we do. Go help him, and catch us up later if you can."

"But he told me to leave," I muttered.

"Doesn't matter," Alice insisted. "Your place is with him, not us."

"No!" Debbie objected. "We can't find our way to the Mountain alone!"

Alice pulled a map out of her rucksack. "I'm sure Darren can point us in the right direction."

"No!" Debbie cried again, clutching me tight. "I'm afraid I'll never see you again if you leave!"

"I must," I sighed. "Alice is right — I have to help Harkat. I'd rather stay with you, but I'd feel like a traitor if I did."

There were hard tears in Debbie's eyes, but she blinked them back and nodded tensely. "OK. If that's the way you want it."

"It's the way it has to be," I said. "You'd do the same thing in my place."

"Possibly." She smiled weakly, then, hiding her feelings behind a businesslike façade, she grabbed the map off Alice, laid it on the ground and told me to ink in the route to Vampire Mountain.

I quickly outlined the easiest route, pointed out a couple of alternate paths in case the first was blocked, and told them how to find their way through the maze of tunnels which led up the inside of the Mountain to the Halls where the vampires lived. Then, without any long goodbyes, I kissed Debbie quickly and thrust the rucksack with my newly recovered diary into Alice's hands. I asked her to look after it for me.

I wished both women well, then turned and raced back for camp. I tried not to dwell on all that could happen to them on their way to the Mountain, and offered up a quick prayer to the gods of the vampires as I ran, asking them to watch over the ex-Chief Inspector and the teacher I loved.

I was on the edge of the camp when I spotted Mr Tiny and Harkat in an open field. In front of the pair stood a shimmering arched doorway, unconnected to anything else. The edges of the doorway glowed red. Mr Tiny also glowed, his suit, hair and skin pulsing a dark, vibrant, crimson shade. The space within the edges of the doorway was a dull grey colour.

Mr Tiny heard me coming, looked over his shoulder and smiled like a shark. "Ah — Master Shan! I thought you might turn up."

"Darren!" Harkat snapped furiously. "I told you not to come! I won't take you with ... me. You'll have to—"

Mr Tiny laid a hand on the Little Person's back and shoved him through the doorway. There was a grey flash, then Harkat disappeared. I could see the field through the grey veil of the doorway — but no sign of Harkat.

"Where's he gone?" I shouted.

"To search for the truth." Mr Tiny smiled, edged aside and gestured towards the glowing doorway. "Care to search with him?"

I stepped up to the doorway, gazing uneasily at the glowing red edges and the grey sheen between. "Where does this lead?" I asked.

"Another place," Mr Tiny answered obscurely, then laid a hand on my right shoulder and looked at me intently. "If you follow Harkat, you might never return. Think seriously about this. If you go with Harkat and die, you won't be here to face Steve Leonard when the time comes, and your absence might have terrible repercussions for vampires everywhere. Is your short, grey-skinned friend worth such an enormous risk?"

I didn't have to think twice about that. "Yes," I answered simply, and stepped through into unnatural, otherworldly greyness.

CHAPTER FIVE

A SUN burnt brightly in the clear sky above the wasteland, highlighting the arid earth and bare rocky hills. A coarse red dust covered much of the land, choking the dry soil. When strong winds blew, the dust rose in sheets, making breathing almost impossible. At such times I pulled on one of Harkat's spare masks – it blocked out the worst of the grainy particles – and the two of us sought shelter and waited for calm to descend.

It had been two weeks – roughly – since Mr Tiny brought us to this desolate land and abandoned us. Two weeks crossing barren valleys and dead hills, where nothing lived except a few hardy lizards and insects, which we caught and ate whenever we could. They tasted disgusting but you can't be choosy if you're stranded in a desert without food or water.

Water was our main concern. Walking in the heat and dust was thirsty work, but water was in scarce supply and we didn't have any canteens to store it in when we found the occasional pool. We'd fashioned primitive containers from the skins of lizards, but they didn't hold much. We had to drink sparingly.

Harkat was angry with me for disobeying his wishes — he ranted at me nonstop for a few days — but his temper gradually abated. Although he hadn't thanked me for choosing to accompany him on his quest, I knew he was secretly grateful.

A fortnight earlier, Mr Tiny followed us through the doorway, which collapsed into dust after him. There'd been a brief moment of disorientation when I stepped through, a grey cloud obscuring my vision. As the cloud cleared, I saw that I was standing in a round, shallow, lifeless valley — and although it had been day when I stepped through the doorway, here it was night, albeit an uncommonly clear night, bright with a full moon and a sky filled with twinkling star clusters.

"Where are we?" Harkat asked, his large green eyes filled with wonder.

Mr Tiny tapped his nose. "That would be telling. Now, boys," he said, squatting and signalling us to squat beside him. He drew a simple compass in the dust at his feet, and pointed to one of the arrows. "That's west, as you'll see by the position of the sun tomorrow. Go in that direction until you come to the hunting grounds of a black panther. You have to kill the panther to find out where to go next."

Smiling, he stood and turned to leave.

"Wait!" I stopped him. "Is that all you're going to tell us?"

"What more would you like to know?" he asked politely.

"Loads!" I shouted. "Where are we? How did we get here? What happens if we walk east instead of west? How will Harkat find out who he used to be? And what the hell does a panther have to do with any of it?"

Mr Tiny sighed impatiently. "I thought you would have developed an appreciation for the unknown by now," he grumbled. "Don't you realize how exciting it is to set out on an adventure without any idea of what's coming next? I'd give my wellies and glasses to experience the world the way you do, as something strange and challenging."

"Forget the wellies and glasses!" I snapped. "Just give with some answers!"

"You can be very rude sometimes," Mr Tiny complained, but squatted again and paused thoughtfully. "There's much I can't and won't tell you. You'll have to discover for yourselves where we are — although it won't make much difference if you don't. You got here, obviously, through a mechanism either of magic or incredibly evolved technology — I'm not saying which. If you don't follow the trail west, you'll die, probably quite horribly. As for Harkat finding out who he is, and the panther..."

Mr Tiny considered the question in silence, before answering. "Somewhere on this world lies a lake – more a glorified pond, really – which I like to refer to as the Lake of Souls. In it you can glimpse the faces of many trapped souls, people whose spirits did not leave Earth when they died. The soul of the person Harkat used to be lies within. You must find the Lake, then fish for his soul. If you succeed, and Harkat learns and acknowledges the truth about himself, your quest will be complete and I'll see that you're guided safely home. If not..." He shrugged.

"How do we find this Lake ... of Souls?" Harkat asked.

"By following instructions," Mr Tiny said. "If you locate and kill the panther, you'll learn where to go next. You'll also discover a clue to your previous identity, which I've been gracious enough to toss in for free."

"Couldn't you just cut the crap and tell us?" I groaned.

"No," Mr Tiny said. He stood and looked down at us seriously. "But I'll say this much, boys — the panther's the least of your worries. Step warily, trust in your instincts, and never let your guard down. And don't forget," he added to Harkat, "as well as learning who you were, you must acknowledge it. I can't step in until you've admitted the truth out loud.

"Now," he smiled, "I really must be going. Places to be, things to do, people to torment. If you've further questions, they'll have to wait. Until next time, boys." With a wave, the short, mysterious man turned and left us, walking east until the darkness swallowed him, stranding us in the unnamed, alien land.

We found a small pool of water and drank deeply from it, sinking our heads into the murky liquid, ignoring the many tiny eels and insects. Harkat's grey skin looked like damp cardboard when he pulled up, having drunk his fill, but it swiftly resumed its natural colour as the water evaporated under the unforgiving sun.

"How far do you think we've come?" I groaned, stretching out in the shade of a prickly bush with small purple flowers. This was the first sign of vegetation we'd encountered, but I was too exhausted to display any active interest.

"I've no idea," Harkat said. "How long have we … been travelling?"

"Two weeks — I think."

After the first hot day, we'd tried travelling by night, but the path was rocky and treacherous underfoot — not to mention hard on my bare feet! After stumbling many times, ripping our clothes and cutting ourselves, we elected to brave the blistering sun. I wrapped my jumper around my head to ward off the worst of the rays — the sun didn't affect Harkat's grey skin, though he sweated a lot — but while that prevented sunstroke, it didn't do much against sunburn. My upper body had been roasted all over, even through the material of my shirt. For a few days I'd been sore and irritable, but I'd recovered quickly — thanks to my healing abilities as a half-vampire — and the red had turned to a dark, protective brown. The soles of my feet had also hardened — I barely noticed the absence of shoes now.

"With all the climbing and back tracking we've … had to do, we can't be making more than … a couple of miles an hour," Harkat said. "Allowing for fourteen or fifteen hours of sunlight … per day, we probably cover twenty-five or thirty miles. Over two weeks that's..." He frowned as he calculated. "Maybe four hundred in total."

I nodded feebly. "Thank the gods we're not human — we wouldn't have lasted a week at this pace, in these conditions."

Harkat sat up and tilted his head left, then right — the Little Person's ears were stitched under the skin of his scalp, so he had to cock his head at a sharp angle to listen intently. Hearing nothing, he focused his green eyes on the land around us. After a brief study of the area, he turned towards me. "Has the smell altered?" he asked. He didn't have a nose, so he relied on mine.

I sniffed the air. "Slightly. It doesn't smell as tangy as it did before."

"That's because there's less ... dust," he said, pointing to the hills around us. "We seem to be leaving the ... desert behind. There are a few plants and patches ... of dry grass."

"About time," I groaned. "Let's hope there are animals too — I'll crack up if I have to eat another lizard or bug."

"What do you think those twelve-legged ... insects were that we ate yesterday?" Harkat asked.

"I've no idea, but I won't be touching them again — my stomach was in bits all night!"

Harkat chuckled. "They didn't bother me. Sometimes it helps to have no ... taste buds, and a stomach capable of digesting ... almost anything."

Harkat pulled his mask up over his mouth and breathed through it in silence, studying the land ahead. Harkat had spent a lot of time testing the air, and didn't think it was poisonous to him — it was slightly different to the air on Earth, more acidic — but he kept his mask on anyway, to be safe. I'd coughed a lot for the first few days, but I was OK now — my hardened lungs had adapted to the bitter air.

"Decided where we are yet?" I asked after a while. That was our favourite topic of conversation. We'd narrowed the possibilities down to four options. Mr Tiny had somehow sent us back into the past. He'd transported us to some far-off world in our own universe. He'd slipped us into an alternate reality. Or this was an illusion, and our bodies were lying in a field in the real world, while Mr Tiny fed this dream scene into our imaginations.

"I believed in the ... illusion theory at first," Harkat said, lowering his mask. "But the more I consider it, the less ... certain I am. If Mr Tiny was making this world up, I think ... he'd make it more exciting and colourful. It's quite drab."

"It's early days," I grunted. "This is probably just to warm us up."

"It certainly warmed *you* up," Harkat grinned, nodding at my tan.

I returned his smile, then stared up at the sun. "Another three or four hours till nightfall," I guessed. "It's a shame neither of us knows more about star systems, or we might be able to tell where we were by the stars."

"It's a bigger shame that we ... don't have weapons," Harkat noted. He stood and studied the land in front of us again. "How will we defend ourselves against the ... panther without weapons?"

"Something will turn up," I reassured him. "Mr Tiny wouldn't throw us in out of our depth, not this early on — it'd spoil his fun if we perished quickly."

"That's not very comforting," Harkat said. "The idea that we're being kept alive ... only to die horribly later, for Mr Tiny's benefit ... doesn't fill me with joy."

"Me neither," I agreed. "But at least it gives us hope."

On that uncertain note, the conversation drew to a close, and after a short rest we filled our meagre lizard-skin pouches with water and marched on through the wasteland, which grew more lush — but no less alien — the further we progressed.

CHAPTER SIX

A WEEK after leaving the desert behind, we entered a jungle of thick cactus plants, long snaking vines, and stunted, twisted trees. Very few leaves grew on the trees. Those that did were long and thin, a dull orange colour, grouped near the tops of the trees.

We'd come across traces of animals – droppings, bones, hair – but didn't see any until we entered the jungle. There we found a curious mix of familiar yet strange creatures. Most of the animals were similar to those of Earth – deer, squirrels, monkeys – but different, usually in size or colouring. Some of the differences weren't so readily apparent — we captured a squirrel one day, which turned out to have an extra set of sharp teeth when we examined it, and surprisingly long claws.

We'd picked up dagger-shaped stones during the course of our trek, which we'd sharpened into knives. We now made more weapons out of thick sticks and bones of larger animals. They wouldn't be much use against a panther, but they helped us frighten off the small yellow monkeys which jumped from trees on to the heads of their victims, blinded them with their claws and teeth, then finished them off as they stumbled around.

"I never heard of monkeys like that," I remarked one morning as we watched a group of the simians bring down and devour a huge boar-like animal.

"Me neither," Harkat said.

As we watched, the monkeys paused and sniffed the air suspiciously. One ran to a thick bush and screeched threateningly. There was a deep grunt from within the bush, then a larger monkey — like a baboon, only an odd red colour — stepped out and shook a long arm at the others. The yellow monkeys bared their teeth, hissed and threw twigs and small pebbles at the newcomer, but the baboon ignored them and advanced. The smaller monkeys retreated, leaving the baboon to finish off the boar.

"I guess size matters," I muttered wryly, then Harkat and I slipped away and left the baboon to feed in peace.

The next night, while Harkat slept — his nightmares had stopped since coming to this new world — and I stood guard, there was a loud, fierce roar from somewhere ahead of us. The night was usually filled with the nonstop sounds of insects and other nocturnal creatures, but at the roar all noise ceased. There was total silence — once the echoes of the roar subsided — for at least five minutes.

Harkat slept through the roar. He was normally a light sleeper, but the air here agreed with him and he'd been dozing more deeply. I told him about it in the morning.

"You think it was ... our panther?" he asked.

"It was definitely a big cat," I said. "It might have been a lion or tiger, but my money's on the black panther."

"Panthers are usually very quiet," Harkat said. "But I guess they could be ... different here. If this is his territory, he should come by ... this way soon. Panthers are on constant patrol. We must prepare." During his time in Vampire Mountain, when he'd been working for Seba Nile, Harkat had spoken with several vampires who'd hunted or fought with lions and leopards, so he knew quite a lot about them. "We must dig a pit to ... lure it into, catch and truss a deer, and also find some ... porcupines."

"Porcupines?" I asked.

"Their quills can stick in the panther's ... paws, snout and mouth. They might slow it down or ... distract it."

"We're going to need more than porcupine quills to kill a panther," I noted.

"With luck, we'll startle it when ... it comes to feed on the deer. We can jump out and frighten it into ... the pit. Hopefully it will die there."

"And if it doesn't?" I asked.

Harkat grinned edgily. "We're in trouble. Black panthers are really leopards, and leopards are ... the worst of the big cats. They're fast, strong, savage and ... great climbers. We won't be able to outrun it or ... climb higher than it."

"So if plan A fails, there's no plan B?"

"No." Harkat chuckled dryly. "It'll be straight to plan P — *Panic!*"

We found a clearing with a thick bush at one end where we'd be able to hide. We spent the morning digging a deep pit with our hands and the rough tools we'd fashioned from branches and bones. When the pit was done, we harvested a couple of dozen thick branches and sharpened the tips, creating stakes that we were going to place in the base of the pit.

As we were climbing into the pit to plant the stakes, I stopped at the edge and started to tremble — remembering another pit that had been filled with stakes, and the friend I'd lost there.

"What's wrong?" Harkat asked. Before I could answer, he read it in my eyes. "Oh," he sighed. "Mr Crepsley."

"Isn't there any other way to kill it?" I groaned.

"Not without proper equipment." Harkat took my stakes from me and smiled encouragingly. "Go hunt for porcupines. I'll handle this ... end of the operation."

Nodding gratefully, I left Harkat to plant the stakes and went looking for porcupines or anything else to use against the panther. I hadn't thought much about Mr Crepsley lately — this harsh world had demanded my full attention — but the pit brought it all crashing back. Again I saw him drop and heard his screams as he died. I wanted to leave the pit and panther, but that wasn't an option. We had to kill the predator to learn where to go next. So I quashed thoughts of Mr Crepsley as best I could and immersed myself in work.

I picked some of the sturdier cacti to use as missiles against the black panther, and made mud-balls using leaves and fresh mud from a nearby stream — I hoped the mud might temporarily blind the panther. I searched hard for porcupines, but if any were in the vicinity, they were keeping an ultra low profile. I had to report back quill-less to Harkat in the afternoon.

"Never mind," he said, sitting by the edge of the completed pit. "Let's create a cover for this and ... catch a deer. After that we're in the lap ... of the gods."

We built a thin cover for the pit out of long twigs and leaves, laid it over the hole and went hunting. The deer here were shorter than those on Earth, with longer heads. They couldn't run as fast as their Earth counterparts, but were still pretty swift. It took a while to track down a lame straggler and bring it back alive. It was dusk by the time we tied it to a stake close to the pit, and we were both tired after our long, taxing day.

"What happens if the panther attacks during the night?" I asked, sheltering under a skin I'd sliced from a deer with a small stone scraper.

"Why do you always have to anticipate ... the worst?" Harkat grumbled.

"Somebody has to," I laughed. "Will it be plan P time?"

"No," Harkat sighed. "If he comes in the dark, it's ... KYAG time."

"KYAG?" I echoed.

"Kiss Your Ass Goodbye!"

*　　*　　*

There was no sign of the panther that night, though we both heard deep-throated growls, closer than the roars of the night before. As soon as dawn broke, we ate a hasty breakfast — berries we'd picked after seeing monkeys eat them — and positioned ourselves in the thick covering bush opposite the staked deer and pit. If all went according to plan, the panther would attack the deer. With luck it'd come at it from the far side of the pit and fall in. If not, we'd leap up whilst it was dragging off the deer and hopefully force it backwards to its doom. Not the most elaborate plan in the world, but it would have to do.

We said nothing as the minutes turned to hours, silently waiting for the panther. My mouth was dry and I sipped frequently from the squirrel skin beakers (we'd replaced the lizard-skin containers) by my side, though only small amounts — to cut out too many toilet trips.

About an hour after midday I laid a hand on Harkat's grey arm and squeezed warningly — I'd seen something long and black through the trees. Both of us stared hard. As we did, I saw the tip of a whiskered nose stick out from around a tree and sniff the air testingly — the panther! I kept my mouth closed, willing the panther to advance, but after a few hesitant seconds it turned and padded away into the gloom of the jungle.

Harkat and I looked questioningly at one another. "It must have smelt us," I whispered.

"Or sensed something wrong," Harkat whispered back. Lifting his head slightly, he studied the grazing deer by the pit, then jerked a thumb backwards. "Let's get further away. I think it will return. If we aren't here, it might be … tempted to attack."

"We won't have a clear view if we withdraw any further," I noted.

"I know," Harkat said, "but we've no choice. It knew something was wrong. If we stay here, it'll also know when … it returns, and won't come any closer."

I followed Harkat as he wriggled further back into the bush, not stopping until we were almost at the end of the briars and vines. From here we could only vaguely see the deer.

An hour passed. Two. I was beginning to abandon hope that the panther would return, when the sound of deep breathing drifted towards us from the clearing. I caught flashes of the deer jumping around, straining to break free of its rope. Something growled throatily — the panther. Even more promising — the growls were coming from the far side of the pit. If the panther attacked the deer from there, it would fall straight into our trap!

Harkat and I lay motionless, barely breathing. We heard twigs snap as the panther closed in on the deer, not masking its sounds any longer. Then there was a loud snapping sound as a heavy body crashed through the covering over the pit and landed heavily on the stakes. There was a ferocious howl and I had to cover my ears with my hands. That was followed by silence, disturbed only by the pounding of the deer's hooves on the soil as it leapt around by the edge of the pit.

Harkat slowly got to his feet and stared over the bush at the open pit. I stood and stared with him. We glanced at each other and I said uncertainly, "It worked."

"You sound like you didn't ... expect it to," Harkat grinned.

"I didn't," I laughed, and started towards the pit.

"Careful," Harkat warned me, hefting a knobbly, heavy wooden club. "It could still be alive. There's nothing more dangerous than ... a wounded animal."

"It'd be howling with pain if it was alive," I said.

"Probably," Harkat nodded, "but let's not take any ... needless risks." Stepping in front of me, he moved off to the left and signalled me to go right. Raising a knife-like piece of bone, I circled away from Harkat, then we slowly closed on the pit from opposite directions. As we got nearer, we each drew one of the small cacti we'd tied to our waists — we also had mud-balls strapped on — to toss like grenades if the panther was still alive.

Harkat came within sight of the pit before I did and stopped, confused. As I got closer, I saw what had bewildered him. I also drew to a halt, not sure what to make of it. A body lay impaled on the stakes, blood dripping from its many puncture wounds. But it wasn't the body of a panther — it was a red baboon.

"I don't understand," I muttered. "Monkeys can't make the kind of growling or howling sounds we heard."

"But how did..." Harkat stopped and fear flashed into his eyes. "The monkey's throat!" he gasped. "It's been ripped open! The panther must—"

He got no further. Even as I was leaping to the same conclusion — the panther had killed the baboon and dropped it into the pit to fool us! — there was a blur of movement in the upper branches of the tree closest to me. Whirling, I caught a very brief glimpse of a long, thick, pure black object flying through the air with outstretched claws and gaping jaws — then the panther was upon me, roaring triumphantly as it dragged me to the ground for the kill!

CHAPTER SEVEN

THE ROAR was critical. If the panther had clamped its fangs clean around my throat, I wouldn't have stood a chance. But the animal was excited – probably by having outsmarted us – and tossed its head, growling savagely as we rolled over and came to a stop with the powerful beast on top of me.

As it roared, Harkat reacted with cool speed and launched a cactus missile. It could have bounced off the animal's head or shoulders, but the luck of the vampires was with us, and the cactus sailed clean between the panther's fearsome jaws.

The panther instantly lost interest in me and lurched aside, spitting and scratching at the cactus stuck in its mouth. I crawled away, panting, scrabbling for the knife I'd dropped. Harkat leapt over me as my fingers closed around the handle of the bone, and brought his club down upon the head of the panther.

If the club had been made of tougher material, Harkat would have killed the panther — he could do immense damage with most axes or clubs. But the wood he'd carved it from proved unworthy of the task, and the club smashed in half as it cracked over the panther's hard skull.

The panther howled with pain and rage, and turned on Harkat, spitting spines, its yellow teeth reflecting the gleam of the afternoon sun. It swiped at his squat grey head and opened up a deep gash down the left side of his face. Harkat fell backwards from the force of the blow and the panther leapt after him.

I didn't have time to get up and lunge after the panther — it would be on Harkat before I crossed the space between us — so I sent my knife flying through the air at it. The bone deflected harmlessly off the creature's powerful flanks, but it distracted the beast and its head snapped around. Harkat used the moment to grab a couple of the mud-balls hanging from his blue robes. When the panther faced him again, Harkat let it have the mud-balls between the eyes.

The panther squealed and turned a sharp ninety degrees away from Harkat. It scraped at its eyes with its left paw, wiping the mud away. As it was doing that, Harkat grabbed the lower half of his broken club and jammed the splintered end into the panther's ribcage. The club penetrated the panther's body, but only slightly, drawing blood but not puncturing the panther's lungs.

That was too much for the panther — it went berserk. Even though it couldn't see properly, it threw itself at Harkat, hissing and spitting, swiping with its deadly claws. Harkat ducked out of the way, but the panther's claws snagged on the hem of his robes. Before he could free himself, the predator was on him, working blindly, its teeth gnashing together in search of Harkat's face.

Harkat wrapped his arms tight around the panther and squeezed, trying to snap its ribs or suffocate it. While he did that, I leapt on the panther's back and raked at its nose and eyes with another cactus head. The panther caught the cactus with its teeth and ripped it clear of my grasp — almost taking my right thumb with it!

"Get off!" Harkat wheezed as I clung to the panther's heaving shoulders and scrabbled for another cactus.

"I think I can—" I started to shout.

"*Off!*" Harkat roared.

There was no arguing with a cry like that. I let go of the panther and slumped to the ground. As I did, Harkat locked his hands even tighter together and spun, looking for the pit through the green blood streaming into his wide left eye. Finding it, he clutched the struggling panther close to his chest, stumbled towards the pit — and threw himself in!

"Harkat!" I screamed, reaching out automatically, as though I could grab and save him. The picture of Mr Crepsley falling into the pit of stakes in the Cavern of Retribution flashed through my head, and my insides turned to lead.

There was an ugly thud and an agonizing screech as the panther was impaled on the stakes. No sound came from

Harkat, which made me think he'd landed beneath the panther and died instantly.

"*No!*" I moaned, picking myself up and hobbling towards the edge of the pit. I was so worried about Harkat that I almost toppled into the pit myself! As I stood on the edge, arms swinging wildly to correct my balance, there was a low groan and I saw Harkat's head turn. He'd landed on top of the panther — he was alive!

"Harkat!" I shouted again, joyously this time.

"Help ... me ... up," he gasped. The panther's limbs were still twitching, but they no longer presented a threat — it was nearing the final stages of its death throes and wouldn't have had the strength to kill Harkat even if it wished to.

Lying on my stomach, I reached down into the pit and offered Harkat my hand, but he couldn't reach. He was lying flat on the panther, and although the creature — and the baboon underneath — had taken the worst of the stakes, several had pierced Harkat, a few in his legs, a couple in his stomach and chest, and one through the flesh of his upper left arm. The wounds to his legs and body didn't look too serious. The one through his arm was the problem — he was stuck on the stake and couldn't raise his right hand high enough to clutch mine.

"Wait there," I said, looking around for something to lower to him.

"As if ... I could go ... anywhere!" I heard him mutter sarcastically.

We didn't have any rope, but there were plenty of strong vines growing nearby. Hurrying to the nearest, I sawed at it with my fingernails, cutting off a two metre length. I grabbed it tightly near both ends and tugged sharply to test it. The vine didn't snap under the strain, so I returned to the pit and fed down one end to Harkat. The Little Person grabbed it with his free right hand, waited until I'd got a good grip on my end, then yanked his left arm free of the stake. He gasped tightly as his flesh slid off the piercing wood. Grasping the vine tight, he swung his feet on to the wall of the pit and walked up it, pulling on the vine at the same time.

Harkat was almost at the top when his feet slipped. As his legs dropped, I realized his falling weight would drag us both down if I held on to the rope. I released it with snake-like speed, collapsed to my stomach and clutched for Harkat's hands.

I missed his hands, but my fingers closed on the left sleeve of his blue robes. There was a terrifying ripping sound and I thought I'd lost him, but the material held, and after a few dangerous, dangling seconds I was able to haul the Little Person up out of the pit.

Rolling on to his back, Harkat stared up at the sky, his grey, stitched-together face looking even more like a corpse's than usual. I tried to get up, but my legs were trembling, so I flopped beside him and the two of us lay there in silence, breathing heavily, marvelling inwardly at the fact that we were still alive.

CHAPTER EIGHT

I PATCHED Harkat up as best I could, cleaning out his wounds with water from the stream, slicing my jumper into strips to use as bandages. If I'd been a full-vampire I could have used my spit to close his cuts, but as a half-vampire I lacked that ability.

The wounds to his face — where the panther had clawed him — should have been stitched, but neither of us had any thread or needles. I suggested improvising and using a small bone and animal hair, but Harkat waved the idea away. "I've enough stitches," he grinned. "Let it heal as it likes. I can't get any uglier ... than I already am."

"That's true," I agreed, and laughed as he swatted me round the back of my head. I swiftly grew serious again. "If infection sets in..."

"Looking on the bright side as usual," he groaned, then shrugged. "If it sets in, I'm finished — no ... hospitals here. Let's not worry ... about it."

I helped Harkat to his feet and we returned to the edge of the pit to gaze down at the panther. Harkat was limping worse than normal — he'd always had a slight limp in his left leg — but he said he wasn't in much pain. The panther was a metre and a half in length and thickly built. As we stared at it, I could hardly believe we'd bested it in the fight. Not for the first time in my life, I got the feeling that if vampire gods existed, they were keeping a close watch on me and lending a helping hand whenever I strayed out of my depth.

"You know what worries me ... the most?" Harkat asked after a while. "Mr Tiny said the panther was ... the *least* of our worries. That means there's worse ahead!"

"Now who's being pessimistic?" I snorted. "Want me to go down and get the panther out?"

"Let's wait until morning," Harkat said. "We'll build a good fire, eat, rest ... and drag the panther ... up tomorrow."

That sounded good to me, so while Harkat made a fire — using flinty stones to create sparks — I butchered the deer and set about carving it up. Once upon a time I might have let the deer go, but vampires are predators. We hunt and kill without remorse, the same as any other animal of the wilds.

The meat, when we cooked it, was tough, stringy and unappealing, but we ate ravenously, both aware of how fortunate we were not to *be* the main course that night.

I climbed down into the pit in the morning and prised the panther off the stakes. Leaving the baboon where it lay I passed the panther's carcass up to Harkat. It wasn't as easy as it sounds — the panther was very heavy — but we were stronger than humans, so it wasn't one of our harder tasks.

We studied the panther's gleaming black corpse, wondering how it would tell us where to go. "Maybe we have to slice it open," I suggested. "There might be a box or canister inside."

"Worth trying," Harkat agreed, and rolled the panther over on its back, presenting us with its smooth, soft stomach.

"Wait!" I shouted as Harkat prepared to make the first cut. The hair on the panther's underside wasn't quite as dark as elsewhere. I could see the stretched skin of its stomach — and there was something drawn on it! I searched among our makeshift knives for one with a long, straight edge, then scraped away some of the hairs on the dead panther's stomach. Thin raised lines were revealed.

"That's just scar tissue," Harkat said.

"No," I disagreed. "Look at the circular shapes and the way they spread out. They've been carved deliberately. Help me scrape the entire stomach clear."

It didn't take long to shave the panther and reveal a detailed map. It must have been gouged into the panther's stomach many years ago, maybe when it was a cub. There was a small X at the extreme right of the map, which seemed to indicate our current position. Towards the left an area was circled, and something had been written within the circle.

"Go to the home of the world's largest toad," I read aloud. "Grab the gelatinous globes."

That's all it said. We read it a few more times, then shared a puzzled look. "Any idea what 'gelatinous' means?" Harkat asked.

"I think it's got something to do with jelly," I answered uncertainly.

"So we've got to find the world's ... largest toad, and grab globes made out of jelly?" Harkat sounded dubious.

"This is Mr Tiny we're dealing with," I reminded him. "He makes jokes out of everything. I think our best bet's simply to follow the map from here to the circle and worry about the rest once we get there."

Harkat nodded, then set about the panther's stomach with a sharp stone knife, cutting free the map. "Here," I stopped him. "Let me. I've got nimbler fingers."

As I carefully cut around the edges of the map and sliced the panther's flesh away from its insides, Harkat strolled around the dead beast, mulling something over. As I peeled the map free of the panther and wiped the inside of it clean on a patch of grass, Harkat stopped. "Do you recall Mr Tiny saying he'd ... thrown in a clue to my identity?" he asked.

I cast my thoughts back. "Yes. Maybe that's what the message within the circle means."

"I doubt it," Harkat replied. "Whoever I was before I died, I'm pretty ... sure I wasn't a toad!"

"Maybe you're a frog prince," I giggled.

"Ha bloody ha," Harkat said. "I'm sure the writing's got nothing ... to do with me. There must be something else."

I studied the dead panther. "If you want to root around in its guts, feel free," I told Harkat. "I'm content with the map."

Harkat crouched beside me and flexed his stubby grey fingers, intent on ripping out the panther's insides. I shifted away, not wanting to be part of the messy task. As I did, my eyes flicked to the panther's mouth. Its lips were curled up over its teeth in a frozen death snarl. I laid a hand on Harkat's left arm and said softly, "Look."

When Harkat saw what I was pointing at, he reached over to the panther's mouth and prised its stiff lips entirely clear of its fangs. There were small black letters etched into most of the creature's teeth — an A, a K, an M and others. "There!" Harkat grunted with excitement. "That must be it."

"I'll hold the head up," I said, "so that you can read all the—"

But before I'd finished, Harkat had grasped one of the panther's largest teeth with his fingers and attacked its gums with a knife held in his right. I saw that he was fixed on extracting all the teeth, so I left him to it while he hacked them loose.

When Harkat was done, he took the teeth to the stream and washed them clean of blood. When he returned, he scattered the teeth on the ground and we bent over them to try and decipher the mystery. There were eleven teeth in all, host to a variety of letters. I arranged them alphabetically so that we could see exactly what we had. There were two A's, followed by a single D, H, K, L, M, R, S, T and U.

"We must be able to make a ... message out of them," Harkat said.

"Eleven letters," I mused. "It can't be a very long message. Let's see what we can come up with." I shifted the letters around until I got three words — ASK MUD RAT — with two letters left over, H and L.

Harkat tried and got SLAM DARK HUT.

As I was juggling them around again, Harkat groaned, pushed me aside and began rearranging the teeth purposefully. "Have you worked it out?" I asked, slightly disappointed that he'd beaten me to the punch.

"Yes," he said, "but it's not a clue — just Mr Tiny ... being smug." He finished laying out the teeth and waved at them bitterly — HARKAT MULDS.

"What's the point of that?" I grumbled. "That's a waste of time."

"Mr Tiny loves playing with time," Harkat sighed, then wrapped the teeth in a piece of cloth and tucked them away inside his robes.

"What are you hanging on to them for?" I asked.

"They're sharp," Harkat said. "They might come in useful." He stood and walked over to where the map was drying in the sun. "Will we be able to use this?" he asked, studying the lines and squiggles.

"If it's accurate," I replied.

"Then let's get going," Harkat said, rolling the map up and sticking it inside his robes along with the teeth. "I'm anxious to meet the world's ... largest toad." He looked at me and grinned. "And to see if there's any ... family resemblance."

Laughing, we broke camp quickly and set off through the trees, eager to leave behind the clouds of flies and insects gathering to feast on the corpse of the defeated lord of the jungle.

CHAPTER NINE

ABOUT THREE weeks later, we came to the edge of a huge swamp — the area marked on the map by the circle. It had been a relatively easy trek. The map had been plainly drawn and was simple to follow. Though the terrain was tricky to negotiate – lots of wiry bushes to cut through – it didn't present any life-threatening problems. Harkat's wounds had healed without complications but he was left with three very noticeable scars on the left side of his face — almost as if he'd been marked by an especially eager vampaneze!

A foul smell of putrid water and rotting plants emanated from the swamp. The air was thick with flying insects. As we stood and watched, we spotted a couple of water snakes attack, kill and devour a large rat with four yellow eyes.

"I don't like the look of this," I muttered.

"You haven't seen the worst yet," Harkat said, pointing to a small island off to our left, jutting out of the waters of the swamp. I couldn't see what he was talking about at first — the island was bare except for three large logs — but then one of the "logs" moved.

"Alligators!" I hissed.

"Very bad news for *you*," Harkat said.

"Why me in particular?" I asked.

"*I* wrestled the panther," he grinned. "The alligators are *yours*."

"You've a warped sense of humour, Mulds," I growled, then stepped back from the edge of the swamp. "Let's circle around and try to find the toad."

"You know it's not going to be ... on the outskirts," Harkat said. "We'll have to wade in."

"I know," I sighed, "but let's at least try and find an entry spot that isn't guarded by alligators. We won't get very far if that lot get a whiff of us."

We walked for hours along the rim of the swamp, without sight or sound of a toad, though we did find lots of small brown frogs. We saw plenty more snakes and alligators too. Finally we came to a section with no visible predators. The water was shallow and slightly less pungent than elsewhere. It was as good a place as any to wet our toes.

"I wish I had Mr Tiny's ... Wellington boots," Harkat grumbled, knotting the hem of his blue robes above his knees.

"Me too," I sighed, rolling up the bottoms of my jeans. I paused as I was about to set foot in the water. "I just thought of something. This stretch of swamp could be full of piranha — that might be why there are no alligators or snakes!"

Harkat stared at me with something close to loathing in his round green eyes. "Why can't you keep stupid thoughts ... like that to yourself?" he snapped.

"I'm serious," I insisted. I got down on my hands and knees and peered into the still waters of the swamp, but it was too cloudy to see anything.

"I think piranha only attack when ... they scent blood," Harkat said. "If there are piranha, we should ... be OK as long as we don't cut ourselves."

"It's times like these that I really hate Mr Tiny," I groaned. But since there was nothing else for it, I stepped into the swamp. I paused, ready to leap out at the first hint of a bite, then waded ahead cautiously, Harkat following close behind.

A few hours later, as dusk was lengthening, we found an uninhabited island. Harkat and I hauled ourselves out of the swampy water and collapsed with exhaustion. We then slept, me sheltered beneath the deer blanket I'd been using these last few weeks, Harkat beneath the fleshy map we'd stripped from the black panther's stomach. But we didn't sleep deeply. The swamp was alive with noises — insects, frogs and the occasional unidentifiable splash. We were bleary-eyed and shivering when we rose the following morning.

One good thing about the filthy swamp was that the water level remained fairly low. Every so often we'd hit a dip and one or both of us would slip and disappear under the murky water, only to bob up spluttering and cursing moments later. But most of the time the water didn't reach higher than our thighs. Another bonus was that although the swamp was teeming with insects and leeches, they didn't bother us — our skin was obviously too tough and our blood off-putting.

We avoided the alligators, circling far around them whenever we saw one. Although we were attacked several times by snakes, we were too quick and strong for them. But we had to remain on constant alert — one slip could be the end of us.

"No piranha so far," Harkat noted as we rested. We'd been working our way through a long swath of tall reeds, full of irritating sticky seeds which had stuck to my hair and clothes.

"In cases like this, I'm delighted to be proved wrong," I said.

"We could spend months ... searching for this toad," Harkat commented.

"I don't think it'll take that long," I said. "By the law of averages, it should take ages to locate anything specific in a swamp this size. But Mr Tiny has a way of fiddling with laws. He wants us to find the toad, so I'm sure we will."

"If that's the case," Harkat mused, "maybe we should just ... do nothing and wait for the toad to ... come to us."

"It doesn't work that way," I said. "Mr Tiny's set this up, but we have to sweat to make it happen. If we sat on the edge of the swamp — or if we hadn't marched west when he said — we'd lose touch with the game and would no longer be under his influence — meaning he couldn't stack the odds in our favour."

Harkat studied me curiously. "You've been thinking about this ... a lot," he remarked.

"Not much else to do in this godsforsaken world," I laughed.

Flicking off the last of the seeds, we rested a few more minutes, then set off, silent and grim-faced, wading through the murky waters, our eyes peeled for predators as we moved ever further into the heart of the swamp.

As the sun was setting, a deep-throated croaking noise drifted to us from the middle of an island covered by thick bushes and gnarly trees. We knew at once that it was our toad, just as we'd instantly recognized the panther by its roar. Wading up to the rim of the island, we paused to consider our options.

"The sun will be gone in a few ... minutes," Harkat said. "Perhaps we should wait for ... morning."

"But the moon will be almost full tonight," I pointed out. "This might be as good a time as any to act — bright enough for us to see, but dark enough for us to hide."

Harkat looked at me quizzically. "You sound as though you ... fear this toad."

"Remember Evanna's frogs?" I asked, referring to a group of frogs that guarded the witch's home. They had sacs of poison along the sides of their tongues – it was deadly if it got into your bloodstream. "I know this is a toad, not a frog, but we'd be fools to take it for granted."

"OK," Harkat said. "We'll go in when the moon's up. If we don't like the ... look of it, we can return tomorrow."

We crouched on the edge of the island while the moon rose and illuminated the night sky. Then, drawing our weapons — a knife for me, a spear for Harkat — we pushed through the damp overhanging fronds and crept slowly past the various trees and plants. After several minutes we came to a clearing at the centre of the island, where we paused under cover of a bush and gawped at the spectacular sight ahead.

A wide moat ran around a curved mound of mud and reeds. To the left and right of the moat, alligators lay in wait, four or five on each side. On the mound in the middle lay the toad — and it was a *monster!* Two metres long, with a huge, knobbly body, an immense head with bulging eyes, and an enormous mouth. Its skin was a dark, crinkled, greeny brown colour. It was pockmarked all over, and out of the holes oozed some sort of slimy yellow pus. Thick black leeches slowly slid up and down its hide, like mobile beauty spots, feeding on the pus.

As we stared incredulously at the giant toad, a crow-like bird flew by overhead. The toad's head lifted slightly, then its mouth snapped open and its tongue shot out, impossibly long and thick. It snatched the bird from the air. There was a squawk and a flurried flapping of wings. Then the crow disappeared and the toad's jaw moved up and down as it swallowed the hapless bird.

I was so taken aback by the toad's appearance that I didn't notice the small clear balls surrounding it. It was only when Harkat tapped my arm and pointed that I realized the toad was sitting on what must be the 'gelatinous globes'. We'd have to cross the moat and sneak the globes out from underneath it!

Withdrawing, we huddled in the shadows of the bushes and trees to discuss our next move. "Know what we need?" I whispered to Harkat.

"What?"

"The world's biggest jam jar."

Harkat groaned. "Be serious," he chastized me. "How are we going to get the … globes without that thing taking our heads off?"

"We'll have to sneak up from behind and hope it doesn't notice," I said. "I was watching its tongue when it struck the crow. I didn't spot any poison sacs along the sides."

"What about the alligators?" Harkat asked. "Are they waiting to attack the toad?"

"No," I said. "I think they're protecting it or living in harmony with it, like the leeches."

"I never heard of alligators doing that," Harkat noted sceptically.

"And *I* never heard of a toad bigger than a cow," I retorted. "Who knows how this mad world functions? Maybe all the toads are that size."

The best we could do would be to create a distraction, nip in, grab the globes, and get out again — fast! Retreating to the edge of the island, we waded through the swamp in search of something we could use to distract the alligators. We killed a couple of large water rats, and captured three live creatures unlike anything we'd seen before. They were shaped like turtles, except with see-through, soft shells and nine powerful fins. They were harmless — speed was their single natural defence. We only caught them when they became entangled in weeds on a mud bank as we were chasing them.

Returning to the island, we crept up on the monstrous toad at the centre and paused in the bushes. "I've been thinking," Harkat whispered. "It makes more sense for only ... one of us to move on the toad. The other should hold on to the ... rats and turtles, and throw them to ... the alligators to provide cover."

"That sounds sensible," I agreed. "Any thoughts on who should go in?"

I expected Harkat to volunteer, but he smiled sheepishly and said, "I think *you* should go."

"Oh?" I replied, momentarily thrown.

"You're faster than me," Harkat said. "You stand a better chance of ... making it back alive. Of course, if you ... don't want to..."

"Don't be stupid," I grunted. "I'll do it. Just make sure you keep those 'gators occupied."

"I'll do my best," Harkat said, then slipped off to the left, to find the ideal position to launch the rats and turtle-like creatures.

I nudged my way around to the rear of the toad, so I could sneak up on it without being seen, and wriggled down to the edge of the moat. There was a stick lying nearby which I stuck into the water, testing its depth. It didn't seem deep. I was sure I could wade the six or seven metres towards the toad's base.

There was a rustling motion off to my left and one of the turtle creatures went zooming through the air, landing amidst the alligators on the far right side. One of the dead rats was quickly hurled among the other alligators on the left of the moat. As soon as the alligators began snapping at each other and fighting for the morsels, I lowered myself into the cold, clammy water. It was filled with soggy twigs, dead insects and slime from the toad's sores. I ignored the disgusting mess and waded across to where the toad was squatting, its eyes fixed on the bickering alligators.

There were several jelly-like globes near the edge of the toad's perch. I picked up a couple, meaning to stuff them inside my shirt, but their soft shells were broken. They lost their shape and a sticky clear fluid oozed out of them.

Glancing up, I saw another of the turtles flying through the air, followed by the second dead rat. That meant Harkat only had one of the turtles held in reserve. I had to act fast. Slithering forward on to the mound, I reached for the shiny globes lying closest to the giant toad. Most were covered with pus. It was warm, with the texture of vomit, and the stench made me gag. Holding my breath, I wiped the pus away and found a globe that wasn't broken. I sifted through the shells and found another, then another. The globes were different sizes, some only five or six centimetres in diameter, some twenty centimetres. I packed loads of the globes inside my shirt, working quickly. I'd just about gathered enough when the toad's head turned and I found myself on the end of its fierce, bulging gaze.

I reacted swiftly and spun away, stumbling back towards the island across the moat. As I lunged to safety, the toad unleashed its tongue and struck me hard on my right shoulder, knocking me flat. I came up gasping, spitting out water and bits of jelly and pus. The toad lashed me with its tongue again, connected with the top of my head and sent me flying a second time. As I came up out of the water, dazed, I caught sight of several objects sliding into the moat beyond the mound. I lost all interest in the toad and its tongue. I had a far greater threat to worry about. The alligators had finished with the scraps Harkat had thrown them. Now they were coming after a fresh snack — *me!*

CHAPTER TEN

TURNING MY back on the alligators, I scrambled for the bank. I might have made it if the toad hadn't struck me again with its tongue, this time whipping the tip of it around my throat and spinning me back towards it. The toad hadn't enough power to pull me all the way to the mound, but I landed close to it. As I sprang to my feet, gasping for breath, I spotted the first of the onrushing alligators and knew I'd never make it to the bank in time.

Standing my ground, I prepared to meet the alligator's challenge. My aim was to clamp its jaws shut and keep them closed — it couldn't do much damage with its tiny front claws. But even assuming I could do that, I'd no way of dealing with the rest of the pack, which were coming fast on the lead alligator's tail.

I glimpsed Harkat splashing into the water, rushing to my aid, but the fight would be long over by the time he reached me. The first alligator homed in on me, eyes glinting cruelly, snout lifting as it bared its fangs — so many! so long! so sharp! — to crush me. I drew my hands apart and started bringing them together...

... when, on the bank to my right, a figure appeared and screeched something unintelligible while waving its arms high in the air.

There was a lightning-bright flash in the sky overhead. I instinctively covered my eyes with my hands. When I removed them a few seconds later, I saw that the alligator had missed me and run aground on the bank. The other alligators were all in a muddle, swimming around in circles and crashing into one another. On the mound, the toad had lowered its head and was croaking deeply, paying no attention to me.

I gazed from the alligators to Harkat — he'd stopped in confusion — then at the figure on the bank. As it lowered its arms, I saw that it was a person —— a woman! And as she stepped forward, out of the shadows of the trees, revealing her long straggly hair and body-wrapping ropes, I recognized her.

"*Evanna?*" I roared in disbelief.

"That was pretty finely timed, even by my standards," the witch grunted, coming to a halt at the edge of the moat.

"*Evanna?*" Harkat cried.

"Is there an echo?" the witch sniffed, then glanced around at the alligators and toad. "I've cast a temporary blinding spell on the creatures, but it won't last long. If you value your lives, get out of there, and quick!"

"But how … what … where…" I stuttered.

"Let's talk about it on … dry land," Harkat said, crossing over to join me, carefully skirting the thrashing alligators. "Did you get the globes?"

"Yes," I said, pulling one out from within my shirt. "But how did she—"

"Later!" Harkat snapped, pushing me towards safety.

Suppressing my questions, I stumbled to the bank and crawled out of the mucky water of the moat. Evanna caught me by the back of my shirt and hauled me to my feet, then grabbed Harkat's robes and pulled him up too. "Come on," she said, retreating. "We'd best not be here when their sight clears. That toad has a nasty temper and might bound after us."

Harkat and I paused to consider what would happen if a toad that size leapt upon us. Then we hurried after the departing witch as fast as our weary legs could carry us.

Evanna had established her camp on a grassy isle a few hundred metres from the island of the toad. A fire was burning when we crawled out of the swamp, a vegetable stew bubbling in a pot above it. Replacement clothes were waiting for us, blue robes for Harkat, dark brown trousers and a shirt for me.

"Get out of those wet rags, get dry, and get dressed," Evanna ordered, going to check on the stew.

Harkat and I stared from the witch, to the fire, to the clothes.

"This probably sounds like a stupid question," I said, "but have you been expecting us?"

"Of course," Evanna said. "I've been here for the past week. I guessed you wouldn't arrive that soon, but I didn't want to risk missing you."

"How did you know we … were coming?" Harkat asked.

"Please," Evanna sighed. "You know of my magical powers and my ability to predict future events. Don't trouble me with unnecessary questions."

"So tell us why you're here," I encouraged her. "And why you rescued us. As I recall, you've always said you couldn't get involved in our battles."

"Not in your fight with the vampaneze," Evanna said. "When it comes to alligators and toads, I have a free hand. Now why don't you change out of your damp clothes and eat some of this delicious stew before you pester me with more of your dratted questions?"

Since it was uncomfortable standing there wet and hungry, we did as the witch advised. After a quick meal, as we were licking our fingers clean, I asked Evanna if she could tell us where we were. "No," she said.

"Could you transport Darren … back home?" Harkat asked.

"I'm going nowhere!" I objected immediately.

"You just narrowly survived being … swallowed by alligators," Harkat grunted. "I won't let you risk your … life any—"

"This is a pointless argument," Evanna interrupted. "I don't have the power to transport either of you back."

"But *you* were able to ... come here," Harkat argued. "You must be able to ... return."

"Things aren't as simple as they seem," Evanna said. "I can't explain it without revealing facts which I must keep secret. All I'll say is that I didn't get here the way you did, and I can't open a gateway between the reality you know and this one. Only Desmond Tiny can."

There was no point in quizzing her further — the witch, like Mr Tiny, couldn't be drawn on certain issues — so we dropped it. "Can you tell us anything about the quest we're on?" I asked instead. "Where we have to go next or what we must do?"

"I can tell you that I am to act as your guide on the next stretch of your adventure," Evanna said. "That's why I intervened — since I'm part of your quest, I can play an active role in it, at least for a while."

"You're coming with us?" I whooped, delighted at the thought of having someone to show us the way.

"Yes," Evanna smiled, "but only for a short time. I will be with you for ten, maybe eleven days. After that you're on your own." Rising, she started away from us. "You may rest now," she said. "Nothing will disturb your slumber here. I'll return in the afternoon and we'll set off."

"For where?" Harkat asked. But if the witch heard, she didn't bother to respond, and seconds later she was gone. Since there was nothing else we could do, Harkat and I made rough beds on the grass, lay down and slept.

CHAPTER ELEVEN

AFTER BREAKFAST, Evanna guided us out of the swamp and south across more hard, barren land. It wasn't as lifeless as the desert we'd crossed, but very little grew on the reddish soil, and the animals were tough-skinned and bony.

Over the days and nights that followed, we slyly probed the witch for clues about where we were, who Harkat had been, what the gelatinous globes were for, and what lay ahead. We slid the questions into ordinary conversations, hoping to catch Evanna off guard. But she was sharp as a snake and never let anything slip.

Despite her annoying reluctance to reveal anything of our circumstances, she was a welcome travelling companion. She arranged the sleeping quarters every night – she could set up a camp within seconds – and told us what we could and couldn't eat (many of the animals and plants were poisonous or indigestible). She also spun tales and sung songs to amuse us during the long, harsh hours of walking.

I asked her several times how the War of the Scars was going, and what Vancha March and the other Princes and Generals were up to. She only shook her head at such questions and said this was not the time for her to comment.

We often discussed Mr Crepsley. Evanna had known the vampire long before I did and was able to tell me what he'd been like as a younger man. I felt sad talking about my lost friend, but it was a warm sort of sadness, not like the cold misery I experienced in the early weeks after he'd died. One night, when Harkat was asleep and snoring loudly (Evanna had confirmed what he'd already suspected — he could breathe the air here — so he'd dispensed with his mask), I asked Evanna if it was possible to communicate with Mr Crepsley. "Mr Tiny has the power to speak with the dead," I said. "Can you?"

"Yes," she said, "but we can only speak to those whose spirits remain trapped on Earth after they die. Most people's souls move on — though nobody knows for sure where they go, not even my father."

"So you can't get in touch with Mr Crepsley?" I asked.

"Thankfully, no," she smiled. "Larten has left the realm of the physical for ever. I like to think he is with Arra Sails and his other loved ones in Paradise, awaiting the rest of his friends."

Arra Sails was a female vampire. She and Mr Crepsley had been "married" once. She died when a vampire traitor —

Kurda Smahlt — sneaked a band of vampaneze into Vampire Mountain. Thinking about Arra and Kurda set me to pondering the past, and I asked Evanna if there'd been any way to avoid the bloody War of the Scars. "If Kurda had told us about the Lord of the Vampaneze, would it have made a difference? Or what if he'd become a Prince, taken control of the Stone of Blood and forced the Generals to submit to the vampaneze? Would Mr Crepsley be alive? And Arra? And all the others who've died in the war?"

Evanna sighed deeply. "Time is like a jigsaw puzzle," she said. "Imagine a giant box full of billions of pieces of millions of puzzles — that is the future. Beside it lies a huge board, partially filled with bits of the overall puzzle — that is the past. Those in the present reach blindly into the box of the future every time they have a decision to make, draw a piece of the puzzle out and slot it into place on the board. Once a piece has been added, it influences the final shape and design of the puzzle, and it's useless trying to fathom what the puzzle would have looked like if a different piece had been picked." She paused. "Unless you're Desmond Tiny. He spends most of his time considering the puzzle and contemplating alternative patterns."

I thought about that for a long time before speaking again. "What you're saying is that there's no point worrying about the past, because we can't change it?"

"Basically," she nodded, then leant over, one green eye shining brightly, one brown eye gleaming dully. "A mortal can drive himself mad thinking about the nature of the universal puzzle. Concern yourself only with the problems of the present and you will get along fine."

It was an odd conversation, one I returned to often, not just that night when I was trying to sleep, but during the quieter moments of the testing weeks ahead.

Eleven days after Evanna had rescued me from the jaws of the alligator, we came to the edge of an immense lake. At first I thought it was a sea — I couldn't see to the far side — but when I tested the water, I found it fresh, although very bitter.

"This is where I'll leave you," Evanna said, gazing out over the dark blue water, then up into the cloud-filled sky. The weather had changed during the course of our journey — clouds and rain were now the norm.

"What's the lake called?" Harkat asked, hoping — like me — that this was the Lake of Souls, though we both knew in our hearts that it wasn't.

"It has no name," Evanna said. "It's a relatively new formation, and the sentient beings of this planet have yet to discover it."

"You mean there are people here?" Harkat asked sharply.

"Yes," the witch replied.

"Why haven't we seen any?" I asked.

"This is a large planet," Evanna said, "but people are few. You may run into some before your adventure draws to a close, but don't get sidetracked — you're here to discover the truth about Harkat, not cavort with the natives. Now, would you like a hand making a raft, or would you rather do it yourselves?"

"What will we need a raft for?" I asked.

Evanna pointed to the lake. "Three guesses, genius."

"Can't we track around it?" Harkat enquired.

"You can, but I don't advise it."

We sighed — when Evanna said something like that, we knew we hadn't much of a choice. "What will we build it from?" I asked. "It's been a few days since I spotted any trees."

"We're close to the wreck of a boat," Evanna said, heading off to the left. "We can strip it bare and use the wood."

"I thought you said none of the ... people here had found this lake," Harkat said, but if the witch heard the query, she paid it no heed.

About a kilometre up the pebbly lake shore, we found the bleached remains of a small wooden boat. The first planks we pulled off were soggy and rotten, but there were stronger planks underneath. We stacked them in a tidy pile, sorting them by length.

"How are we going to bind them?" I asked when we were ready to begin construction. "There aren't any nails." I wiped rain from my forehead — it had been drizzling steadily for the last hour.

"The builder of the boat used mud to bind the planks," Evanna said. "He had no rope or nails, and no intention of sailing the boat — he merely built it to keep himself busy."

"Mud won't keep a raft together once we ... get out on the water," Harkat noted dubiously.

"Indeed," Evanna smirked. "That's why we are going to tie the planks tightly with ropes." The squat witch began unwrapping the ropes she kept knotted around her body.

"Do you want us to look away?" I asked.

"No need," she laughed. "I don't plan to strip myself bare!"

The witch reeled off an incredibly long line of rope, dozens of metres in length, yet the ropes around her body didn't diminish, and she was as discreetly covered when she stopped as she'd been at the outset. "There!" she grunted. "That should suffice."

We spent the rest of the day constructing the raft, Evanna acting as the designer, performing magical shortcuts when our backs were turned, making our job a lot quicker and easier than it should have been. It wasn't a large raft when finished, two and a half metres long by two wide, but we could both fit on it and lie down in comfort. Evanna wouldn't tell us how wide the lake was, but said we'd have to sail due south and sleep on the raft a few nights at least. The raft floated nicely when we tested it and although we had no sails, we fashioned oars out of leftover planks.

"You should be fine now," Evanna said. "You won't be able to light a fire, but fish swim close to the surface of the lake. Catch and eat them raw. And the water is unpleasant but safe to drink."

"Evanna…" I began, then coughed with embarrassment.

"What is it, Darren?" the witch asked.

"The gelatinous globes," I muttered. "Will you tell us what they're for?"

"No," she said. "And that's not what you wanted to ask. Out with it, please. What's bothering you?"

"Blood," I sighed. "It's been ages since I last drank human blood. I'm feeling the side effects — I've lost a lot of my sharpness and strength. If I carry on like this, I'll die. I was wondering if I could drink from *you*?"

Evanna smiled regretfully. "I would gladly let you drink from me, but I'm not human and my blood's not fit for consumption — you'd feel a lot worse afterwards! But don't worry. If the fates are kind, you'll find a feeding source shortly. If they're not," she added darkly, "you'll have greater problems to worry about.

"Now," the witch said, stepping away from the raft, "I must leave you. The sooner you set off, the sooner you'll arrive at the other side. I've just this to say — I've saved it until now because I had to — and then I'll depart. I can't tell you what the future has in store, but I can offer this advice — to fish in the Lake of Souls, you must borrow a net which has been used to trawl for the dead. And to access the Lake, you'll need the holy liquid from the Temple of the Grotesque."

"*Temple of the Grotesque?*" Harkat and I immediately asked together.

"Sorry," Evanna grunted. "I can tell you that much, but nothing else." Waving to us, the witch said, "Luck, Darren Shan. Luck, Harkat Mulds." And then, before we could reply, she darted away, moving with magical speed, disappearing out of sight within seconds into the gloom of the coming night.

Harkat and I stared at one another silently, then turned and manoeuvred our meagre stash of possessions on to the raft. We divided the gelatinous globes into three piles: one for Harkat, one for me and one in a scrap of cloth tied to the raft, then set off in the gathering darkness across the cold, still water of the nameless lake.

CHAPTER TWELVE

WE ROWED for most of the night, in what we hoped was a straight line (there seemed to be no currents to drag us off course), rested for a few hours either side of dawn, then began rowing again, this time navigating south by the position of the sun. By the third day we were bored out of our skulls. There was nothing to do on the calm, open lake, and no change in scenery — dark blue underneath, mostly unbroken grey overhead. Fishing distracted us for short periods each day, but the fish were plentiful and easy to catch, and soon it was back to the rowing and resting.

To keep ourselves amused, we invented games using the teeth Harkat had pulled from the dead panther. There weren't many word games we could play with such a small complement of letters, but by giving each letter a number, we were able to pretend the teeth were dice and indulge in simple gambling games. We didn't have anything of value to bet, so we used the bones of the fish we caught as gambling chips, and made believe they were worth vast amounts of money.

During a rest period, as Harkat was cleaning the teeth — taking his time, to stretch the job out — he picked up a long incisor, the one marked by a K, and frowned. "This is hollow," he said, holding it up and peering through it. Putting it to his wide mouth, he blew through it, held it up again, then passed it to me.

I studied the tooth against the grey light of the sky, squinting to see better. "It's very smooth," I noted. "And it goes from being wide at the top to narrow at the tip."

"It's almost as though ... a hole has been bored through it," Harkat said.

"How, and what for?" I asked.

"Don't know," Harkat said. "But it's the only one ... like that."

"Maybe an insect did it," I suggested. "A parasite which burrows into an animal's teeth and gnaws its way upwards, feeding on the material inside."

Harkat stared at me for a moment, then opened his mouth as wide as he could and gurgled, "Check my teeth quick!"

"Mine first!" I yelped, anxiously probing my teeth with my tongue.

"Your teeth are tougher ... than mine," he said. "I'm more vulnerable."

Since that was true, I leant forward to examine Harkat's sharp grey teeth. I studied them thoroughly, but there was no sign that any had been invaded. Harkat checked mine next, but

I drew a clean bill of health too. We relaxed after that — though we did a lot of prodding and jabbing with our tongues over the next few hours! — and Harkat returned to cleaning the teeth, keeping the tooth with the hole to one side, slightly away from the others.

That fourth night, as we slept after many hours of rowing, huddled together in the middle of the raft, we were woken by a thunderous flapping sound overhead. We bolted out of our sleep and sat up straight, covering our ears to drown out the noise. The sound was like nothing I'd heard before, impossibly heavy, as though a giant was beating clean his bed sheets. It was accompanied by strong, cool gusts of wind which set the water rippling and our raft rocking. It was a dark night with no break in the clouds, and we couldn't see what was making the noise.

"What is it?" I whispered. Harkat couldn't hear my whisper over the noise, so I repeated myself, but not too loudly, for fear of giving our position away to whatever was above.

"No idea," Harkat replied, "but there's something ... familiar about it. I've heard it before ... but I can't remember where."

The flapping sounds died away as whatever it was moved on, the water calmed and our raft steadied, leaving us shaken but unharmed. When we discussed it later, we reasoned it must have been some huge breed of bird. But in my gut, I sensed that wasn't the answer, and by Harkat's troubled expression and inability to fall back asleep, I was sure he sensed it too.

We rowed quicker than usual in the morning, saying little about the sounds we'd heard the night before, but gazing up often at the sky. Neither of us could explain why the noise had so alarmed us — we just felt that we'd be in big trouble if the creature came again, by the light of day.

We spent so much time staring up at the clouds that it wasn't until early afternoon, during a brief rest period, that we looked ahead and realized we were within sight of land. "How far do you think ... it is?" Harkat asked.

"I'm not sure," I answered. "Four or five kilometres?" The land was low-lying, but there were mountains further on, tall grey peaks which blended with the clouds, which was why we hadn't noticed them before.

"We can be there soon if we ... row hard," Harkat noted.

"So let's row," I grunted, and we set to our task with renewed vigour. Harkat was able to row faster than me — my strength was failing rapidly as a result of not having any human blood to drink — but I stuck my head down and pushed my muscles to their full capacity. We were both eager to make the safety of land, where at least we could find a bush to hide under if we were attacked.

We'd covered about half the distance when the air overhead reverberated with the same heavy flapping sounds that had interrupted our slumber. Gusts of wind cut up the water around us. Pausing, we looked up and spotted something hovering far above. It seemed small, but that was because it was a long way up.

"What the hell is it?" I gasped.

Harkat shook his head in answer. "It must be immense," he muttered, "for its wings to create ... this much disturbance from that high up."

"Do you think it's spotted us?" I asked.

"It wouldn't be hovering there otherwise," Harkat said.

The flapping sound and accompanying wind stopped and the figure swooped towards us with frightening speed, becoming larger by the second. I thought it meant to torpedo us, but it pulled out of its dive ten or so metres above the raft. Slowing its descent, it unfurled gigantic wings and flapped to keep itself steady. The sound was ear shattering.

"Is that ... what I ... think it is?" I roared, clinging to the raft as waves broke over us, eyes bulging out of my head, unable to believe that this monster was real. I wished with all my heart that Harkat would tell me I was hallucinating.

"Yes!" Harkat shouted, shattering my wishes. "I knew I ... recognized it!" The Little Person crawled to the edge of the raft to gaze at the magnificent but terrifying creature of myth. He was petrified, like me, but there was also an excited gleam in his green eyes. "I've seen it before ... in my nightmares," he croaked, his voice only barely audible over the flapping of the extended wings. "It's a *dragon!*"

CHAPTER THIRTEEN

I'D NEVER in my life seen anything as wondrous as this dragon, and even though I was struck numb with fear, I found myself admiring it, unable to react to the threat it posed. Though it was impossible to accurately judge its measurements, its wingspan had to be twenty metres. The wings were a patchy light green colour, thick where they connected to its body, but thin at the tips.

The dragon's body was seven or eight metres from snout to the tip of its tail. It put me in mind of a snake's tapered body — it was scaled — though it had a round bulging chest which angled back towards the tail. Its scales were a dull red and gold colour underneath. From what I could see of the dragon's back, it was dark green on top, with red flecks. It had a pair of long forelegs, ending in sharp claws, and two shorter limbs about a quarter of the way from the end of its body.

Its head was more like an alligator's than a snake's, long

and flat, with two yellow eyes protruding from its crown, large nostrils, and a flexible lower jaw which looked like it could open wide to consume large animals. Its face was a dark purple colour and its ears were surprisingly small, pointed and set close to its eyes. It had no teeth that I could see, but the gums of its jaws looked hard and sharp. It had a long, forked tongue which flicked lazily between its lips as it hung in the air and gazed upon us.

The dragon observed us for a few more seconds, wings beating steadily, claws flexing, pupils opening and dilating. Then, tucking in its wings, it dived sharply, forelegs stretched, talons exposed, mouth closed — aiming for the raft!

With startled yells, Harkat and I snapped to attention and threw ourselves flat. The dragon screamed by overhead. One of its claws connected with my left shoulder and sent me crashing into Harkat.

As we pushed ourselves apart, I sat up, rubbing my bruised shoulder, and saw the dragon turn smoothly in the air, reverse and begin another dive. This time, instead of throwing himself on to the raft, Harkat grabbed his oar and thrust it up at the dragon, roaring a challenge at the monster. The dragon screeched angrily in reply — a high-pitched sound — and swerved away.

"Get up!" Harkat yelled at me. As I struggled to my feet, he thrust my oar into my hands, got to his knees and rowed desperately. "You keep it off ... if you can," he gasped. "I'll try and get us ... to shore. Our only hope is to ... make land and hope we can ... hide."

Holding the oar up was agony, but I ignored the pain in my shoulder and kept the piece of wood aloft, pointed at the dragon like a spear, silently willing Harkat to row even quicker. Above, the dragon circled, yellow eyes focused on the raft, occasionally screeching.

"It's assessing us," I muttered.

"What?" Harkat grunted.

"It's making a study. Noting our speed, analyzing our strengths, calculating our weaknesses." I lowered my oar. "Stop rowing."

"Are you crazy?" Harkat shouted.

"We'll never make it," I said calmly. "We're too far out. We'd best save our strength for fighting."

"How the hell do you think ... we're going to fight a dragon?" Harkat snorted.

"I don't know," I sighed. "But we can't out-pace it, so we might as well be fresh when it attacks."

Harkat stopped rowing and stood beside me, staring at the dragon with his unblinking green eyes. "Maybe it won't attack," he said with hollow optimism.

"It's a predator," I replied, "like the panther and alligators. It's not a question of *if* it will attack, but *when.*"

Harkat looked from the dragon to the shore and licked his lips. "What if we swam? We wouldn't be as visible ... in the water. That might make it harder ... for it to grab us."

"True," I agreed, "but we wouldn't be able to defend ourselves. We won't jump unless we have to. In the meantime, let's sharpen our oars." Drawing one of my knives, I whittled away at the end of my oar. Harkat did the same with his. Within seconds of us setting to work on the oars, the dragon – perhaps sensing our intent – attacked, cutting short our preparations.

My immediate instinct was to duck, but I stood firm beside Harkat and we both raised our oars defensively. The dragon didn't pull out of its dive this time, but swooped even lower than before and barrelled into us with its hard head and shoulders, wings tucked in tight. We jabbed at it with our oars, but they snapped off its hard scales without causing the slightest bit of damage.

The dragon collided with the raft. The force of the blow sent us flying clear of the raft, deep under water. I came up gasping and thrashing wildly. Harkat was several metres adrift of me, also winded and bruised from the encounter. "Got to … make the … raft!" he shouted.

"No use!" I cried, pointing at the wreckage of the raft, which had been shattered to splinters. The dragon was hovering overhead, almost perpendicular to the sea, tail curled up into its scaly body. I swam to where Harkat was bobbing up and down, and we gazed up fearfully at the flying lizard.

"What's it waiting for?" Harkat wheezed. "We're at its mercy. Why isn't it finishing … us off?"

"It seems to be puffing itself up," I noted, as the dragon closed its mouth and breathed in through its widening nostrils. "It's almost as though it's getting ready to…" I stopped, my face whitening. "Charna's guts!"

"What?" Harkat snapped.

"Have you forgotten what dragons are famous for?"

Harkat stared at me, clueless, then clicked to it. "They breathe fire!"

Our eyes locked on the dragon's chest, which was expanding steadily. "Watch it closely," I said, grabbing hold of Harkat's robes. "When I say 'dive', power for the bottom of the lake as hard as you can, and stay under till your breath runs out."

"It'll still be here ... when we come up," Harkat said dejectedly.

"Probably," I agreed, "but if we're lucky, it only has one burst of fire in it."

"What are you basing that ... judgement on?" Harkat asked.

"Nothing." I grinned shakily. "I'm just hoping."

There was no time for further exchanges. Above us, the dragon's tail curled down and back, and its head swung towards us. I waited until what I deemed the last possible instant, then, "*Dive!*" I screamed, and together Harkat and I rolled over and dived down deep, thrusting hard with our hands and feet.

As we descended, the water around us lit up redly. It then grew warm and began to bubble. Kicking even harder, we swam clear of the danger zone, down into the darkness of the deeper water. Once safe, we stopped and looked up. The lake had darkened again and we couldn't see the dragon. Clinging tight to each other, we held our mouths shut, waiting for as long as our breath would hold.

As we floated in silence and fear, there was a huge splash and the dragon came slicing through the water towards us. There was no time to evade it. Before we knew what was happening, the dragon hooked us with its claws, dragged us deeper down into the lake, then turned and struck for the surface.

Bursting free of the water, the dragon screeched triumphantly and rose into the air, Harkat trapped in one of its claws, me in the other. It had hold of my left arm, gripping me tightly, and I couldn't wriggle free.

"Darren!" Harkat screamed as we rose higher into the sky and surged towards shore. "Can you ... get loose?"

"No!" I shouted. "You?"

"I think so! It only has hold ... of my robes."

"Then free yourself!" I yelled.

"But what about—"

"Never mind me! Get free while you can!"

Harkat cursed bitterly, then grabbed hold of the back of his robes where the dragon had caught him, and tugged sharply. I didn't hear the ripping over the sound of the dragon's wings, but suddenly Harkat was free and falling, landing with an almighty splash in the lake beneath.

The dragon hissed with frustration and circled around, obviously meaning to go after Harkat again. We were almost over land now, at the very edge of the lake. "Stop!" I roared helplessly at the dragon. "Leave him alone!" To my astonishment, the dragon paused when I shouted, and gazed at me with a strange expression in its giant yellow eyes. "Leave him," I muttered desperately. Then, giving way to blind panic, I screamed at the beast, "Let me go, you son of a—"

Before I could complete the curse, the dragon's claws unexpectedly retracted, and suddenly I was dropping through the sky like a stone. I had just enough time to worry about whether I was over the lake or over land. Then I hit hard — *earth or water?* — and the world went black.

CHAPTER FOURTEEN

WHEN MY eyes opened, I was lying in a hammock. I thought I was back in the Cirque Du Freak. I looked over to tell Harkat about a weird dream I'd had – full of black panthers, giant toads and dragons – but when I did, I saw that I was in a poorly built shack. There was a strange man standing close by, studying me with beady eyes and stroking a long curved knife.

"Who are you?" I shouted, falling out of the hammock. "Where am I?"

"Easy," the man chuckled, laying his knife aside. "Sorry t' trouble ye, young 'un. I was watching over ye while ye slept. We get an awful lot o' crabs and scorpions here. I didn't want 'em getting stuck into ye while ye was recovering. Harkat!" he bellowed. "Yer wee friend's awake!"

The door to the shack swung open and Harkat stepped in. The three scars from his fight with the panther were as prominent as usual, but he didn't look any the worse for wear otherwise. "Afternoon, Sleeping Beauty," he grinned. "You've been out for ... almost two days."

"Where are we?" I asked, standing shakily. "And who's this?"

"Spits Abrams," the stranger introduced himself, stepping forward into the beam of sunlight shining through a large hole in the roof. He was a broad, bearded man of medium height, with small eyes and bushy eyebrows. His black hair was long and curly, tied back with coloured pieces of string. He wore a faded brown jacket and trousers, a dirty white vest, and knee-high black boots. He was smiling and I could see that he was missing several teeth, while the others were discoloured and jagged. "Spits Abrams," he said again, sticking out a hand. "Pleased t' meet ye."

I took the man's hand – he had a strong grip – and shook it warily, wondering who he was and how I'd wound up here.

"Spits rescued you from the lake," Harkat said. "He saw the dragon attack ... and drop you. He dragged you out and was ... waiting for you to dry when *I* waded out. He got a shock when ... he saw me, but I convinced him I was harmless. We carried you here, to his ... home. We've been waiting for you ... to wake."

"Many thanks, Mr Abrams," I said.

"'Tain't nowt t' be thanking me fer," he laughed. "I jest fished ye out, same as any other fisherman would've."

"You're a fisherman?" I asked.

"Of a sort," he beamed. "I used t' be a pirate 'fore I ended up here, and 'twas people I fished fer. But since there ain't much grows round these parts, I've been eating mostly fish since I came — and fishing fer 'em."

"A pirate?" I blinked. "A real one?"

"Aaarrr, Darren lad," he growled, then winked.

"Let's go outside," Harkat said, seeing my confusion. "There's food on the fire and ... your clothes are dry and repaired."

I realized I was only wearing my underpants, so I hurried out after Harkat, found my clothes hanging on a tree, and slipped them on. We were close to the edge of the lake, on a meagre green patch amidst a long stretch of rocky soil. The shack was built in the shelter of two small trees. There was a tiny garden out back.

"That's where I grows me potatoes," Spits said. "Not fer eating — though I has one 'r two when I takes a fancy — but fer brewing poteen. My grandfather came from Connemara — in Ireland — and he used t' make a living from it. He taught me all his secrets. I never bothered before I washed up here — I prefer whisky — but since spuds is all I can grow, I has t' make do."

Dressed, I sat by the fire and Spits offered me one of the fish speared on sticks over the flames. Biting into the fish, I ate ravenously, silently studying Spits Abrams, not sure what to make of him.

"Want some poteen to wash that down with?" Spits asked.

"I wouldn't," Harkat advised me. "I tried it and it made ... my eyes water."

"I'll give it a miss then," I said. Harkat had a high tolerance for alcohol, and could drink just about anything. If the poteen had made his eyes water, it'd probably blow my head clean off my neck.

"Yerra, go on," Spits encouraged me, passing over a jug filled with a clear liquid. "It might blind ye, but 'twon't kill ye. 'Twill put hairs on yer chest!"

"I'm hairy enough," I chuckled, then leant forward, nudging the jug of poteen aside. "I don't want to be rude, Spits, but who are you and how did you get here?"

Spits laughed at the question. "That's what this 'un asked too, the first time he saw me," he said, pointing at Harkat with his thumb. "I've told him all about myself these last couple o' days — did a helluva lot o' talking fer a man who ain't said a word fer five or six years! I won't go through the whole thing again, just give ye the quick lowdown."

Spits had been a pirate in the Far East in the 1930s. Although piracy was a "dying art" (as he put it), there were still ships which sailed the seas and attacked others in the years before World War II, plundering them of their spoils. Spits found himself working on one of the pirate ships after years of ordinary naval service (he said he was shanghaied, though his eyes shifted cagily, and I got the feeling he wasn't being honest). "The *Prince o' Pariahs* was 'er name." He beamed proudly. "A fine ship, small but speedy. We was the scourge o' the waters wherever we went."

It was Spits's job to fish people out of the sea if they jumped in when they were boarded. "Two reasons we didn't like leaving 'em there," he said. "One was that we didn't want 'em to drown — we was pirates, not killers. The other was that the ones who jumped was normally carrying jewels or other such valuables — only the rich is that scared of being robbed!"

Spits got that shifty look in his eyes again when he was talking about fishing people out, but I said nothing about it, not wanting to offend the man who'd rescued me from the lake.

One night, the *Prince of Pariahs* found itself at the centre of a fierce storm. Spits said it was the worst he'd ever experienced, "and I been through just about everything that old sow of a sea can throw at a man!" As the ship broke apart, Spits grabbed a sturdy plank, some jugs of whisky and the nets he used to fish for people, and jumped overboard.

"Next thing I know, I'm in this lake," he finished. "I dragged myself out and there was a small man in big yellow galoshes waiting fer me." *Mr Tiny!* "He told me I'd come to a place far from the one I knew, and I was stuck. He said this was a land o' dragons, awful dangerous fer humans, but there was a shack where I'd be safe. If I stayed there and kept a watch on the lake, two people would come along eventually, and they could make my dreams come true. So I sat back, fished, found spuds growing nearby and brought some back fer me garden, and I been waiting ever since, five 'r six years near as I can figure."

I thought that over, staring from Spits to Harkat and back again. "What did he mean when he said we'd be able to make your dreams come true?" I asked.

"I suppose he meant ye'd be able t' get me home." Spits's eyes shifted nervously. "That's the only dream this old sailor has, t' get back where there's women and whisky, and not a drop o' water bigger than a puddle in sight — I've had enough o' seas and lakes!"

I wasn't sure I believed that was all the pirate had on his mind, but I let the matter drop and instead asked if he knew anything about the land ahead. "Not a whole lot," he answered. "I've done some exploring, but the dragons keep me pinned here most o' the time — I don't like wandering off too far with them demons waiting to pounce."

"There's more than one?" I frowned.

"Aaarrr," he said. "I ain't sure how many, but definitely four 'r five. The one that went after ye is the biggest I've seen, though mebbe there's bigger that don't bother with this lake."

"I don't like the sound of that," I muttered.

"Me neither," Harkat said. Then, turning to Spits, he said, "Show him the net."

Spits ducked behind the shack and emerged dragging a stringy old net, which he untangled and spread on the ground. "Two o' me nets slipped through with me," he said. "I lost t'other one a couple o' years back when a huge fish snatched it out o' my hands. I been keeping this 'un safe, in case of an emergency."

I remembered what Evanna had told us, that we'd need a net which had been used to fish for the dead if we were to find out who Harkat had been. "Think this is the net we need?" I asked Harkat.

"Must be," he answered. "Spits says he didn't use his nets to … fish for the dead, but this has to be it."

"Course I never fished fer the dead!" Spits boomed, laughing weakly. "What'd I do that fer? Mind, I been thinking about it since Harkat asked, and I recall a couple o' people who drowned when I was fishing 'em out. So I guess it probably *has* been used to drag up corpses — accidentally, like."

Spits's eyes practically shot out of his sockets, they were darting so swiftly from side to side. There was definitely something the ex-pirate wasn't telling us. But I couldn't pump him for information without indicating that I didn't believe him, and this was no time to risk making an enemy.

After eating, we discussed what to do next. Spits didn't know anything about a Temple of the Grotesque. Nor had he seen any people during his long, lonely years here. He'd told Harkat that the dragons usually approached the lake from the southeast. The Little Person was of the opinion that we should go in that direction, though he couldn't say why — just a gut feeling. Since I'd no personal preference, I bowed to his wishes and we agreed to head southeast that night, moving under cover of darkness.

"Ye'll take me along, won't ye?" Spits asked eagerly. "I'd feel awful if ye went without me."

"We don't know what we're … walking into," Harkat warned the grizzly ex-pirate. "You could be risking your life … by coming with us."

"Nowt t' worry about!" Spits guffawed. "'Twon't be the first time I risked it. I remember when the *Prince o' Pariahs* sailed into a trap off the Chinese coast…"

Once Spits got talking about his adventures on the pirate ship, there was no stopping him. He regaled us with wild, bawdy tales of the plundering they'd done and battles they'd engaged in. As he spoke, he sipped from his jug of poteen, and as the day wore on his voice got louder and his tales got wilder — he told some extra spicy stories about what he'd got up to during shore leave! Eventually, with the sun starting to set, he dozed off and curled up into a ball beside the fire, clutching his almost empty jug of poteen close to his chest.

"He's some character," I whispered, and Harkat chuckled softly.

"I feel sorry for him," Harkat said. "To be stuck here alone for ... so long must have been dreadful."

"Yes," I agreed, but not wholeheartedly. "But there's something 'off' about him, isn't there? He makes me feel uneasy, the way his eyes flick left and right so beadily when he's lying."

"I noticed that too," Harkat nodded. "He tells all sorts of lies — last night he ... said he'd been engaged to a Japanese princess — but it's ... only when he talks about his job on the ... *Prince of Pariahs* that he gets the *really* shifty look."

"What do you think he's hiding?" I asked.

"I've no idea," Harkat replied. "I doubt it matters — there are ... no pirate ships here."

"At least none that we've seen," I grinned.

Harkat studied the sleeping Spits — he was drooling into his unkempt beard — then said quietly, "We can leave him behind … if you'd prefer. He'll be asleep for hours. If we leave now and walk … fast, he'll never find us."

"Do you think he's dangerous?" I asked.

Harkat shrugged. "He might be. But there must be a reason why … Mr Tiny put him here. I think we should take him. And his net."

"Definitely the net," I agreed. Clearing my throat, I added, "There's his blood too. I need human blood — and soon."

"I thought of that," Harkat said. "It's why I didn't stop him … drinking. Do you want to take some now?"

"Maybe I should wait for him to wake and ask him," I suggested.

Harkat shook his head. "Spits is superstitious. He thinks I'm a demon."

"A demon!" I laughed.

"I told him what I really … was, but he wouldn't listen. In the end I settled for persuading him … that I was a harmless demon — an imp. I sounded him out about vampires. He believes in them, but thinks they're … evil monsters. Said he'd drive a stake through … the heart of the first one he met. I think you should drink … from him while he's asleep, and never … tell him what you really are."

I didn't like doing it — I'd no qualms about drinking secretly from strangers, but on the rare occasions when I'd had to drink from people I knew, I'd always asked their permission — but I bowed to Harkat's greater knowledge of Spits Abrams's ways.

Sneaking up on the sleeping sot, I bared his lower left leg, made a small cut with my right index nail, clamped my mouth around it and sucked. His blood was thin and riddled with alcohol — he must have drunk huge amounts of poteen and whisky over the years! — but I forced it down. When I'd drunk enough, I released him and waited for the blood around the cut to dry. When it had, I cleaned it and rolled the leg of his trousers down.

"Better?" Harkat asked.

"Yes." I burped. "I wouldn't like to drink from him often — there's more poteen than blood in his veins! — but it'll restore my strength and keep me going for the next few weeks."

"Spits won't wake until morning," Harkat noted. "We'll have to wait ... until tomorrow night to start, unless you ... want to risk travelling by day."

"With dragons roaming overhead? No thanks! Anyway, an extra day of rest won't hurt — I'm still recovering from our last run-in."

"By the way, how did you ... get it to drop you?" Harkat asked as we settled down for the night. "And why did it ... fly away and leave us?"

I thought back, recalled yelling at the dragon to let me go, and told Harkat what had happened. He stared at me disbelievingly, so I winked and said, "I always did have a way with dumb animals!" And I left it at that, even though I was equally bewildered by the dragon's strange retreat.

CHAPTER FIFTEEN

I THOUGHT Spits would have a sore head when he awoke, but he was in fine form — he said he never suffered from hangovers. He spent the day tidying up the shack, putting everything in order in case he ever returned. He stashed a jug of poteen away in a corner and packed the rest in a large sack he planned to carry slung over his shoulder, along with spare clothes, his fishing net, some potatoes and dried fish slices. Harkat and I had almost nothing to carry – apart from the panther's teeth and gelatinous globes, most of which we'd managed to hang on to – so we offered to divide Spits's load between us, but he wouldn't hear of it. "Every man to a cross of his own," he muttered.

We took it easy during the day. I hacked my hair back from my eyes with one of Spits's rusty blades. We'd replaced our handmade knives, most of which we'd lost in the lake, with real knives that Spits had lying around.

Harkat stitched together holes in his robes with bits of old string.

When night fell, we set off, heading due southeast towards a mountain range in the distance. Spits was surprisingly morose to be leaving his shack — "'Tis the closest thing to a home I've had since running away t' sea when I was twelve," he sighed — but several swigs of poteen improved his mood and by midnight he was singing and joking.

I was worried that Spits would collapse — his legs were wobbling worse than the jelly-like globes we were carting — but as drunk as he got, his pace never wavered, though he did stop quite often to "bail out the bilge water". When we made camp beneath a bushy tree in the morning, he fell straight asleep and snored loudly all day long. He woke shortly before sunset, licked his lips and reached for the poteen.

The weather worsened over the next few nights, as we left the lowlands and scaled the mountains. It rained almost constantly, harder than before, soaking our clothes and leaving us wet, cold and miserable — except Spits, whose poteen warmed and cheered him up whatever the conditions. I decided to try some of Spits's home-brewed concoction, to see if it would combat the gloom. One swallow later, I was rolling on the ground, gasping for breath, eyes bulging. Spits laughed while Harkat poured water down my throat, then urged me to try it again. "The first dram's the worst," he chuckled. Through wheezing coughs, I firmly declined.

It was difficult to know what to make of Spits Abrams. A lot of the time he came across as a funny old sailor, crude and coarse, but with a soft centre. But as I spent more time with him, I thought that a lot of his speech patterns seemed deliberately theatrical — he spoke with a broad accent on purpose, to give the impression he was scatterbrained. And there were times when his mood darkened and he'd mutter ominously about people who'd betrayed him in one way or another.

"They thought they was so high and mighty!" he growled one night, weaving drunkenly under the cloudy sky. "Better than dumb old Spits. Said I was a monster, not fit t' share a ship with 'em. But I'll show 'em! When I gets me hands on 'em, I'll make 'em suffer!"

He never said how he intended to "get his hands on" whoever "'em" were. We hadn't told Spits what year we'd come from, but he knew time had moved on — he often made reference to "yer generation" or said "things was different in my day". I couldn't see any way back for Spits, and he couldn't either — a common refrain of his when he was feeling sorry for himself was, "Here I is and here I'll die." Yet still he swore to get his own back on "them what done me wrong", despite the fact that the people he disliked would have been dead and buried decades ago.

Another night, while he was telling us about his tasks on board the *Prince of Pariahs*, he stopped and looked at us with a steady blank expression. "I had t' kill every now and then," he said softly. "Pirates is vagabonds. Even though we didn't kill those we robbed, we sometimes had t'. If people refused t' surrender, we had t' put a stop to 'em. Couldn't afford t' let 'em off the hook."

"But I thought you didn't board the ships you attacked," I said. "You told us you fished out people who jumped overboard."

"Aaarrr," he grinned bleakly, "but a man in the water can struggle just as much as one on deck. A woman too. Sometimes I had t' teach 'em a lesson." His eyes cleared a little and he grinned sheepishly. "But that was rare. I only mention it so ye know ye can rely on me if we gets into a tight spot. I ain't a killer, but I'll do it if me back's against a wall, or t' save a friend."

Harkat and I didn't doze much that day. Instead we kept a wary watch on the snoring Spits. Although we were stronger and fitter than him, he posed a worrying threat. What if he got into a drunken fit and took it into his head to kill us in our sleep?

We discussed the possibility of leaving the ex-pirate behind, but it didn't seem fair to strand him in the mountains. Although he was able to keep pace beside us during our marches, he had no sense of direction and would have become lost in no time if he'd been by himself. Besides, we might have need of his fishing skills if we made it to the Lake of Souls. Both of us could catch fish with our hands, but neither of us knew much about angling.

In the end we chose to keep Spits with us, but agreed not to turn our backs on him, to take turns sleeping, and to cut him loose if he ever threatened violence.

We made slow but steady progress through the mountains. If the weather had been finer, we'd have raced through, but all the rain had led to mudslides and slippery underfoot conditions. We had to walk carefully, and were often forced to backtrack and skirt around an area made inaccessible by the rain and mud.

"Does it normally rain this much?" I asked Spits.

"T' tell the truth, this has been one o' the better years," he chortled. "We gets very hot summers — long, too — but the winters are dogs. Mind, it'll probably break in another night or two — we ain't hit the worst o' the season yet, and it's rare t' get more'n a week or so o' nonstop rain at this time o' year."

As though the clouds had been listening, they eased up the next morning — affording us a welcome view of blue sky — and by night, when we set off, it was the driest it had been since we landed at Spits's shack.

That same night, we topped a small peak and found ourselves on a sharp decline into a long, wide chasm leading out of the mountain ridges. The base of the chasm was flooded with rainwater, but there were ledges along the sides which we'd be able to use. Hurrying down the mountain, we located one of the broader ledges, tied a rope around ourselves to form a chain, me in front, Spits in the middle, Harkat behind, and set off over the fast-flowing river, edging forwards at a snail's pace. Spits even went so far as to cork his jug of poteen and leave it untouched!

Day dawned while we were on the ledge. We hadn't seen any caves in the cliff, but there were plenty of large holes and cracks. Untying ourselves, each of us crawled into a hole to rest, out of sight of any passing dragons. It was extremely uncomfortable, but I was exhausted after the hard climb and fell asleep immediately, not waking until late in the day.

After a quick meal — the last of Spits's dried fish slices — we tied ourselves together again and set off. It began to drizzle shortly afterwards, but then it cleared for the rest of the night and we progressed without interruption. The ledge didn't run all the way to the end of the chasm, but there were ledges above and beneath it which we were able to transfer to, making the journey in stages. Shortly before daybreak we came to the end of the chasm and crawled down to a flat plain which spread out for many kilometres ahead of us, ending in a massive forest which stretched left and right as far as we could see.

We debated our options. Since none of us wanted to sleep in a hole in the cliff again, and the route to the forest was littered with bushes we could hide under if we spotted a dragon, we decided to head for the trees straightaway. Forcing our tired legs on, we jogged briskly over the plain, Spits feeding himself with poteen, somehow managing not to spill a drop despite the jolting of his arms as he ran.

We made camp just within the edge of the forest. While Harkat kept an eye on Spits, I slept soundly until early afternoon. Harkat and I caught a wild pig soon after that, which Spits gleefully roasted over a quickly constructed fire. We tucked into our first hot meal since leaving for the mountains more than two weeks earlier — delicious! Wiping our hands clean on the grass afterwards, we set off in a general southeast direction — it was hard to tell precisely with all the tree cover — prepared for a long, gloomy trek through the forest.

To our surprise, we cleared the trees a few hours before sunset — the forest was long, but narrow. We found ourselves standing at the top of a small cliff, gazing down on fields of the tallest, greenest grass I'd ever seen. No trees grew in the fields, and though there must have been many streams feeding the soil to produce such greenery, they were hidden by the towering stalks of grass.

Only one object stood out against the otherwise unbroken sea of green — a huge white building a couple of kilometres directly ahead, which shone like a beacon under the evening sun. Harkat and I shared a glance and said simultaneously, with a mixture of excitement and tension, "The Temple of the Grotesque!"

Spits stared suspiciously at the building, spat over the edge of the cliff, and snorted. "Trouble!"

CHAPTER SIXTEEN

THE STALKS of grass grew thickly together, a couple of metres high. We had to chop our way through, like hacking a path through a jungle. It was hard, slow work, and night had fallen before we reached the temple. Studying it by the light of a strong moon, we were impressed by its stature. Made of large rough stones which had been painted white, it stood thirty-five or forty metres high. A square building, its walls were about a hundred metres in length, and supported a flat roof. We did a full circuit of the exterior and there was only one entrance, a huge open doorway, five metres wide by eight or nine high. We could see the flicker of candlelight from within.

"I don't like the look o' this place," Spits muttered.

"Me neither," I sighed. "But if it's the Temple of the Grotesque, we have to go in and find the holy liquid that Evanna told us about."

"Ye two can trust a witch's word if ye like," Spits grunted, "but I ain't having nowt t' do with dark forces! If ye want t' enter, best o' luck. I'll wait out here."

"Afraid?" Harkat grinned.

"Aaarrr," Spits replied. "Ye should be too. Ye can call this the Temple o' the Grotesque if ye like, but I knows what it really is — a Temple o' Death!" And he stormed off to find a hiding place in a patch of nearby grass.

Harkat and I shared Spits's gloomy opinion, but we had to venture in. Knives drawn, we crept to the doorway and were about to enter, when the sound of chanting drifted to us over the clear night air. We paused uncertainly, then drew back to where Spits was hiding in the grass.

"Changed yer minds?" he hooted.

"We heard something," Harkat told him. "It sounded like voices — *human* ... voices. They were chanting."

"Where'd they come from?" Spits asked.

"To our left," I told him.

"Will I go check 'em out while ye explore yer temple?"

"I think it would be best if we all ... went to check," Harkat said. "If there are people here, this temple ... must be theirs. We can ask them about it and ... maybe they can help us."

"Ye're awfully simple-minded fer a demon," Spits laughed cynically. "Never trust a stranger, that's what I says!"

That was good advice, and we paid heed to it, quietly sliding through the grass — which didn't grow so thickly here — cautiously closing in on the chanting. A short way beyond the temple, we came to the edge of a clearing. In it was a small, peculiar-looking village. The huts were made of grass and built very low to the ground, no more than a metre high. Either we'd come to a village of pygmies, or the huts were only used as shelters to sleep beneath. Rough grey robes were bundled in a pile in the centre of the village. Dead sheep-like animals were stacked one on top of another, close to the robes.

As we were taking in the sight of the village, a naked man appeared through the grass to our right. He was of ordinary height and build, a light brown colour, but with lanky pink hair and dull white eyes. He walked to the mound of dead sheep, dragged one out and returned the way he'd come, pulling the sheep by its rear legs. Without discussing it, Spits, Harkat and I set off after him, keeping to the edge of the village, still hidden in the grass.

The chanting — which had died down — began again as we approached the spot where the man had disappeared into the grass. We found a path of many footprints in the soft earth and traced them to a second, smaller clearing. There was a pond at the centre, around which thirty-seven people stood, eight men, fifteen women and fourteen children. All were naked, brown-skinned, pink-haired and white-eyed.

Two men hung the dead sheep over the pond, stretched lengthways by its legs, while another man took a knife of white bone or stone and sliced the animal's stomach open. Blood and guts plopped into the pond. As I strained my neck, I saw that the water was a dirty red colour. The men held the sheep over the pond until the blood stopped dripping, then slung the carcass to one side and stood back as three women stepped forward.

The women were old and wrinkled, with fierce expressions and bony fingers. Chanting louder than anyone else, they stooped, swirled the water of the pond around with their hands, then filled three leather flasks with it. Standing, they beckoned the other people forward. As they filed past the first woman, she raised her flask high and poured the red water over their heads. The second woman wet her fingers with the water and drew two rough circular diagrams on everybody's chest. The third pressed the mouth of her flask to their lips, and they drank the putrid water within.

After the three women had attended to all of the people, they moved in a line back to the village, eyes closed, chanting softly. We slipped off to one side, then trailed after them, frightened and perplexed, but incredibly curious.

In the village, the people pulled on the grey robes, each of which was cut away in front to reveal their chest and the round crimson signs. Only one person remained unclothed — a young boy, of about twelve or thirteen. When all were dressed, they formed a long line, three abreast, the trio of old women who'd handled the flasks at the fore and the naked boy by himself in front of everybody else. Chanting loudly, they marched in a procession towards the temple. We waited until they'd passed, then followed silently, intrigued.

At the entrance to the temple, the procession stopped and the volume of the chanting increased. I couldn't understand what they were saying — their language was alien to me — but one word was repeated more than any other, and with great emphasis. "Kulashka!"

"Any idea what 'Kulashka' means?" I asked Harkat and Spits.

"No," Harkat said.

Spits began to shake his head, then stopped, eyes widening, lips thinning with fear. "Saints o' the sailors!" he croaked, and fell to his knees.

Harkat and I gawped at Spits, then looked up and saw the cause of his shock. Our jaws dropped as we set eyes on the most nightmarishly monstrous creature imaginable, wriggling out of the temple like a mutant worm.

It must have been human once, or descended from humans. It had a human face, except its head was the size of six or seven normal heads. And it had dozens of hands. No arms — and no legs or feet — just loads of hands sticking out of it like pin heads in a pincushion. It was a couple of metres wide and maybe ten or eleven metres long. Its body tapered back like a giant slug. It crept forward slowly on its hundreds of fingers, dragging itself along, though it looked capable of moving more quickly if it wished. It had just one enormous bloodshot eye, hanging low on the left side of its face. Several ears dotted its head in various places, and there were two huge, bulging noses set high above its upper lip. Its skin was a dirty white colour, hanging from its obscene frame in saggy, flabby folds, which quivered wildly every time it moved.

Evanna had named the monster well. It was utterly and

totally grotesque. No other word could have conveyed its repulsive qualities as simply and clearly.

As I recovered from my initial shock, I focused on what was happening. The naked boy was on his knees beneath the Grotesque, arms spread wide, roaring over and over, "Kulashka! Kulashka! Kulashka!"

As the boy roared and the people chanted, the Grotesque paused and raised its head. It did this like a snake, arching its body back so that the front section came up. From where we were hiding I got a closer look at its face. It was lumpy and ill formed, as though it had been carved from putty by a sculptor with a shaky hand. There were scraps of hair everywhere I looked, nasty dark tufts, more like skin growths than hair. I saw no teeth inside its gaping maw of a mouth, except for two long, curved fangs near the front.

The Grotesque lowered itself and slithered around the group of people. It left a thin, slimy trail of sweat. The sweat oozed from pores all over its body. I caught the salty scent, and although it wasn't as overpowering as that of the giant toad, it was enough to make me clamp my hand over my nose and mouth so that I didn't throw up. The people — the Kulashkas, for want of a better word — didn't mind the stench though. They knelt as their ... god? king? pet? ... whatever it was to them, passed and rubbed their faces in its trail of sweat. Some even stuck out their tongues and licked it up!

When the Grotesque had circled all of its worshippers, it returned to the boy at the front. Raising its head again, it leant forward and stuck out its tongue, a huge pink slab, dripping with thick globs of saliva. It licked the boy's face. He didn't flinch, but smiled proudly. The Grotesque licked him again, then wrapped its unnatural body around him once, twice, three times, and suffocated him with its fleshy coils, the way a boa constrictor kills its victims.

My first impulse was to rush to the boy's aid when I saw him disappearing beneath the sweaty flesh of the Grotesque, but I couldn't have saved him. Besides, I could see that he didn't wish to be saved. It was clear by his smile that he considered this an honour. So I stayed crouched low in the grass and kept out of it.

The Grotesque crushed the life out of the boy — he cried out once, briefly, as the creature made splinters of his bones — then unwrapped itself and set about swallowing him whole. Again, in this respect, it acted like a snake. It had a supple lower jaw which stretched down far enough for the monster to get its mouth around the boy's head and shoulders. By using its tongue, jaw and some of its hands, it slowly but steadily fed the rest of the boy's body down its eager throat.

As the Grotesque devoured the boy, two of the women entered the temple. They emerged shortly afterwards, clasping two glass vials, about forty centimetres long, with thick glass walls and cork stoppers. A dark liquid ran about three-quarters of the way to the top of each vial — it had to be Evanna's "holy liquid".

When the Grotesque had finished devouring the boy, a man stepped forward and took one of the vials. Stepping up to the beast, he held the vial aloft and chanted softly. The Grotesque studied him coldly. I thought it meant to kill him too, but then it lowered its head and opened its enormous mouth. The man reached into the Grotesque's mouth, removed the cork from the vial and raised it to one of the creature's fangs. Inserting the tip of the fang into the vial, he pressed the glass wall hard against it. A thick, viscous substance oozed out of the fang and trickled down the side of the tube. I'd seen Evra milking poison from his snake's fangs many times — this was exactly the same.

When no more liquid seeped from the fang, the man corked the vial, handed it back to the woman, took the second vial and milked the Grotesque's other fang. When he'd finished, he stepped away and the monster's mouth closed. The man passed the vial back, joined the rest of the group, and began chanting loudly along with everyone else. The Grotesque studied them with its single red eye, its inhumanly human-like head swaying from side to side in time with the chanting. Then it slowly turned and scuttled back into the temple on its carriage of fingers. As it entered, the people followed, in rows of three, chanting softly, vanishing into the gloom of the temple after the Grotesque, leaving us shaken and alone outside, to withdraw and discuss the sinister spectacle.

CHAPTER SEVENTEEN

"YE'RE CRAZY!" Spits hissed, keeping his voice down so as not to attract the attention of the Kulashkas. "Ye want t' go into that devil's lair and risk yer lives, fer the sake o' some bottles o' poison?"

"There must be something ... special about it," Harkat insisted. "We wouldn't have been told we ... needed it if it wasn't important."

"Nowt's worth throwing yer lives away fer," Spits snarled. "That monster will have ye both fer pudding, and still be hungry after."

"I'm not sure about that," I muttered. "It fed like a snake. I know about snakes from when I shared a tent with Evra — a snake-boy," I added for Spits's benefit. "A child would take a long time to digest, even for a beast of that size. I doubt it'll need to eat again for a few days. And a snake normally sleeps while it's digesting."

"But this ain't a snake," Spits reminded me. "It's a ... what did ye call it?"

"Grotesque," Harkat said.

"Aaarrr. Ye never shared a tent with a Grotesque, did ye? So ye know nothing about 'em. Ye'd be mad t' risk it. And what about that crazy pink-haired mob? If they catch ye, they won't be long offering ye up t' that giant mongrel o' theirs."

"What do you think the deal ... is with them?" Harkat asked. "I believe they worship the Grotesque. That's why they ... sacrificed the boy."

"A fine how-d'ye-do!" Spits huffed. "'Tis one thing t' go killing a stranger, but t' willingly give up one o' yer own — madness!"

"They can't do it often," I noted. "There aren't many of them. They'd die out if they made a human sacrifice every time the beast was hungry. They must feed it with sheep and other animals, and only offer up a human on special occasions."

"Should we try ... talking to them?" Harkat asked. "Many civilized people in the past ... offered human sacrifices to their gods. They might not be violent."

"I've no intention of putting them to the test," I said quickly. "We can't walk away from this — we saw them milk the snake's fangs, and I'm pretty certain that poison is the holy liquid we need. But let's not push our luck. There's no telling what the people of this world are like. The Kulashkas might be lovely folk who welcome strangers with open arms — or they might feed us to the Grotesque the instant they set eyes on us."

"We're stronger than them," Harkat said. "We could fight them off."

"We don't know that," I disagreed. "We've no idea what these people are capable of. They could be ten times as strong as you or me. I say we hit the temple, grab the vials, and beat it quick."

"Forget the vials!" Spits pleaded. He'd been drinking heavily from his jug since we'd retreated to safety and was trembling worse than normal. "We can come back later if we need 'em."

"No," Harkat said. "Darren's right about the Kulashkas. But if we're going to launch a … quick raid, we need to do it while the Grotesque is sleeping. We have to go after the … holy liquid now. You don't have to come … if you don't want."

"I won't!" Spits said quickly. "I ain't gonna chuck my life away on a crazy thing like this. I'll wait out here. If ye don't return, I'll carry on ahead and look fer yer Lake o' Souls myself. If it holds the dead like ye say, I might meet ye there!" He chuckled wickedly at that.

"Will we go while it's dark," I asked Harkat, "or wait for morning?"

"Wait," Harkat said. "The Kulashkas might have sung themselves … to sleep by then." The pink-haired people had returned to their village an hour after making their sacrifice, and had been singing, dancing and chanting ever since.

We lay back and rested as the moon crossed the cloudless sky (typical — when we wanted clouds for cover, there weren't any!), listening to the music of the strange Kulashkas. Spits kept sipping from his jug of poteen, his beady eyes getting smaller and smaller, tugging at the strands of his tied-back hair, muttering darkly about block-headed fools and their just comeuppances.

The noise from the Kulashka village died away towards morning, and by dawn there was silence. Harkat and I shared a questioning glance, nodded and stood. "We're going," I told Spits, who was half dozing over his jug.

"Wha'?" he grunted, head snapping up.

"We're going," I said again. "Wait here. If we're not back by night, go your own way and don't worry about us."

"I won't wait that long," he sniffed. "I'll be gone by midday, with 'r without ye."

"Suit yourself," I sighed, "but you'd be less visible in the dark. It would be safer."

Spits's features softened. "Ye're mad," he said, "but ye've more guts than any pirate I ever sailed with. I'll wait till sunset and keep the poteen ready — ye might be glad of it if ye survive."

"We might at that," I grinned, then spun away with Harkat and pushed through the tall covering grass to the doorway of the Temple of the Grotesque.

We stopped at the door of the temple, gripping our knives close by our sides, inhaling the foul sweaty stench of the beast. "What if there are guards?" I whispered.

"Knock them out," Harkat said. "Kill them only if we ... must. But I doubt there'll be any — they would have ... come out with the Grotesque if there were."

Taking deep, nervous breaths, we slid inside the temple, back to back, moving slowly and warily. Candles jutted from the walls, not a huge number, but enough to light our way. We were in a short, narrow corridor, covered by a low roof. A large room lay ahead. We paused at the entrance. The room was enormous. The roof was supported by giant pillars, but there were no other dividing structures. In the centre of the temple, the Grotesque was curled around a raised circular platform, upon which we saw a tall, hollow, upright crystal cylinder packed with vials like the ones the Kulashkas had used to milk the monster's venom.

"No lack of holy liquid," I whispered to Harkat.

"The trouble will be ... getting to it," he replied. "I think the Grotesque's body goes ... all the way around the altar."

I hadn't thought of the platform as an altar, but now that I looked again, I saw that Harkat was right — the cylinder holding the vials had the appearance of some religious relic.

We started across the room to the altar, the only sound our shallow breathing. The Grotesque's head was buried underneath its fleshy rear, so it shouldn't have a view of us if it was awake — though I hoped with all my being that it wasn't! There was a path leading directly from the doorway to the altar, lit by tall candles, but we approached the altar from the side, where we'd be less conspicuous.

We soon ran into an unexpected obstacle. The floorboards at the sides of the path were rotten and creaked heavily as we crossed them. "The path must be the only one reinforced from below," I hissed as we stopped to ponder our options. "By the echoes of the creaks, there's a pit beneath the boards."

"Should we return to ... the path?" Harkat asked.

I shook my head. "Let's continue — but tread carefully!"

Despite our attempts to proceed with care, a few metres further on, Harkat's left foot snapped through a board and his leg shot down into darkness. He gasped painfully but bit down on a cry. My eyes snapped to where the Grotesque was coiled, to see if it had stirred, but it was in the same position as before. The fingers close to its head twitched a few times — I hoped that meant it was asleep and dreaming.

Stooping, I examined the board around Harkat's leg, carefully snapped more of it away to increase the width of the hole, then helped ease him out of it and back on to slightly sturdier boards.

"Are you hurt?" I asked softly.

"Cut," Harkat answered, probing his leg. "Not bad."

"We can't chance these boards any longer," I said. "We'll have to use the path."

Together we hobbled back to the path, where we rested a minute, before advancing to the altar. By the luck of the vampires the Grotesque slept on. Once there, we walked around the putrid monster, looking for a gap where we could mount the altar. But the Grotesque had fully encircled it, chunks of its flesh draped off it in places. This close to the beast, I couldn't help but stare and marvel that such a thing could have come to exist. What troubled me most was its obviously human features. It was like a nightmare come to life — but a human nightmare. What was its history? How had it been born?

Having walked around the Grotesque a couple of times, I tore my gaze away. Not daring to talk this close to the creature,

I tucked my knife away and made hand signals at Harkat, indicating that we'd have to jump over the monster at its narrowest point, close to where its tail lapped over its head. Harkat didn't look thrilled with that idea, but there was no other way of getting to the altar, so he nodded reluctantly. I made a second set of hand signals, to the effect that I could jump and Harkat should remain where he was, but he shook his head and held up two stubby grey fingers, to show we should both go.

I jumped first. I crouched low, then leapt over the muscular coils of the giant beast. I landed softly, but spun quickly, not wishing to stand with my back to the Grotesque. It hadn't moved. Stepping aside, I nodded for Harkat to join me. He didn't leap quite as smoothly, but his feet cleared the monster, and I caught him as he landed, steadying him and muffling the sound.

We checked to make sure we hadn't disturbed the Grotesque, then faced the tall cylinder and studied the vials resting on see-through shelves within. Those at the top hadn't been filled, but there were dozens underneath, heavy with the thick poison from the Grotesque's fangs. The Kulashkas must have been milking the giant for decades to have amassed such a collection.

There was a frosty crystal front to the cylinder. I eased it open, reached inside, and pulled out a vial. It was cool and surprisingly heavy. I slipped it inside my shirt, pulled out a second vial and passed it to Harkat. He held it up to the light of the candles, scrutinizing the liquid inside.

As I was reaching for more vials, there was a shout from just inside the temple door. Looking up, startled, we saw two

Kulashka children, a boy and girl. I raised my fingers to my lips and waved at the children, hoping they'd stop shouting, but that only agitated them more. The girl turned and shot out the doorway, doubtless fleeing to wake the adults. The boy remained and raced towards us, yelling and clapping, grabbing a candle to use as a weapon.

I knew instantly that we'd have to forget the rest of the vials. Our only hope was to get out quick, before the Grotesque awoke or the Kulashkas poured into the temple. The pair of vials we'd stolen would have to do. Leaving the door of the cylinder hanging open, I stepped down to where Harkat was waiting and we got ready to jump. But before we could leap, the Grotesque's rear section swished back, its head whipped up, and we found ourselves gazing straight into its furious red eye — and at its bared, sabre-like fangs!

CHAPTER EIGHTEEN

WE FROZE on the altar, mesmerized by the Grotesque's glinting, demonic eye. As we stood rooted, helpless, its body unfurled and its head rose a metre or two, arcing backwards. It was preparing to attack, but by raising its head, it broke eye contact with us. We snapped out of our daze, realized what was about to happen, and dropped to the floor as the monster struck.

One of the Grotesque's long fangs caught me between my shoulder blades as I hit the floor. It dug into my flesh and ripped down my back. I yelled with pain and fear, rolled over as the beast released me, and slithered behind the crystal cylinder.

The Grotesque jabbed at me as I retreated but missed. It let out a bellow, like a giant baby's angry cry, then turned on Harkat. He was lying on his back, with his face and stomach exposed, an easy target. The Grotesque raised itself up to strike. Harkat got ready to throw his vial of poison at it. The Grotesque shrieked fiercely and withdrew a couple of metres, the fingers near its tail carrying it away from Harkat, the fingers near its head wriggling at him like dozens of snakes or eels. A detached part of me noticed that there were small holes on each finger where its nails would be if it was human, and the sweat came out of these holes in steady streams.

Harkat scrambled around to where I was sheltering. "My back!" I gasped, turning so that he could examine it. "How bad is it?"

Harkat studied my wound swiftly, then grunted. "It's not very deep. It'll leave the mother of ... all scars, but it won't kill you."

"Unless there was poison in the fang," I muttered.

"The Kulashkas milked it," Harkat said. "Fresh poison couldn't ... have formed already — could it?"

"Not in a snake," I said, "but there's no telling with this thing."

I had no time to worry about it. The Grotesque slid around the altar, to attack us again. We backpedalled, keeping the cylinder between us and the Grotesque's bobbing head.

"Any plans for ... getting out?" Harkat asked, drawing a knife but keeping his vial of poison in his left hand.

"I'm taking this second by second," I panted.

We retreated steadily, circling around the cylinder again and again, the monster following impatiently, spitting and growling, its tongue flicking between its lips, ready to strike the instant we relaxed our guard. The Kulashka boy was standing on the path to the altar, cheering the Grotesque on.

A minute later, the rest of the Kulashkas poured into the temple. Most were carrying weapons, and their faces were filled with fury. Hurrying to the altar, they spread out around it, crawled over the Grotesque and moved in on us, murder in their angry white eyes.

"This would be a good time to try talking to them," I said sarcastically to Harkat, but he took my wry advice seriously.

"We mean no harm!" he shouted. "We want to be ... your friends."

The Kulashkas stopped and murmured with astonishment when Harkat spoke. One of the men – I guessed it was their chief – stepped ahead of the others and pointed a spear at us. He shouted a question at Harkat but we couldn't understand what he was saying.

"We don't speak your language," I said, following Harkat's lead, keeping one eye on the man and one on the Grotesque, which was still scrabbling after us, though it had pulled back slightly to make room for the Kulashkas. The chief shouted at us again, but slower this time, emphasizing each word. I shook my head. "We can't understand you!" I cried.

"Friends!" Harkat tried desperately. "Amigos! Comrades! Buddies!"

The Kulashka stared at us uncertainly. Then his expression hardened and he barked something at the rest of his clan. Nodding, they advanced, their weapons raised offensively, herding us towards the fangs of the giant Grotesque.

I stabbed at one of the Kulashka women with my knife, a warning gesture, trying to ward her off, but she ignored me and continued to close in, along with the others. Even the children were converging on us, small knives and spears held fast in their tiny hands.

"Let's try the poison!" I screamed at Harkat, pulling out my vial. "They might scatter if we throw it at their eyes!"

"OK!" he roared, and held his vial up high.

When the Kulashkas saw the vial in Harkat's grey hand, they froze with fear and most took a hasty step backwards. I was confused by their reaction, but seized on their fear and raised mine as well. When they saw another of the vials, the men, women and children spilt back off the platform, chattering fearfully, wildly waving their hands and weapons at us.

"What's going on?" I asked Harkat.

"They're afraid of the ... poison," he said, waving his vial at a handful of the Kulashka women — they screamed and spun away, covering their faces with their hands. "It's either really sacred ... to them, or really dangerous!"

The Grotesque, seeing the Kulashkas grind to a halt, slid over the women and made for Harkat. One of the men darted ahead of the monster and waved his arms at it, shouting at the top of his lungs. The Grotesque paused, then swatted the man aside with its huge head and fixed its gaze on us again. It was snarling now — it meant to throw itself at us and finish us off. I drew back my vial to hurl at the beast, but a woman dashed between me and the Grotesque and waved her arms like the man had. This time the monster didn't swat the Kulashka aside, but stared fiercely at her as she crooned a song and waved her arms above her head.

When she had the full attention of the Grotesque, the woman stepped away from the altar and led the beast aside. The rest of the Kulashkas filed into the gap the Grotesque had left and stared at us hatefully — but also fearfully.

"Keep your vial up!" Harkat warned me, shaking his at the Kulashkas, who flinched miserably. Following a quick conference, a few of the women chased the children out of the temple and ran after them, leaving only the men and the sturdier, more warlike women.

The chief lowered his spear and again tried to communicate, making gestures with his hands, pointing to the Grotesque, the altar and the vials. We tried making sense of his signals, but couldn't.

"We don't understand!" I shouted, frustrated. I pointed to my ears, shook my head and shrugged.

The chief cursed — I didn't need to speak his language to know that — then took a deep breath and said something to his clan. They hesitated. He barked the words again, and this time they parted, clearing a space between us and the path to the temple doorway. The chief pointed at the path, then us, then back at the path. He looked at us questioningly to see if we understood.

"You're going to … let us go?" Harkat asked, repeating the Kulashka's gestures.

The chief smiled, then raised a warning finger. He pointed to the vials in our hands, then at the cylinder behind us. "He wants us to replace the vials first," I whispered to Harkat.

"But we need the … holy liquid," Harkat objected.

"This is no time to dig your heels in!" I hissed. "They'll kill us if we don't do what they say!"

"What's to stop them killing … us anyway?" Harkat asked. "The vials are all that's … keeping us safe. If we abandon them, why shouldn't they … cut us down dead?"

I licked my lips nervously, gazing at the Kulashka chief, who repeated his gestures, smiling warmly this time. I pointed to his spear when he finished. He looked at it, then tossed it away. He snapped at the rest of the Kulashkas and they too disposed of their weapons. Then they took another few steps away from us, spreading wide their empty hands.

"We have to trust them," I sighed. "Let's quit while we're ahead, put the vials back, and pray they're people of their word."

Harkat delayed for another frustrating moment, then nodded gruffly. "OK. But if they kill us on … our way out, I'll never speak … to you again."

I laughed at that, then stepped up to the crystal cylinder to return the vial of poison to its rightful place. As I did, a bearded man stumbled out of the shadows of the temple, waving a jug over his head and whooping loudly. "Fear not, lads! The fleet's here t' save ye!"

"Spits!" I bellowed. "No! We're sorting this out! Don't—"

I never finished. Spits raced past the chief and smashed him over the head with a long curved knife. The chief fell, screaming, blood pumping from his scalp. The other Kulashkas yelled with confusion and anger, then dived for their weapons.

"You moron!" I roared at Spits as he bounded on to the altar. "What the hell are you doing?"

"Saving ye!" the ex-pirate yelled with delight. He was weaving heavily from side to side, drunker than I'd ever seen him, his eyes barely focused. "Gimme that bottle o' pus," he grunted, snatching Harkat's vial from him. "If this is what the freaks is scared of, this is what we'll let 'em have!"

Spits raised the vial to lob at the Kulashkas. A loud shriek stopped him — the Grotesque was returning! Either the woman controlling it had been distracted by Spits's wild entrance, or she'd decided to set the beast on us. Either way, it was scampering towards us on its fingers at a frightening speed. In a couple of seconds it would be on us and the fight would be over.

Yelping with a drunken mixture of excitement and terror, Spits tossed the vial at the Grotesque. The glass missed its head, but connected with its long, fleshy body and smashed open. The instant it did, there was a huge explosion and the Grotesque and the floorboards beneath it disappeared in a spray of blood, flesh, bone and splintered wood.

The explosion blasted us from the platform and sent the Kulashkas crashing to the floor like bowling pins. I had just enough presence of mind to cradle my vial close to my chest as I fell, then tucked it inside my shirt to keep it safe as I rolled over on to my back in the aftermath of the blast. I now knew why the Kulashkas were so afraid of the vials — the Grotesque's venom was liquid explosive!

As I sat up, stunned, ears ringing, eyes stinging, I saw that the Grotesque wasn't the only casualty. Several of the Kulashkas — those who'd been closest to the monster — were lying dead on the floor. But I hadn't time to feel sorry for the Grotesque worshippers. The blast had also shattered a couple of the huge pillars supporting the roof, and as I watched, one pillar tipped over and crashed into another, which toppled into another and then another, like giant dominoes. Gazing up at the ceiling, I saw a series of cracks run across it, then huge chunks of the roof broke loose and cascaded down around the collapsing pillars. Within a matter of seconds the temple was going to fold in on itself, crushing all who lay within!

CHAPTER NINETEEN

THOSE KULASHKAS still alive and alert to the danger fled for the doorway. Some made it to safety, but most were trapped beneath the pillars and roof, which caved in around them as they ran. Stumbling to my feet, I set off after the Kulashkas, but Harkat grabbed me. "We'll never make it!" he gasped.

"There's no other way out!" I screamed in reply.

"Have to ... shelter!" he yelled, dragging me away from the main path. He hobbled across the floorboards, his green eyes darting from left to right as he watched for falling debris.

"We're in fer it now!" Spits hollered, popping up beside us, eyes alight with crazy drunken glee. "Face the heavenly stairs and cough up yer prayers!"

Harkat ignored the ex-pirate, dodged a chunk of heavy masonry, paused, then started jumping up and down on the spot. I thought he'd lost his mind, until I saw the hole in the floor where his foot had gone through earlier. Twigging to his plan, I bounced up and down beside him on the fragile floorboards. I didn't know how deep the pit was beneath, or if we'd be safe in it, but we couldn't fare any worse below than up here.

"What in the devil's name are ye—" Spits began. He got no further, because at that point the floor gave way and the three of us plummeted into darkness, yelling wildly as we fell.

We landed in a heap several metres beneath the temple, on a hard stone floor, Spits on top of Harkat and me. Groaning, I shoved Spits off — he'd been knocked out during the landing — and looked up. I saw part of the roof give way far overhead and come crashing down. Yelping, I stumbled to my feet and dragged Spits off to one side, cursing at Harkat to follow. There was a fierce, thunderous roar at our heels as we only just cleared the section of falling roof, which exploded upon contact with the floor and showered us with splinters and chips of stone.

Coughing — the force of the impact had raised a thick cloud of dust — we pushed ahead blindly, dragging Spits between us, into darkness and what we hoped was safety from the crumbling Temple of the Grotesque. After several frantic metres we came to a hole in the ground. Exploring with my hands, I said, "I think it's a tunnel — but it drops sharply!"

"If it gets covered over ... we'll be trapped," Harkat said.

There was a heavy bang overhead and the floorboards above us creaked ominously. "We don't have a choice!" I yelled, and crawled into the tunnel, bracing myself against the walls with my hands and feet. Harkat shoved Spits after me, then came himself — the tunnel was only just wide enough to accommodate his bulky body.

We clung near the top of the tunnel a few seconds, listening to the sounds of the destruction. I peered down the tunnel, but there was no light, and no way of telling how long it was. Spits's body weighed a ton and my feet began to slip. I tried digging in with my nails but the stone was too smooth and tough. "We have to slide!" I bellowed.

"What if we can't get ... back up?" Harkat asked.

"One crisis at a time!" I shouted, and let go. I lay flat on my back, allowing my body to shoot down the tunnel. It was a short, fast ride. The tunnel dropped sharply for many metres, then gradually levelled out. I came to a stop several seconds later at the end of the tunnel, where I stretched out a foot, searching for the floor. I hadn't found it when the unconscious Spits barrelled into the back of me and sent me sprawling out into open space.

I opened my mouth to yell, but hit the ground before I could — the mouth of the tunnel was only a metre or two off the floor. Relieved, I got to my knees — and was promptly knocked flat when Spits toppled out on top of me. Swearing blindly, I pushed him off and was rising again when Harkat shot out of the tunnel and bowled me over.

"Sorry," the Little Person muttered, easing himself off. "Are you OK?"

"I feel like I've been run over by a steamroller," I groaned, then sat up and took deep breaths of the musty air, letting my head clear.

"We've escaped being crushed by ... the temple," Harkat noted after a while, as the noises echoing through the tunnel decreased and then ceased.

"For whatever good it'll be," I grunted. I couldn't see my friend in the gloom of the underground cavern. "If there's no way out, we'll face a slow, miserable death. We might wind up wishing we'd been squashed by a falling pillar."

Beside me, Spits groaned feebly, then muttered something unintelligible. There was the sound of him sitting up, then, "What's happening? Where have the lights gone?"

"The lights, Spits?" I asked innocently.

"I can't see!" he gasped. "It's pitch black!"

"Really?" I said, eager to punish him for fouling things up with the Kulashkas. "*I* can see fine. How about you, Harkat?"

"Perfectly," Harkat murmured. "I wish I had ... sunglasses, it's so bright."

"My eyes!" Spits howled. "I'm blind!"

We let Spits suffer a while, before telling him the truth. He berated us with some choice insults for scaring him, but soon calmed down and asked what our next move would be.

"I guess we walk," I answered, "and see where we end up. We can't go back, and there are walls to the left and right—" I could tell by the echoes of our voices "—so it's straight ahead until a choice presents itself."

"I blame ye fer this," Spits muttered. "If ye hadn't gone prancing about in that bloody temple, we'd be waltzing through the fields now, with all the fresh air in the world t' breathe."

"*We* weren't the ones who … tossed bombs when there wasn't a need!" Harkat snapped. "We'd agreed a deal with … the Kulashkas. They were letting us go."

"That lot?" Spits snorted. "They'd've strung ye up and had ye fer breakfast!"

"I'll string *you* up if you don't … shut your mouth," Harkat growled.

"What's eating him?" Spits asked me, stung by Harkat's tone.

"Many Kulashkas died because of you," I sighed. "If you'd stayed outside like you were supposed to, they needn't have."

"Who cares about that lot?" Spits laughed. "They ain't of our world. What's the difference if some of 'em got squished?"

"They were people!" Harkat roared. "It doesn't matter what … world they were from. We had no right … to come in here and kill them! We—"

"Easy," I hushed him. "We can't put it right now. Spits was only trying to help, in his clumsy, drunken way. Let's concentrate on finding a way out, and leave the finger-pointing for another time."

"Just keep him away … from me," Harkat grumbled, pushing to the front and taking the lead.

"That's not very polite," Spits complained. "I thought, as an imp, he'd be delighted to cause havoc."

"Be quiet," I snapped, "or I'll change my mind and set him on you!"

"Crazy pair o' landlubbers," Spits snorted, but kept further comments to himself and fell in behind me as I stumbled after Harkat.

We limped along in silence for a number of minutes, disturbed only by the sound of Spits slurping from his jug of poteen (no fear *that* got broken in the explosion!). It was completely dark in the tunnel. I couldn't see Harkat, even though he was only a metre or so ahead of me, so I concentrated on my sense of hearing, following him by sound alone. His large grey feet made a very distinctive noise, and because I was focusing on that, I didn't hear the other sounds until they were almost upon us.

"Stop!" I hissed suddenly.

Harkat came to an instant standstill. Behind me, Spits stumbled into my back. "What're ye—" he began.

I clamped a hand over his mouth, finding it with little difficulty from the stink of his breath. "Not a word," I whispered, and through the throb of his lips I felt his heartbeat pick up speed.

"What's wrong?" Harkat asked quietly.

"We're not alone," I said, straining my ears. There were very slight rustling sounds all around us, ahead, at the sides, behind. The sounds stopped for a few seconds when we stopped, but then picked up again, slightly slower and quieter than before.

"Something just crawled over my right foot," Harkat said.

I felt Spits stiffen. "I've had enough o' this," he muttered fearfully, and made to pull away and run.

"I wouldn't do that," I said softly. "I think I know what this is. If I'm right, running would be a *very* bad idea."

Spits trembled but held his nerve and stood his ground. Releasing him, I bent to the ground slowly, as gracefully as I could, and gently laid a hand on the floor of the tunnel. A few seconds later, something crawled over my fingers, something with hairy legs ... two ... four ... six ... eight.

"Spiders," I whispered. "We're surrounded by spiders."

"Is that all?" Spits laughed. "I'm not scared o' a few wee spiders! Stand aside, boys, and I'll stamp 'em out fer ye."

I sensed Spits raising a foot into the air. "What if they're poisonous?" I said. He froze.

"I've a better one," Harkat said. "Maybe these are babies. This is a world of ... giants — the Grotesque and that monstrous toad. What if there are giant ... spiders too?"

At that, I froze like Spits had, and the three of us stood there, sweating in the darkness, listening ... waiting ... helpless.

CHAPTER TWENTY

"THEY'RE CRAWLING up my leg," Spits said after a while. He hadn't lowered his foot and was trembling wildly.

"And mine," Harkat said.

"Let them," I said. "Spits — lower your foot, as slowly as you can, and make sure you don't squash any of the spiders."

"Can you talk to them and ... control them?" Harkat asked.

"I'll try in a minute," I said. "First I want to find out if these are all we have to deal with." I'd been fascinated by spiders when I was a kid. That's how I got mixed up with Mr Crepsley, through his performing tarantula, Madam Octa. I had a gift for communicating with arachnids and had learnt to control them with my thoughts. But that had been on Earth. Would my powers extend to the spiders here?

I penetrated the darkness with my ears. There were hundreds, maybe thousands of spiders in the tunnel, covering the floor, walls and ceiling. As I listened, one dropped on to my head and began exploring my scalp. I didn't brush it off. Judging from the noise and the feel of the spider on my head, these were medium-sized tarantulas. If there were any giant spiders, they weren't moving — maybe because they were waiting for us to walk into their lair?

I carefully raised my right hand and touched my fingers to the side of my head. The spider found them a few seconds later. It tested the new surface, then crawled on to my hand. I brought my hand and the spider down and around, so that I was facing it (even though I couldn't see it). Taking a deep breath, I focused my attention on the spider and began talking to it inside my head. When I'd done this in the past, I'd used a flute to help focus my thoughts. This time I just had to wing it and hope for the best.

"Hello, little one. Is this your home? We're not intruders — we're just passing through. I can tell you're a beauty. Intelligent too. You can hear me, can't you? You understand. We're not going to harm you. We just want safe passage." As I continued talking to the spider, reassuring it of our peaceful intentions, flattering it and trying to get inside its head, I extended my range of thought and directed my words at the spiders around us. It's not necessary to control every spider in a huge pack, just those nearest to you. If you have the talent and experience, you can then use those spiders to control the rest. I could do that with spiders in my own world — were this lot the same, or were we doomed flies caught in an underground web?

After a couple of minutes, I put my abilities to the test. Bending, I let the spider crawl off my fingers on to the floor, then addressed the group around us. "We need to move on now, but we don't want to hurt any of you. You'll have to spread out of our way. We can't see you. If you stay bunched together, we won't be able to avoid you. Move, my beauties. Slip to the sides. Let us pass freely."

Nothing happened. I feared the worst but kept on trying, talking to them, urging them to part. I'd have been more authoritative with normal spiders, and ordered them out of our way. But I didn't know how these would react to direct commands, and didn't want to risk angering them.

For two or three minutes I spoke to the spiders, asking them to move. Then, when I was almost on the point of quitting and making a break for freedom, Harkat said, "They're climbing off me."

"Me too," Spits croaked a moment later. He sounded on the verge of tears.

All around us the spiders were retreating, slowly edging out of our way. I stood, relieved, but didn't break mental contact with them. I kept on talking inside my head, thanking them, congratulating them, keeping them on the move.

"Is it safe to advance?" Harkat asked.

"Yes," I grunted, anxious not to lose my concentration. "But slowly. Feel in front with your toes every time you take a step."

I went back to communicating my thoughts to the spiders. Harkat edged ahead, one sliding step after another. I followed, keeping close, maintaining my link with the spiders. Spits stumbled along behind, holding on to my sleeve with one hand, clutching his bottle of poteen to his chest with his other.

We walked for a long time in this way, many of the spiders keeping pace with us, new recruits joining them further along the tunnel. No signs of any giants. It was hard work talking to them for such an extended amount of time, but I didn't let my concentration slip.

Finally, after twenty or thirty minutes, Harkat stopped and said, "I've come to a door."

Stepping up beside him, I laid a hand on hard, smooth wood. It was covered in cobwebs, but they were old and dry, and brushed away easily at my touch. "How do you know it's a door?" I asked, momentarily breaking contact with the spiders. "Maybe the tunnel's just blocked off." Harkat found my right hand and guided it to a metal handle. "Does it turn?" I whispered.

"Only one way to ... find out," he said, and together we twisted it down. There was almost no resistance, and the door swung inwards the instant the latch was retracted. A soft buzzing noise greeted us from inside. The spiders around us scuttled backwards half a metre.

"I don't like this," I hissed. "I'll go in alone and check it out." Moving ahead of Harkat, I entered the room and found myself standing on cold, hard tiles. I flexed my bare toes a few times, to be certain.

"What's wrong?" Harkat asked when he didn't hear me moving.

"Nothing," I said. Remembering the spiders, I re-established contact and told them to stay where they were. Then I took a step forward. Something long and thin brushed against my face — it felt like a giant spider leg! I ducked sharply — the spiders had guided us into a trap! We were going to be devoured by monster arachnids! We had to run, get out, flee for our lives! We...

But nothing happened. I wasn't seized by long, hairy spider legs. There was no sound of a giant spider creeping towards me, intent on finishing me off. In fact there were no sounds at all, except for the strange buzzing and the fast, hard beating of my heart.

Rising slowly, I stretched out my arms and explored. My left hand found a long, narrow piece of cord hanging from above. Wrapping my fingers around it, I tugged softly. It resisted, so I tugged again, slightly harder. There was a click, then a harsh white light flooded the room.

I winced and covered my eyes — the light was blinding after the blackness of the tunnel. Behind me, I heard Harkat and Spits spin aside to avoid the glare. The spiders took no notice of it — living in utter darkness, they must have discarded their sense of sight some time in the past.

"Are you OK?" Harkat roared. "Is it a trap?"

"No," I muttered, spreading my fingers slightly in front of my eyes, allowing my pupils to adjust. "It's just a..." I stopped as my fingers parted. Lowering my hands, I gazed around, bewildered.

"Darren?" Harkat said. When I didn't answer, he poked his head through the door. "What's...?" He stopped when he saw what I was looking at, and stepped into the room, speechless. Spits did the same moments later.

We were in a large kitchen, like any modern kitchen back on Earth. There was a fridge – the source of the buzzing – a sink, cupboards, a bread bin, a kettle, even a clock over the table, though the hands had stopped. Closing the door to the room to keep the spiders out, we quickly searched the cupboards. We found plates, mugs, glasses, cans of food and drink (no labels or dates on the cans). There was nothing in the fridge when we opened it, but it was in full working order.

"What's going on?" Spits asked. "Where'd all this stuff come from? And what's that?" Hailing from the 1930s, he'd never seen a fridge like this before.

"I don't–" I started to answer, then stopped, my eyes falling on a saltcellar on the table — there was a piece of paper underneath, with a note scribbled across it. Removing the saltcellar, I scanned the note in silence, then read it out loud.

"'Top of the morning to you, gentlemen! If you've made it this far, you're doing splendidly. After your narrow escape in the temple, you've earned a rest, so put your feet up and tuck into the refreshments — courtesy of this kitchen's previous owner, who never got round to enjoying them. There's a secret exit tunnel behind the refrigerator. It's a few hundred metres to the surface. After that, you face a short walk to the valley wherein lies the Lake of Souls. Head due south and you can't miss it. Congratulations on overcoming the obstacles to date. Here's hoping all goes well in the final stretch. Best regards, your dear friend and sincere benefactor — Desmond Tiny.'"

Before discussing the note, we nudged the fridge aside and checked behind it. Mr Tiny had told the truth about the tunnel, though we wouldn't know for sure where it led until we explored it.

"What do you think?" I asked Harkat, sitting and pouring myself one of the fizzy drinks from the cupboard. Spits was busy examining the fridge, oohing and aahing with wonder at the advanced technology.

"We have to do as ... Mr Tiny says," Harkat replied. "We were heading in a general ... southerly direction anyway."

I glanced at the note again. "I don't like the bit about 'here's hoping all goes well in the final stretch'. It sounds as though he thinks it *won't*."

Harkat shrugged. "He might have said that ... just to worry us. At least we know we're ... close to the—"

We were startled by a shrill cry. Leaping to our feet, we saw Spits turning away from one of the cupboards, which he'd moved on to after the fridge. He was shaking and there were tears in his eyes.

"What is it?" I yelled, thinking it must be something dreadful.

"It's ... it's..." Spits held up a bottle full of a dark golden liquid, and broke into a wet-eyed grin. "It's *whisky!*" he croaked, and his face was as awe-filled as the Kulashkas' had been when they knelt before their Grotesque god.

Several hours later, Spits had drunk himself into a stupor and lay snoring on a rug on the floor. Harkat and I had eaten a filling meal and were resting against a wall, discussing our

adventures, Mr Tiny and the kitchen. "I wonder where all this
... came from?" Harkat said. "The fridge, food and drinks ...
are all from our world."

"The kitchen too," I noted. "It looks to me like a nuclear
fallout shelter. I saw a programme about places like this.
People built underground shelters and stocked them with
imperishable goods."

"You think Mr Tiny transported an entire ... shelter
here?" Harkat asked.

"Looks that way. I've no idea why he'd bother, but the
Kulashkas certainly didn't build this place."

"No," Harkat agreed. He was silent a moment, then said,
"Did the Kulashkas remind you ... of anyone?"

"What do you mean?"

"There was something about their appearance ... and the
way they talked. It took me a while to work it out ... but now
I have it. They were like the Guardians of the Blood."

The Guardians of the Blood were strange humans who
lived in Vampire Mountain and disposed of dead vampires in
exchange for their internal organs. They had white eyes like
the Kulashkas, but no pink hair, and spoke in a strange
language which, now that I thought about it, did seem quite
like the Kulashkas'.

"There *were* similarities," I said hesitantly, "but differences
too. The hair was pink, and the eyes were a duller white
colour. Anyway, how could they be related?"

"Mr Tiny might have transported ... them here," Harkat
said. "Or maybe this is where the Guardians of the ... Blood
originally came from."

I mused that one over for a while, then rose and walked to the door.

"What are you doing?" Harkat asked as I opened the door on to the tunnel.

"Checking out a hunch," I said, crouching low and casting about with my eyes. Most of the spiders had left but a few were still close by, hunting for food or resting. I made mental contact with one and summoned it. It crawled on to my left hand and lay snugly in my palm as I lifted it to the light and examined it. It was a large grey spider with unusual green spots. I studied it from all sides, to be absolutely certain, then set it on the floor of the tunnel and closed the door again.

"Ba'Shan's spiders," I said to Harkat. "They're the spiders Madam Octa created when she bred with Ba'Halen's spiders in Vampire Mountain."

"You're certain?" Harkat asked.

"They were named in my honour by Seba. I'm positive." I sat down again beside Harkat, my forehead creased as I picked away at the puzzle. "Mr Tiny must have brought them here, like the kitchen, so I guess he could have brought some of the Guardians of the Blood too. But Ba'Shan's spiders aren't blind and the Guardians don't have pink hair. If Mr Tiny did bring them here, it must have been decades ago in this world's time, if not longer — they'd need that long to transform."

"It seems like a lot of effort to ... go to," Harkat said. "Maybe he wanted the Guardians to build ... the Temple of the Grotesque. And the kitchen might just have ... been for a joke. But why bring the spiders?"

"I don't know," I said. "When you put them all together, they don't add up. There's something more to this, a bigger picture which we're missing."

"Maybe the answer's in the kitchen," Harkat said, rising and slowly surveying the tiles, table and cupboards. "The details are so fine. Maybe the answer is hidden ... among them." He wandered around the room, gradually winding his way over to the fridge, where several postcards were attached by magnets to the door. They were from various tourist attractions on Earth — Big Ben, the Eiffel Tower, the Statue of Liberty, and so on. I'd seen them earlier but paid no attention.

"Maybe there are clues or further ... instructions on the back of these," Harkat said, taking down one of the cards. Turning it over, he studied it in silence, then quickly grabbed another, and another.

"Anything?" I asked. Harkat didn't answer. He was gazing down at the postcards, his lips moving silently. "Harkat? Are you OK? Is something wrong?"

Harkat's gaze flicked over me, then returned to the postcards. "No," he said, tucking the cards away inside his tattered blue robes. He reached for the others.

"Can I see the cards?" I asked.

Harkat paused, then said softly, "No. I'll show them to you ... later. No point distracting ourselves now." That raised my interest, but before I could press to see the postcards, Harkat sighed. "It's a shame we don't ... have any of the holy liquid. I suppose we'll just have to..." He stopped when he saw me grin and reach inside my shirt. "No way!" he whooped.

I held up the vial I'd tucked away after being blown from the altar. "Am I brilliant or what?" I smirked.

"If you were a girl … I'd kiss you!" Harkat cheered, rushing over.

I passed the vial to him and forgot about the postcards. "How do you think it works?" I asked as he turned the vial around, careful not to slosh the explosive liquid. "With all that force in its venom, surely the Grotesque should have blown its head off the first time it sunk its fangs into something."

"It must not be explosive … to begin with," Harkat guessed. "Maybe an element in the air … reacts with the poison after its release … and changes it."

"A pretty big change," I laughed, then took the vial back. "How do you think we're supposed to use it?"

"There must be something … we have to blow up," Harkat said. "Perhaps the Lake is covered … and we have to blast a way through. What puzzles me more are the … globes." He picked out one of the gelatinous globes from within his robes and tossed it up and down. "They must serve a … purpose, but I can't for the life of … me think what it is."

"I'm sure it'll become clear," I smiled, tucking the vial away. Pointing at the sleeping Spits, I said, "We should apologize to him when he wakes up."

"What for?" Harkat snorted. "Killing the Kulashkas and almost … getting us killed too?"

"But don't you see? He was *meant* to. Mr Tiny wanted us to come here, but we wouldn't have if Spits hadn't barged in. Without him, we'd have no holy liquid. And even if we'd managed to sneak a vial out of the temple, we wouldn't have known about its explosive properties — we'd have blown ourselves to bits!"

"You're right," Harkat chuckled. "But I think an apology … would be wasted. All Spits cares about now … is his whisky. We could call him every foul … name in the world, or praise him … to the heavens, and he wouldn't notice."

"True!" I laughed.

We lay down after that and rested. I spent the quiet moments before sleep thinking about our adventures and the puzzle this world presented, and wondering what awful, life-threatening obstacles lay in wait for us at the end, in the valley of the Lake of Souls.

CHAPTER TWENTY-ONE

AFTER A long sleep and a hot meal, courtesy of a small gas stove, we packed some tins and drinks (Spits made the three remaining bottles of whisky his first priority), along with a few of the longer knives, and exited the underground kitchen. I switched off the light before we left — a force of habit from the time when my mum would roar whenever I left lights on around the house.

The tunnel was a couple of hundred metres long and ended in the side of a riverbank. The exit was blocked with loose stones and sandbags, but they were easy to remove. We had to jump into the river and wade across to dry land, but the water was shallow. On the far bank we got undercover quickly and hurried away through the tall stalks of grass. We were anxious not to run into any Kulashka survivors.

It was midday when we left the kitchen. Although we'd previously travelled at night, we marched steadily all day, hidden by the tall grass. We stopped late in the night to sleep, and set off early the next morning. That evening we cleared the grasslands. We were delighted to leave the tall grass behind — we were covered in burs and insects and nicked all over from the sharp edges of the blades. The first thing we did was find a pool of water and wash ourselves clean. After that we ate, rested a few hours, then headed south, reverting to our previous pattern of walking by night and sleeping by day.

We expected to come upon the valley at every bend – Mr Tiny had said it was a short walk – but another night passed without any sight of it. We were worried that we'd taken the wrong path, and discussed backtracking, but early the next night the ground rose to a peak and we instinctively knew that our goal lay on the other side. Harkat and I hurried up the rise, leaving Spits to catch up in his own time (he'd been drinking heavily and was making slow progress). It took us half an hour to reach the top. Once there, we saw that we were at the head of the valley — and we also saw the enormity of the task ahead.

The valley was long and green, with a small lake – a glorified pond, as Mr Tiny had accurately called it – set in the centre. Apart from that, the valley was featureless — except for five dragons resting around the edge of the water!

We stood staring down into the valley at the dragons. One looked like the creature which had attacked us on the raft. Two were smaller and slimmer, probably females — one had a grey head, the other white. The remaining two were much smaller — infants.

As we studied the dragons, Spits approached, panting heavily. "Well, lads," he wheezed, "is this the valley or ain't it? If it is, let's sing a wee sea shanty t' celebrate our—"

We jumped on him before he burst into song, and smothered his startled cries. "What's going on?" he yelped through my fingers. "Are ye mad? 'Tis me — Spits!"

"Quiet!" I hushed him. "Dragons!"

He snapped out of his drunkenness. "Let me see!" We rolled off and let him wriggle forward to the edge of the overhang. His breath caught in his throat when he saw the dragons. He lay there for a minute, studying them silently, then returned to our side. "I recognize two of 'em. The biggest is the one that attacked ye in the lake by my shack. I've seen the one with the grey head too, but not the others."

"Do you think they're just … resting?" Harkat asked.

Spits tugged on his straggly beard and grimaced. "The grass round the Lake has been trampled flat in a big wide circle. 'Twouldn't have got that way if they'd only been here a while. I think this is their den."

"Will they move on?" I asked.

"No idea," Spits said. "Mebbe they will — though I doubt it. They're safe from attack here — they'd see anything coming long before it reached 'em — and the land around is teeming with animals and birds for 'em to feed on. Plus, my lake's not far off — as the dragon flies — with all the fish they could wish fer."

"They've children too," Harkat noted. "Animals normally stay where … they are when they're rearing their young."

"So how are we going to get to the Lake of Souls?" I asked.

"Are ye sure that *is* the Lake?" Spits asked. "It looks awful small t' be home to a load o' dead souls."

"Mr Tiny said it would be small," I told him.

"There could be another lake nearby," Spits said hopefully.

"No," Harkat grunted. "This is it. We'll just have to keep watch and ... wait for them to leave — they have to hunt ... for food. We'll move in when they go and ... hope they don't return too quickly. Now, who wants to creep forward and ... take first watch?"

"I'll go," I said, then snatched Spits's bottle from him as he made to slug back a shot. I also grabbed his sack, where his other bottles were stowed.

"Hey!" he protested.

"No more whisky until this is over," I told him. "You're taking the next watch — and you're taking it sober."

"You can't boss me about!" he griped.

"Yes I can," I growled. "This is serious business. I'm not having you fly off the handle like you did in the temple. You can have some whisky before you go on watch, and when you come off, but between those times — not a drop."

"And if I refuse?" he snarled, reaching towards his long curved knife.

"We'll break the whisky bottles," I said simply, and his face went white.

"I'd kill ye if ye did!" he croaked.

"Aaarrr," I grinned, "but that wouldn't bring yer whisky back!" Handing the bottle and sack to Harkat, I winked at Spits. "Don't worry — when we're through, you can drink all the whisky you want." Then I hurried forward to find a bush to hide behind and observe the dragons.

We kept watch for almost a week before accepting that we'd have to revise our plan. At least three dragons remained in the valley at any given time, usually the two young ones and a female, though sometimes the male took one of the youngsters hunting with him. There was no way of telling when the absent dragons would return — sometimes the male was gone overnight, while other times he'd sweep back to his family within minutes, a bleating sheep or goat clutched between his claws.

"We'll just have to . . . sneak in one night and hope . . . they don't spot us," Harkat said as we debated our options. We were in a rough cave we'd dug in the soil of the hill, to hide us from the dragons when they took flight.

"Them dragons have awful good eyesight," Spits said. "I seen 'em spot prey from hundreds o' feet up on nights as black as a shark's soul."

"We could try burrowing to the Lake," I suggested. "The soil isn't hard-packed — I'm sure I could dig a way through."

"And when you broke through . . . to the Lake?" Harkat asked. "The water would flood the tunnel . . . and we'd all drown."

"We ain't chancing that!" Spits said quickly. "I'd rather be ate by one o' them demons than drowned!"

"There must a way to get past them," I groaned. "Maybe we could use the explosive Grotesque poison — wait until they're grouped together, sneak up close and lob it among them."

"I doubt we'd be able to … get close enough," Harkat said. "And if even one of them survived…"

"If we had more'n one vial, we'd have nowt to worry about," Spits sighed. "We could walk in and toss a vial at 'em any time they came near. Mebbe we should go back t' the temple and search fer more vials."

"No," I frowned. "That's not the answer — even if they didn't blow up during the blast, they'd be buried under rubble. But you're on to something…" I took out my vial of "holy liquid" and examined it. "Mr Tiny knew that we'd crash through the floorboards and make our way to the kitchen, so maybe he also knew we'd only grab a single vial."

"Then one must be enough," Harkat muttered, taking the vial from me. "There must be a way we can … use it to get to the Lake."

"'Tis a pity Boom Boom Billy ain't with us," Spits chuckled. When we looked at him blankly, he explained. "Boom Boom Billy was a wonder with bombs. He knew all about dynamite and gunpowder, and how t' blow things up. The cap'n often said Billy was worth his weight in gold." Spits chortled. "Which made it all the funnier when he blew himself up trying t' crack open a chest full of ingots!"

"You've got a warped sense of humour, Spits," I sniffed. "I hope that one day you—" I stopped, eyes narrowing. "*Bombs!*" I exclaimed.

"You have an idea?" Harkat asked excitedly.

I shushed him with a wave of a hand, thinking furiously. "If we could make bombs out of the 'holy liquid'..."

"How?" Harkat asked. "We know nothing about ... bombs, and even if we did, we don't ... have anything to make them with."

"Don't be so sure about that," I said slowly. Reaching inside my shirt, I took out the piece of cloth I'd wrapped my share of the gelatinous globes in, and carefully unrolled them on to the floor. Picking up a jelly-like ball, I squeezed it softly between my fingers, watching the thin liquid within ooze from side to side. "By themselves, these globes are worthless," I said. "The 'holy liquid' is worthless too — by itself. But if we put them together..."

"Are you thinking of covering ... the globes with the liquid?" Harkat asked.

"No," I said. "It would drop off on to the ground and explode. But if we could inject it *into* the globes..." I trailed off into silence, sensing I was close to the answer, but unable to make the final leap in logic.

With a sudden grunt, Harkat beat me to the punch. "The tooth!" He dug through his robes for the bag of teeth he'd taken from the black panther.

"What're they?" Spits asked, never having seen the teeth before.

Harkat didn't answer, but sorted through them until he found the hollow tooth with the K carved on it. Holding it up, he blew through the tooth to make sure it was clear, then passed it to me, his green eyes shining brightly. "You have smaller fingers," he said.

Picking up a globe, I brought the tip of the tooth close to it, then stopped. "We'd better not try this here," I said. "If something goes wrong..."

"Agreed," Harkat said, shuffling towards the mouth of the cave. "Besides, we'll have to test them ... to make sure they work. We'd best do that ... out of earshot of the dragons."

"What 're ye on about?" Spits whined. "Ye ain't making sense!"

"Just follow close behind," I winked. "You'll see!"

We made our way to a copse of thick, stunted trees a few kilometres away. Once there, Harkat and Spits huddled behind a fallen trunk, while I squatted in a clearing and laid several gelatinous globes and the panther's tooth on the earth around me. With extreme care, I uncorked the vial of explosive poison. It smelt like cod-liver oil. I set the vial down, lay out flat on my stomach and placed one of the globes directly in front of me. With my left hand, I gently jabbed the sharp, narrow end of the panther's tooth into the globe. When it was sticking in half a centimetre, I picked up the vial with my right hand, brought its lip to the rim of the tooth, and poured.

I was sweating furiously as the first drops trickled into the tooth — if they exploded this close to my face, I was dead meat. But, like treacle, the liquid rolled slowly down the hole inside the tooth, then into the soft gelatinous globe.

I filled the tooth to the top – it didn't hold very much – then removed the vial and waited for all the liquid to seep into the globe. It took a minute, but eventually the globe had absorbed all of the deadly poison from the tooth.

Keeping my hands steady, I removed the tip of the tooth from the top of the globe and held my breath, watching the jelly-like material close over the tiny hole, until it was no more than a pinprick in the skin of the globe. Once it had closed as far as it was going to, I corked the vial, set the tooth aside, and stood. "It's done," I called to Harkat and Spits.

Harkat crept over. Spits stayed where he was, eyes wide, hands over his head. "Take the vial and tooth," I told Harkat. "Lay them where Spits is, so they're out of harm's way."

"Do you want me to ... come back to help?" Harkat asked.

I shook my head. "I can throw it further than you. I'll test it myself."

"But you're a half-vampire," he said. "You took a vow never to use ... missile-firing weapons or bombs."

"We're on another world — as far as we know — and facing a bunch of dragons — I think this qualifies as an exceptional circumstance," I said dryly.

Harkat grinned, then swiftly retreated with the vial, my share of the globes and the panther's tooth. When I was alone, I crouched, took hold of the poison-filled globe, and cautiously picked it up. I winced as my fingers tightened around the globe, expecting it to blow up in my face — but it didn't. I turned the globe over, to see if any of the liquid spilt out. Detecting no leaks, I stood, swung my arm back, then lobbed the globe at a gnarly tree in the distance.

The instant the globe was out of my hand, I ducked and covered my head with my hands, following the globe's flight through the cracks between my fingers. It soared cleanly ahead, before connecting with the tree. When it hit the trunk, the shell of the globe smashed, the liquid splashed with great force over the wood, and the air was rent with the sound of a sharp explosion. My fingers snapped closed and I buried my face in the ground. When, a few seconds later, I raised my head and opened my eyes, I saw the top half of the tree topple over, torn to shreds in the middle.

Getting up slowly, I studied the shattered tree, then turned and smiled at Harkat and Spits, who were also on their feet. Taking a cheeky bow, I hooted, "Move over Boom Boom Billy — there's a new kid in town!"

Then Harkat and Spits were racing towards me, whooping with excitement, eager to make some bombs of their own.

CHAPTER TWENTY-TWO

EARLY AFTERNOON the next day. We'd been waiting for the male dragon to go hunting. Ideally, we'd like to have waited until he took one of the females or young dragons with him, but he usually only made short trips when accompanied. Our best bet was to make our move when he was off hunting by himself, in the hope that he wouldn't return while we were in the valley.

Finally, near the end of my watch, the dragon unfurled his long wings and took to the sky. I hurried off to alert Harkat and Spits.

We'd filled the remaining thirty-two globes with liquid from the vial. The vial was still about a third full, and I carried it in my shirt, keeping it in reserve. Harkat and I had divided the globes between us, giving none to Spits, even though he'd argued bitterly for a share. There were two reasons why we kept the globes from him. Firstly, it was our aim to scare off the dragons, not kill them. Neither of us wished to destroy such mystical, marvellous creatures, and we couldn't trust Spits not to go bomb-happy. The second reason was that we needed him to concentrate on fishing. The pirate had held on to his net, despite all we'd been through — he had it wrapped around his chest — and he was the best qualified to fish for Harkat's soul. (We weren't sure what form the souls in the Lake would take, or how we'd recognize Harkat's, but we'd worry about that when — if! — we got there.)

"Ready?" I asked, crawling out of our makeshift cave, four small globes cradled in my hands.

"Ready," Harkat said. He was carrying six of the globes — his hands were bigger than mine.

"Aaarrr," Spits growled, still sour about not being given any bombs. He'd been in a foul mood most of the week, due to the tiny amount of whisky we'd limited him to.

"When this is over," I tried to cheer him up, "you can drink all the whisky you like and get steaming drunk, OK?"

"I like the sound o' that!" he chuckled.

"Are you looking forward to ... getting home?" Harkat asked.

"Home?" Spits frowned, then grinned sickly. "Aaarrr. 'Twill be great. I wish we was there already." His eyes shifted nervously and he looked away quickly, as though he'd been caught stealing.

"We'll go in three abreast," I told Spits, shuffling to the top of the hill. "You take the middle. Head straight for the Lake. We'll protect you."

"What if the dragons don't flee from the bombs?" Spits asked. "Will ye let 'em have it in the gob?" Spits thought we were crazy for not wanting to blow up the dragons.

"We'll kill them if we have to," I sighed. "But only if there's no other way."

"And only after they've ... eaten you," Harkat added, then laughed when Spits cursed loudly at him.

Forming a line, we checked ourselves one last time. Harkat and I were carrying everything we owned in our pockets, and Spits had his sack slung over his shoulder. Taking deep breaths, we shared crooked grins, then started down into the valley, where the four dragons were waiting.

A young dragon spotted us first. It was playing with its sibling — the pair often chased each other around the valley, like two overgrown kittens. When it saw us, it drew up short, flapped its wings and screeched warningly. The heads of the female dragons shot up, their hot yellow eyes fierce above their long purple faces.

The female with the grey head got to her feet, spread her wings, flapped them firmly and soared into the air. She circled around, screeching, then directed her snout at us and zoomed in. I could see her nostrils expanding as she prepared to blow fire.

"I'll deal with this one," I called to Harkat, stepping forward and holding up one of the larger globes. I judged my moment finely, waited until the dragon was almost directly overhead, then threw the globe hard into the earth and ducked. It exploded, sending soil and pebbles flying up into the dragon's face. She screamed with panic and veered sharply away to the left.

The second female took to the air at the sound of the explosion, and the young dragons followed, adopting a position several metres above their mothers, who hovered side by side.

While the dragons hung in the air, we hurried towards the Lake of Souls, Harkat and I watching our every footstep, all too aware of the consequences if we stumbled and smashed the deadly globes. Spits was muttering over and over, "Better be worth it! Better be worth it! Better be..."

The female dragons split up and attacked us on two fronts at the same time, swooping out of the sky like a couple of comets. Harkat and I waited, then threw our globes at the same time, confusing the dragons with loud explosions and blinding geysers of earth and stones.

The dragons dogged our steps all the way to the Lake, attacking in turn or together every minute or so, only pulling clear when we launched our globes. One of the young dragons tried to join in, but its mother shot a warning streak of fire at it, frightening it back to its previous safe height.

As we progressed, I realized the dragons were intelligent creatures. After the first few explosions, they no longer flew into the blasts but pulled up short as soon as they saw us lobbing the globes. On a couple of occasions I tried to outfox them by just pretending to toss a globe, but they obviously saw through my ploy and only withdrew when I actually launched one.

"They'll keep coming until we run out of globes!" I roared at Harkat.

"Looks that way!" Harkat yelled back. "Have you been keeping track ... of how many you've used?"

"I think seven or eight."

"Me too," Harkat said. "That only leaves us with about ... half our original supply. Enough to get us to the ... Lake — but not to get back!"

"If we're going to retreat, we'll have to do it now," I noted.

To my surprise, Spits answered before Harkat could. "No!" he yelled, his face alight. "We're too close t' pull back!"

"Spits seems to be getting into the spirit of the adventure," I laughed.

"The time he picks to ... develop a backbone!" Harkat snorted in reply.

We hurried on to the Lake and arrived a couple of minutes later, having used another two globes. The female dragons pulled away when they saw us draw up to the edge of the Lake. They hovered in the air with their children, high above our heads, observing suspiciously.

Spits was the first to gaze into the water of the Lake of Souls, while Harkat and I kept a watch on the dragons. After a few seconds he fell to his knees and moaned softly. "It's beautiful! All I ever dreamt, and more!"

Staring over my shoulder to see what he was babbling about, I found myself gazing into murky blue water, in which swam hundreds upon hundreds of shimmering human figures. Their bodies and faces were pale and ill defined, some swelling out and sucking in, almost like a fish puffing itself up and returning to its normal size. Others were squashed into tiny balls or stretched out to impossible lengths. All swam in slow, mournful circles, listless, oblivious to distractions, their blinking eyes or flexing fingers the only signs that they weren't totally lifeless. A few of the shapes drifted towards the upper levels of the Lake every now and then, but none broke the surface of the water. I got the impression that they couldn't.

"The souls of the dead," Harkat whispered. Both of us had turned our backs on the dragons, momentarily captivated by the spectacle of the Lake.

Most of the figures twisted slowly as they swam, so that their faces revolved in and out of sight. Every face was a picture of loneliness and sorrow. This was a lake of misery. Not agony — nobody seemed to be in pain — just sadness. I was studying the faces, filled with a sense of pity, when I spotted one I knew. "By the black blood of Harnon Oan!" I shouted, taking an involuntary step back.

"What is it?" Harkat asked sharply — he thought I'd found the person he used to be.

"*Murlough!*" It was less than a breath on my lips. The first vampaneze I ever encountered. Consumed by madness, he'd lost control and had been killing people in Mr Crepsley's home city. We'd tracked him down and Mr Crepsley killed him. The vampaneze looked exactly the way he had when he died, only his purple sheen was muted by the water of the Lake and the depth he was swimming at.

As I watched, Murlough sunk downwards, slowly dropping from sight into the lower reaches of the Lake. A shiver ran down my spine. I'd never thought to look upon

Murlough's face again. It had dredged up many bad memories. I was lost in thought, transported to the past, reliving those long ago nights, wondering what other souls I might find here. Not Mr Crepsley — Evanna had told me his soul was in Paradise. But what about the first vampaneze I'd killed? Gavner Purl? Arra Sails? Kur—

"Beautiful," Spits murmured, breaking my train of thought. He looked up at me and his eyes were wet with happy tears. "The little man in the yellow galoshes told me 'twould be like this but I never believed it till now. "All my dreams would come true", he said. Now I know he wasn't lying."

"Never mind your dreams!" I snapped, recalling the danger we were in. I put Murlough from my thoughts and spun to keep both eyes on the dragons. "Get fishing, quick, so we can get out of here!"

"I'll get fishing, sure enough," Spits giggled, "but if ye thinks I'm leaving this pool o' sunken treasures, ye're crazier than them Kulashkas!"

"What do you mean?" Harkat asked, but Spits didn't answer immediately, only unravelled his net with measured care and fed it into the still water of the Lake of Souls.

"I was considered a prize on the *Prince o' Pariahs*," the pirate said softly. "Nobody cooked as fine a meal as Spits Abrams. The cap'n used to say I was second in importance only t' Boom Boom Billy, and when Billy blew himself up, I became the most valuable man aboard. Every pirate would've sold his mother fer a bowl o' Spits's famous stew, or a slice of his delicious roast meat."

"He's cracking up!" I yelled.

"I don't think so," Harkat said nervously, studying Spits as he focused on his net, lips drawn back over his teeth, eyes burning with a frightening inner light.

"They never asked where the meat came from," Spits continued, swishing his net through the water. The souls in the Lake parted and swam around the net automatically, but their glum expressions didn't change. "Even when we'd been at sea fer months on end, and all the other supplies had run out, I was able t' slap up as much meat as they could eat."

The pirate paused and his mouth grew tight with anger. "When they found out, they said I wasn't human and didn't deserve t' live. But they knew. Deep down, they must've guessed, and they went on chewing regardless. 'Twas only when a new man caught me and made a fuss that they had to admit it. Hypocrites!" he roared. "They was a stinking bunch o' lying, double-faced hypocrites, fit only t' roast in the fires o' hell!"

Spits's face grew crafty and he laughed maniacally, drawing his net out, checking its condition, then lowering it back into the water. "But since the devil couldn't be bothered with 'em, I'll treat 'em to a fire of me own. Aaarrr! They thought they'd seen the last o' Spits Abrams when they tossed me overboard. But we'll see who has the last laugh when they're draped on a spit, sizzling slowly over my flames!"

"What's he talking about?" I croaked.

"I think I understand," Harkat whispered, then spoke to Spits. "How many of the people ... that you fished from the sea ... did you *kill*?"

"Most of 'em," Spits giggled. "In the heat o' battle, nobody took any notice of them what jumped overboard. I kept the occasional one alive, t' show off t' the cap'n and crew. But I slit the throats o' most and hid the bodies in the galley."

"And then you carved them ... up, cooked them and served them ... to the pirates," Harkat said hollowly, and I felt my stomach churn.

"*What?*" I gasped.

"That's Spits's big secret," Harkat said sickly. "He was a cannibal and he turned his ... crewmates into cannibals too!"

"They loved it!" Spits howled. "They'd've gone on eating Spits's grub fer ever and said nowt if that new lad hadn't walked in on me while I was carving up a nice fat vicar and his wife! After that, they acted disgusted and treated me like a monster."

"I've eaten human flesh," Harkat said quietly. "Little People will eat anything. When I first came back from the dead, my thoughts ... weren't my own, and I ate with the rest. But we only ate the flesh ... of those who'd died naturally. We didn't kill. And we didn't take pleasure ... from it. You *are* a monster, even to someone ... like me."

Spits sneered. "Come off it, imp! I know why ye're really here — t' feast yer chops on Spits's stew! Shan boy too!" His eyes fixed on me and he winked crookedly. "Ye thought I didn't know what ye was, but Spits ain't as dumb as he lets on. Ye're a bloodsucker! Ye fed from me when ye thought I was asleep. So don't play the innocents, lads — 'twon't work!"

"You're wrong, Spits," I said. "I drink blood to survive, and Harkat's done things in the past that he's ashamed of.

But we aren't killers or cannibals. We don't want any part of your unholy feast."

"We'll see if ye think that way when ye smell the cooking," Spits cackled. "When yer lips are drooling and yer bellies growling, ye'll come running, plates out, begging fer a thick, juicy slice o' thigh."

"He's completely out of his mind," I whispered to Harkat, then called aloud to Spits. "Have you forgotten the dragons? *We'll* get roasted and eaten if we stand around gabbing!"

"They won't bother us," Spits said confidently. "The Tiny man told me. He said as long as I stayed within eight feet o' the Lake, the dragons couldn't harm me — they can't come this close. There's a spell on the Lake. Unless a living person jumps or falls in, the dragons can't come near."

Spits stopped dragging on his net and gazed at us calmly. "Don't ye see, lads? We don't ever need t' leave. We can stay here the rest of our lives, fishing fer dinner each day, all the water we can drink. Tiny said he'd drop by if we made it, and promised t' provide me with pots and material t' build fires. We'll have t' eat our catch raw till then, but I've ate humans raw before — not as tasty as when cooked, but ye won't have cause fer complaint."

"*That's* your dream!" Harkat hissed. "Not to return to our world, but to stay ... here for ever, fishing for the souls ... of the dead!"

"Aaarrr!" Spits laughed. "Tiny told me all about it. The souls don't have bodies in the water — them's just ghosts that we see. But once they're dragged on to dry land, they become real, the way they was before they died. I'll be able t' kill 'em again and carve 'em up any way I like. An unending supply — including the souls o' the cap'n and most o' the others on the *Prince o' Pariahs*! I can have revenge on top of a full stomach!"

There was a heavy thud behind us — the male dragon had returned and set down close to where we were standing. I raised a globe to throw at him, but then I saw that he wasn't coming any closer. Spits was right about the dragons not being able to approach the Lake.

"We can't let you do it," I said. Focusing on Spits, I started walking towards him.

"Ye can't stop me," he sniffed. "If ye don't want t' stay, ye can leave. I'll fish up the imp's soul and ye can take yer chances with the dragons. But there's nowt ye can do t' make me go with ye. I'm staying."

"No," I said. "We won't let you."

"Stay back!" Spits warned, lowering his net and drawing a knife. "I like ye both — ye're decent sorts fer a vampire and an imp! — but I'll slice the skin clean off yer bones if I have t'!"

"Don't try, Spits," Harkat said, stepping up behind me. "You've seen us in action. You know we're stronger and faster . . . than you. Don't make us hurt you."

"I ain't scared o' ye!" Spits shouted, backing away, waving his knife at us. "Ye need me more than I need ye! Unless ye back off, I won't fish yer soul out, and this'll all have been fer nowt!"

"I don't care," Harkat said softly. "I'd rather blow my chance . . . and die, than leave you here to torment the souls . . . of the dead and feed upon them."

"But they're bad 'uns!" Spits howled. "These ain't the souls o' good people — they're the souls o' the lost and damned, who couldn't get int' heaven."

"It doesn't matter," Harkat said. "We won't let you ... eat them."

"Crazy pair o' landlubbers," Spits snarled, coming to a halt. "Ye think ye can rob me o' the one thing that's kept me going all these years alone in this hellhole? 'Twasn't enough fer ye t' rob me o' me whisky — now ye wants t' take me meat away too! Well damn ye, demons o' the dark — damn ye both t' hell!"

With that shrill cry, Spits attacked, slicing wildly with his knife. We had to leap back quickly to avoid being gutted by the raging ex-pirate. Spits raced after us, whooping gleefully, chopping with his knife. "Gonna slice ye up and cook ye!" he howled. "The dead can wait — I'll feast on *yer* flesh tonight! I'm gonna see what ye're made of inside. I never ate a vampire or imp before — 'twill make fer an interesting comparison!"

"Spits!" I roared, ducking out of the way of his knife. "Stop now and we'll let you live! Otherwise we'll have to kill you!"

"Only one man'll be doing any killing today!" Spits retorted. "Spits Abrams, scourge o' the seas, lord o' the Lake, sultan o' chefs, king o'–"

Before Spits got any further, Harkat slid inside his stabbing range and grabbed his knife arm. Spits screamed at the Little Person and punched him with his free fist. When that didn't have any effect, he pulled a whisky bottle out of his sack and prepared to break it over Harkat's head.

"No you don't!" I grunted, seizing Spits's forearm. I squeezed tightly, until I heard bones cracking. Spits screeched painfully, dropped the bottle and spun away from me. I released him and he retreated sharply, breaking free of Harkat's grip, collapsing on the ground a couple of metres away.

"Quit it!" I yelled as Spits staggered to his feet and drew another bottle, cradling his injured arm across his chest.

"Never!" he cried. "I've still got one good hand. That'll be enough t'—" He stopped when he saw us freeze, our eyes widening. "What're ye up t' now?" he asked suspiciously. We couldn't answer, only gaze wordlessly at the space behind him. Spits sensed that we weren't trying to trick him, and whipped around to see what we were staring at. He found himself gazing up into the fierce cold eyes of the male dragon.

"Is that all that's bothering ye?" Spits hooted. "Didn't I tell ye they couldn't come next nor near us as long as we stayed..."

He trailed off into silence. He looked down at his feet, then at us, then at the Lake — which was about four or five metres away from where he was standing!

Spits could have made a run for it, but didn't. With a bitter smile, he shook his head, spat into the grass, and muttered, "*Aaarrr!*" The dragon opened its mouth wide when Spits said that — as though he'd been awaiting an order — and blew a huge ball of fire over the stranded ex-pirate. Spits disappeared in flames and Harkat and I had to cover our eyes and turn aside from the heat.

When we looked again, a fiery Spits was stumbling towards us, arms thrashing, face invisible beneath a mask of red flames. If he was screaming, we couldn't hear him over the crackle of his burning hair and clothes. We lunged out of his way as Spits staggered closer. He continued past us, oblivious to our presence, and didn't stop until he reached the edge of the Lake of Souls and toppled in.

Snapping out of our daze, we raced to the Lake in case there was anything we could do to help Spits. But we were too late. He was already deep under water, arms still moving, but weakly. As we watched, the shimmering shades of the dead surrounded the pirate's body, as though guiding it on its way. Spits's arms gradually stopped waving, then his body sunk deeper into the water, until it vanished from sight in the murky gloom of the soul-filled depths.

"Poor Spits," Harkat croaked. "That was awful."

"He probably deserved it," I sighed, "but I wish it could have happened some other way. If only he'd—"

A roar stopped the words dead in my throat. My head shot around and I spotted the male dragon, hovering in the air close above us, eyes gleaming. "Don't worry," Harkat said. "We're close to the Lake. It can't..." The words died on his lips and he stared at me, his green eyes filling with fear.

"The spell!" I moaned. "Spits said it would only last until a living person fell into the Lake! And he was still alive when..."

As we stood trembling, the dragon — no longer bound by the spell — opened his jaws wide and coughed a ball of fire straight at us — meaning to finish us off the same way he'd killed Spits!

CHAPTER TWENTY-THREE

I REACTED quicker to the flames than Harkat — I'd been badly burnt many years earlier, and had no wish to suffer the same fate again. I hurled myself into the Little Person, knocked him clear of the blast and rolled after him. As the flames zipped past us, out over the water of the Lake — momentarily illuminating the faces of the dead trapped within — I reached for a globe and hurled it at the ground beneath the dragon. There was a large explosion and the dragon peeled away, roaring — this was his first exposure to our explosives.

"Hurry!" I shouted at Harkat. "Give me your globes, grab the net and fish your soul out!"

"I don't know how ... to fish!" Harkat howled.

"There's no better time to learn!" I bellowed, then threw another globe as one of the females swooped upon us.

Harkat swiftly unloaded his globes and laid them on the ground by my feet. Then, grabbing Spits's abandoned net, he pulled it out of the Lake, paused a moment to clear his thoughts, and slowly fed the net in. As he did, he muttered softly, "I seek my soul, spirits … of the dead. I seek my soul, spirits … of the dead. I seek my—"

"Don't talk!" I yelled. "Fish!"

"Quiet!" Harkat hissed. "This is the way. I sense it. I must call upon my soul to … lure it into the net."

I wanted to ask how he'd figured that out, but there was no time — the male and both females were attacking, the females from the left and right, the male floating out over the Lake, in front of us. Scaring off the females with two hastily thrown globes, I studied the dragon angling down towards the surface of the Lake. If I threw a globe at the Lake, it wouldn't burst. That meant I'd have to aim for the dragon itself, and possibly kill him. It seemed a shame, but there were no other options.

I was getting a fix on the dragon when an idea struck me. Hurling the globe out on to the water in front of the approaching beast, I grabbed a nearby pebble, took careful aim, and sent it flying at the globe. It struck just as the dragon was nearing the globe, showering the creature's face with a seething funnel of water.

The dragon pulled out of its attack and arced away into the air, screeching its frustration. The females almost sneaked in while I was dealing with the male, but I spotted them just in time and scattered them with another blast. While the dragons regrouped overhead, I did a quick globe count — eight remained, plus the vial.

I wanted to tell Harkat to hurry, but his face was knitted together fiercely as he bent over the net, whispering softly to the souls in the Lake, searching for the soul of the person he used to be. To disturb him would be to delay him.

The dragons attacked again, in the same formation as before, and once again I successfully repelled them, leaving myself with five lonely-looking globes. As I picked up three more, I considered aiming to kill — after these three, I'd be down to my final pair — but as I studied the dragons circling in the air, I was again struck by their awesome majesty. This was their world, not ours. We had no right to kill them. What if these were the only living dragons, and we wiped out an entire species just to save our own necks?

As the dragons attacked once more, I still wasn't sure what I intended to do with the explosive globes. Clearing my mind, I allowed my self-defence mechanism to kick in and make the choice for me. When I found my hands pitching the globes short of the dragons, scaring them off but not killing them, I nodded grimly. "So be it," I sighed, then called to Harkat, "I can't kill them. After the next attack, we're done for. Do you want to take the globes and—"

"I have it!" Harkat shouted, hauling ferociously on the net, the strings of which tightened and creaked alarmingly. "A few more seconds! Buy me just a . . . few more seconds!"

"I'll do what I can," I grimaced, then faced the dragons, which were homing in on us as before, patiently repeating their previous manoeuvre. For the final time I sent the females packing, then pulled out the vial, tossed it on to the surface of the Lake, and smashed it with a pebble. Some glass must have struck the male dragon when the vial exploded, because he roared with pain as he peeled away.

Now that there was nothing else to do, I hurried to Harkat and grabbed hold of the net. "It's heavy!" I grunted, feeling the resistance as we tugged.

"A whopper!" Harkat agreed, grinning crazily.

"Are you OK?" I roared.

"I don't know!" he shouted. "I'm excited but terrified! I've waited so long ... for this moment, and I still ... don't know what to expect!"

We couldn't see the face of the figure caught in the strands of the net — it was turned away from us — but it was a man, light of build, with what looked to be dirty blond hair. As we pulled the spirit out of the Lake, its form glittered, then became solid, a bit at a time, first a hand, then an arm, followed by its other hand, its head, chest...

We had the rescued soul almost all the way out when I caught sight of the male dragon zooming towards us, his snout bleeding, pain and fury in his large yellow eyes. "Harkat!" I screamed. "We're out of time!"

Glancing up, Harkat spotted the dragon and grunted harshly. He gave the net one last desperate tug. The body in the net shot forward, its left foot solidifying and clearing the water with a pop similar to a gun's retort. As the dragon swooped down on us, its mouth closed, nostrils flaring, working on a fireball, Harkat spun the body over on to its back, revealing a pale, confused, horrified face.

"What the—?" I gasped.

"It can't be!" Harkat croaked, as the man in the net — impossibly familiar — stared at us with terror-filled eyes.

"Harkat!" I roared. "That can't be who you were!" My gaze flicked to the Little Person. "Can it?"

"I don't know," Harkat said, bewildered. He stared at the dragon — now almost upon us — then down at the man lying shivering on the shore. "Yes!" he shouted suddenly. "That's me! I'm him! I know who I was! I..."

As the dragon opened its mouth and blew fire at us with all the force it could muster, Harkat threw his head back and bellowed at the top of his voice, "I was the vampire traitor — *Kurda Smahlt!*"

Then the dragon's fire washed over us and the world turned red.

CHAPTER TWENTY-FOUR

I FELL to the ground, clamping my lips and eyes shut. Clambering to my knees, I tried to crawl out of the ball of fire before I was consumed to the bone—

—then paused when I realized that although I was surrounded by the dragon's flames, there wasn't any heat! I opened my left eyelid a fraction, ready to shut it again quick. What I saw caused both my eyes to snap open and my jaw to drop with astonishment.

The world around me had stopped. The dragon hung frozen over the Lake, a long line of fire extending from its mouth. The fire covered not just me, but Harkat and the naked man – *Kurda Smahlt!* – on the ground. But none of us was burnt. The static flames hadn't harmed us.

"What's going on?" Harkat asked, his words echoing hollowly.

"I haven't a clue," I said, running a hand through the

frozen fire around me — it felt like warm fog.

"Over ... there!" the man on the ground croaked, pointing to his left.

Harkat and I followed the direction of the finger and saw a short, tubby man striding towards us, beaming broadly, playing with a heart-shaped watch.

"*Mr Tiny!*" we shouted together, then cut through the harmless flames — Harkat grabbed Kurda under the arms and dragged him out — and hurried to meet the mysterious little man.

"Tight timing, boys!" Mr Tiny boomed as we came within earshot. "I didn't expect it to go that close to the wire. A thrilling finale! Most satisfying."

I stopped and stared at Mr Tiny. "You didn't know how it would turn out?" I asked.

"Of course not," he smirked. "That's what made it so much fun. A few more seconds and you'd have been toast!"

Mr Tiny stepped past me and held out a cloak to Harkat and his naked companion. "Cover the poor soul," Mr Tiny punned.

Harkat took the cloak and draped it around Kurda's shoulders. Kurda said nothing, just stared at the three of us, his blue eyes wide with suspicion and fear, trembling like a newborn baby.

"What's going on?" I snapped at Mr Tiny. "Harkat can't have been Kurda — he was around long before Kurda died!"

"What do you think, Harkat?" Mr Tiny asked the Little Person.

"It's me," Harkat whispered, studying Kurda intensely. "I don't know how … but it is."

"But it can't—" I began, only for Mr Tiny to interrupt curtly.

"We'll discuss it later," he said. "The dragons won't stay like this indefinitely. Let's not be here when they unfreeze. I can control them normally, but they're in quite an agitated state and it would be safer not to press our luck. They couldn't harm me, but it would be a shame to lose all of you to their fury at this late stage."

I was anxious for answers, but the thought of facing the dragons again enabled me to hold my tongue and follow quietly as Mr Tiny led us out of the valley, whistling chirpily, away from the lost remains of Spits Abrams and the other dead spirits held captive in the Lake of Souls.

Night. Sitting by a crackling fire, finishing off a meal which two of Mr Tiny's Little People had prepared. We were no more than a kilometre from the valley, out in the open, but Mr Tiny assured us that we wouldn't be disturbed by dragons. On the far side of the fire stood a tall, arched doorway, like the one we'd entered this world by. I longed to throw myself through it, but there were questions which needed to be answered first.

My eyes returned to Kurda Smahlt, as they had so often since we'd pulled him out of the Lake. He was extremely pale and thin, his hair untidy, his eyes dark with fear and pain. But otherwise he looked exactly as he had the last time I saw him, when I'd foiled his plans to betray the vampires to the vampaneze. He'd been executed shortly afterwards, dropped into a pit of stakes until he was dead, then cut into pieces and cremated.

Kurda felt my eyes upon him and glanced up shamefully. He no longer shook, though he still looked very uncertain. Laying aside his plate, he wiped around his mouth with a scrap of cloth, then asked softly, "How much time has passed since I was put to death?"

"Eight years or so," I answered.

"Is that all?" He frowned. "It seems much longer."

"Do you remember everything that happened?" I asked.

He nodded bleakly. "My memory's as sharp as ever, though I wish it wasn't — that drop into the pit of stakes is something I'd rather never think about again." He sighed. "I'm sorry for what I did, killing Gavner and betraying the clan. But I believed it was for the good of our people — I was trying to prevent a war with the vampaneze."

"I know," I said softly. "We've been at war since you died, and the Vampaneze Lord has revealed himself. He..." I gulped deeply. "He killed Mr Crepsley. Many others have died as well."

"I'm sorry," Kurda said again. "Perhaps if I'd succeeded, they'd still be alive." He grimaced as soon as he said that, and shook his head. "No. It's too easy to say 'what if' and paint a picture of a perfect world. There would have been death and misery even if you hadn't exposed me. That was unavoidable."

Harkat hadn't said much since we'd sat down — he'd been studying Kurda like a baby watching its mother. Now his eyes roamed to Mr Tiny and he said quietly, "I know I was Kurda. But *how*? I was created years before ... Kurda died."

"Time is relative," Mr Tiny chuckled, roasting something that looked suspiciously like a human eyeball on a stick over the fire. "From the present, I can move backwards into the past, or forward into any of the possible futures."

"You can travel through time?" I asked sceptically.

Mr Tiny nodded. "That's my one great thrill in life. By playing with time, I can subtly influence the course of future events, keeping the world on a chaotic keel — it's more interesting that way. I can help or hinder humans, vampires and vampaneze, as I see fit. There are limits to what I can do, but I work broadly and actively within them.

"For reasons of my own, I decided to help young Master Shan," he continued, addressing his words to Harkat. "I've laid many plans around that young man, but I saw, years ago, that he was doomed for an early grave. Without someone to step in at vital moments — for instance, when he fought with the bear on his way to Vampire Mountain, and later with the wild boars during his Trials of Initiation — he would have perished long ago.

"So I created Harkat Mulds," he said, this time speaking to me. He swallowed the eyeball he'd been cooking and belched merrily. "I could have used any of my Little People, but I needed someone who'd cared about you when he was alive, who'd do that little bit extra to protect you. So I went into a possible future, searched among the souls of the tormented dead, and found our old friend Kurda Smahlt."

Mr Tiny slapped Kurda's knee. The one-time General flinched. "Kurda was a soul in agony," Mr Tiny said cheerfully. "He was unable to forgive himself for betraying his people, and was desperate to make amends. By becoming Harkat Mulds and protecting you, he provided the vampires with the possibility of victory in the War of the Scars. Without Harkat, you would have died long ago, and there would have been no hunt for the Lord of the Vampaneze — he would simply have led his forces to victory over the vampires."

"But I didn't know ... that I used to be Kurda!" Harkat protested.

"Deep down you did," Mr Tiny disagreed. "Since I had to return your soul to the past, I had to hide the truth of your identity from you — if you'd known who you were, you might have tried to directly interfere with the course of the future. But on a subconscious level, you knew. That's why you fought so bravely beside Darren, risking your life for his on numerous occasions."

I thought about that in silence for a long while, as did Harkat and Kurda. Time travel was a difficult concept to get my head around, but if I overlooked the paradox of being able to send a soul from the future into the past to alter the present — and didn't question how it was achieved — I could see the logic. Kurda had betrayed the vampires. Ashamed, his soul remained bound to Earth. Mr Tiny offered him the chance of redemption — by returning to life as a Little Person, he could make amends for his foul deeds.

"There's something I don't understand," Kurda said, then winced. "Actually, there's *loads* I don't understand, but one thing in particular. My plan to betray the vampires would have succeeded if Darren hadn't interfered. But you say

Darren would have died without my aid as Harkat Mulds. So, in effect, I helped Darren mastermind my own downfall!"

Mr Tiny shook his head. "You would have perished regardless of the outcome. Your death was never in question — merely the manner of it."

"What puzzles *me* the most," Harkat muttered, "is how ... the two of us can be here at the same ... time. If I'm Kurda and he's ... me, how can we exist together?"

"Harkat's wiser than he looks," Mr Tiny noted with a chuckle. "The answer is that you *can't* — at least, not for very long. While Kurda remained in the Lake of Souls, Harkat was free to roam the world. Now that Kurda has emerged, one must make way for the other."

"What do you mean?" I asked sharply.

"Kurda and Harkat share the same soul," Mr Tiny explained, "but while a soul can be split, it can only lay claim to one body at any given time — although there *are* ways to protect a newly formed body for a while, if you send it into the past, which is how Harkat was previously able to function at the same time as Kurda." As the original, Kurda has a natural claim to existence. Even now, the strands of Harkat's form are unravelling. Within a day his body will dissolve, releasing his share of their soul. A split soul can never be rejoined — Harkat and Kurda are two different people. Since this is the case, Harkat's half of their soul must depart this world. It's nature's way."

"You mean Harkat's going to die?" I yelled.

"He's dead already," Mr Tiny chuckled.

"Stop splitting hairs!" I growled. "Will Harkat perish if we stay here?"

"He'll perish wherever you are," Mr Tiny replied. "Now that Kurda's soul has been given form, only he has the power to spare Harkat's body."

"If I can save Harkat, I will," Kurda said immediately.

"Even if it costs you your own newly restored life?" Mr Tiny asked slyly.

Kurda stiffened. "What are you talking about?"

Mr Tiny stood and stretched. "There's much I can't tell you," he said. "But I'll explain as best I can. There are two ways in which I can create a Little Person — from a soul's resurrected body – the one which forms when a person is fished from the Lake of Souls – or from their corpse. With Harkat, I used Kurda's original remains."

"But Kurda's body was burnt to ashes," I interrupted.

"No," Mr Tiny said. "When I decided to use Kurda's soul, I returned to the time of his death and convinced the Guardians of the Blood to switch his body with another's. I used Kurda's bones to make Harkat. The deal I then made with him was that in return for his new body, he'd travel with Darren and protect him, and later, if he did as instructed, I'd free his soul — he wouldn't have to return to the Lake.

"Well, Harkat has performed admirably and is most deserving of his reward. If Kurda chooses, he can walk away a free man now. He can live out the rest of his renewed life, however long or short that proves to be. Harkat's body will fall apart, his soul will be freed, and I'll have upheld my end of the bargain."

"To live again!" Kurda whispered, eyes bright.

"*Or*," Mr Tiny added with cruel relish, "we can strike a new deal and Kurda can sacrifice himself."

Kurda's eyes narrowed. "Why would I do that?" he snapped.

"You and Harkat share a soul, but it's a soul which I have helped divide into two parts. If you let me destroy your new body, your part of your shared spirit will depart this realm instead of Harkat's. Harkat will become your soul's sole physical vessel. I can't guarantee him immunity from the Lake of Souls in that case, but he may return home with Darren and live out his life. His future will be his own — if he lives a good life and dies well, the Lake will have no claim on him."

"That's a despicable choice to present me with," Kurda growled.

"I don't make the laws," Mr Tiny shrugged. "I just obey them. One of you can live — the other must bid farewell to life. I could make the call and just kill one of you, but wouldn't you rather decide for yourselves?"

"I suppose," Kurda sighed, then looked at Harkat and grinned. "No offence, but if we were to decide on the basis of good looks, I'd win hands down."

"And if we judged it ... on loyalty," Harkat responded, "*I* would win, since I have ... never betrayed my friends."

Kurda grimaced. "Would you want to live?" he asked Harkat. "The Lake is a hellish place. Mr Tiny's offering you a guaranteed escape. Maybe you want to take it?"

"No," Harkat said. "I don't want to let go ... of life. I'd rather go back with Darren and take my chances."

Kurda looked at me. "What do you reckon, Darren?" he asked softly. "Should I grant Harkat life or set his soul free?"

I started to answer but Harkat cut in. "Darren has nothing to do ... with this. Much of my memory – *your* ... memory – is returning. A lot is clear now. I know you the same way I ... know myself. You always went your own way ... even to the point of betraying your people ... when you thought it was for their best. Be the man in death that ... you were in life. Decide for yourself."

"He put that quite well," Mr Tiny murmured.

"Couldn't have said it better myself," Kurda agreed, grinning sickly. Standing, he turned in a complete, slow circle, studying the dark world beyond the light of the fire, thinking deeply. Then he sighed and faced Mr Tiny. "I've had my fill of life. I made my choices and accepted the consequences. This is Harkat's time. I belong to death — let it have me."

Mr Tiny smiled strangely, almost warmly. "Your decision makes no sense to me but I admire you for it. I promise your death will be swift and painless, and your departure for whatever glories or terrors which lie beyond will be instant."

Mr Tiny stepped over to the arched doorway. He held up his heart-shaped watch and it glowed a deep red colour. Within seconds the doorway and the small man's face were glowing too. "Through you go, boys — the home fires are burning and your friends are waiting."

"Not yet!" I shouted. "I want to know where we are and how Evanna got here and why you stocked that kitchen underground and where the dragons came from and why—"

"Your questions must wait," Mr Tiny stopped me. His face was glowing red and he looked more frightening than anything we'd faced during the course of our journey. "Go now, or I'll leave you here to the dragons."

"You wouldn't!" I snorted, but I was in no position to call his bluff. Walking to the doorway, followed by Harkat, I stopped and gazed back at Kurda Smahlt, about to face death for the second time. There was so much I wanted to say to him, so much I wanted to ask him. But there was no time. "Thank you," I whispered simply.

"Yes — thank you," Harkat added.

"What's a life between friends?" Kurda laughed, then grew serious. "Make it count. Lead a good life, so you'll have no regrets when you die. That way your soul will fly free, and you won't be at the beck and call of meddlers like Desmond Tiny."

"If not for we meddlers, who would hold the fabric of the universe together?" Mr Tiny countered. Then, before we could pursue the conversation any further, he barked, "You must go now — or stay for ever!"

"Goodbye, Kurda," Harkat said numbly.

"Farewell, *Sire*," I saluted him.

Kurda didn't answer, just waved shortly and turned his head aside. I think he was crying. And then, leaving many questions unanswered, but having successfully achieved what we set out to, Harkat and I turned away from the living corpse, the Lake of Souls, the dragons, the Grotesque and other creatures of this twisted place, and walked through the glowing doorway, back to the world of our own.

CHAPTER TWENTY-FIVE

MR TALL was waiting for us when we stepped through the doorway, standing beside a fire much like the one we'd left behind, close to the vans and tents of the Cirque Du Freak, but separated from the campsite by a row of trees. His small mouth was stretched into a smile as he stepped forward to shake our hands. "Hello, Darren. Hello, Harkat. I'm delighted about your safe return."

"Hello, Hibernius," Harkat greeted the Cirque owner — it was the first time he'd ever called him that.

"Ah!" Mr Tall beamed. "Your mission was a success — as Kurda, you always called me Hibernius."

"Good to see you again ... old friend," Harkat said. His voice hadn't changed, but he somehow sounded different.

As we sat around the fire, I asked where our other friends were. Mr Tall told us most were sleeping — it was late and everyone was tired after that night's performance.

"I've known for the last week that you were due to return — if you managed to make it back alive — but I wasn't sure of the exact date. I've been making a fire and waiting beside it for several nights. I could wake the others, but it would be better to wait and announce your return in the morning."

We agreed to let our friends slumber. Harkat and I began telling Mr Tall about our adventures in the mysterious world through the glowing doorway (which crumbled to ash shortly after we stepped through). Mr Tall was fascinated and listened in rapt silence, asking virtually no questions. We only meant to tell him the highlights — and save the majority of the tale for when we had more listeners — but once we started, we couldn't stop, and over the next few hours we told him all that had happened. The only time he interrupted was when we mentioned Evanna — he stopped us there and asked a lot of questions about her.

There was a long silence at the end, as the three of us stared into the dying embers of the fire and thought about our battles and narrow escapes, the fate of the deranged Spits Abrams, the wondrous dragons, the great revelation and Kurda's unenviable choice.

"Will Mr Tiny really kill Kurda?" I asked after a while.

Mr Tall nodded sadly. "A soul can divide but it cannot share two bodies. But Kurda made the right choice — Harkat will remember most of what Kurda experienced while alive, and in that way Kurda will live on. Had Kurda chosen life, all of Harkat's memories would have been lost to the world. This way they both win."

"A cheery thought to end on," Harkat said, smiling. He yawned and stared up at the moon. "How much time has passed since ... we were away?"

"Time has been the same for us as for you," Mr Tall said. "Some three months have slipped by. It is summer now."

"Any news about the War of the Scars?" I asked.

"None," Mr Tall said shortly.

"I hope Debbie and Alice reached Vampire Mountain," I muttered. During my months away, I'd only rarely stopped to wonder what was happening back home. Now I was anxious to catch up on all that I had missed.

"I wouldn't trouble myself if I were you," Mr Tall said, seeing the questions in my eyes. "This is where you and Harkat are meant to be right now. The War of the Scars will find you again when destiny decrees. For the time being, relax and enjoy this calm between the storms."

Mr Tall stood and smiled at us. "I'll leave you now. Get as much sleep as you need — I'll see that you are not disturbed." As he turned to leave, he paused and glanced back at Harkat. "It would be wise to wear your mask again, now that the air is no longer safe."

"Oh!" Harkat gasped. "I forgot!" Digging out a mask, he tied it around his mouth, breathed through it a few times to make sure there weren't any rips, then lowered it so that he could speak clearly. "Thanks."

"Don't mention it," the tall man chuckled.

"Mr Tall," I said quietly, as he turned to leave again. "Do you know where we were? Was that world a different planet, the past, an alternate reality?"

The Cirque owner said nothing and didn't look back — just shook his head and hurried on towards the camp.

"He knows," I sighed. "But he won't tell."

Harkat grunted. "Did you bring anything ... back with you?" he asked.

"Only my clothes," I said. "And I don't plan on hanging on to these rags — they can go straight in the bin!"

Harkat smiled, then rifled through his robes. "I still have the postcards I took ... from the underground kitchen, as well as ... the panther's teeth." He spilt the teeth on to the grass and turned them so all the letters were face up. He idly began arranging them to form his name, but as he got to the end of "Harkat", he stopped, quickly scanned all the teeth, and groaned.

"What's wrong?" I asked sharply.

"Remember Mr Tiny saying at the ... start that we'd find a clue to who I was ... when we killed the panther?" Harkat quickly rearranged the letters on the teeth to form another name — *KURDA SMAHLT!*

I stared at the letters, then groaned like Harkat had. "The answer was in front of us all along — your name's an anagram! If we'd spent more time on the letters after we'd killed the panther, we could have solved the puzzle and skipped the rest of the ordeal!"

"I doubt it would have been ... that simple," Harkat laughed. "But at least I now know where ... my name came from. I used to wonder ... how I'd picked it."

"On the subject of names," I said, "are you sticking with Harkat Mulds or reverting to your original name?"

"Harkat Mulds or Kurda Smahlt," Harkat muttered, and said the names a few more times. "No," he decided. "Kurda's the person I used ... to be. Harkat's the person I've become. We are the same in some ways ... but different in many others. I want to be known ... as Harkat."

"Good," I said. "It would have been very confusing otherwise."

Harkat cleared his throat and looked at me oddly. "Now that you know the truth ... about me, does it change anything? As Kurda, I betrayed you and ... all the vampires. I killed Gavner Purl. I will understand if you don't ... think as highly of me as you ... did before."

"Don't be stupid," I grinned. "I don't care who you used to be — it's who you *are* that matters. You've long made up for any mistakes in your previous life." I frowned. "But does this change how *you* feel about *me*?"

"What do you mean?" Harkat asked.

"The reason you stuck by me before was that you needed my help to find out who you were. Now that you know, maybe you'd like to head off and explore the world by yourself. The War of the Scars isn't your battle any longer. If you'd rather go your own way..." I trailed off into silence.

"You're right," Harkat said after a couple of thoughtful moments. "I'll leave first thing in ... the morning." He stared seriously at my glum features, then burst out laughing. "You idiot! Of course I won't go! This is my war as much as ... it's yours. Even if I hadn't been a ... vampire, I wouldn't leave. We've been through too much ... together to split up now.

Maybe when the war is over ... I'll seek a path of my own. For the time being I still feel ... bound to you. I don't think we're meant ... to part company yet."

"Thanks," I said simply. It was all that needed to be said.

Harkat gathered up the panther's teeth and put them away. Then he studied the postcards, turned one over and gazed at it moodily. "I don't know if I should ... mention this," he sighed. "But if I don't, it will ... gnaw away at me."

"Go on," I encouraged him. "Those cards have been bothering you since you found them in the kitchen. What's the big mystery?"

"It has to do with ... where we were," Harkat said slowly. "We spent a lot of time wondering where ... we'd been taken — the past, another world ... or a different dimension."

"So?" I prodded him when he stalled.

"I think I know the answer," he sighed. "It ties it all together, why ... the spiders were there ... and the Guardians of the Blood, if that's ... who the Kulashkas really were. And the kitchen. I don't think Mr Tiny put the kitchen ... there — I think it was in place ... all along. It was a nuclear fallout shelter, built to ... survive when all else fell. I think it was put to the test ... and it passed. I hope I'm wrong, but I'm ... afraid I'm not."

He passed a postcard to me. On the front was a picture of Big Ben. There was writing on the back, a typical tourist's account of their holiday — "Having a great time, weather good, food fab." The name at the bottom and the name and address on the right-hand side of the postcard meant nothing to me.

"What's the big deal?" I asked.

"Look at the postmark," Harkat whispered.

What I saw confused me. "That date can't be right," I muttered. "That's not for another twelve years."

"They're all like that," Harkat said, passing the rest of the postcards to me. "Twelve years ahead … fifteen … twenty … more."

"I don't get it," I frowned. "What does it mean?"

"I don't think we were in the past or … on a different world," Harkat said, taking the postcards back and tucking them away. He stared at me ominously with his large green eyes, hesitated a moment, then quickly mumbled the words which turned my insides cold. "I think that barren, monster-filled wasteland … was the *future!*"

TO BE CONTINUED…

DARREN SHAN
LORD OF THE SHADOWS

THE SAGA OF DARREN SHAN

BOOK 11

For:

Bas – my globetrotting gal

OBE's
(Order of the Bloody Entrails) to:
Maiko "Greenfingers" Enomoto
Megumi "The Voice" Hashimoto
"Queen" Tomoko Taguchi
"Eagle-eyed" Tomoko Aoki
Yamada "Papa" san

And everybody else on the Japanese Shan team who worked
so hard to make June 2003 such a special time for me

Editing Crew:
Gillie "The Don" and Zoë "The Mom"

Guiding Lights:
The Christopher Little Posse

PROLOGUE

IN THE distance a wave of blood was building. Red, towering, topped with spitting heads of fire. On a vast plain, a mass of vampires waited. All three thousand or so faced the onrushing wave. At the rear, separated from the crowd, I stood alone. I was trying to push forward – I wanted to be with the rest of the clan when the wave hit – but an invisible force held me back.

As I struggled, roaring silently – my voice didn't work here – the wave swept ever nearer. The vampires pulled closer together, terrified but proud, facing their deaths with dignity. Some were pointing spears or swords at the wave, as though they could fight it back.

Closer now, almost upon them, half a kilometre high, stretching in an unbroken line across the horizon. A wave of crackling flames and boiling blood. The moon disappeared behind the crimson curtain and a blood-red darkness descended.

The foremost vampires were eaten by the wave. They screamed in agony as they were crushed, drowned or burnt to death, their bodies tossed about like pieces of cork within the heart of the scarlet wave. I reached out to them — my people! — and prayed to the gods of the vampires to free me, so that I could die with my blood brothers and sisters. But still I couldn't break through the invisible boundary.

More vampires vanished beneath the breaking surf of fire and blood, lost to the wave of merciless red. A thousand lives extinguished ... fifteen hundred warriors eliminated ... two thousand souls sent soaring to Paradise ... twenty-five hundred death howls ... three thousand corpses, bobbing and burning in the flames.

And then only I was left. My voice returned, and with a desolate cry I collapsed to my knees and glared hatefully up at the crest of the wave as it teetered overhead. I saw faces within the walls of flaming blood — my friends and allies. The wave was taunting me with them.

Then I saw something hovering in the air above the wave, a creature of myth but oh so real. A dragon. Long, glittering, scaled, terrifyingly beautiful. And on its back — a person. A figure of pulsating darkness. It was almost as though his body had been created from shadows.

The shadow man laughed when he saw me, and his laugh was a ghostly cackle, evil and mocking. At his command, the dragon swooped lower, so that it was only a few metres above me. From here I could see its rider's features. His face was a mass of dancing patches of darkness, but when I squinted I recognized him — Steve Leopard.

"All must fall to the Lord of the Shadows," Steve said softly, and pointed behind me. "This is my world now."

Turning around, I saw a vast area of wasteland dotted with corpses. Over the dead bodies crawled giant toads, hissing black panthers, grotesque human mutants, and more nightmarish creatures and shapes. Cities burnt in the far distance, and great mushroom clouds of smoke and flames filled the air overhead.

I faced Steve again and roared a challenge at him. "Face me on the ground, you monster! Fight me now!"

Steve only laughed, then waved an arm at the wave of fire. There was a moment of hushed calm. Then the wave crashed to earth around me and I was swept away, face burning, lungs filling with blood, surrounded by the bodies of the dead. But what terrified me most before I was swallowed by eternal blackness was that I'd snatched one final glimpse of the Lord of the Shadows before I died. And this time it wasn't Steve's face I saw — it was *mine*.

CHAPTER ONE

MY EYES snapped open. I wanted to scream, but there was a hand over my mouth, rough and powerful. Fear gripped me. I lashed out at my attacker. Then my senses returned and I realized it was just Harkat, muffling my screams so that I didn't disturb any of the sleepers in the neighbouring caravans and tents.

I relaxed and tapped Harkat's hand to show that I was OK. He released me and stepped back, his large green eyes alive with concern. He handed me a mug of water. I drank deeply from it, then wiped a shaking hand across my lips and smiled weakly. "Did I wake you?"

"I wasn't asleep," Harkat said. The grey-skinned Little Person didn't need much sleep and often went two or three nights without dozing. He took the mug from me and set it down. "It was a bad one this ... time. You started screaming five or six ... minutes ago, and only stopped now. The same nightmare?"

"Isn't it always?" I muttered. "The wasteworld, the wave of fire, the dragon, the ... Steve," I finished quietly. I'd been haunted by the nightmare for almost two years, screaming myself awake at least a couple of times a week. In all those months I hadn't told Harkat about the Lord of the Shadows and that wretched face I always saw at the end of the nightmare. As far as he knew, Steve was the only monster in my dreams — I didn't dare tell him that I was as scared of myself as I was of Steve Leopard.

I swung my legs out of my hammock and sat up. I could tell by the darkness that it was only three or four in the morning, but I knew I wouldn't be able to sleep any more. The nightmare always left me shaken and wide awake.

Rubbing the back of my neck, I found myself studying Harkat out of the corner of my eye. Although he wasn't the source of my nightmares, I could trace their origins back to him. The Little Person had been built from the remains of a corpse. For most of his new life he hadn't known who he was. Two years ago, Mr Tiny — a man of immense power, with the ability to travel through time — transported us to a barren wasteworld and sent us off on a quest to discover Harkat's previous identity. We fought a variety of wild creatures and twisted monstrosities before finally fishing Harkat's original body out of the Lake of Souls, a holding place for damned spirits.

Harkat used to be a vampire called Kurda Smahlt. He'd betrayed the vampire clan in a bid to prevent war with our blood cousins, the purple-skinned vampaneze. To make up for his sins, he'd agreed to become Harkat Mulds and travel back into the past to be my guardian.

I'm Darren Shan, a Vampire Prince. I'm also one of the hunters of the Lord of the Vampaneze — a.k.a. Steve Leopard. Steve was destined to lead the vampaneze to victory over the vampires. If he won, he'd wipe us out entirely. But a few of us – the hunters – had the ability to stop him before he came fully into his powers. If we found and killed him before he matured, the war would be ours. By helping me as Harkat, Kurda hoped to help the clan and prevent their destined destruction at the hands of the vampaneze. In that way he could put right some of the wrongs he'd committed.

Having learnt the truth about Harkat, we returned to our own world — rather, our own *time*. Because what we worked out later was that the wasteworld wasn't an alternative universe or Earth in the past, as we'd first thought — it was Earth in the future. Mr Tiny had given us a glimpse of what was to come if the Lord of the Shadows came to power.

Harkat thought the ruined world would only come to pass if the vampaneze won the War of the Scars. But I knew about a prediction which I hadn't shared with anybody else. When the hunt for Steve was finally concluded, there would be one of two possible futures. In one, Steve became the Lord of the Shadows and destroyed the world. In the other future, the Lord of the Shadows was *me*.

That's why I woke in a cold sweat, to the sound of my own screams, so often. It wasn't just fear of the future, but fear of myself. Would I somehow play a part in creating the barren, twisted world I'd seen in the future? Was I damned to become a monster like Steve, and wreck all that I held dear? It seemed impossible, but the uncertainties gnawed away at me all the same, prompted by the ever-repeating nightmares.

I spent the time before dawn chatting with Harkat, small talk, nothing serious. He'd suffered terrible nightmares before finding out the truth about himself, so he knew exactly what I was going through. He knew what to say to calm me down.

When the sun rose and the Cirque camp started to come to life around us, we made an early start on our day's chores. We'd been with the Cirque Du Freak since returning from our gruelling quest in the wasteworld. We knew nothing about what was happening in the War of the Scars. Harkat wanted to return to Vampire Mountain, or at least make contact with the clan — now that he knew he had once been a vampire, he was more concerned than ever for them. But I held off. I didn't feel the time was right. I had a hunch that we were meant to remain with the Cirque, and that destiny would decide our course as and when it saw fit. Harkat strongly disagreed with me – we'd had some very heated arguments about it – but he reluctantly followed my lead — though I'd sensed recently that his patience was coming to an end.

We performed a variety of jobs around the camp, helping out wherever we were needed — moving equipment, mending costumes, feeding the Wolf Man. We were handymen. Mr Tall – the owner of the Cirque Du Freak – had offered to find more responsible, permanent positions for us, but we didn't know when we'd have to leave. It was easier to stick to simple tasks and not get too involved in the long-term running of the show. That way we wouldn't be missed too much when the time came to part company with the freakish folk.

We'd been performing on the outskirts of a large city, in an old, run-down factory. Sometimes we played in a big top which we transported around with us, but Mr Tall always liked to take advantage of local venues whenever possible. This was our fourth and final show in the factory. We'd be moving on in the morning, to pastures new. None of us knew where we'd be going yet — Mr Tall made those decisions and usually didn't tell us until we'd broken camp and were already on the move.

We put on a typically tight, exciting show that night, built around some of the longest-serving performers — Gertha Teeth, Rhamus Twobellies, Alexander Ribs, Truska the bearded lady, Hans Hands, Evra and Shancus Von. Usually the Vons rounded off the show, treating audiences to one final scare when their snakes slid from the shadows overhead. But Mr Tall had been experimenting with different line-ups recently.

On stage, Jekkus Flang was juggling knives. Jekkus was one of the Cirque helpers, like Harkat and me, but tonight he'd been billed as a star attraction and was entertaining the crowd with a display of knife tricks. Jekkus was a good juggler, but his act was pretty dull compared to the others. After a few minutes, a man in the front row stood up as Jekkus balanced a long knife on the tip of his nose.

"This is rubbish!" the man shouted, climbing on to the stage. "This is meant to be a place of magic and wonder — not juggling tricks! I could see stuff like this at any circus."

Jekkus took the knife from his nose and snarled at the intruder. "Get off the stage, or I'll cut you up into tiny pieces!"

"You don't worry me," the man snorted, taking a couple of large paces over to Jekkus, so they were eyeball to eyeball. "You're wasting our time and money. I want a refund."

"Insolent scum!" Jekkus roared, then lashed out with his knife and cut off the man's left arm just below the elbow! The man screamed and grabbed for the falling limb. As he was reaching for his lost forearm, Jekkus struck again and cut off the man's other arm in the same place!

People in the audience erupted with panic and surged to their feet. The man with the jagged stumps beneath his elbows tottered towards the edge of the stage, desperately waving his half-arms around, face white with apparent shock. But then he stopped — and laughed.

The people in the front rows heard the laughter and stared up at the stage suspiciously. The man laughed again. This time his laughter carried further, and people all around relaxed and faced the stage. As they watched, tiny hands grew out of the stumps of the man's arms. The hands continued to grow, followed by wrists and forearms. A minute later, the man's arms had returned to their natural length. He flexed his fingers, grinned, and took a bow.

"Ladies and gentlemen!" Mr Tall boomed, appearing suddenly on stage. "Put your hands together for the fabulous, the amazing, the incredible *Cormac Limbs!*"

Everybody realized they'd been the victims of a practical joke — the man who'd stepped out of the audience was a performer. They clapped and cheered as Cormac sliced off his fingers one by one, each of which grew back quickly. He could cut off any part of his body — though he'd never tried chopping off his head! Then the show finished for real and the crowd poured out, babbling with excitement, wildly discussing the mystical mysteries of the sensational Cirque Du Freak.

Inside, Harkat and I helped with the tidying up. Everyone involved was vastly experienced, and we could normally clear everything away within half an hour, sometimes less. Mr Tall stood in the shadows while we worked. That was odd — he normally retired to his van after a show — but we took little notice of it. You grew used to oddness when you worked with the Cirque Du Freak!

As I was stacking several chairs away, to be removed to a truck by other hands, Mr Tall stepped forward. "A moment, please, Darren," he said, removing the tall red hat he wore whenever he went on stage. He took a map out of the hat — the map was much larger than the hat, but I didn't question how he'd fitted it inside — and unrolled it. He held one end of the map in his large left hand and nodded for me to take the other end.

"This is where we are now," Mr Tall said, pointing to a spot on the map. I studied it curiously, wondering why he was showing me. "And this is where we will be going next," he said, pointing to a town a hundred and sixty kilometres away.

I looked at the name of the town. My breath caught in my throat. For a moment I felt dizzy and a cloud seemed to pass in front of my eyes. Then my expression cleared. "I see," I said softly.

"You don't have to come with us," Mr Tall said. "You can take a different route and meet up with us later, if you wish."

I started to think about it, then made a snap gut decision instead. "That's OK," I said. "I'll come. I want to. It ... it'll be interesting."

"Very well," Mr Tall said briskly, taking back the map and rolling it up again. "We depart in the morning."

With that, Mr Tall slipped away. I felt he didn't approve of my decision, but I couldn't say why, and I didn't devote much thought to it. Instead, I stood by the stacked-up chairs, lost in the past, thinking about all the people I'd known as a child, especially my parents and younger sister.

Harkat limped over eventually and waved a grey hand in front of my face, snapping me out of my daze. "What's wrong?" he asked, sensing my disquiet.

"Nothing," I said, with a confused shrug. "At least, I don't think so. It might even be a good thing. I..." Sighing, I stared at the ten little scars on my fingertips and muttered without looking up, "I'm going home."

CHAPTER TWO

ALEXANDER RIBS stood, rapped his ribcage with a spoon and opened his mouth. A loud musical note sprang out and all conversation ceased. Facing the boy at the head of the table, Alexander sang, "He's green, he's lean, snot he's never seen, his name is Shancus — happy birthday!"

Everybody cheered. Thirty performers and helpers from the Cirque Du Freak were seated around a huge oval table, celebrating Shancus Von's eighth birthday. It was a chilly April day, and most people were wrapped up warmly. The table was overflowing with cakes, sweets and drinks, and we were digging in happily.

When Alexander Ribs sat down, Truska — a woman who could grow her beard at will — stood and sung another birthday greeting. "The only things he fears is his mother's flying ears, his name is Shancus — happy birthday!"

Merla snapped one of her ears off when she heard that

and flicked it at her son. He ducked and it flew high over his head, then circled back to Merla, who caught and reattached it to the side of her head. Everyone laughed.

Since Shancus had been named in my honour, I guessed I'd better chip in with a verse of my own. Thinking quickly, I stood, cleared my throat, and chanted, "He's scaly and he's great, today he has turned eight, his name is Shancus — happy birthday!"

"Thanks, godfather," Shancus smirked. I wasn't really his godfather, but he liked to pretend I was — especially when it was his birthday and he was looking for a cool present!

A few others took turns singing birthday greetings to the snake-boy, then Evra stood and wrapped up the song with, "Despite the pranks you pull, your mum and I love you, pesky Shancus — happy birthday!"

There was lots of applause, then the women at the table shuffled over to hug and kiss Shancus. He pulled a mortified expression, but I could see he was delighted by the attention. His younger brother, Urcha, was jealous and sat a little way back from the table, sulking. Their sister, Lilia, was rooting through the piles of presents Shancus had received, seeing if there was anything of interest to a five-year-old girl.

Evra went to try and cheer up Urcha. Unlike Shancus and Lilia, the middle Von child was an ordinary human and he felt he was the odd one out. Evra and Merla had a tough time making him feel special. I saw Evra slip a small present to Urcha, and heard him whisper, "Don't tell the others!" Urcha looked much happier after that. He joined Shancus at the table and tucked into a pile of small cakes.

I made my way over to where Evra was beaming at his family. "Eight years," I remarked, clapping Evra on his left shoulder (some of his scales had been sliced away from his right shoulder a long time ago, and he didn't like people touching him there). "I bet it feels like eight weeks."

"You don't know how right you are," Evra smiled. "Time flies when you have kids. You'll find out yourself one—" He stopped and grimaced. "Sorry. I forgot."

"Don't worry about it," I said. As a half-vampire, I was sterile. I could never have children. It was one of the drawbacks to being part of the clan.

"When are you going to show the snake to Shancus?" Evra asked.

"Later," I grinned. "I gave him a book earlier. He thinks that's his real present — he looked disgusted! I'll let him enjoy the rest of the party, then hit him with the snake when he thinks the fun is over."

Shancus already owned a snake, but I'd bought a new one for him, larger and more colourful. Evra helped me choose it. His old snake would be passed on to Urcha, so both boys would have cause to celebrate tonight.

Merla called Evra back to the party — Lilia had got stuck in wrapping paper and needed to be rescued. I watched my friends for a minute or two, then turned my back on the festivities and walked away. I wandered through the maze of vans and tents of the Cirque Du Freak, coming to a halt near the Wolf Man's cage. The savage man-beast was snoring. I took a small jar of pickled onions out of my pocket and ate one, smiling sadly as I remembered where my taste for pickled onions had come from.

That memory led to others, and I found myself looking back over the years, recalling major events, remarkable triumphs, and sickening losses. The night of my blooding, when Mr Crepsley pumped his vampiric blood into me. Slowly coming to terms with my appetite and powers. Sam Grest — the original pickled onion connoisseur. My first girlfriend, Debbie Hemlock. Learning about the vampaneze. The trek to Vampire Mountain. My Trials, where I'd had to prove myself worthy of being a child of the night. Failing and running away. The revelation that a Vampire General — Kurda Smahlt — was a traitor, in league with the vampaneze. Exposing Kurda. Becoming a Prince.

The Wolf Man stirred and I walked on, not wanting to wake him. My mind continued to turn over old memories. Kurda telling us why he'd betrayed the clan — the Lord of the Vampaneze had arisen and stood poised to lead his people into war against the vampires. The early years of the War of the Scars, when I'd lived in Vampire Mountain. Leaving the safety of the fortress to hunt for the Vampaneze Lord, accompanied by Mr Crepsley and Harkat. Meeting Vancha March, the third hunter — only he, Mr Crepsley or I could kill the Vampaneze Lord. Travelling with a witch called Evanna. Clashing with the Lord of the Vampaneze, unaware of his identity until afterwards, when he'd escaped with his protector, Gannen Harst.

I wanted to stop there — the next set of memories was the most painful — but my thoughts raced on. Returning to the city of Mr Crepsley's youth. Running into Debbie again — an adult now, a teacher. Other faces from the past — R.V. and Steve Leopard. The former used to be an eco-warrior, a man who blamed me for the loss of his hands. He'd become a vampaneze and was part of a plot to lure my allies and me underground, where the Lord of the Vampaneze could kill us.

Steve was part of that plot too, though at first I thought he was on our side. Steve was my best friend when we were kids. We went to the Cirque Du Freak together. He recognized Mr Crepsley and asked to be his assistant. Mr Crepsley refused — he said Steve had evil blood. Later, Steve was bitten by Mr Crepsley's poisonous tarantula. Only Mr Crepsley could cure him. I became a half-vampire to save Steve's life, but Steve didn't see it that way. He thought I'd betrayed him and taken his place among the vampires. He became hell-bent on revenge.

Underground in Mr Crepsley's city. Facing the vampaneze in a chamber Steve had named the Cavern of Retribution. Me, Mr Crepsley, Vancha, Harkat, Debbie and a police officer called Alice Burgess. A huge fight. Mr Crepsley faced the man we thought was the Lord of the Vampaneze. He killed him. But then Steve killed Mr Crepsley by knocking him into a pit of stakes. A gut-churning blow, made all the worse when Steve revealed the shocking truth — *he* was the real Lord of the Vampaneze!

I reached the last of the tents and stopped, gazing around, half-dazed. We'd set up camp in an abandoned football stadium. It used to be the home ground of the local football team, but they'd moved to a new, purpose-built stadium some years ago. The old stadium was due to be demolished — apartment blocks were to be built over the ruins — but not for several months yet. It was an eerie feeling, staring around at thousands of empty seats in the ghost stadium.

Ghosts… That put me in mind of my next, bizarre quest with Harkat, in what we now knew was a shade of the future. Once again I began to wonder if that ruined future world was unavoidable. Could I prevent it by killing Steve, or was it destined to come no matter who won the War of the Scars?

Before I got too worked up about it, someone stepped up beside me and said, "Is the party over?"

I looked around and saw the scarred, stitched-together, grey-skinned face of Harkat Mulds. "No," I smiled. "It's winding down, but it hasn't finished yet."

"Good. I was afraid I'd miss it." Harkat had been out on the streets most of the day, handing out fliers for the Cirque Du Freak — that was one of his regular jobs every time we arrived at a new venue. He stared at me with his round, green, lidless eyes. "How do you feel?" he asked.

"Strange. Worried. Unsure of myself."

"Have you been out there yet?" Harkat waved a hand at the town beyond the walls of the stadium. I shook my head. "Are you going to go, or do you plan ... to hide here until we leave?"

"I'll go," I said. "But it's hard. So many years. So many memories." This was the real reason I was so fixed on the past. After all these years of travel, I'd returned home to the town where I was born and had lived all my human life.

"What if my family's still here?" I asked Harkat.

"Your parents?" he replied.

"And Annie, my sister. They think I'm dead. What if they see me?"

"Would they recognize you?" Harkat asked. "It's been a long time. People change."

"Humans do," I snorted. "But I've only aged four or five years."

"Maybe it wouldn't be a bad thing to ... see them again," Harkat said. "Imagine their joy if they learnt that ... you were still alive."

"No," I said forcefully. "I've been thinking about that ever since Mr Tall told me we were coming here. I *want* to track them down. It would be wonderful for me — but terrible for them. They buried me. They've done their grieving and have hopefully moved on with their lives. It wouldn't be fair to bring back all those old pains and torments."

"I'm not sure I agree with that," Harkat said, "but it's ... your decision. So stay here with the Cirque. Lay low. Hide."

"I can't," I sighed. "This is my home town. I've got an itch to walk the streets again, see how much has changed, look for old faces that I used to know. I want to find out what happened to my friends. The wise thing would be to keep my head down — but when did *I* ever do the wise thing?"

"And maybe trouble would find you ... even if you did," Harkat said.

"What do you mean?" I frowned.

Harkat glanced around uneasily. "I have a strange feeling about ... this place," he croaked.

"What sort of a feeling?" I asked.

"It's hard to explain. Just a feeling that this is ... a dangerous place, but also the place where ... we're meant to be. Something's going to happen here. Don't you sense it?"

"No — but my thoughts are all over the place right now."

"We've often discussed your decision to ... stay with the Cirque," Harkat reminded me, making little of the many arguments we'd had about whether or not I should leave and seek out the Vampire Generals. He believed I was hiding from my duty, that we should seek out the vampires and resume the hunt for the Vampaneze Lord.

"You're not starting that again, are you?" I groaned.

"No," he said. "The opposite. I now think you were right. If we hadn't stuck with the Cirque ... we wouldn't be here now. And, as I said, I think we're ... meant to be here."

I studied Harkat silently. "What do you think will happen?" I asked quietly.

"The feeling isn't that specific," Harkat said.

"But if you had to guess?" I pressed.

Harkat shrugged awkwardly. "I think we might run into ... Steve Leonard, or find a clue which ... points towards him."

My insides tightened at the thought of facing Steve again. I hated him for what he'd done to us, especially killing Mr Crepsley. But just before he died, Mr Crepsley warned me not to devote my life to hatred. He said it would twist me like Steve. So although I hungered for the chance to get even, I worried about it too. I didn't know how I'd react when I saw him again, whether I'd be able to control my emotions or give in to blind, hateful rage.

"You're frightened," Harkat noted.

"Yes. But not of Steve. I'm frightened of what *I* might do."

"Don't worry," Harkat smiled. "You'll be OK."

"What if..." I hesitated, afraid I'd jinx myself. But that was silly, so I came out with it. "What if Steve tries to use my family against me? What if he threatens my parents or Annie?"

Harkat nodded slowly. "I thought of that already. It's the sort of sick stunt I can ... imagine him pulling."

"What will I do if he does?" I asked. "He already sucked Debbie into his insane plot to destroy me — not to mention R.V. What if–"

"Easy," Harkat soothed me. "The first thing is to find out if ... they still live here. If they do, we can arrange protection ... for them. We'll establish a watch around their house ... and guard them."

"The two of us can't protect them by ourselves," I grunted.

"But we're not by ourselves," Harkat said. "We have many friends in ... the Cirque. They'll help."

"You think it's fair to involve them?" I asked.

"They may already be involved," Harkat said. "Their destinies are tied to ours, I think. That may be another reason why you felt ... you had to stay here." Then he smiled. "Come on — I want to get to the party before ... Rhamus scoffs all the cakes!"

Laughing, I put my fears behind me for a while and walked back through the campsite with Harkat. But if I'd known just how closely the destinies of my freakish friends were connected with mine, and the anguish I was steering them towards, I'd have about-faced and immediately fled to the other end of the world.

CHAPTER THREE

I DIDN'T go exploring that day. I stayed at the Cirque Du Freak and celebrated Shancus's birthday. He loved his new snake, and I thought Urcha was going to float away with joy when he found out Shancus's old snake was to be his. The party went on longer than expected. The table was loaded up with more cakes and buns, and not even the ever-hungry Rhamus Twobellies could finish them off! Afterwards we prepared for that night's show, which went ahead smoothly. I spent most of the show in the wings, studying faces in the audience, looking for old neighbours and friends. But I didn't see anybody I recognized.

The next morning, while most of the Cirque folk were sleeping, I slipped out. Although it was a bright day, I wore a light anorak over my clothes, so I could pull the hood up and mask my face if I had to.

I walked rapidly, thrilled to be back. The streets had changed a lot — new shops and offices, many redecorated or redesigned buildings — but the names were the same. I ran into memories on every block. The shop where I bought my football boots. Mum's favourite clothes boutique. The cinema where we'd taken Annie to her first film. The newsagent where I shopped for comics.

I wandered through a vast complex which used to be my favourite computer arcade. It was under new ownership and had grown beyond recognition. I tried out some of the games, and smiled as I remembered how excited I'd get when I'd come here on a Saturday and blast away a few hours on the latest shoot-'em-up.

Moving away from the central shopping area, I visited my favourite parks. One was now a housing estate but the other was unchanged. I saw a groundsman tending to a bed of flowers — old William Morris, my friend Alan's grandfather. William was the first person from the past I'd seen. He hadn't known me very well, so I was able to walk right past him and study him up-close without fear of being spotted.

I wanted to stop and chat with Alan's grandfather, and ask for news about Alan. I was going to tell him that I was one of Alan's friends, that I'd lost touch with him. But then I remembered that Alan was now an adult, not a teenager like me. So I walked on, silent, unobserved.

I was anxious to check out my old house. But I didn't feel ready — I trembled with nerves every time I thought about it. So I wandered through the centre of town, past banks, shops, restaurants. I caught glimpses of half-remembered faces — clerks and waiters, a few customers — but nobody I'd known personally.

I had a bite to eat in a café. The food wasn't especially good, but it had been Dad's favourite place — he often brought me here for a snack while Mum and Annie were doing damage in the shops. It was nice to sit in the familiar surroundings and order a chicken and bacon sandwich, like in the old days.

After lunch, I strolled past my original school — a really eerie feeling! A new wing had been added, and there were iron railings around the perimeter, but apart from that it looked just the way I remembered. Lunch break was ending. I watched from underneath the shadows of a tree while the students filed back into class. I saw some teachers too. Most were new, but two caught my attention. One was Mrs McDaid. She'd taught languages, mostly to older students. I'd had her for half a term when my regular teacher was on a leave of absence.

I'd been much closer to the other teacher — Mr Dalton! I'd had him for English and history. He'd been my favourite teacher. He was chatting with some of his students as he entered class after lunch, and by their smiles I saw he was still as popular as ever.

It would have been great to catch up with Mr Dalton. I was seriously thinking about waiting for school to finish, then going to see him. He'd know what had happened to my parents and Annie. I needn't tell him I was a vampire — I could say I had an anti-ageing disease, which kept me looking young. Explaining away my "death" would be tricky, but I could cook up some suitable story.

One thing held me back. A few years ago, in Mr Crepsley's home city, I'd been branded a killer by the police, and my name and photo had been flashed all over the TV and newspapers. What if Mr Dalton had heard about that? If he knew I was alive, and thought I was a murderer, he might alert the authorities. Safer not to take the risk. So I turned my back on the school and slowly walked away.

It was only then that it struck me that Mr Dalton wouldn't be the only one who might have picked up on the "Darren Shan — serial killer!" hysteria. What if my parents had heard about it! Mr Crepsley's city was in a different part of the world, and I wasn't sure how much news travelled between the two countries. But it was a possibility.

I had to sit down on a street bench while I considered that horrific potential. I could only begin to imagine how shocking it would have been if, years after they'd buried me, Mum and Dad had spotted me on the news, under a caption branding me a killer. How had I never thought about it before?

This could be a real problem. As I'd told Harkat, I didn't intend going to see my family — too painful for everyone. But if they already knew I was alive, and were living with the misbelief that I was a killer, I'd have to set the record straight. But what if they *didn't* know?

I had to do some research. I'd passed a brand new, ultra-modern library earlier that morning. Hurrying back to it, I asked a librarian for assistance. I said I was doing a school project and had to pick some local story from the last three years to write about. I asked to examine all the issues of the main local paper, as well as the national paper which my mum and dad used to read. I figured, if word of my exploits in Mr Crepsley's city had spread this far, there'd be a mention of me in one of those two papers.

The librarian was happy to help. She showed me where the microfiche were stored, and how to use them. Once I'd got the knack of getting them up on screen and scanning from one page to the next, she left me to my own devices.

I started with the earliest editions of the national paper, from a few months before I ran into trouble with the law. I was looking for any mention of Mr Crepsley's city and the killers plaguing it. I made quick time, glancing only at the international sections. I found a couple of references to the murders — and they were both mocking! Apparently journalists here were amused by the vampire rumours which had swept the city, and the story was treated as light entertainment. There was a short piece in one issue, relaying the news that the police had caught four suspects, and then carelessly let all four escape. No names, and no mention of the people Steve had killed when he broke out.

I was relieved but angered at the same time. I knew the pain the vampaneze had brought to that city, the lives they'd destroyed. It wasn't right that such a grim story should be turned into the stuff of funny urban legends, simply because it happened in a city far away from where these people lived. They wouldn't have found it so amusing if the vampaneze had struck here!

I made a quick check on issues from the next few months, but the paper had dropped the story after news of the escape. I turned to the local paper. This was slower going. The main news was at the front, but local interest stories were scattered throughout. I had to check most of the pages of each edition before I could move on to the next.

Although I tried not to dwell on articles unrelated to me, I couldn't stop myself from skimming the opening paragraphs of the more interesting stories. It wasn't long before I was catching up with all the news — elections, scandals, heroes, villains; policemen who'd been highly commended, criminals who'd given the town a bad name; a big bank raid; coming third in a national tidy towns competition.

I saw photographs and read clips about several of my school friends, but one in particular stood out — Tom Jones! Tommy was one of my best friends, along with Steve and Alan Morris. We were two of the best footballers in our class. I was the goal-scorer, leading the line up front, while Tommy was the goal-stopper, pulling off spectacular saves. I'd often dreamt of going on to be a professional footballer. Tommy had taken that dream all the way and become a goalkeeper.

There were dozens of photos and stories about him. Tom Jones (he'd shortened the "Tommy") was one of the best keepers in the country. Lots of articles poked fun at his name – there was also a famous singer called Tom Jones – but nobody had anything bad to say about Tommy himself. After working his way up through the amateur ranks, he'd signed for a local team, made a name for himself, then played abroad for five years. Now he was back home, part of the best team in the country. In the most recent editions, I read how local football fans were buzzing with excitement at the prospect of this year's cup semi-final — it was being held in our town, and Tommy's team was in it. Of course, they'd have been a lot happier if their own team had qualified, but this was the next best thing.

Reading about Tommy brought a smile to my face — it was great to see one of my friends doing so well. The other good news was that there was no mention of me. Since this was quite a small town, I was sure word would have spread if anyone had heard about me in connection with the killings. I was in the clear.

But there was no mention of my family in the papers either. I couldn't find the name "Shan" anywhere. There was only one thing for it — I'd have to dig around for information in person by going back to the house where I used to live.

CHAPTER FOUR

THE HOUSE took my breath away. It hadn't changed. Same colour door, same style curtains, same small garden out the back. As I stood gazing at it, gripping the top of the fence, I almost expected a younger version of myself to come bounding out the back door, clutching a pile of comics, on his way over to Steve's.

"May I help you?" someone asked behind me.

My head snapped round and my eyes cleared. I didn't know how long I'd been standing there, but by my white knuckles, I guessed it had been a few minutes at least. An elderly woman was standing close by, studying me suspiciously. Rubbing my hands together, I smiled warmly. "Just looking," I said.

"At what, precisely?" she challenged me, and I realized how I must appear to her — a rough-faced teenager, gazing intently into a deserted back yard, checking out the house. She thought I was a burglar casing the joint!

"My name's Derek Shan," I said, borrowing an uncle's first name. "My cousins lived here. In fact, they still might. I'm not sure. I'm in town to see some friends, and I thought I'd pop over and find out if my relatives were here or not."

"You're related to Annie?" the woman asked, and I shivered at the mention of the name.

"Yes," I said, fighting hard to keep my voice steady. "And Dermot and Angela." My parents. "Do they still live here?"

"Dermot and Angela moved away three or four years ago," the woman said. She stepped up beside me, at ease now, and squinted at the house. "They should have left sooner. That was never a happy house, not since their boy died." The woman looked sideways at me. "You know about that?"

"I remember my dad saying something," I muttered, ears turning red.

"I wasn't living here then," the woman said. "But I've heard all about it. He fell out of a window. The family stayed on, but it was a miserable place after that. I don't know why they stuck around so long. You can't enjoy yourself in a house of bitter memories."

"But they did stay," I said, "until three or four years ago? And then moved on?"

"Yes. Dermot had a mild heart attack. He had to retire early."

"Heart attack!" I gasped. "Is he OK?"

"Yes." The woman smiled at me. "I said it was mild, didn't I? But they decided to move when he retired. Left for the coast. Angela often said she'd like to live by the sea."

"What about Annie?" I asked. "Did she go with them?"

"No. Annie stayed. She still lives here — her and her boy."

"*Boy?*" I blinked.

"Her son." The woman frowned. "Are you sure you're a relative? You don't seem to know much about your own family."

"I've lived abroad most of my life," I said truthfully.

"Oh." The woman lowered her voice. "Actually, I suppose it's not the sort of thing you talk about in front of children. What age are you, Derek?"

"Sixteen," I lied.

"Then I guess you're old enough. My name's Bridget, by the way."

"Hello, Bridget." I forced a smile, silently willing her to get on with the story.

"The boy's a nice enough child, but he's not really a Shan."

"What do you mean?" I frowned.

"He was born out of wedlock. Annie never married. I'm not even sure anyone except her knows who the father is. Angela claimed they knew, but she never told us his name."

"I guess lots of women choose not to marry these days," I sniffed, not liking the way Bridget was talking about Annie.

"True," Bridget nodded. "Nothing wrong with wanting the child but not the husband. But Annie was on the young side. She was just sweet sixteen when the baby was born."

Bridget was glowing, the way gossips do when they're telling a juicy story. I wanted to snap at her, but it was better to hold my tongue.

"Dermot and Angela helped rear the baby," Bridget continued. "He was a blessing in some ways. He became a replacement for their lost son. He brought some joy back into the house."

"And now Annie looks after him by herself?" I asked.

"Yes. Angela came back a lot during the first year, for weekends and holidays. But now the boy's more independent, Annie can cope by herself. They get along as well as most, I guess." Bridget glanced at the house and sniffed. "But they could do with giving that old wreck a slap of paint."

"I think the house looks fine," I said stiffly.

"What do sixteen-year-old boys know about houses?" Bridget laughed. Then she bid me good day and went about her business. I was going to call her back, to ask when Annie would be home. But then I decided not to. Just as easy — and more exciting — to wait out here and watch for her.

There was a small tree on the other side of the road. I stood by it, hood up over my head, checking my watch every few minutes as though I was waiting to meet somebody. The street was quiet and not many people passed.

The day darkened and dusk set upon the town. There was a bite in the air but it didn't trouble me — half-vampires don't feel the cold as much as humans. I thought about what Bridget had said while I was waiting. Annie, a mother! Hard to believe. She'd been a kid herself the last time I saw her. From what Bridget said, Annie's life hadn't been the easiest. Being a mother at sixteen must have been rough. But it sounded like she had things under control now.

A light went on in the kitchen. A woman's silhouette passed from one side to the other. Then the back door opened and my sister stepped out. There was no mistaking her. Taller, with long brown hair, much plumper than she'd been as a girl. But the same face. The same sparkling eyes, and lips which were ready to turn up into a warm-hearted smile at a moment's notice.

I stared at Annie as though in a trance. I wasn't able to tear my eyes away. I was trembling, and my legs felt like they were about to give way, but I couldn't turn my gaze aside.

Annie walked to a small washing line in the back yard, from which a boy's clothes were hanging. She blew into her hands to warm them, then reached up and took the clothes down, one garment at a time, folding each over the crook of her left arm.

I stepped forward and opened my mouth to call her name, all thoughts of not announcing myself forgotten. This was Annie — my sister! I *had* to talk to her, hold her again, laugh and cry with her, catch up on the past, ask about Mum and Dad.

But my vocal chords wouldn't work. I was choked up with emotion. All I managed was a thin croak. Closing my mouth, I walked across the road, slowing as I came to the fence. Annie had gathered all the clothes from the line and was returning to the kitchen. I gulped deeply and licked my lips. Blinked several times in quick succession to clear my head. Opened my mouth again—

—and stopped when a boy inside the house shouted, "Mum! I'm home!"

"About time!" Annie yelled in reply, and I could hear the love in her voice. "I thought I told you to bring in the clothes."

"Sorry. Wait a sec…" I saw the boy's shadow as he entered the kitchen and hurried over to the back door. Then he emerged, a chubby boy, fair-haired, very pleasant looking.

"Do you want me to take some of those?" the boy said.

"My hero," Annie laughed, handing half of the load over to the boy. He went in ahead of her. She turned to shut the door and caught a glimpse of me. She paused. It was quite dark. The light was behind her. She couldn't see me very well. But if I stood there long enough … if I called out to her…

I didn't.

Instead I coughed, pulled my hood tight around my face, spun and walked away. I heard the door close behind me, and it was like the sound of a sharp blade slicing me adrift from the past.

Annie had her own life. A son. A home. Probably a job. Maybe a boyfriend or somebody special. It wouldn't be fair if I popped up, opening old wounds, making her part of my dark, twisted world. She enjoyed peace and a normal life — much better than what I had to offer.

So I left her behind and slunk away quickly, through the streets of my old town, back to my real home — the Cirque Du Freak. And I sobbed my heart out every painful, lonely step of the way.

CHAPTER FIVE

I COULDN'T bear to talk to anybody that night. I sat by myself in a seat high up in the football stadium while the show was in progress, thinking about Annie and her child, Mum and Dad, all that I'd lost and missed out on. For the first time in years I felt angry with Mr Crepsley for blooding me. I found myself wondering what life would be like if he'd left me alone, wishing I could go back and change the past.

But there was no point tormenting myself. The past was a closed book. I could do nothing to alter it, and wasn't even sure I would if I could — if I hadn't been blooded, I wouldn't have been able to tip the vampires off about Kurda Smahlt, and the entire clan might have fallen.

If I'd returned home ten or twelve years earlier, my feelings of loss and anger might have been stronger. But I was an adult now, in all but looks. A Vampire Prince. I'd learnt to deal with heartache. That wasn't an easy night. Tears flowed freely. But by the time I drifted off to sleep a few hours before dawn, I'd resigned myself to the situation, and knew there would be no fresh tears in the morning.

I was stiff with the cold when I awoke, but worked it off by jogging down the tiers of the stadium to where the Cirque was camped. As I was making for the tent I shared with Harkat, I spotted Mr Tall. He was standing by an open fire, roasting sausages on a spit. He beckoned me over and threw a handful of sausages to me, then speared a fresh batch and stuck them over the flames.

"Thanks," I said, eagerly munching the piping-hot sausages.

"I knew you would be hungry," he replied. He looked at me steadily. "You have been to see your sister."

"Yes." It didn't surprise me that he knew. Mr Tall was an insightful old owl.

"Did she see you?" Mr Tall asked.

"She saw me briefly, but I left before she got a good look."

"You behaved correctly." He turned the sausages over and spoke softly. "You are about to ask me if I will help protect your sister. You fear for her safety."

"Harkat thinks something's going to happen," I said. "He's not sure what, but if Steve Leopard's part of it, he might use Annie to hurt me."

"He won't," Mr Tall said. I was surprised by his directness — normally he was very cagey when it came to revealing anything about the future. "As long as you stay out of her life, your sister will be under no direct threat."

"What about *in*direct threat?" I asked warily.

Mr Tall chuckled. "We are all under indirect threat, one way or another. Harkat is correct — this is a time and place of destiny. I can say no more about it, except leave your sister alone. She is safe that way."

"OK," I sighed. I wasn't happy about leaving Annie to fend for herself, but I trusted Hibernius Tall.

"You should sleep some more now," Mr Tall said. "You are tired."

That sounded like a good plan. I scoffed another sausage, turned to leave, then stopped. "Hibernius," I said without facing him, "I know you can't tell me what's going to happen, but before we came here, you said I didn't have to come. It would have been better if I'd stayed away, wouldn't it?"

There was a long silence. I didn't think he was going to respond. But then, softly, he said, "Yes."

"What if I left now?"

"It is too late," Mr Tall said. "Your decision to return set a train of events in motion. That train cannot be derailed. If you left now, it would only serve the purpose of the forces you oppose."

"But what if—" I said, turning to push the issue. But Mr Tall had disappeared, leaving only the flickering flames and a stick speared with sausages lying on the grass next to the fire.

That evening, after I'd rested and enjoyed a filling meal, I told Harkat about my trip home. I also told him about my short conversation with Mr Tall and how he'd urged me not to get involved with Annie.

"Then you were right," Harkat grunted. "I thought you should involve yourself with ... your family again, but it seems I was wrong."

We were feeding scraps of meat to the Wolf Man, part of our daily chores. We stood at a safe distance from his cage, all too aware of the power of his fearsome jaws.

"What about your nephew?" Harkat asked. "Any family resemblance?"

I paused, a large sliver of meat in my right hand. "It's strange, but I didn't think of him as that until now. I just thought of him as Annie's son. I forgot that also makes him my nephew." I grinned crookedly. "I'm an uncle!"

"Congratulations," Harkat deadpanned. "Did he look like you?"

"Not really," I said. I thought of the fair-haired, chubby boy's smile, and how he'd helped Annie bring in the washing. "A nice kid, from what I saw. Handsome, of course, like all the Shans."

"Of course!" Harkat snorted.

I was sorry I hadn't taken more notice of Annie's boy. I didn't even know his name. I thought about going back to ask about him – I could hang about and collar Bridget the gossip again – but dismissed the idea immediately. That was precisely the kind of stunt which could backfire and bring me to Annie's notice. Best to forget about him.

As we were finishing off, I saw a young boy watching us from behind a nearby van. He was studying us quietly, taking care not to attract attention. In the normal run of things, I'd have ignored him — children often came nosing around the Cirque site. But my thoughts were on my nephew and I found myself more interested in the boy than I'd otherwise have been.

"Hello!" I shouted, waving at him. The boy's head instantly vanished behind the van. I would have left it, but moments later the boy stepped out and walked towards us. He looked nervous – understandable, since we were in the presence of the snarling Wolf Man – but he was fighting hard not to show it.

The boy stopped a few metres away and nodded curtly. "Hello," he mumbled. He was scrawny. He had dark blond hair and bright blue eyes. I put his age at somewhere in the region of ten or eleven, maybe a little bit older than Annie's kid, though there couldn't have been much of an age difference. For all I knew they might even be going to school together!

The boy said nothing after greeting us. I was thinking about my nephew and comparing this boy to him, so I said nothing either. Harkat finally broke the silence. "Hi," he said, lowering the mask he wore to filter out air, which was poisonous to him. "I'm Harkat."

"Darius," the boy said, nodding at Harkat, not offering to shake hands.

"And I'm Darren," I smiled.

"You two are with the freak show," Darius said. "I saw you yesterday."

"You've been here before?" Harkat asked.

"A couple of times. I've never seen a freak show before. I tried buying a ticket but nobody will sell me one. I asked the tall guy — he's the owner, isn't he? — but he said it wasn't suitable for children."

"It is a bit on the gruesome side," I said.

"That's why I want to see it," he grunted.

I laughed, remembering what I'd been like at his age. "Tell you what," I said. "Why don't you walk around with us? We can show you some of the performers and tell you about the show. If you still want a ticket, maybe we can sort one out for you then."

Darius squinted at me suspiciously, then at Harkat. "How do I know I can trust you?" he asked. "You might be a pair of kidnappers."

"Oh, you have my word we won't … kidnap you," Harkat purred, treating Darius to his widest grin, displaying his grey tongue and sharp, pointed teeth. "We might feed you to the Wolf Man … but we won't kidnap you."

Darius yawned to show he wasn't impressed by the theatrical threat, then said, "What the hell, I've nothing better to do." Then he tapped his foot and raised an eyebrow impatiently. "Come on!" he snapped. "I'm ready!"

"Yes, master," I laughed, and led the harmless-looking boy on a tour of the Cirque.

CHAPTER SIX

WE WALKED Darius around the site and introduced him to Rhamus Twobellies, Cormac Limbs, Hans Hands and Truska. Cormac was busy and didn't have time to show the boy how he could re-grow his limbs, but Truska sprouted a short beard for him, then sucked the hairs back into her face. Darius acted like he wasn't impressed, but I could see the wonder in his eyes.

Darius was strange. He didn't say much, and kept his distance, always a couple of metres away from Harkat and me, as though he still didn't trust us. He asked lots of questions about the performers and the Cirque Du Freak, which was normal. But he didn't ask anything about me, where I was from, how I'd come to join the show or what my tasks involved. He didn't ask about Harkat either. The grey-skinned, stitched-together Little Person was like nothing most people had ever seen. It was common for newcomers to pump him for information. But Darius seemed uninterested in Harkat, as if he already knew everything about him.

He also had a way of staring at me oddly. I'd catch him looking at me, when he thought my attention was elsewhere. It wasn't a threatening look. There was just something about the flickering of his eyes that for some reason unsettled me.

Harkat and I weren't hungry, but when we passed one of the open campfires and saw a pot of bubbling soup, I heard Darius's stomach rumble. "Want to eat?" I asked.

"I'm having dinner when I go home," he said.

"How about a snack, to keep you going?"

He hesitated, then licked his lips and nodded quickly. "But just a small bowl of soup," he snapped, as though we meant to force-feed him.

While Darius was downing the soup, Harkat asked if he lived nearby.

"Not far off," he answered vaguely.

"How did you find out ... about the show?"

Darius didn't look up. "A friend of mine — Oggy Bas — was here. He was going to take some seats — we often come here when we want seats or railings. It's easy to get in and nobody cares what we take. He saw the circus tent and told me. I thought it was an ordinary circus until I came exploring yesterday."

"What sort of a name is Oggy Bas?" I asked.

"Oggy's short for Augustine," Darius explained.

"Did you tell Oggy what the Cirque Du ... Freak really was?" Harkat asked.

"Nah," Darius said. "He's got a big mouth. He'd tell

everybody and they'd all come. I like being the only one who knows about it."

"So you're a boy who knows how to keep a secret," I chuckled. "Of course, the downside is that since nobody knows you're here, if we *did* kidnap you or feed you to the Wolf Man, nobody would know where to look."

I was joking, but Darius reacted sharply. He half-bolted to his feet, dropping the unfinished bowl of soup. Acting instinctively, I snatched for the bowl, and with my vampire speed I caught it before it hit the ground. But Darius thought I meant to strike him. He threw himself backwards and roared, "Leave me alone!"

I took a surprised step back. The other people around the fire were gawping at us. Harkat's green eyes were on Darius, and there was more than just surprise in his expression — he looked wary too.

"Easy," I half-laughed, lowering the bowl, then raising my hands in a gesture of friendship. "I'm not going to hurt you."

Darius sat up. He was blushing angrily. "I'm OK," he mumbled, getting to his feet.

"What's wrong, Darius?" Harkat asked quietly. "Why so edgy?"

"I'm OK," Darius said again, glaring at Harkat. "I just don't like people saying stuff like that. It's not funny, creatures like you making threats like that."

"I didn't mean it," I said, ashamed for having frightened the boy. "How about I get a ticket to tonight's show for you, to make up for scaring you?"

"I ain't scared," Darius growled.

"Of course you aren't," I smiled. "But would you like a ticket anyway?"

Darius pulled a face. "How much are they?"

"It's free," I said. "Courtesy of the house."

"OK then." That was as close as Darius got to saying thanks.

"Would you like one for Oggy too?" I asked.

"No," Darius said. "He wouldn't come. He's a scaredy cat. He doesn't even watch horror movies, not even the really old and boring ones."

"Fair enough," I said. "Wait here. I'll be back in a couple of minutes."

I tracked down Mr Tall. When I told him what I wanted, he frowned and said all the tickets for tonight's show had been sold. "But surely you can find a spare one somewhere," I laughed. There was always lots of space in the aisles and it was usually never a problem to stick in a few extra chairs.

"Is it wise, inviting a child to the show?" Mr Tall asked. "Children tend to fare unfavourably here. Yourself, Steve Leonard, Sam Grest." Sam was a boy who'd had a fatal run-in with the Wolf Man. He was the first person I'd drunk blood from. Part of his spirit — not to mention his taste for pickled onions! — still lived on within me.

"Why mention Sam?" I asked, confused. I couldn't remember the last time Mr Tall had made a reference to my long-dead friend.

"No reason in particular," Mr Tall said. "I just think this is a dangerous place for children." Then he produced a ticket out of thin air and handed it to me. "Give it to the boy if you wish," he grumbled, as if I'd squeezed an inconvenient favour out of him.

I walked back slowly to Darius and Harkat, wondering why Mr Tall had behaved in such a curious manner. Had he been trying to warn me not to let Darius get too closely involved with the Cirque Du Freak? Was Darius like Sam Grest, eager to leave home and travel around with a band of magical performers? By inviting him to the show, was I setting him up for a fall like Sam's?

I found Darius standing where I'd left him. He didn't look like he'd moved a muscle. Harkat was on the other side of the fire, keeping a green eye on the boy. I hesitated before giving Darius his ticket. "What do you think of the Cirque Du Freak?" I asked.

"It's OK," he shrugged.

"How would you feel about joining?"

"What do you mean?" he asked.

"If there was an opening, and you had the chance to leave home, would—"

"No way!" he snapped before I finished.

"You're happy at home?"

"Yes."

"You don't want to travel around the world?"

"Not with you lot."

I smiled and gave him the ticket. "That's OK then. The show starts at ten. Will you be able to come?"

"Of course," Darius said, pocketing the ticket without looking at it.

"What about your parents?" I asked.

"I'll go to bed early, then sneak out," he said, and giggled slyly.

"If you're caught, don't tell them about us," I warned him.

"As if!" he snorted, then waved sharply and left. He looked at me one final time before he passed out of sight, and again there was something odd about his gaze.

Harkat walked around the fire and stared after the boy.

"A strange kid," I commented.

"More than just strange," Harkat murmured.

"What's wrong?" I asked.

"I don't like him," Harkat said.

"He was a bit sullen," I agreed, "but lots of kids his age are like that. I was that way myself when I first joined the Cirque Du Freak."

"I don't know." Harkat's eyes were full of doubt. "I didn't buy his story about his ... friend, Oggy. If he's such a scaredy cat, what was he ... doing exploring up here by himself?"

"You're getting suspicious in your old age," I laughed.

Harkat shook his head slowly. "You didn't pick up on it."

"What?" I frowned.

"When he accused us of threatening him, he said ... 'creatures like you'."

"So?"

Harkat smiled thinly. "I'm quite obviously *not* human. But what tipped him off to the fact ... that *you* aren't either?"

A sudden chill ran through me. Harkat was right — the boy had known more about us than he should have. And I realized now what it was about Darius's gaze which had disturbed me. When he thought I wasn't looking, his eyes kept going to the scars on my fingertips, the standard marks of a vampire — like he knew what they meant!

CHAPTER SEVEN

HARKAT AND I weren't sure what to make of Darius. It seemed unlikely that the vampaneze would recruit children. But there was the twisted mind of their leader, Steve Leopard, to take into account. This could be one of his evil, hate-fuelled games. We decided to take the boy to one side when he came to the show, and pump him for information. We wouldn't resort to torture or anything so drastic — just try to scare a few answers out of him.

We were supposed to help the performers get ready for the show, but we told Mr Tall we were busy and he assigned our tasks to other members of the troupe. If he knew about our plans for Darius, he didn't say so.

There were two entrances to the big top. Shortly before the audience started to arrive, Harkat and I each took up a position close to one of the entry points, where we could watch for Darius. I was still worried about being recognized by somebody who'd known me in the past, so I stood in the shadows beside the entrance, disguised in a set of Harkat's blue robes, the hood pulled up to hide my face. I watched silently as the early birds trickled in, handing their tickets to Jekkus Flang (Mr Tall was on the other entrance). With every third or fourth customer, Jekkus threw their ticket into the air, then launched a knife at it, spearing it through the middle and pinning it to a nearby post.

As the trickle of people turned into a steady stream, and Jekkus pinned more and more tickets to the pole, the tickets and knives took on the outline of a hanged man. People chuckled edgily when they realized what Jekkus was doing. A few paused to commend him on his knife-throwing skills, but most hurried past to their seats, some glancing backwards at the figure of the hanged man, perhaps wondering if it was an omen of things to come.

I ignored the hanged man — I'd seen Jekkus perform this trick many times before — and focused on the faces in the crowd. It was hard to note everybody who passed in the crush, especially short people. Even if Darius entered this way, there was no guarantee I'd spot him.

Towards the end of the line, as the last members of the audience were filing in, Jekkus gave a gasp of surprise and abandoned his post. "Tom Jones!" he shouted, bounding forward. "What an honour!"

It was the town's famous goalkeeper, Tom Jones — my old school friend!

Tommy smiled awkwardly and shook Jekkus's hand.

"Hi," he coughed, looking around to see if anyone else had noticed him. Apart from those nearest us, nobody had — all eyes were fixed on the stage, as everyone awaited the start of the show.

"I've seen you play!" Jekkus enthused. "I don't get to many games — the curse of travelling — but I've made it to a few. You're awesome! Do you think we'll win tomorrow? I wanted to get a ticket, but they were sold out."

"It's a big match," Tommy said. "I could try to get one for you, but I don't think—"

"That's OK," Jekkus interrupted. "I'm not trying to shake you down for free tickets. Just wanted to wish you good luck. Now, speaking of tickets, could I see yours?"

Tommy gave his ticket to Jekkus, who asked if Tommy would sign it for him. Tommy obliged and Jekkus pocketed the ticket, beaming happily. He offered to find a seat for Tommy near the front, but Tommy said he was happy to sit at the back. "I don't think it would be good for my image if word got out that I came to shows like this," he laughed.

As Tommy made his way to one of the few free seats, I breathed a sigh of relief — he hadn't seen me. The luck of the vampires was on my side. I waited a few more minutes, until the final stragglers had been admitted, then crept out as Jekkus closed off the entrance. I linked up with Harkat.

"Did you see him?" I asked.

"No," Harkat said. "You?"

"No. But I saw an old friend." I told him about Tom Jones.

"Could it be a setup?" Harkat asked.

"I doubt it," I said. "Tommy wanted to come to the Cirque Du Freak the last time it was in town. He's here for the match tomorrow. He must have heard about the show and picked up a ticket — easy when you're a celebrity."

"But isn't it a bit too coincidental that ... he's here the same time as us?" Harkat persisted.

"He's here because his team's in the cup semi-final," I reminded Harkat. "Steve couldn't have engineered that — even the Lord of the Vampaneze has his limits!"

"You're right," Harkat laughed. "I really am getting paranoid!"

"Let's forget about Tommy," I said. "What about Darius? Could he have got in without us seeing him?"

"Yes," Harkat said. "It was impossible to identify ... everyone who entered. A child could have easily ... passed without us noticing."

"Then we've got to go inside and look for him," I said.

"Steady on." Harkat stopped me. "Although your friend Tommy's being here is most likely ... nothing to worry about, let's not tempt fate. If you go in, your hood might slip ... and he might see you. Leave it to me."

While I waited outside, Harkat entered the tent and patrolled the aisles, checking the faces of every audience member as the show got under way. More than half an hour passed before he emerged.

"I didn't see him," Harkat said.

"Maybe he wasn't able to sneak away from home," I said.

"Or maybe he sensed we were ... suspicious of him," Harkat said. "Either way, we can't do anything except ...

keep watch the rest of the time we're here. He might come sneaking around ... by day again."

Although it was anticlimactic, I was glad Darius hadn't shown. I hadn't been looking forward to threatening the boy. It was better this way, for all concerned. And the more I thought about it, the more ridiculous our reaction seemed. Darius had certainly known more about us than any child should, but maybe he'd simply read the right books or found out about us on the Internet. Not many humans know about the true marks of a vampire, or that Little People exist, but the truth (like they used to say on that famous TV show) is out there! There were any number of ways a clued-up kid could have found out the facts about us.

Harkat wasn't as relaxed as I was, and he insisted we stay outside the entrances until the show finished, in case Darius turned up late. There was no harm in being cautious, so I kept watch throughout the rest of the show, listening to the gasps, screams and applause of the people inside the tent. I slipped away a few minutes before the end and collected Harkat. We hid in a van as the crowd poured out, and only emerged when the final excited customer had left the stadium.

We gathered with most of the performers and backstage crew in a tent behind the big top, for the post-show party. There wasn't a celebration after each performance, but we liked to let our hair down every once in a while. It was a hard life on the road, driving long distances, working doggedly, keeping a low profile so as not to attract attention. It was good to chill out every so often.

There were a few guests in the tent — police officers, council officials, wealthy businessmen. Mr Tall knew how to grease the right palms, to make life easy for us.

Our visitors were particularly interested in Harkat. The normal audience members hadn't seen the grey-skinned Little Person. This was a chance for the special guests to experience something different, which they could boast about to their friends. Harkat knew what was expected of him and he let the humans examine him, telling them a bit about his past, politely answering their questions.

I sat in a quiet corner of the tent, munching a sandwich, washing it down with water. I was getting ready to leave when Jekkus Flang pushed his way through a knot of people and introduced me to the guest he'd just led into the tent. "Darren, this is the world's best goalkeeper, Tom Jones. Tom, this is my good friend and fellow workmate, Darren Shan."

I groaned and closed my eyes. So much for the luck of the vampires! I heard Tommy gasp with recognition. Opening my eyes, I forced a smile, stood, shook Tommy's hand — his eyes were bulging out of his head — and said, "Hello, Tommy. It's been a long time. Can I get you something to drink?"

CHAPTER EIGHT

TOMMY WAS astonished to see me alive when I'd been declared dead and buried eighteen years earlier. Then there was the fact that I only looked a handful of years older. It was almost too much for him to comprehend. For a while he listened to me talk, nodding weakly, not taking anything in. But eventually his head cleared and he focused on what I was saying.

I spun him a far-fetched but just about believable tale. I felt bad, lying to my old friend, but the truth was stranger than fiction — it was simpler and safer this way. I said I had a rare disease which prevented me from ageing normally. It was discovered when I was a child. The doctors gave me five or six years to live. My parents were devastated by the news, but since we could do nothing to prevent it, we told no one and tried to lead a normal life for as long as we could.

Then the Cirque Du Freak came to town.

"I ran into an extraordinary physician," I lied. "He was travelling with the Cirque, making a study of the freaks. He said he could help me, but I'd have to leave home and travel with the Cirque — I'd need constant monitoring. I talked it over with my parents and we decided to fake my death, so I could leave without arousing suspicions."

"But for heaven's sake, why?" Tommy exploded. "Your parents could have left with you. Why put everyone through so much pain?"

"How would we have explained it?" I sighed. "The Cirque Du Freak is an illegal travelling show. My parents would have had to give up everything and gone undercover to be with me. It wouldn't have been fair on them, and it would have been dreadfully unfair on Annie."

"But there must have been some other way," Tommy protested.

"Maybe," I said. "But we hadn't much time to think it over. The Cirque Du Freak was only in town for a few days. We discussed the proposal put forward by the physician and accepted it. I think the fact that I'm still alive all these years later, against all medical odds, justifies that decision."

Tommy shook his head uncertainly. He'd grown up to be a very large man, tall and broad, with huge hands and bulging muscles. His black hair was receding prematurely — he'd be bald in a few more years. But despite his physical presence, his eyes were soft. He was a gentle man. The idea of letting a child fake his death and be buried alive was repulsive to him.

"What's done is done," I said. "Maybe my parents should have searched for another way. But they had my best interests at heart. Hope was offered and they seized it, regardless of the terrible price."

"Did Annie know?" Tommy asked.

"No. We never told her." I guessed Tommy had no way of contacting my parents directly, to check out my story, but he could have gone to Annie. I had to sidetrack him.

"Not even afterwards?" Tommy asked.

"I talked about it with Mum and Dad — we keep in touch and meet up every few years — but we never felt the time was right. Annie had her own problems, having a baby so young."

"That *was* tough," Tommy agreed. "I was still living here. I didn't know her very well, but I heard all about it."

"That must have been just before your football career took off," I said, leading him away from talk about me. We discussed his career after that, some of the big matches he'd been involved in, what he planned to do when he retired. He wasn't married but he had two kids from a previous relationship, when he'd lived abroad.

"I only get to see them a couple of times a year and during the summer," he said sadly. "I hope to move over there when I quit football, to be closer to them."

Most of the performers, crew and guests had departed by this stage. Harkat had seen me talking with Tommy and made a sign asking if I wanted him to stick around. I signalled back that I was OK and he'd left with the others. A few people still sat and talked softly in the tent, but nobody was near Tommy and me.

Talk turned to the past and our old friends. Tommy told me Alan Morris had become a scientist. "Quite a famous one too," he said. "He's a geneticist — big into cloning. A controversial area, but he's convinced it's the way forward."

"As long as he doesn't clone himself!" I laughed. "One Alan Morris is enough!"

Tommy laughed too. Alan had been a close friend of ours, but he could be a bit of a pain at times.

"I've no idea what Steve's up to," Tommy said, and the laughter died on my lips. "He left home at sixteen. Ran off without a word to anyone. I've spoken to him on the phone a few times, but I've only seen him once since then, about ten years ago. He returned home for a few months when his mother died."

"I didn't know she was dead," I said. "I'm sorry. I liked Steve's Mum."

"He sold off the house and all her effects. He shared an apartment with Alan for a while. That was before..." Tommy stopped and glanced at me oddly. "Have *you* seen Steve since you left?"

"No," I lied.

"You don't know anything about him?"

"No," I lied again.

"Nothing at all?" Tommy pressed.

I forced a chuckle. "Why are you so concerned about Steve?"

Tommy shrugged. "He got into some trouble the last time he was here. I thought you might have heard about it from your parents."

"We don't discuss the past," I said, elaborating on the lie I'd concocted. I leant forward curiously. "What did Steve do?" I asked, wondering if it was in any way linked to his vampaneze activities.

"Oh, I don't rightly remember," Tommy said, shifting uncomfortably — he was lying. "It's old history. Best not to bring it up. You know what Steve was like, always in one form of trouble or another."

"That's for sure," I muttered. Then my eyes narrowed. "You said you've talked to him on the phone?"

"Yeah. He rings every so often, asks what I'm up to, says nothing about what he's doing, then hangs up!"

"When was the last time he rang?"

Tommy thought about it. "Two, maybe three years ago. A long time."

"Have you a contact number for him?"

"No."

A shame. I'd thought for a moment that Tommy might be my path back to Steve, but it seemed he wasn't.

"What's the time?" Tommy asked. He looked at his watch and groaned. "If my manager finds out how late I've been out, he'll sack me! Sorry, Darren, but I really have to go."

"That's OK," I smiled, standing to shake his hand. "Maybe we could meet up again after the match?"

"Yeah!" Tommy exclaimed. "I'm not travelling back with the team — I'm staying here for the night, to see some relatives. You can come to the hotel after the game and... Actually, how'd you like to come see me play?"

"At the semi-final?" My eyes lit up. "I'd love to. But didn't I hear you telling Jekkus the tickets were sold out?"

"Jekkus?" Tommy frowned.

"The guy with the knives — your number-one fan."

"Oh." Tommy grimaced. "I can't give away tickets to all my fans. But family and friends are a different story."

"I wouldn't be sitting near anyone who knew me, would I?" I asked. "I don't want the truth about me going any further — Annie might hear about it."

"I'll get you a seat away from the others," Tommy promised. Then he paused. "You know, Annie's not a girl any more. I saw her a year ago, the last time I was here for a match. She struck me as being very level-headed. Maybe it's time to tell her the truth."

"Maybe," I smiled, knowing I wouldn't.

"I really think you should," Tommy pressed. "It would be a shock, like it was for me, but I'm sure she'd be delighted to know you're alive and well."

"We'll see," I said.

I walked Tommy out of the tent, through the campsite and stadium tunnels to where his car was parked. I bid him goodnight at the car, but he stopped before getting in and stared at me seriously. "We must talk some more about Steve tomorrow," he said.

My heart skipped a beat. "Why?" I asked as casually as I could.

"There are things you should know. I don't want to get into them now — it's too late — but I think..." He trailed off into silence, then smiled. "We'll talk about it tomorrow. It might help you make up your mind about some other things."

And on that cryptic note he said farewell. He promised to send over a ticket in the morning, gave me his hotel name and mobile number, shook my hand one last time, got into his car and drove away.

I stood outside the walls of the stadium a long while, thinking about Tommy, Annie and the past — and wondering what he'd meant when he said we needed to talk some more about Steve.

CHAPTER NINE

WHEN I told Harkat about the match, he reacted with automatic suspicion. "It's a trap," he said. "Your friend is an ally of ... Steve Leonard."

"Not Tommy," I said with absolute certainty. "But I've a feeling he might in some way be able to direct us to him, or set us on his trail."

"Do you want me to come with ... you to the match?" Harkat asked.

"You wouldn't be able to get in. Besides," I laughed, "there'll be tens of thousands of people there. In a crowd like that, I think I'll be safe!"

The ticket was delivered by courier and I set off in good time for the match. I arrived an hour before kickoff. A huge crowd milled around outside the stadium. People were singing and cheering, decked out in their club colours, buying drinks, hot dogs and burgers from the street vendors. Troops of police kept a close watch on the situation, making sure rival fans didn't clash.

I mingled for a while, strolling around the stadium, relishing the atmosphere. I bought a hot dog, a match programme, and a hat with Tommy's picture on it, sporting the slogan, "He's not unusual!" There were lots of hats and badges dedicated to Tommy. There were even CDs by the singer Tom Jones, with photos of Tommy taped across the covers!

I took my seat twenty minutes before kickoff. I had a great view of the floodlit pitch. My seat was in the middle of the stadium, just a few rows behind the dugouts. The teams were warming up when I arrived. I got a real buzz out of seeing Tommy in one of the goals, stopping practice shots. To think one of my friends was playing in a cup semi-final! I'd come a long way since childhood and put most of my human interests behind me. But my love of football came flooding back as I sat, gazing down at Tommy, and I felt a ball of pure childish excitement build in the pit of my stomach.

The teams left the pitch to get ready for kickoff, then re-emerged a few minutes later. All the seats in the stadium had been filled and there was a huge cheer as the players marched out. Most people stood up, clapping and hollering. The ref tossed a coin to decide which way the teams would play, then the captains shook hands, the players lined up, the ref blew his whistle, and the match got underway.

It was a brilliant game. Both teams went all-out for the win. Tackles flew in fast and hard. Play shifted from one end to the other, both sides attacking in turn. There were lots of chances to score. Tommy made some great saves, as did the other keeper. A couple of players blasted wide or over the bar from good positions, to a chorus of jeers and groans. After forty-three minutes, the teams seemed like they'd be heading in level at half-time. But then there was a quick break, a defender slipped, a forward had a clear shot at goal, and he sent the ball flying into the left corner of the net, past the outstretched fingers of a flailing Tom Jones.

Tommy and his team-mates looked dejected as they trudged off at half-time, but their fans – and the locals who'd come to cheer for Tommy – kept on singing, "One-nil down, two-one up, that's the way to win the cup!"

I went to get a drink but the size of the queue was frightening — the more experienced fans had slipped out just before the half-time whistle. I walked around to stretch my legs, then returned to my seat.

Although they were a goal down, Tommy's team looked the more confident when they came out after the break. They attacked from the start of the half, knocking their opponents off the ball, pushing them back, driving hard for goal. The game grew heated and three players were booked within the first quarter of an hour. But their new found hunger was rewarded in the sixty-fourth minute when they scored a scrappy goal from a corner to pull level.

The stadium erupted when Tommy's team scored. I was one of the thousands who leapt from their seats and punched the air with joy. I even joined in with the song to the silenced fans of the other team, "You're not singing, you're not singing, you're not singing any more!"

Five minutes later, I was chanting even louder when, from another corner, the team scored again to go two-one up. I found myself hugging the guy next to me – a total stranger! – and jumping up and down with glee. I could hardly believe I was behaving this way. What would the Vampire Generals say if they saw a Prince acting so ridiculously!

The rest of the game was a tense affair. Now that they were a goal down, the other team had to attack in search of an equalizer. Tommy's team-mates were forced further back inside their own half. There were dozens of desperate defensive tackles, lots of free kicks, more yellow cards. But they were holding out. Tommy had to make a few fairly easy saves, but apart from that his goal wasn't troubled. With six minutes to go, the win looked safe.

Then, in virtually an action replay of the first goal, a player slipped free of his defender and found himself in front of goal, with only Tommy to beat. Once again the ball was struck firmly and accurately. It streaked towards the lower left corner of the net. The striker turned away to celebrate.

But he'd reacted too soon. Because this time, somehow, Tommy got down and across, and managed to get a few fingers to the ball. He only barely connected, but it was enough to tip the ball out around the post.

The crowd went wild! They were chanting Tommy's name and singing, "It's not unusual, he's the greatest number one!" Tommy ignored the songs and stayed focused on the corner, directing his defenders. But the save had sapped the other team of their spirit, and though they kept coming forward for the final few minutes, they didn't threaten to score again.

When the whistle blew, Tommy's team wearily embraced each other, then shook their opponents' hands and swapped jerseys. After that they saluted their fans, acknowledging their support. We were all on our feet, applauding, singing victory songs, a lot of them about the incredible Tom Jones.

Tommy was one of the last players to leave the pitch. He'd swapped his jersey with his opposite number and the pair were walking off together, discussing the game. I roared Tommy's name as he came level with the dugouts, but of course he couldn't hear me over the noise of the crowd.

Just as Tommy was about to vanish down the tunnel to the dressing-rooms, a commotion broke out. I heard angry yells, then several sharp bangs. Most of the people around me didn't know what was happening. But I'd heard these sounds before — gunfire!

I couldn't see down the tunnel from where I was, but I saw Tommy and the other goalkeeper stop, confused, then back away from the tunnel entrance. I immediately sensed danger. "Tommy!" I screamed, then knocked aside the people nearest me and forced my way down towards the pitch. Before I got there, a steward reeled out of the tunnel, blood pouring from his face. When the people in front of me saw that, they panicked. Turning, they pushed away from the pitch, halting my advance and forcing me back.

As I struggled to break free, two figures darted out of the tunnel. One was a shaven-headed, shotgun-toting vampet with a disfigured, half-blown-away face. The other was a bearded, purple-skinned, crazy vampaneze with silver and gold hooks instead of hands.

Morgan James and R.V.!

I screamed with fresh fear when I saw the murderous pair, and shoved aside everyone around me, drawing upon the full extent of my vampiric powers. But before I could bruise a way through, R.V. homed in on his target. He bounded past the dugouts, ignored the players, coaching staff and stewards on the pitch, and bore down on a startled Tom Jones.

I don't know what flashed through Tommy's mind when he saw the burly, purple monster streaking towards him. Maybe he thought it was a practical joke, or a weird fan coming to hug him. Either way, he didn't react, raise his hands to defend himself, or turn to run. He just stood, staring dumbly at R.V.

When R.V. reached Tommy, he pulled back his right hand – the one with the gold hooks – then jabbed the blades sharply into Tommy's chest. I froze, feeling Tommy's pain from where I was trapped in the crowd. Then R.V. jerked his hooked hand back, shook his head with insane delight, and retreated down the tunnel, following Morgan James, who fired his gun to clear a path.

On the pitch, Tommy stared stupidly down at the red, jagged hole in the left side of his chest. Then, with almost comical effect, he slid gracelessly to the ground, twitched a few times, and lay still — the terrible, unmistakable stillness of the dead.

CHAPTER TEN

BURSTING FREE of the crowd, I stumbled on to the pitch. Those around me were staring at the fallen goalkeeper, paralyzed with shock. My first instinct was to run to Tommy. But then my training kicked in. Tommy had been killed. I could grieve for him later. Right now I had to focus on R.V. and Morgan James. If I hurried after them, I might catch up before they got away.

Tearing my gaze away from Tommy, I ducked down the tunnel, past the players, staff and stewards who had yet to recover their senses. I saw more shot-up bodies but didn't stop to check whether they were living or dead. I had to be a vampire, not a human. A killer, not a carer.

I raced down the tunnel until it branched off in two directions. Left or right? I stood, panting, scanning the corridors for clues. Nothing to my left, but there was a small red mark on the wall to my right — blood.

I picked up speed again. A voice at the back of my mind whispered, "You have no weapons. How will you defend yourself?" I ignored it.

The corridor led to a dressing room, where most members of the winning team had gathered. The players weren't aware of what had happened on the pitch. They were cheering and singing. The corridor branched again here. The path to the left led back towards the pitch, so I took another right turn, praying to the gods of the vampires that I'd chosen correctly.

A long sprint. The corridor was narrow and low-ceilinged. I was panting hard, not from exertion but sorrow. I kept thinking about Tommy, Mr Crepsley, Gavner Purl — friends I'd lost to the vampaneze. I had to fight the sorrow, or it would overwhelm me, so I thought about R.V. and Morgan James instead.

R.V. was once an eco-warrior. He'd tried to free the Wolf Man at the Cirque Du Freak. I'd stopped him but not before the Wolf Man had bitten his hands off. R.V. fled, survived, and blamed me for his misfortune. Some years later, he was discovered by Steve Leopard. Steve told the vampaneze to blood him, and the pair plotted my downfall. R.V. had been in the Cavern of Retribution when Mr Crepsley was killed. That was the last time I'd seen him.

Morgan James was an ex-police officer. A vampet, one of the humans the vampaneze had recruited. Like the other vampets, he dressed in a brown shirt and black trousers, shaved his head, painted circles of blood around his eyes, and had a "V" tattooed above either ear. Since he hadn't been blooded, he was free to use missile-firing weapons such as guns. Vampaneze, like vampires, swear an oath when they're blooded not to use such weapons. James had also been in the Cavern of Retribution. During the battle he was shot, and the left side of his face had been torn into fleshy strips by the bullet.

A treacherous, deadly pair. Again I found myself wondering what I'd do if I caught up with them — I hadn't any weapons! But again I ignored that problem and concentrated on the chase.

The end of the corridor. A door swinging ajar. Two police officers and a steward lying slumped against the wall — dead. I cursed R.V. and Morgan James, and swore revenge.

I kicked the door wide open and ducked out. I was at the rear of the stadium, the quietest part of the area, backing on to a housing estate. The police out here had been attracted to the sides of the stadium — there was some kind of a disturbance at the front, no doubt timed to tie in with the assault.

Ahead of me I saw R.V. and Morgan James enter the estate. By the time the police turned their attention this way, the killers would be gone. I started after them. Stopped. Hurried back inside the stadium and frisked the dead police officers. No guns, but both had been carrying truncheons. I took the clubs, one for each hand, then fled after my prey.

It was dark on the estate, especially after the brightness of the stadium. But I had the extra-sharp vision of a half-vampire, so I was able to negotiate my way without any problems. The road branched off at regular intervals, seven or eight houses per stretch. I paused briefly at each junction, looking left and right. No sign of R.V. and Morgan James. Forward again.

I wasn't sure if they knew I was following. I assumed they knew I was at the match, but they might not have counted on me being the first to break out of the stadium and pursue them. The element of surprise *might* be on my side, but I warned myself not to count on it.

I came to the last junction. Left or right? I stood in the road, head twisting one way, then the other. I couldn't see anyone. I'd lost them! Should I take a direction at random or backtrack and—

There was a soft screeching sound to my left — a blade scraping against a wall. Then someone hissed, "Quiet!"

I turned. There was a tiny alley between two houses, the source of the noise. The nearest street lights had been smashed. The only illumination came from across the road. I had a bad feeling about this – the screech and hiss had been far too convenient – but I couldn't back off now. I advanced.

I stopped a couple of metres shy of the alley and edged out into the middle of the road. My knuckles were white from gripping the truncheons. I came into gradual sight of the alley. Nobody near the dark mouth. The alley only ran back five or six metres, and even in the poor light I could see all the way to the rear wall. Nobody was there. I breathed out shakily. Maybe my ears had been playing tricks. Or else the sound had been a TV or radio. What should I do now? I was back where I'd been moments before, no idea which way to—

Something moved in the alley, low down on the floor. I stiffened and lowered my sights. And now I saw them, crouched where it was darkest, one hugging either wall, practically invisible in the shadows.

The figure to my left chuckled, then stood — R.V. I raised the truncheon in my left hand defensively. Then the figure to my right rose, and Morgan James stepped forward, bringing up his shotgun, pointing it at me. I began to raise the truncheon in my right hand against him, then realized how worthless it would be if he fired.

I took another step back, meaning to run, when a voice spoke from the darkness behind R.V. "No guns," it said softly. Morgan James immediately lowered the barrel of his shotgun.

I should have run, but I couldn't, not without putting a face to that voice. So I stood my ground, squinting, as a third shape formed and stepped out from behind R.V. It was Gannen Harst, the prime protector of the Lord of the Vampaneze.

Part of me had expected this, and instead of panicking, I experienced something close to relief. The waiting was over. Whatever destiny had in store for me, it started here. One final encounter with the Vampaneze Lord. At the end of it, I'd kill him — or he'd kill me. Either way was better than the waiting.

"Hello, Gannen," I said. "Still hanging out with madmen and scum, I see."

Gannen Harst bristled but didn't reply. "Lord," he said instead, and a fourth ambusher stepped out from behind Morgan James, more familiar than any of the others.

"Good to see you again, Steve," I said cynically as the grey-haired Steve Leopard slid into view. I was partly focused on Gannen Harst, R.V. and Morgan James — but mostly on Steve. I was judging the gap between us, wondering what sort of damage I could do if I hurled my truncheons at him. I didn't care about the other three — killing the Vampaneze Lord was my first priority.

"He doesn't look surprised to see us," Steve remarked. He hadn't stepped out as far as Gannen Harst, and was protected by the body of Morgan James. I might be able to hit him from this angle — but it was a very big *might*.

"Let me have him," R.V. snarled, taking a step towards me. The last time I'd seen him, he'd been wearing red contact lenses, and had painted his skin purple, to look more like a vampaneze. But his eyes and skin had changed naturally over the past two years, and though his colouring was slight in comparison to a mature vampaneze, it was genuine.

"Stay where you are," Steve said to R.V. "We can all have a slice of him later. Let's finish the introductions first. Darius."

From behind Steve, the boy called Darius stepped out. He was wearing green robes, like Steve. He was shivering, but his face was set sternly. He was holding a large arrow-gun, one of Steve's inventions. It was pointed at me.

"Have you started blooding children now?" I growled

disgustedly, still waiting for Steve to move out a little more, ignoring the threat of the boy's arrow-gun.

"Darius is an exception," Steve said, smiling. "A most worthy ally and a valuable spy."

Steve took a half-step towards the boy. This was my chance! I began to draw my right hand back, careful not to give my intentions away, totally focused on Steve. Another second or two and I could make my play...

Then Darius spoke.

"Shall I shoot him now, Dad?"

DAD?

"Yes, son," Steve replied.

SON?

While my brain spun and whirled like a dervish, Darius steadied his aim, gulped, pulled the trigger, and shot a steel-tipped arrow straight at me.

CHAPTER ELEVEN

THE ARROW struck me high in my right shoulder, knocking me backwards. I roared with agony, grabbed the shaft of the arrow and pulled. The shaft broke off in my hand, leaving the head stuck deep in my flesh.

For a moment the world around me turned red. I thought I was going to pass out. But then the crimson haze faded and the road and houses swam back into focus. Over the sound of my pained panting, I heard footsteps coming towards me. Sitting up — grinding my teeth together to fight back a wave of fresh pain — I saw Steve leading his small band in for the kill.

I'd let go of the truncheons when I fell. One had rolled away, but the other was close by. I snatched for it and for the shaft of the arrow — the splintered end could be used as a crude dagger. When Gannen Harst saw this, he stepped in front of Steve. "Fan out!" he commanded R.V.

and Morgan James. They swiftly obeyed. The boy, Darius, was behind Steve. He looked sick. I don't think he'd ever shot anyone before.

"Keep back!" I hissed, waving my pitiful weapons at them.

"Make us," R.V. giggled.

"Uhr'd luhk tuh shee im truhy!" said Morgan James, who could only speak in a slur since his accident.

"We won't let him try anything," Gannen Harst said quietly. He hadn't drawn his sword yet, but his right hand was hanging purposefully by his scabbard. "He's a dangerous foe, even injured — don't forget that."

"You think too much of the boy," Steve purred, looking at me over his protector's shoulder. "He won't even be able to get up with a wound like that."

"Won't I?" I snorted, and pushed myself to my feet just to spite him. A red curtain descended for the second time, but again it passed after a couple of seconds. When my sight cleared, I saw Steve grinning wickedly — he'd goaded me to my feet on purpose, to string more entertainment out of me.

Waving the arrow shaft around at the four men, I backed away. Each step was torture, the pain in my right shoulder flaring up at the slightest movement. It was clear I couldn't get very far, but Gannen was taking no chances. He sent R.V. to my left and James to my right, blocking my route in both directions.

I stopped, weaving heavily on my feet, woozily trying to formulate a plan. I knew only Steve could kill me — Des

Tiny had predicted doom for the vampaneze if anybody other than their Lord killed any of the vampire hunters — but the others could hold me down for him.

"Let's finish him off quickly," Gannen Harst said, finally drawing his sword. "He is at our mercy. Let's not waste time."

"Take it easy," Steve chuckled. "I want to see him bleed a bit more."

"And if he bleeds to death from your son's arrow?" Gannen snapped.

"He won't," Steve said. "Darius shot exactly where I trained him to." Steve glanced back at the boy and caught his troubled look. "Are you OK?"

"Yes," Darius croaked. "I just didn't think it would be so ... so..."

"Bloody," Steve said. He nodded understandingly. "You did good work tonight. You don't have to watch the rest if you don't want to."

"How did ... *you* end up with ... a son?" I gasped, playing for time, hoping an escape would present itself.

"A long, twisted story," Steve said, facing me again. "One I'll delight in telling you before I drive a stake through your heart."

"You got that ... the wrong way round." I laughed bleakly. "*I'll* be the one doing ... the killing tonight."

"Optimistic to the last," Steve smirked. He cocked a devilish eyebrow at me. "How did Tommy die — with dignity, or like that squealing pig Crepsley?"

At that, something snapped inside me. I screamed a foul insult at Steve and, without thinking, hurled my truncheon at him. With blind luck, it struck his forehead and he dropped with a startled grunt.

Gannen Harst instinctively swung away from me, to check on his Lord. As soon as he made his move, I made mine. Jumping at Morgan James, I lashed out with the arrow shaft. He took a quick step back to avoid being speared. As he did, I smashed into him with my wounded right shoulder. I howled with pain as the arrow head was forced deeper into my flesh, but my ploy worked — James toppled over.

The path ahead was momentarily clear. I stumbled forward, grasping my right shoulder with my left hand, pressing hard around the hole where the arrow head was buried, trying to stem the flow of blood, weeping with agony. Behind me I heard Steve shout, "I'm OK! Chase him! Don't let him get away!"

If I hadn't been injured, I might have had enough of a head start on them. But I could manage nothing faster than a slow jog. It was only a matter of seconds before they'd catch up with me.

As I lurched away, my pursuers hot on my heels, a door to one of the houses on my left opened and a large man stuck his head out. "What's all the noise about?" he shouted angrily. "Some of us are trying to—"

"Help!" I screamed on impulse. "Murder!"

The man threw the door all the way open and stepped out. "What's going on?" he yelled.

I looked back at Steve and the others. They'd come to a halt. I had to make the most of their confusion.

"Help!" I screamed at the top of my lungs. "Killers! They've shot me! Help!"

Lights began flicking on in the neighbouring houses, and curtains were swished back. The man who'd come out started towards me. Steve sneered, reached over his shoulder, produced an arrow-gun and fired at the man. Gannen Harst knocked the arrow-gun aside just before Steve fired, so the arrow whizzed wide of its mark. But the man had seen Steve's intent and he ran back inside his house before he could be fired upon again.

"What are you doing?" Steve furiously challenged Gannen Harst.

"We must get out of here!" Gannen shouted.

"Not without killing him!" Steve yelled, jerking his arrow-gun at me.

"Then kill him, quick, and let's go!" Gannen responded.

Steve stared at me, eyes filled with hatred. Behind him, R.V. and Morgan James were looking on with hungry longing, eager to see me die. Darius was further removed from the gang — I couldn't tell if he was watching or not.

Steve raised his arrow-gun, took a couple of steps closer, trained his sights on me, then...

...lowered it, unfired. "No," he said sullenly. "This is too easy. Too fast."

"Don't be foolish!" Gannen roared. "You have to kill him! This is the predicted fourth encounter. You must do it now, before—"

"I'll do what I please!" Steve yelled, turning on his mentor. For a moment I thought he meant to attack his closest ally. But then he got hold of himself and smiled tightly. "I know what I'm doing, Gannen. I can't kill him this way."

"If not now, then when?" Gannen snarled.

"Later," Steve said. "When the time is right. When I can torment him at my leisure and make him feel the pain I felt when he betrayed me and pledged himself to Creepy Crepsley."

"And Mr Tiny's prophecy?" Gannen hissed.

"Stuff it!" Steve smirked. "I'll create my own destiny. That mug in the wellies doesn't rule my life."

Gannen's red eyes were ablaze with rage. This was madness. He wanted Steve to kill me, to settle the War of the Scars once and for all. He would have argued the point, but more doors were opening and people were poking their heads out. Gannen realized they were in danger of attracting too much unwanted attention. He shook his head, then grabbed Steve, spun him away from me and pushed him back the way they'd come, ordering R.V. and Morgan James to retreat.

"Catch you later, vampire-gator!" Steve laughed, waving at me as Gannen shepherded him away.

I wanted to respond with a suitable insult, but I lacked the strength. Besides, I had to get out of there as sharply as Steve and his gang. If the people came out and found me, I'd be in major trouble. It would mean the police, hospital, recognition and arrest — I was still a wanted fugitive. The general public here might not know about the alleged killer, Darren Shan, but I was sure the police did.

Turning my back on the emerging humans, I staggered to the end of the block, where I rested a moment, leaning against a wall. I wiped sweat from my forehead and tears from my eyes, then checked the hole in my shoulder — still bleeding. There was no time to examine it further. People were spilling out on to the street. It wouldn't be long before news of the killings at the stadium trickled through. Then they'd be on their phones to the police, telling them all about the disturbance.

Pushing myself away from the wall, I stumbled left and started down a path which would hopefully lead me away from the housing estate. I tried to jog but it was too painful. I slowed to the fastest walk I could manage, bleeding with every step I took, head ringing, desperately wondering how far I could struggle on before I collapsed from loss of blood or shock.

CHAPTER TWELVE

I CLEARED the housing estate a few minutes later. In the distance police sirens screamed like banshees in the night. The stadium would be their first priority, but once word reached them of the scuffle on the housing estate, units would be sent to investigate.

As I stood bent over, panting for breath, I studied the path I'd taken and saw little puddles of blood marking my course — a clear trail for anyone who followed. If I was to progress any further undetected, I'd have to do something about my wound.

I examined the hole. There was a tiny bit of shaft sticking out of it, attached to the arrow head. I took hold of the light piece of wood, closed my eyes, bit down hard, and pulled.

"Charna's guts!"

I fell back, shivering, fingers twitching, mouth opening and shutting rapidly. For maybe a minute, I knew only pain. The houses around me could have collapsed and I wouldn't have noticed.

Gradually the pain abated and I was able to study the wound again. I hadn't managed to pull the head out, but I'd drawn it closer towards the hole, plugging it up. Blood still oozed out but it wasn't flowing steadily like it had been. That would have to do. Tearing a long strip off my shirt, I balled it up and pressed it over the wound. After a few deep breaths, I got to my feet. My legs were shaking like a newborn lamb's, but they held. I made sure I wasn't dripping blood, then resumed my sluggish flight.

The next ten or fifteen minutes passed in a slow, agonized blur. I had enough sense left to keep moving, but I wasn't able to take note of street names or plot a course back to the Cirque Du Freak. All I knew was that I couldn't stop.

I kept to the sides of streets and alleys, so I could grab a fence for support or lean against a wall to rest. I didn't pass many people. Those I did pass ignored me. That surprised me, even in my dazed state, until I realized how I must look. A teenager, reeling along the path, head bowed, body crooked over, moaning softly — they thought I was drunk!

Eventually I had to stop. I was at the end of my rope. If I didn't sit down and rest, I'd drop in the middle of the street. Luckily I was close to a dark alley. I fell into it and crawled away from the streetlights, deep into welcome shadows. I stopped beside a large black garbage bin, sat up against the wall by which it was set, and dragged my legs in.

"Just ... a short ... rest," I wheezed, laying my head on

my knees, wincing at the pain in my shoulder. "A few ... minutes ... and then I can..."

I got no further. My eyelids fluttered shut and I flaked out, at the mercy of any who happened to chance upon me.

My eyes opened. It was later, darker, colder. I felt like I was encased in a block of ice. I tried lifting my head, but even that small effort proved too much for me. I blacked out again.

The next time I awoke, I was choking. Some stinging liquid was being forced down my throat. For a confused moment I thought I was a raw half-vampire again, and that Mr Crepsley was trying to force me to drink human blood. "No!" I mumbled, slapping at the hands holding my head. "Not gonna ... be like you!"

"Hold him still!" someone grunted.

"It's not that easy," the person holding me complained. "He's stronger than he looks." Then I felt a body pressing down on mine and a voice whispered in my ear, "Steady, kid. We're only trying to help."

My head cleared slightly and I stopped struggling. Blinking, I tried to focus on the faces of the men around me, but it was either too dark or my sight was clouded with pain. "What ... are you?" I gasped, meaning were they friends or foes.

The man holding me must have misheard my question, and thought I'd asked *who* were they. "I'm Declan," he said. "This is Little Kenny."

"Open wide," Little Kenny said, pressing the rim of a bottle to my lips. "This is cheap and nasty, but it'll warm you up."

I drank reluctantly, unable to argue. My stomach filled with a sickening fire. When Little Kenny took the bottle away, I leant my head back against the wall and groaned. "What time ... is it?" I asked.

"We don't bother with watches," Declan chuckled. "But it's late, maybe one or two in the morning." He took hold of my chin, turned my head left and right, then picked at the strip of shirt which was stuck to my shoulder with dried blood.

"Ow!" I yelped.

Declan released me immediately. "Sorry," he said. "Does it hurt much?"

"Not ... as much ... as it did," I muttered. Then my head began to swim and I half-blacked out again. When I recovered, the two men were huddled together a metre away, discussing what to do with me.

"Leave him," I heard Little Kenny hiss. "He can't be more than sixteen or seventeen. He's no good to us."

"Every person matters," Declan disagreed. "We can't afford to be picky."

"But he's not one of *us*," Little Kenny said. "He probably has a family and home. We can't start recruiting normal people, not until we're told."

"I know," Declan said. "But there's something different about him. Did you see his scars? And he didn't get that wound fighting in the playground. We should take him back with us. If the ladies choose not to keep him, we can get rid of him easily enough."

"But he'll know where we are!" Little Kenny objected.

"The shape he's in, I doubt he even knows what town this is!" Declan snorted. "He's got more things to worry about than marking the route we take."

Little Kenny grumbled something I couldn't hear, then said, "OK, but don't forget it was your choice, not mine. I'm not taking the blame for this."

"Fine," Declan said, and returned to my side. He rolled my eyelids all the way up and I got my first clear look at him. He was a large, bearded man, dressed in shabby clothes, covered in grime — a tramp. "Kid," he said, snapping his fingers in front of my eyes. "You awake? Do you know what's going on?"

"Yes." I glanced over at Little Kenny and saw that he was also a tramp.

"We're taking you back with us," Declan said. "Can you walk?"

I assumed that they meant to take me to a mission house or homeless shelter. That wasn't as preferable as the Cirque Du Freak, but it was better than a police station. I wet my lips and locked gazes with Declan. "No ... police," I moaned.

Declan laughed. "See?" he said to Little Kenny. "I told you he was our kind of people!" He took hold of my left arm and told Little Kenny to take my right. "This will hurt," he warned me. "You ready for it?"

"Yes," I said.

They pulled me to my feet. The pain in my shoulder flared back into life, my brain ignited with fireworks, and my stomach lurched. Doubling over, I was sick on the alley floor. Declan and Little Kenny held me while I vomited, then hauled me up.

"Better?" Declan asked.

"No!" I gasped.

He laughed again, then shuffled around, dragging me with him, so we were facing the entrance of the alley. "We'll carry you as best we can," Declan said. "But try to use your legs — it'll make life easier for all of us."

I nodded to show I understood. Declan and Little Kenny linked hands behind my back, put their other hands on my chest to support me, then led me away.

Declan and Little Kenny were a strange pair of guardian angels. They encouraged me along with a series of curses, pushes and pulls, kicking my feet every so often to goad me into short bursts of self-momentum. We rested every few minutes, leaning against walls or lampposts, Declan and Little Kenny panting almost as hard as I was. They obviously weren't accustomed to this much exercise.

Even though it was the middle of the night, the town was abuzz. Word of the stadium slaughter had spread, and people had taken to the streets in outrage. Police cars passed us regularly, sirens blaring, flashlights glaring.

We marched in plain view of the police and angry citizens, but nobody took any notice of us. With Declan and Little Kenny holding me, I looked like the third of a trio of drunk tramps. One policeman did stop and shout at us to get the hell off the streets — hadn't we heard what happened?

"Yes, sir," Declan mumbled, half-saluting the policeman. "Going home right now. Don't suppose you could arrange a lift for us?"

The policeman snorted and turned away. Declan chuckled, then led us on again. When we were out of earshot, he said to Little Kenny, "Have you any idea what all the fuss is about?"

"Something to do with football, I think," Little Kenny said.

"How about you?" Declan asked me. "Do you know what people are up in arms about?"

I shook my head. Even if I'd wanted to tell them the truth, I couldn't have. The pain was worse than ever. I had to keep my teeth ground tightly together to stop myself from screaming out loud.

We carried on walking. I half-hoped I'd black out again, to numb myself to the pain. I didn't even care that Declan and Little Kenny would probably dump me in a gutter to die, rather than drag my deadweight body along. But I stayed awake, if not entirely alert, and managed to swing my legs into action when prompted.

I'd no idea where I was being taken, and I wasn't able to raise my head to mark the way. When we finally came to a halt in front of an old, brown-faced building, Little Kenny darted forward to open a door. I tried looking up to see what the number was. But even that was beyond me, and I could only stare at the ground through half-closed eyes as Declan and Little Kenny dragged me inside and laid me on a hard wooden floor.

Little Kenny stayed with me, keeping watch, as Declan went upstairs. They'd lain me on my left side, but I rolled over on to my back and stared up at the ceiling. I could feel my last sparks of consciousness flickering out. As I watched, my eyes played tricks and I imagined the ceiling was shimmering, like sea water in a light breeze.

I heard Declan coming back with somebody. He was talking quickly and quietly. I tried turning my head to see who he was bringing, but the scene on the ceiling was too captivating to turn away from. Now I was imagining boats, sails filled with the breeze, circling the sea/ceiling above me.

Declan stopped by my side and examined me. Then he stepped back and the person with him bent over to look. That's when I knew I was really losing my grip on reality, because in my delirium I thought the person was Debbie Hemlock, my ex-girlfriend. I smiled weakly at the ludicrous thought of running into Debbie here. Then the woman standing over me exclaimed, "Darren! Oh my—"

And then there was only darkness, silence and dreams.

CHAPTER THIRTEEN

"Ow! IT'S hot!" I winced.

"Don't be a baby," Debbie smiled, pressing a spoon of steaming hot soup to my lips. "It's good for you."

"Not if it scalds my throat," I grumbled. I blew on the soup to cool it, swallowed, then smiled at Debbie as she dipped the spoon into the bowl again. Harkat stood guard by the door. Outside I could hear Alice Burgess talking with one of their street people. I felt incredibly safe as I lay there, sipping soup, like nothing in the world could harm me.

It had been five days since Declan and Little Kenny rescued me. The first few days passed in a haze. I'd been wracked with pain and a high fever, senses in disarray, subject to nightmares and delusions. I kept thinking Debbie and Alice were imaginary. I'd laugh when they talked to me, convinced my brain was playing tricks.

But as the fever broke and my senses returned, the faces of the women remained constant. When I finally realized it really was Debbie, I threw my arms around her and hugged her so hard, I almost fainted again!

"Would you like some soup?" Debbie asked Harkat.

"No," Harkat replied. "Not hungry."

I asked Debbie to fetch Harkat and Mr Tall even before she'd told me what she and Alice were doing here. When my worried friend arrived — Mr Tall didn't come — I told him about Steve and his gang, and about Steve being Darius's father. Harkat's round green eyes almost doubled in size when he heard that. I wanted him to leave and contact the Vampire Generals, but he refused. He said he had to stay to protect me, and wouldn't go until I was fit again. I argued the point, but it was no good. He hadn't left the room since then, except for the occasional toilet break.

Debbie spooned the last of the soup into my mouth, wiped around my lips with a napkin, and winked. She'd hardly changed in the two years we'd been parted. The same lush dark skin, beautiful brown eyes, full lips, and tightly cropped hair. But she was more physically developed than before. She was leaner, more muscular, and she moved with a fighter's fluid grace. Her eyes were always alert. She was never totally at ease, ready to respond to any threat at an instant's notice.

The last time we'd met, Debbie and Alice had been on their way to Vampire Mountain. They were troubled by the rise of the vampaneze and shaven-headed vampets — they thought they'd turn on humanity next if they won the War of the Scars. They decided that the vampires should create their own human force to combat the threat of the gun-wielding vampets. They planned to offer their services to the Generals, and hoped to put together a small army to battle the vampets, leaving the vampires free to tackle the vampaneze.

I didn't think the Generals would accept their proposal. Vampires have always distanced themselves from humans, and I thought they'd reject Debbie and Alice automatically. But Debbie told me that Seba Nile – the quartermaster of Vampire Mountain, and an old friend of Mr Crepsley's and mine – had spoken on their behalf. He said times had changed and the Generals needed to change with them. Vampires and vampaneze had sworn an oath never to use missile-firing weapons, but the vampets hadn't. Many vampires were being shot by the shaven-headed curs. Seba said something had to be done about it, and this was their chance to fight the vampets on level terms.

As the oldest living vampire, Seba was greatly respected. Upon his recommendation Debbie and Alice were accepted, albeit with reluctance. For several months they'd trained in the vampire ways, mostly at the hands of my old task master, Vanez Blane. The blind vampire taught them to fight and think as creatures of the night. It wasn't easy – the ever-wintry Vampire Mountain was a hard place to survive if you lacked the hot blood of the vampires – but they'd clung to each other for support and stuck with it, earning the admiration even of those Generals who'd greeted them with suspicion.

Ideally they'd have trained for several years, learning the ways of vampire warfare. But time was precious. The vampets were growing in number, taking part in more and more battles, killing more and more vampires. Once Debbie and Alice had covered the basics, they set out with a small band of Generals to assemble a makeshift army. Debbie told me Seba and Vanez longed to come with them, for one last taste of adventure in the outside world. But they served the clan best in Vampire Mountain, so they stayed, loyal servants to the end.

The door to my room opened and Alice stepped in. Alice Burgess used to be a police chief inspector and she looked even more warrior-like than Debbie. She was taller and broader, with more pronounced muscles. Her white hair was cut ultra-short, and though she was extremely light-skinned, there was nothing soft about her complexion. She looked as pale and deadly as a snowstorm.

"The police are searching the neighbourhood," Alice said. "They'll be here in an hour or less. Darren will have to hide again."

The building was old and had once been used as a church by a shady preacher. He'd created a couple of secret rooms, almost impossible to find. They were stuffy and uncomfortable, but safe. I'd stayed in one of them three times already, to avoid the police searches which had been in full flow since the massacre at the football stadium.

"Any word from Vancha?" I asked, sitting up and pushing the bed covers back.

"Not yet," Alice said.

As the other surviving hunter, Vancha March was the only person apart from me who could freely kill Steve.

Debbie and Alice didn't have a direct line to the Prince, but they'd equipped a number of the younger, more forward-thinking Generals with mobile phones. One would get word to Vancha about the situation here — eventually. I just prayed it wouldn't be too late.

Recruiting an army had proved a lot harder than it sounded. No vampire knew for sure how the vampaneze had put the vampets together, but we could imagine their recruiting strategy — find weak-willed, wicked people, then bribe them with promises of power. "Join us and we'll teach you how to fight and kill. We'll blood you when the time is right and make you stronger than any human. As one of us, you'll live for centuries. Anything you wish for can be yours."

Debbie and Alice faced a much harder task. They needed good people who were willing to fight on the side of right, who recognized the threat the vampets and their masters posed, who wished to avert the prospect of living in a world where a band of killers dominated the night. Crooked, grasping, evil-hearted people were easy to find. Honest, concerned, self-sacrificing people were harder to come by.

They found a few, among police and soldiers – Alice had lots of contacts from her time on the force – but nowhere near enough to counter the threat of the vampets. For half a year they made little or no progress. They were beginning to think it was a waste of time. Then Debbie saw the way forward.

The vampaneze were on the increase. As well as recruiting the vampets, they were blooding more vampaneze assistants than normal, driving up their numbers in a bid to win the War of the Scars by means of force. Since they were more active than usual, they needed to drink more blood, to keep up their energy levels. And when vampaneze drank blood, they killed.

So where were all the bodies?

Vampaneze had survived for six hundred years by feeding cautiously, never killing too many people in any one area, carefully hiding the bodies of their victims. There weren't many of them — never more than three hundred before the War of the Scars — and they were spread across the world. It was relatively easy to keep their presence a secret from humanity.

But now they were on the increase, feeding in groups, killing hundreds of humans every month. There was no way such a drain on humanity could have passed unnoticed by the general public — unless those they fed from weren't officially part of that public.

Tramps. Dossers. Hobos. Vagrants. Mankind had dozens of names for homeless people, those without careers, houses, families or security. Many names — but not a lot of interest. Homeless people were a nuisance, a problem, an eyesore. Whether "ordinary" people felt pity or disgust for them, whether they handed over change when they saw someone begging or walked straight by, one thing united most humans — they knew homeless people existed, but very few took any real notice of them. Who in any town or city could say how many homeless people were living on the streets? Who'd know if those numbers started to drop? Who'd care?

The answer — almost nobody. Except the homeless people themselves. *They'd* know something was wrong. The homeless would listen, pitch in and fight. If not for the vampires, then for themselves — they were victims of the War of the Scars, and stood to lose big time if the vampaneze were triumphant.

So Debbie, Alice and their small band of Generals took their recruiting speeches to the corners of the world most humans know nothing about. They went out on the streets, into homeless shelters and mission churches, down alleys lined with rough beds made of cardboard boxes and wads of newspapers. They moved freely among the people of this subworld, facing suspicion and danger, spreading their message, in search of allies.

And they found them. There was a grapevine among the homeless, similar to that of the vampire clan. Though most lacked phones, they kept in touch with one another. It was amazing how fast a rumour could travel, and wherever Alice and Debbie went, they found people who'd heard about the murders and knew they were under attack, even though they had no idea who their attackers were.

Debbie and Alice told the street people about the vampaneze. They encountered scepticism to begin with, but the vampires with them backed them up, demonstrating their powers. In a couple of cities they helped the street folk track down vampaneze and kill them. Word spread rapidly, and over the last several months thousands of street people across the world had pledged themselves to the vampire cause. Most hadn't been trained yet. For now they were serving as eyes and ears, watching for vampaneze, passing on word of their movements.

They'd also chosen a name — *vampirites*.

Harkat helped me out of bed and I hobbled from my room, down the corridor and stairs to the ground floor, where the hidden rooms were located. Alice came with us, to ensure all was in order. We passed Declan along the way. He was on the phone to another nearby vampirite stronghold, warning them of the police search.

The Generals with Debbie and Alice left them eventually, to resume the fight against the vampaneze — all hands were needed in the War of the Scars. A couple kept in touch, meeting up with them every month or two, monitoring their progress. But most of the time the ladies of the shadows – as the vampirites referred to them – travelled alone, choosing places where the vampaneze were active, recruiting fervently.

They'd come to my home town a fortnight ago. There'd been many reports of vampaneze here, and a band of vampirites had already formed to combat them. Debbie and Alice came to raise morale, and also to spread awareness among the street folk. That task accomplished, they'd planned to move on soon. Then I'd turned up, beaten and bleeding, and their plans changed.

I rubbed my right shoulder as I shuffled to the secret room. Alice had removed the arrowhead and stitched me up. The wound had healed cleanly, but it still stung like crazy, and I was a long way off full recovery.

Alice and Harkat moved the furniture which helped mask the entrance to the hidden room at the rear of the house. Then Alice pressed a secret panel and a section of wall slid back to reveal a cramped cell. There was a very dim light set in one of the walls.

"They searched the house thoroughly last time," Alice reminded me, checking that the jug beside the mattress on the floor was filled with water. "You could be in for another long stay."

"I'll be fine," I said, lying down.

"Hold on!" I heard Debbie shout, as Alice was about to close the section of wall on me. She came hurrying to the entrance, carrying a small bag. "I've been waiting until you were strong enough to give this to you. It will help pass the time."

"What is it?" I asked, taking the bag.

"You'll see," Debbie replied, blowing me a kiss and stepping back as the cell was closed off. I waited a minute for my eyes to adjust to the dim light, then reached inside the bag and pulled out several notepads bound together by an elastic band. I broke into a smile — my diary! I'd forgotten it entirely. Now that I cast my thoughts back, I recalled handing the notepads to Alice before leaving with Harkat two years earlier.

I slipped the elastic band off the pads, thumbed through the copy on top, then paused, upended the diary, and went back eighteen years to before I sneaked out to the Cirque Du Freak and met Mr Crepsley. Within minutes I was adrift in the past, and the hours flew by as I focused on my scrawled writing, aware of nothing else.

CHAPTER FOURTEEN

ONCE I got the all clear, I returned to my bedroom and spent the next couple of days bringing my diary up to date. I'd soon filled out the most recent notepad, so Debbie brought me fresh writing material. I wrote all about my adventures with Harkat in the barren wasteland which seemed to be the world of the future. I described my fears, that the world might face destruction regardless of who won the War of the Scars, and that I might be in some way linked to the fall of mankind. I told about discovering Harkat's true identity and returning home. A quick rundown of our recent travels with the Cirque Du Freak. Then the latest cruel chapter, in which Tommy died and I learnt that Steve had a son.

I hadn't thought much about Tommy since that night. I knew the police were scouring the city in search of his killers, and that R.V. and Morgan James had killed eight others and wounded many more in the stadium. But I didn't know what the general public made of the murders, or if I'd been identified as a suspect — maybe Steve was setting me up to take the blame for this.

I asked Debbie to bring me all the local papers from the last few days. There were poor pictures of R.V. (full-vampaneze couldn't be photographed, but R.V.'s molecular system must not have changed yet) and Morgan James, but none of me. There was a brief mention of the incident outside the ground, when I'd been attacked, but the police didn't seem to place much importance on it or link it with the stadium murders.

"Were you close to him?" Debbie asked, tapping a photo of a smiling Tommy Jones. She was sitting on the end of my bed, watching me while I read the papers. She'd been spending a lot of time with me during my recovery, nursing me, chatting with me, telling me about her life.

"We were good friends when we were kids," I sighed.

"Do you think he knew about Steve or the vampaneze?" Debbie asked.

"No. He was an innocent victim. I'm sure of it."

"But didn't he say he had something important to tell you?"

I shook my head. "He said there were things we had to discuss about Steve, but he wasn't specific. I don't think it had anything to do with this."

"It scares me," Debbie said, taking the paper from me and folding it over.

"You're scared because they killed Tommy?" I frowned.

"No — because they did it in front of tens of thousands of people. They must be full of confidence, afraid of nothing. They wouldn't have dared pull a stunt like this a few years ago. They're growing more powerful all the time."

"Over-confidence may prove to be their undoing," I grunted. "They were safer when nobody knew about them. Confidence has brought them out into the light, but they seem to have forgotten — light's no good for creatures of the night."

Debbie put the paper aside. "How's your shoulder?" she asked.

"Not too bad," I said. "But Alice's stitch work leaves a lot to be desired — I'm going to have a terrible scar when the wound heals."

"Another one for the collection," Debbie laughed. Her smile faded. "I noticed a new scar on your back, long and deep. Did you get it when you went away with Harkat?"

I nodded, remembering the monstrous Grotesque, how one of its fangs had caught between my shoulder blades and ripped downwards sharply.

"You still haven't told me what happened, or where you went," Debbie said.

I sighed. "It's not something we need to talk about right now."

"But you found out who Harkat was?"

"Yes," I said and let the matter drop. I didn't like concealing secrets from Debbie, but if that wasteworld really was the future, I saw no reason to burden Debbie with foreknowledge of it.

I woke early the next morning with a terrible headache. There was a small crack between the curtains, and although only a thin shaft of light was visible, I felt as if a strong torch was being shone directly into my eyes. Groaning, I stumbled out of bed and pulled the curtains closed. That helped, but my headache didn't improve. I lay as still as I could, hoping it would go away. When it didn't, I got out of bed again, meaning to go downstairs and get some aspirin. I passed Harkat on my way. He was leaning against a wall, asleep, although his lidless eyes were – as always – wide open.

I had taken a few steps down the stairs when a wave of giddiness overcame me and I fell. I grabbed for the banister, managed to catch it before I toppled over, and slid to a bruising halt halfway down the stairs. Head ringing, I sat up and looked around, dazed, wondering if this was an after-effect of my wounded shoulder. I tried shouting for help but I could only work up a croak.

A short while later, as I lay on the stairs, gathering my strength in an effort to crawl back to my room, Debbie walked by the top of the staircase. She caught sight of me and stopped. I raised my head to call her name, but again I could only form a choked croak.

"Declan?" Debbie asked, taking a step forward. "What are you doing? You haven't been drinking again, have you?"

I frowned. Why had she confused me with Declan? We looked nothing alike.

As Debbie climbed down to help, she realized I wasn't the tramp. She stopped, coming on guard. "Who are you?" she snapped. "What are you doing here?"

"It's ... me," I gasped, but she didn't hear.

"Alice!" Debbie shouted. "Harkat!"

At her cry, Alice and Harkat came running and joined her at the top of the stairs. "Is it one of Declan or Little Kenny's friends?" Alice asked.

"I don't think so," Debbie said.

"Who are you?" Alice challenged me. "Tell us, quick, or—"

"Wait," Harkat interrupted. He stepped past the women and stared hard at me, then grimaced. "As if we haven't enough ... problems!" He hurried down the steps. "It's OK," he told Alice and Debbie as he picked me up. "It's Darren."

"*Darren?*" Debbie exclaimed. "But he's covered in hair!"

And I realized why she hadn't recognized me. Overnight, my hair had sprouted and I'd grown a beard. "The purge!" I wheezed.

"The second phase," Harkat nodded. "You know what ... this means?"

Yes — it meant my time as a half-vampire was almost at an end. Within a few weeks the vampire blood within my veins would transform all of the human cells and I'd become a true, night-hugging, sunlight-fearing creature of the dark.

I explained the purge to Debbie and Alice. My vampire cells were attacking my human cells, converting them. Within weeks I'd be a full-vampire. In the meantime my body would mature rapidly and undergo all kinds of inconveniences. Apart from the hair, my senses would go haywire. I'd suffer headaches. I'd have to cover my eyes and plug up my nose and ears. My sense of taste would desert me. I'd experience sudden bursts of energy then loss of strength.

"It's terrible timing," I complained to Debbie later in the day. Harkat and Alice were busy elsewhere in the house while Debbie helped me cut my hair and shave.

"What's so bad about it?" she asked.

"I'm vulnerable," I said. "My head's pounding. I can't see, hear or smell right. I don't know what my body's going to do from one minute to the next. If we get into a fight with the vampaneze any time soon, I can't be depended upon."

"But you're stronger than normal during the purge, aren't you?"

"Sometimes. But that strength can dwindle away suddenly, leaving me weak and defenceless. And there's no way of predicting when that will happen."

"What about afterwards?" Debbie asked, trimming my fringe. "You'll be a full-vampire?"

"Yes."

"You'll be able to flit and communicate telepathically with other vampires?"

"Not straightaway," I told her. "The ability will be there, but I'll have to develop it. I've got a lot of learning to do over the next few years."

"You don't sound too happy about it," Debbie noted.

I pulled a face. "In many ways I'm glad — I'll finally

be a true vampire, as a Prince should be. I've always felt awkward, being a half-vampire and having so much power. On the other hand I'm facing the end of a way of life. No more sunlight or being able to pass for human. I've enjoyed the best of both worlds since I was blooded. Now I have to leave one of them — the human world — behind for ever." I sighed moodily.

Debbie thought about that in silence, cutting my hair back. Then she said quietly, "You'll be an adult at the end, won't you?"

"Yes," I snorted. "That's another change I'm not sure about. I've been a child or teenager for the better part of thirty years. To leave that behind in the space of a few weeks... It's weird!"

"But wonderful," Debbie said. She stopped cutting and stepped in front of me. "Do you remember when you tried to kiss me a few years ago?"

"Yes," I grimaced. "That's when I was pretending to be a student, and you were my teacher. You hit the roof and ordered me out of your apartment."

"Rightly so," Debbie grinned. "As a teacher — an adult — it would be wrong of me to get involved with a child. I couldn't kiss you then, and I can't kiss you now. It'd feel terribly wrong kissing a boy." Her grin changed subtly, mysteriously. "But in a few weeks, you won't be a boy. You'll be a man."

"Oh," I said, thinking about that. Then my expression changed. I gazed up at Debbie with new understanding and hope, then gently took her hand.

CHAPTER FIFTEEN

A BENEFIT of the purge was that my wound healed quickly and I got my strength back. A couple of days later, I was almost back to full physical fitness, except for my headaches and growing pains.

I was doing press-ups on the floor of my bedroom, working off some of my excess energy, when I heard Debbie squeal downstairs. I stopped instantly and shared a worried look with Harkat, who was standing guard by the door. I hurried to his side and removed one of the earplugs I was wearing to block out the worst of the street noises.

"Should we go down?" Harkat asked, opening the door a crack. We could hear Debbie babbling excitedly, and as we listened, Alice joined her and also began to talk very quickly.

"I don't think anything's wrong," I said, frowning. "They seem happy, as if an old friend has..." I stopped and slapped my forehead. Harkat laughed, then both of us said at exactly the same time, "*Vancha!*"

Throwing the door wide open, we barged down the stairs and found Debbie and Alice chatting with a burly, red-skinned, green-haired man, dressed in purple animal hides and no shoes, with belts of sharp throwing stars — shurikens — looped around his torso.

"Vancha!" I shouted happily, clutching his arms and squeezing tight.

"It is good to see you again, Sire," Vancha said with surprising politeness. Then he burst into a grin and hugged me tight. "Darren!" he boomed. "I've missed you!" Turning to Harkat, he laughed. "I missed you too, ugly!"

"Look who's talking!" Harkat grinned.

"It's great to see you both, but of course I'm most pleased to see the ladies," Vancha said, releasing me and winking at Debbie and Alice. "Female beauty's what we hot-blooded men live for, aye?"

"He's a born flatterer," Alice sniffed. "I bet he says that to every woman he meets."

"Naturally," Vancha murmured, "because all women are beautiful, in one way or another. But you're more beautiful than most, my dear — an angel of the night!"

Alice snorted with contempt, but there was a strange little smile playing at the corners of her lips. Vancha looped his arms around Debbie and Alice and guided us into the living room, as though this was his house and we were the guests. Sitting down, making himself comfortable, he told Debbie to go fetch some food. She told him — in no uncertain terms — that he could do his own fetching while he was here, and he laughed with delight.

It was refreshing to see that the War of the Scars hadn't changed Vancha March. He was as loud and lively as ever. He filled us in on his recent movements, the countries he'd explored, the vampaneze and vampets he'd killed, making it sound like a big, exciting adventure, free from all consequences.

"When I heard that Leonard was here, I came as quickly as I could," Vancha concluded. "I flitted without rest. I haven't missed him, have I?"

"We don't know," I said. "We haven't heard from him since the night he almost killed me."

"But what does your heart tell you?" Vancha asked, his large eyes weighing heavy upon me, his small mouth closed in a tight, expectant line.

"He's here," I said softly. "He's waiting for me — for *us*. I think this is where Mr Tiny's prophecy will be tested. We'll face him on these streets — or beneath — and we'll kill him or he'll kill us. And that will be the end of the War of the Scars. Except..."

"What?" Vancha asked when I didn't continue.

"There was supposed to be one final encounter. Four times our path was due to cross with his. When he had me at his mercy recently, that was the fourth time, but we're both still alive. Maybe Mr Tiny got it wrong. Maybe his prophecy doesn't hold true any longer."

Vancha mulled that one over. "Perhaps you have a point," he said uncertainly. "But as much as I despise Des

Tiny, I have to admit he doesn't make many mistakes when it comes to prophecies — in fact none that I've heard of. He told you *we* would have four chances to kill Leonard, aye?" I nodded. "Then maybe we both have to be there. Perhaps your solo encounter doesn't count."

"It would have counted if he'd killed me," I grunted.

"But he didn't," Vancha said. "Maybe he couldn't. Perhaps it simply wasn't his destiny."

"If you're right, that means we're going to run into him again," I said.

"Aye," Vancha said. "A fight to the death. Except if he wins, he won't kill both of us. Evanna said one of us would survive if we lost." Evanna was a witch, the daughter of Mr Tiny. I'd almost forgotten that part of the prophecy. If Steve won, he'd leave one of us alive, to witness the downfall of the clan.

There was a long, troubled silence as we thought about the prophecy and the dangers we faced. Vancha broke it by clapping loudly. "Enough of the doom and gloom! What about you two?" He nodded at Harkat and me. "How did your quest go? Do we know who Harkat used to be?"

"Yes," Harkat said. He glanced at Debbie and Alice. "I don't wish to be rude, but could you ... leave us alone for a while?"

"Is this *men's* talk?" Alice asked mockingly.

"No," Harkat chuckled. "It's *Prince's* talk."

"We'll be upstairs," Debbie said. "Call us when you're ready."

Vancha stood and bowed as the ladies were leaving. When he sat again, his expression was curious. "Why the secrecy?" he asked.

"It's about who I was," Harkat said, "and where ... we learnt the truth. We don't think we should discuss it ... in front of anybody except a Prince."

"Intriguing," Vancha said, leaning forward eagerly.

We gave Vancha a quick rundown of our quest through the wastelands, the creatures we'd battled, meeting Evanna, the mad sailor – Spits Abrams – and the dragons. He said nothing, but listened enthralled. When we told him about pulling Kurda Smahlt out of the Lake of Souls, Vancha's jaw dropped.

"But it can't be!" he protested. "Harkat was alive before Kurda died."

"Mr Tiny can move through time," I said. "He created Harkat from Kurda's remains, then took him into the past, so that he could serve as my protector."

Vancha blinked slowly. Then his features clouded over with rage — and fear. "Damn that Desmond Tiny! I always knew he was powerful, but to be able to meddle with time itself... What manner of diabolical beast is he?"

It was a rhetorical question, so we didn't attempt to answer it. Instead we finished by telling him how Kurda had chosen to sacrifice himself – he and Harkat shared a soul, so only one of them could live at any given time – leaving us free to return to the present.

"The *present*?" Vancha snapped. "What do you mean?"

Harkat told him about our theory — that the wasteworld was the future. When he heard that, Vancha trembled as though a cold wind had sliced through him. "I never thought the War of the Scars could be that crucial," he said softly. "I knew our future was at stake, but I never dreamt we could drag humanity down with us." He shook his head and turned away, muttering, "I need to think about this."

Harkat and I said nothing while Vancha deliberated. Minutes passed. A quarter of an hour. Half an hour. Finally he heaved a large sigh and turned to face us. "These are grim tidings," he said. "But perhaps not as grim as they seem. From what you've told me, I believe that Tiny did take you into the future — but I also believe he wouldn't have done so without good reason. He might have been simply mocking you, but it might also have been a warning.

"That damned future must be what we face if we lose the War of the Scars. Steve Leonard is the sort who'd level the world and bring it to ruin. But if we win, we can prevent that. When Tiny came to Vampire Mountain, he told us there were two possible futures, didn't he? One where the vampaneze win the war, and one where the vampires win. I think Tiny gave you a glimpse of the former future to drive home the point that we *have* to win this war. It's not just ourselves we're fighting for — it's the entire world. The wasteworld is one future — I'm sure the world where we've won is completely different."

"It makes sense," Harkat agreed. "If both futures currently exist ... he might have been able to choose which ... to take us to."

"Maybe," I sighed, unconvinced. I was thinking again about the vision I'd had shortly after we'd first met Evanna, when Harkat had been plagued by nightmares. Evanna helped me put a stop to them, by sending me into his dreams. In the dream, I'd faced a being of immense power — the Lord of the Shadows. Evanna told me this master of evil was part of the future, and the road there was paved with dead souls. She'd also told me that the Lord of the Shadows could be one of two people — Steve Leopard or *me*.

The uncertainties came rushing back. I was unable to share Vancha and Harkat's view that one future was bright and cheery where the other was dark and miserable. I felt we were heading for big-scale trouble, whichever way the War of the Scars swung. But I kept my opinions to myself — I didn't want to come across as a prophet of doom.

"So!" Vancha laughed, startling me out of my dark thoughts. "We just have to make sure we kill Steve Leonard, aye?"

"Aye," I said, grinning sickly.

"What about me?" Harkat asked. "Does it alter your opinion of me ... now that you know I was once a vampire traitor?"

"No," Vancha said. "I never liked you much anyway." He spat into his right palm, ran the spit through his hair, then winked to show he was joking. "Seriously, you were right not to broadcast the news. We'll keep it to ourselves. I always believed that although Kurda acted stupidly, he acted with the best interests of the clan at heart. But there are many who don't share that view. If they knew the truth about you, it might divide them. Internal argument is the last thing we need. That'd be playing straight into the hands of the vampaneze.

"As for who Harkat is now..." Vancha studied the Little Person. "I know you and trust you. I believe you've learnt from Kurda's faults. You won't betray us again, will you, Harkat?"

"No," Harkat said softly. "But I'm still in favour of a treaty ... between the two clans. If I can help bring that about through peaceful ... means, by talking, I will. This War of the Scars is destroying ... both families of the night, and it threatens to destroy ... even more."

"But you recognize the need to fight?" Vancha said sharply.

"I recognize the need to kill Steve ... Leonard," Harkat said. "After that, I'll push for peace ... if I can. But openly — no plotting or intrigue ... this time."

Vancha considered that in silence, then shrugged. "So be it. I've nothing personal against the vampaneze. If we kill Leonard and they agree to a truce, I'm all for it. Now," he continued, scratching his chin, "where do you think Leonard's holed up?"

"Probably somewhere deep underground," I said.

"You think he's preparing a grand-scale trap, like before?" Vancha asked.

"No," Harkat said. "Vampaneze have been active here. That's why Debbie and Alice came. But if there were dozens of them, like ... the last time, the death count would be higher. I don't think Steve has as many ... vampaneze with him as when we faced him ... in the Cavern of Retribution."

"I hope you're right," Vancha said. He glanced at me sideways. "How did my brother look?" Vancha and Gannen Harst were estranged brothers.

"Tired," I said. "Strained. Unhappy."

"Not hard to imagine why," Vancha grunted. "I'll never understand why Gannen and the others follow a maniac like Leonard. The vampaneze were content the way they were. They didn't seek to crush the vampires or provoke a war. It makes no sense for them to flock to that demon and pledge themselves to him."

"It's part of Mr Tiny's prophecy," Harkat said. "As Kurda, I spent much time with ... the vampaneze, researching their ways. You know about their Coffin of Fire. When a person lies within, it fills ... with flames. All normal people die in it. Only the Lord of the Vampaneze ... can survive. Mr Tiny told the vampaneze that if they didn't ... obey that person and do all that he commanded, they'd ... be wiped from the face of the earth. Most of the vampaneze fight to preserve themselves ... not to destroy the vampires."

Vancha nodded slowly. "Then they're motivated by fear for their lives, not hatred of us. I understand now. After all, isn't that why we're fighting too — to save ourselves?"

"Both fighting for the same reason," Harkat chuckled humourlessly. "Both terrified of the ... same thing. Of course, if neither side fought … both would be safe. Mr Tiny is playing the creatures of the night … for fools, and we're helping him."

"Aye," Vancha grunted disgustedly. "But there's no use moaning about how we got ourselves into this sorry state. The fact is, we fight because we must."

Vancha stood and stretched. There were dark rims around his eyes. He looked like a man who hadn't slept properly for a very long time. The last two years must have been tough for him. Although he hadn't mentioned Mr Crepsley, I was sure the dead vampire was never far from his thoughts. Vancha, like I, probably felt a certain amount of guilt — the two of us had given Mr Crepsley the go-ahead to face the Vampaneze Lord. If either of us had taken his place, he'd be alive now. It looked to me like Vancha had been pushing himself to his limits in his hunt to find the Lord of the Vampaneze — and was rapidly nearing them.

"You should rest, Sire," I said. "If you flitted all the way here, you must be exhausted."

"I'll rest when Leonard is dead," Vancha grunted. "Or myself," he added softly, under his breath. I don't think he realized he'd spoken aloud. "Now!" Vancha said, raising his voice. "Enough self-pity and misery. We're here and Leonard's here — it doesn't take a genius to see that an old-fashioned scrap to the death's on the agenda. The question is, do we wait for him to come to us, or do we seize the initiative and go looking for him?"

"We wouldn't know where … to look," Harkat said. "He could be anywhere."

"So we look everywhere," Vancha grinned. "But where do we start? Darren?"

"His son," I said immediately. "Darius is an unusual name. There can't be too many of them. We ask around, find out where he lives, track Steve through him."

"Use the son to get to the father," Vancha hummed. "Ignoble, but probably the best way." He paused. "The boy worries me. Leonard's a nasty piece of work, a formidable foe. But if his son has the same evil blood, and has been trained in Leonard's wicked ways since birth, he could be even worse!"

"I agree," I said quietly.

"Can you kill a child, Darren?" Vancha asked.

"I don't know," I said, unable to meet his eyes. "I don't think so. Hopefully it won't come to that."

"It's no good hoping," Harkat objected. "Going after the boy is wrong. Just because Steve has no morals doesn't ... mean we should act like savages too. Children should be kept out ... of this."

"So what's your suggestion?" Vancha asked.

"We should return to the ... Cirque Du Freak," Harkat said. "Hibernius might be able to tell us more ... about what we should do. Even if he's unable to help, Steve knows ... where the Cirque is camped. He'll find us there. We can wait for him."

"I don't like the idea of being a sitting target," Vancha growled.

"You'd rather chase children?" Harkat countered.

Vancha stiffened, then relaxed. "Perhaps no-ears has a

point," he said. "It can certainly do no harm to ask Hibernius for his opinion."

"OK," I said. "But we'll wait for night — my eyes can't take the sun."

"So that's why your ears and nose are stuffed!" Vancha laughed. "The purge?"

"Yes. It struck a couple of days ago."

"Will you be able to pull your weight," Vancha asked directly, "or should we wait for it to pass?"

"I'll do my best," I said. "I can't make any guarantees, but I think I'll be OK."

"Very well." Vancha nodded at the ceiling. "What about the ladies? Do we tell them what we're up to?"

"Not all of it," I said. "We'll take them to the Cirque Du Freak and tell them we're hunting Steve. But let's not mention Darius — Debbie wouldn't think much of our plan to use a child."

Harkat snorted but said nothing. After that we called Debbie and Alice down and spent a peaceful afternoon eating, drinking and talking, swapping tales, laughing, relaxing. I noticed Vancha glancing around during quiet moments, as though looking for somebody. I dismissed it at the time, but I now know who he was looking for — *death*. Of us all, only Vancha sensed death in the room that day, its eternal gaze passing from one of us to the other, watching … waiting … choosing.

CHAPTER SIXTEEN

WHEN NIGHT fell, we departed. Declan and Little Kenny bid us farewell. They were settling down in the living room, mobile phones laid in front of them like swords. Debbie and Alice's vampirites had been scouring the town for traces of Steve and the other vampaneze since the massacre in the stadium. Declan and Little Kenny were to coordinate that search in the ladies' absence.

"You have our numbers," Alice said to Declan as we were leaving. "Call if you have anything to report, no matter how trivial it might seem."

"Will do," Declan grinned, saluting clumsily.

"Try not to get yourself shot this time," Little Kenny said to me, winking.

Alice and Debbie had a rented van. We piled in, Harkat and Vancha in the back, covered by several blankets. "If we're stopped and searched, you two will have to break free," Alice told them. "We'll act like we didn't know you were there. It'll be easier that way."

"You mean you'll act the innocent and string us out to dry," Vancha grunted.

"Exactly," Alice said.

Even though it was night and the moon was only half-full, I wore sunglasses. My eyes were especially sensitive that night, and I had a splitting headache. I was also wearing earplugs and had little balls of cotton wool stuffed up my nose.

"Maybe you should stay behind," Debbie said, noting my discomfort as Alice switched on the engine.

"I'm OK," I groaned, squinting against the glare of the headlights, wincing at the roaring grumble of the engine.

"We could walk," Alice said, "but we're more likely to be stopped and searched."

"I'm OK," I said again, hunching down in my seat. "Just don't blow the horn."

The drive to the old football stadium where the Cirque Du Freak was encamped was uneventful. We passed two security checkpoints, but were waved through at each. (I took my glasses off and removed the earplugs and cotton wool as we approached, so as not to arouse suspicion.) Alice parked outside the stadium. We let Harkat and Vancha out of the back and walked in.

A big smile broke across my face as the tents and caravans came into sight — it was good to be home. As we exited the tunnel and made for the campsite, we were spotted by a group of children playing on the outskirts.

One stood, studied us warily, then raced towards us, yelling, "Godfather! Godfather!"

"Not so loud!" I laughed, catching Shancus as he leapt up to greet me. I gave the snake-boy a welcome hug, then pushed him away — my skin was tingling as a result of the purge, and any form of contact was irritating.

"Why are you wearing sunglasses?" Shancus frowned. "It's night."

"You're so ugly, I can't bear to look at you without protection," I said.

"Very funny," he snorted, then reached up, picked the cotton wool out of my left nostril, examined it, stuck it back in, and said, "You're weird!" He looked behind me at Vancha, Debbie and Alice. "I remember you lot," he said. "But not very well. I was only a kid the last time I saw you." Smiling, I made the introductions. "Oh yeah," Shancus said when I told him Debbie's name. "You're Darren's bird."

I spluttered with embarrassment and blushed bright red. Debbie just smiled and said, "Am I, indeed? Who told you that?"

"I heard Mum and Dad talking about you. Dad knows you from when you first met Darren. He said Darren goes googly-eyed when you're around. He–"

"That's enough," I interrupted, wishing I could strangle him. "Why don't you show the ladies how you can stick your tongue up your nose?"

That distracted him, and he spent a couple of minutes showing off, telling Alice and Debbie about the act he performed on-stage with Evra. I caught Debbie smiling at me sideways. I smiled back weakly.

"Is Truska still with the show?" Vancha asked.

"Yes," Shancus said.

"I must look her up later," Vancha muttered, using a ball of spit to slick back his green hair. The ugly, dirty Prince fancied himself as something of a lady's man — even though no ladies ever agreed with him!

"Is Mr Tall in his van?" Harkat asked Shancus.

"I guess," Shancus said. Then he glanced at Debbie and Alice and straightened up. "Come with me," he said officiously. "I'll lead you to him."

All five of us fell in behind the snake-boy as he led us through the campsite. He kept up a running commentary, telling Debbie and Alice who the various tents and caravans belonged to, giving them a rundown of that night's coming show. As we neared Mr Tall's van, we passed Evra, Merla and Urcha. They had the family snakes out in big tubs of water and were carefully scrubbing them down. Evra was delighted to see me and rushed over to check that I was all right. "I wanted to come visit," he said, "but Hibernius told me it wasn't a good idea. He said I might be followed."

"The Cirque's being watched?" Vancha snapped, eyes narrowing.

"He didn't say so in as many words," Evra said. "But I've felt eyes on my back a few times recently, late at night when I've been wandering around. I'm not the only one. We've all been edgy here lately."

"Maybe we shouldn't have ... come back," Harkat said, worried.

"Too late now," Vancha huffed. "Let's go see what Hibernius has to say."

Merla grabbed Shancus as he made to lead the way again. "No you don't," she said. "You've a show to prepare for. You needn't expect me to groom your snake for you every time you want to go and play with your friends."

"Aw, Mum!" Shancus grumbled, but Merla stuck a sponge in Shancus's hand and dragged him over to the snake I'd bought for his birthday.

"I'll catch up with you later," I laughed, feeling sorry for him. "I'll show you my new scar, where I was shot."

"Another one?" Shancus groaned. He turned appealingly to Evra. "How come Darren gets all the excitement? Why can't I get into fights and have scars?"

"Your mother will scar your backside if you don't get busy on that snake," Evra responded, and winked at me over Shancus's head. "Drop by when you have time."

"I will," I promised.

We moved on. Mr Tall was waiting for us at his van. He was standing in the doorway, looking more impossibly towering than ever, eyes dark, face drawn. "I have been expecting you," he sighed, then stood aside and beckoned us in. As I passed him, a strange shiver ran down my spine. It took me a few seconds to realize what the sensation reminded me of — it was the same sort of feeling I got whenever I saw a dead person.

When we were all seated, Mr Tall closed the door, then sat on the floor in the middle of us, legs crossed neatly, huge bony hands resting on his knees. "I hope you do not think me rude for not visiting," he said to me. "I knew you would recover, and I had much to put in order here."

"That's OK," I smiled, taking off my sunglasses and putting them to one side.

"It is good to see you again, Vancha," Mr Tall said, and then welcomed Debbie and Alice.

"Now that the pleasantries are out of the way," Vancha grunted, "let's get down to business. You knew what was going to happen at the football arena, aye?"

"I had my suspicions," Mr Tall said cagily, his lips barely moving.

"But you let Darren go regardless? You let his friend die?"

"I did not 'let' anything happen," Mr Tall disagreed. "Events unfolded the way they had to. It is not my place to interfere in the unravelling of destiny. You know that, Vancha. We have had this conversation before. Several times."

"And I still don't buy it," Vancha grumbled. "If *I* had the power to see into the future, I'd use it to help those I cared about. You could have told us who the Lord of the Vampaneze was. Larten would be alive now if you'd warned us in advance."

"No," Mr Tall said. "Larten would have died. The circumstances might have differed, but his death was inevitable. I could not have altered that."

"You should still have tried," Vancha persisted.

Mr Tall smiled thinly, then looked at me. "You have come to seek guidance. You wish to know where your one-time friend, Steve Leonard, is."

"Can you tell us?" I asked softly.

"No," Mr Tall said. "But rest assured, he will make himself known soon. You will not have to dredge the depths for him."

"Does that mean he's going to attack?" Vancha pressed. "Is he nearby? When does he plan to strike? Where?"

"I grow weary of your questions," Mr Tall growled, his eyes flashing menacingly. "If I could step in and play an active part in the affairs of the vampire clan, I would. It is much harder to stand back and watch passively. Harder than you could ever imagine. You wept for Larten when he died — but *I* grieved for him for thirty years in advance, since glimpsing his probable death."

"You mean you didn't know for ... sure that he'd die?" Harkat asked.

"I knew he would come to the point where it was his life or the Lord of the Vampaneze's, but I could not see beyond that — though I feared the worst."

"And what of our next encounter?" I asked quietly. "When Vancha and I face Steve for the last time — who'll die then?"

"I do not know," Mr Tall said. "Looking into the future is more often than not a painful experience. It is better not to know the fate of your friends and loved ones. I lift the lid off the present as seldom as possible. There are times when I cannot avoid it, when my own destiny forces me to look. But only rarely."

"So you don't know if we'll win or lose?" I asked.

"Nobody knows that," Mr Tall said. "Not even Desmond Tiny."

"But *if* we lose," I said, and there was an edge to my voice now. "If the vampaneze are triumphant, and Steve kills one of us — which will it be?"

"I don't know," Mr Tall said.

"But you could find out," I pressed. "You could look into the future where we've lost and see which of us survived."

"Why should I?" Mr Tall sighed. "What profit would there be in it?"

"I want to know," I insisted.

"Maybe it would be better—" Vancha began to say.

"No!" I hissed. "I *must* know. For two years I've dreamt of the destruction of the clan, and listened to the screams of those who'll perish if we fail. If I'm to die, so be it. But tell me, please, so I can prepare myself for it."

"I cannot," Mr Tall said unhappily. "Nobody can predict which of you will kill the Vampaneze Lord — or die at his hand."

"Then look further ahead," I pleaded. "Go twenty years ahead, or thirty. Do you see Vancha or me in that future?"

"Leave me out of this!" Vancha snapped. "I don't want to mess about with stuff like that."

"Then just look for me," I said, staring hard at Mr Tall.

Mr Tall held my gaze, then said quietly, "You are sure?"

I stiffened. "Yes!"

"Very well." Mr Tall lowered his gaze and closed his eyes. "I cannot be as specific as you state, but I will cast my eyes a number of decades forward and..."

Mr Tall trailed off into silence. Vancha, Harkat, Debbie, Alice and I watched, awed, as his face twitched and glowed a light red colour. The owner of the Cirque Du Freak seemed to stop breathing and the temperature of the air dropped several degrees. For five minutes he held that pose, face glowing and twitching, lips sealed. Then he breathed out, the glow faded, his eyes opened and the temperature returned to normal.

"I have looked," he said, his expression unreadable.

"*And?*" I croaked.

"I did not find you there."

I smiled bitterly. "I knew it. If the clan falls, it will fall because of *me*. I'm the doomed one in the future where we lose."

"Not necessarily," Mr Tall said. "I looked fifty or sixty years ahead, long after the fall of the vampires. You might have died after all of the others had been killed."

"Then bring it forward," I demanded. "Look twenty or thirty years ahead."

"No," Mr Tall said stiffly. "I have already seen more than I wished. I don't want to suffer any further tonight."

"What are you talking about?" I huffed. "What have you suffered?"

"Grief," Mr Tall said. He paused, then glanced at Vancha. "I know you told me not to look for you, old friend, but I couldn't help myself."

Vancha cursed, then braced himself. "Go on. Since this fool's opened the can of worms, we might as well watch them wriggle. Hit me with the bad news."

"I looked into both futures," Mr Tall said hollowly. "I did not mean to, but I cannot control these things. I looked into the future where the vampaneze won the War of the Scars, and also into the future where the vampires won — and although I found Darren in the latter future, I found you in neither." He locked gazes with Vancha and muttered gloomily, "You were killed by the Lord of the Shadows in both."

CHAPTER SEVENTEEN

VANCHA BLINKED slowly. "You're saying I'll die whether we win or lose?" His voice was surprisingly steady.

"The Lord of the Shadows is destined to destroy you," Mr Tall replied. "I cannot say when or how it happens, but it will."

"Who's this Lord of the Shadows?" Harkat asked. I was the only person who'd been told about him. Evanna had warned me not to speak of it to anybody else.

"He's the cruel leader who will ruin the world after the War of the Scars," Mr Tall said.

"I don't get it," Harkat grumbled. "If we kill Steve, then there won't be a … Lord of the bloody Shadows."

"Oh, but there will," Mr Tall said. "The world is set to produce a monster of unimaginable power and fury. His coming is unavoidable. Only his identity is yet to be determined — and that will be decided shortly."

"The wasteworld," Harkat said sickly. "You mean, even if we kill Steve, that's what ... the future will be? The desolate land where Darren and I found ... out the truth about me — that's what lies ... in store?"

Mr Tall hesitated, then nodded. "I could not tell you before. I have never spoken of matters such as this in the past. But we are at the time where no harm can come of revealing it, since nothing can be done to avert it. The Lord of the Shadows is upon us — within twenty-four hours he will be born, and all the world will tremble at his coming."

There was a long, stunned silence. Vancha, Harkat, Debbie and Alice were filled with confusion, especially the latter pair, who knew nothing of the wasteworld of the future. *I* was filled with fear. This was confirmation of all my worst nightmares. The Lord of the Shadows would rise regardless of what happened in the War of the Scars. And not only could I not prevent his coming — in one of the futures, I would *be* him. Which meant, if we won the war, at some stage in the next fifty or sixty years, along with all the other lives I'd ruin, I would kill Vancha too. It seemed impossible. It sounded like a sick joke. But Evanna and Mr Tall both had the gift of reading the future — and both had told me the same thing.

"Let me get this straight," Vancha growled, breaking the silence and disrupting my train of thought. "No matter what happens between us and Steve Leonard – or in the war with the vampaneze – a Lord of the Shadows is going to come along and destroy the world?"

"Yes," Mr Tall said. "Humans are soon to lose control of this planet. The reins of power will be handed over. This is written. What remains to be seen is whether the reins pass to a vampaneze or ... to a vampire." He didn't look at me when he said that. It might have been my imagination, but I got the feeling he had deliberately avoided making eye contact with me.

"But regardless of who wins, I'm for the chop?" Vancha pressed.

"Yes." Mr Tall smiled. "But do not fear death, Vancha, for it comes for us all." His smile dimmed. "For some of us, it comes very soon."

"What are you talking about?" Vancha snapped. "You're not part of this. No vampire or vampaneze would raise a hand against you."

"That might be true," Mr Tall chuckled, "but there are others in this world who do not hold me in such high esteem." He cocked his head sideways and his expression mellowed. "And to prove my point..."

A woman screamed. We all sprang to our feet and rushed to the door, except Mr Tall, who slowly rose behind us.

Alice was first to the door. Flinging it open, she dived out, drew a gun, rolled when she hit the ground, then came to her knees. Vancha was next. He leapt out, pulling a couple of shurikens free, jumping high to launch them from a height if he had to. I was third. I had no weapons, so I sprang over to where Alice was, guessing she'd be able to supply me with something. Harkat and Debbie moved at the same time, Harkat brandishing his axe, Debbie pulling a pistol like Alice's. Behind them, Mr Tall stood in the doorway, gazing up at the sky. Then he stepped down.

There was nobody in sight, but we heard another scream, this time a child's. Then a man gave a shout of panic — it was Evra.

"A weapon!" I yelled at Alice as she got to her feet. With one hand she reached down and produced a short hunting knife from a pouch on her left leg.

"Stay behind me," Alice commanded, homing in on the screams. "Vancha to my left, Debbie and Harkat to my right."

We obeyed the ex-chief inspector, fanned out and advanced. I could sense Mr Tall following, but I didn't look back.

A woman screamed again — Merla, Evra's wife.

People spilt out of the caravans and tents around us, performers and staff, eager to help. Mr Tall roared at them to keep out of this. His voice was thunderous and they quickly bolted back inside. I glanced over my shoulder, stunned by his fierceness. He smiled apologetically. "This is our fight, not theirs," he said by way of explanation.

The "our" surprised me — was Mr Tall finally abandoning his neutrality? — but I hadn't time to dwell upon it. Ahead of me, Alice had cleared the end of a tent and come into sight of the disturbance. A second later, I was on the scene too.

The Vons — except Lilia, who wasn't present — were under attack. Their assailants — R.V., Morgan James and

Steve Leopard's son, Darius! R.V. had killed Evra's snake and was in the process of chopping up Shancus's. Evra was fighting with the hook-handed madman, trying to drag him off. Shancus was in a wrestling lock with Darius. Merla had hold of Urcha, who was gripping his snake for dear life, sobbing pitifully. They were backing away from Morgan James. He was following slowly, smiling a jagged half-faced smile, red circles of blood highlighting his evil little eyes. The nose of his rifle was aimed at Merla's stomach.

Vancha reacted quickest. He sent a shuriken flying at Morgan James's rifle, knocking it off-target. James's finger tightened on the trigger at the contact and the rifle exploded — but the bullet shot wide. Before he could fire again, Merla released Urcha, ripped her right ear loose, and sent it flying at James's face. The ear struck him between the eyes and he fell back, grunting with surprise.

Alerted to our presence, R.V. knocked Evra out of the way and drove after Shancus. He grabbed him from Darius and held him up, laughing, daring us to risk the snake-boy's life.

"I don't have a clear shot!" Alice yelled.

"I've got Morgan James covered!" Debbie shouted back.

"Then take him out!" Alice roared.

"The boy dies if you hurt Morgan!" R.V. retorted, pressing the three blades of his hooked left hand up into the scaly flesh of Shancus's throat. Shancus either didn't realize the danger he was in, or didn't care, because he kept kicking and punching R.V. But we saw the killer's intent and paused.

"Let him go, Hooky," Vancha snarled, moving ahead of the rest of us, hands spread wide. "I'll fight you man to man."

"You're no man," R.V. replied scornfully. "You're scum, like all your race. Morgan! Are you OK?"

"Uh'm fuhn," Morgan James groaned. He picked up his rifle and aimed it at Merla again.

"Not this time!" Harkat shouted, stepping in front of Merla and swinging at James with his axe. James leapt clear of the deadly blade. Across from him, Darius drew a small arrow-gun and fired at Harkat. But he fired too hastily and the arrow flew high of its mark.

I threw myself at Darius, meaning to grab and hold him, as R.V. was holding Shancus. But Shancus's snake was thrashing wildly in its death throes, and I tripped over it before I could bring my hands together around Darius's throat. Flying forward, I crashed into Evra, who was rushing to his son's aid. We both fell over, wrapped in the dying snake's coils.

During the confusion, Morgan James and Darius re-grouped around R.V.

Alice, Debbie, Harkat and Vancha hung back, unable to pursue them for fear that R.V. would kill Shancus.

"Let him go!" Merla screamed, eyes filled with tears of desperation.

"Make me!" R.V. jeered.

"You can't get out of here," Vancha said as R.V. backed away.

"Who's going to stop us?" R.V. mocked him.

Evra was back on his feet and he made to run after the retreating trio. R.V. dug his hooks deeper into Shancus's throat. "No you don't!" he sang, and Evra froze.

"Please," Debbie said, lowering her pistol. "Release the boy and we'll let you leave unharmed."

"You're in no position to make deals," R.V. laughed.

"What do you want?" I shouted.

"The snake-boy," R.V. giggled.

"He's no good to you." I took a determined step forward. "Take me instead. I'll swap for Shancus."

I expected R.V. to leap at my offer, but he only shook his head slyly, red eyes shining. "Stuff it, Shan," he said. "We're taking the boy. If you get in our way, he dies."

I glanced around at my allies — nobody was reacting. The vampaneze had us in a bind. Vancha could move with the speed of a full-vampire, and Debbie and Alice both had guns. But R.V. could kill Shancus before any of us could stop him.

R.V., Morgan James and Darius continued to back away. R.V. and James were grinning, but Darius looked the same way he'd looked after shooting me — scared and slightly sickened.

Then, as the rest of us hesitated, Mr Tall spoke. "I cannot allow this."

R.V. paused uncertainly. "This is none of your business!" he shouted. "Keep your nose out of it."

"You have made it my business," Mr Tall disagreed quietly. "This is my home. These are my people. I must intervene."

"Don't be a—" R.V. yelled, but before he got any further, Mr Tall was upon him. He moved at a supernatural speed which even a vampire couldn't match. In less than a flash of an eye he was in front of R.V., his hands on the lunatic's hooks. He wrenched them away from Shancus's throat, tore two of the hooks off the left hand, and one off the right.

"My hands!" R.V. screamed in agony, as though the gold and silver hooks were part of his flesh. "Leave my hands alone, you—"

Whatever foul name he shouted was lost in the burst of a gun retort. Morgan James, who'd been standing next to R.V., had jammed the tip of his rifle hard into Mr Tall's ribs and pulled the trigger. A bullet fired down the chamber of the rifle at a merciless speed — then ripped through the ribcage of the defenceless Hibernius Tall!

CHAPTER EIGHTEEN

MR TALL'S midriff erupted in a fountain of dark red blood and white chips of bone. For a moment he stood, gripping R.V.'s hooks, as though nothing had happened. Then he collapsed, blood pumping out of the hole, his stomach torn to shreds.

R.V. and Darius stared numbly at Mr Tall as he fell. Then Morgan James screamed at them to run. In a ragged unit they fled, R.V. clutching Shancus, James firing wildly at us over his shoulder.

Nobody followed. Our eyes were all on Mr Tall. He was blinking rapidly, hands exploring the hole in his middle, lips torn back over his small black teeth. I don't think anybody knew how old Mr Tall was, or where he'd come from. But he was older than any vampire, a being of immense magic and power. It was mind-boggling to think that he could have been brought low in so simple and violent a manner.

Debbie snapped to her senses first and rushed towards Mr Tall, dropping her pistol, meaning to go to his aid. The rest of us took a step after her—

—and stopped instantly when somebody spoke from the shadows of a nearby van. "Your concern is commendable, but utterly worthless. Keep back, please."

A small man waddled forward, smiling glibly. He was dressed in a sharp yellow suit and green Wellington boots. He had white hair, thick glasses, and a heart-shaped watch which he was twirling in his left hand. *Desmond Tiny!* Behind him came his daughter, the witch, Evanna — short, muscular, hairy, clad in ropes instead of clothes. She had a small nose, pointed ears, a thin beard, and mismatched eyes, one brown, one green.

We gawped at the strange pair as they stopped beside the gasping Mr Tall and gazed down at him. Evanna's face was strained. Mr Tiny looked only curious. With his right foot, he nudged Mr Tall where he'd been shot. Mr Tall hissed with pain.

"Leave him alone!" Debbie shouted.

"Shut up, please, or I'll kill you," Mr Tiny replied. Though he said it sweetly, I've no doubt he would have struck Debbie down dead if she'd said another word. Fortunately, she realized that too, and she held her tongue, trembling.

"So, Hibernius," Mr Tiny said. "Your time here comes to an end."

"You knew it would," Mr Tall replied, and his voice was remarkably firm.

"Yes," Mr Tiny nodded. "But did *you* know?"

"I guessed."

"You could have turned aside from it. Your fate was never directly linked to these mortals."

"For me, it was," Mr Tall said. He was shivering badly, a dark pool of blood spreading out around him. Evanna took a step aside to avoid the blood, but Mr Tiny let it flow around his boots, staining the soles.

"Tiny!" Vancha snapped. "Can you save him?"

"No," Mr Tiny replied simply. Then he bent over Mr Tall and spread the fingers of his right hand. He placed his middle finger in the centre of Mr Tall's forehead, the adjoining fingers over his eyes, and held the thumb and little finger out at the sides. "Even in death, may you be triumphant," he said with surprising softness then removed his fingers.

"Thank you, Father," Mr Tall said. He glanced up at Evanna. "Goodbye, Sister."

"I will remember you," the witch answered as the rest of us looked on, stunned by the revelation. I'd known about Evanna's twin brother, born, as she was, of a union between Mr Tiny and a wolf. I'd just never guessed it was Mr Tall.

Evanna bent and kissed her brother's forehead. Mr Tall smiled, then his body shook, his eyes went wide, his neck stiffened — and he died.

Mr Tiny stood and turned. There was one round tear of blood in the corner of each eye. "My son is dead," he said, in the same tone he'd have used to comment on the weather.

"We didn't know!" Vancha gasped.

"He never cared to speak of his parentage." Mr Tiny chuckled and kicked the dead Mr Tall's head aside with the heel of his left foot. "I don't know why."

I growled when he kicked Mr Tall, and started towards him angrily. Harkat and Vancha did the same.

"Gentlemen," Evanna said quietly. "If you waste time picking a fight with my father, the killers will escape with the young Von boy."

We stopped short. I'd momentarily forgotten about Shancus and the danger he was in. The others had too. Now that we'd been reminded, we shook our heads and snapped out of our daze.

"We have to chase them," Vancha said.

"But what about Mr Tall?" Debbie cried.

"He's dead," Vancha sniffed. "Let his *family* care for him."

Mr Tiny laughed at that, but we couldn't afford to pay him any further heed. Grouping together without discussing it, the five of us set off. "Wait!" Evra shouted. I looked back and saw him exchange a wordless look with Merla. She half-nodded and he ran after us. "I'm coming too," he said.

Nobody argued. Accepting Evra into our ranks, we raced away from Merla, Urcha, Mr Tiny, Evanna and the dead Mr Tall, and hurried through the campsite in pursuit of Shancus and his kidnappers.

As soon as we cleared the tunnel leading out of the stadium, we saw that our quarry had split. To our right,

R.V. was running away with Shancus, headed into the heart of town. To our left, Morgan James and Darius fled down the hill towards a river which flowed close by the stadium.

Vancha took charge and made a swift decision. "Alice and Evra — with me. We'll go after R.V. and Shancus. Darren, Harkat and Debbie — take Morgan James and the boy."

I'd rather have gone to Shancus's rescue, but Vancha was more experienced than me. Nodding obediently, I swung left with Harkat and Debbie and we set off after the killer and his apprentice. My headache had flared up savagely and I was half-blind as I flailed down the hill. Also, the sounds of my feet on the pavement as I ran were torture on my ears. Still, as a half-vampire I could run faster than Harkat or Debbie, and I'd soon pulled ahead and was rapidly closing the gap on Morgan James and Darius.

James and Darius stopped when they heard me coming and spun to face my charge. I should have waited for Harkat and Debbie, rather than face them on my own, armed only with a knife. But rage had taken hold of me. I forged on heedlessly as they fired, James with his rifle, Darius with his arrow-gun. By the luck of the vampires, their bullets and arrows missed, and seconds later I was upon them, wild with fury, intent on revenge.

James swung at me with the butt of his rifle. It struck my right shoulder, where I'd been shot by Darius. I roared with pain but didn't falter. I stabbed at James with my knife, aiming for his half-mangled face. He ducked, and Darius punched me in the ribs as I slid past. I swatted the boy aside and stabbed at James again. He laughed and grabbed me tight, wrestling me to the ground.

My face was pressed up close to the left side of Morgan James's head. The skin was wrinkled and red, his teeth exposed behind the thin flesh of his lips, his eye a horrible glob in the middle of a ruined, scarred mess.

"Lyhk iht?" James gurgled.

"Lovely!" I sneered, rolling on top of him, poking for his eyes with my thumbs.

"Uh'm gonna duh the shahm tuh yuh!" James vowed, breaking my grip and driving his knee up into my stomach.

"We'll see!" I grunted, falling away slightly, then coming back at him. I managed to stick my knife in, but only into his arm. I was aware of the boy battering me with his arrow-gun, trying to beat me off. I ignored him and focused on Morgan James. I was stronger than the vampet, but he was larger and a seasoned fighter. He wriggled beneath me, digging his knees and elbows into the flesh of my stomach and groin, spitting into my eyes. There was a painful white light building inside my head. I felt like screaming and clapping my hands over my ears. But instead I bit into the flesh of James's upper left arm and ripped a chunk away.

James screeched like a cat and shoved me off, lent strength by his pain. As I fell aside, Darius kicked me hard in the head and I lost my bearings for a second or two. When I recovered, James was on top of me. He pushed my head back with his left hand and brought up my own knife – which I'd dropped in the fight – with his right, meaning to slit my throat.

I grabbed for the knife. Missed. Grabbed again. Knocked it aside. Grabbed a third time — then stopped, tensed my muscles and shut my eyes. James gave a little shiver of delight. He thought I'd given up. What he didn't realize was that I'd caught sight of Harkat behind him, swinging his axe.

There was a whishing sound — Darius started to shout a warning — then a heavy thud. My eyes opened. I caught a glimpse of Morgan James's head rolling away into darkness, severed from its body by one powerful blow of Harkat's axe. Then blood gushed from the stump of James's neck. I shut my eyes again as I was drenched in a burst of hot red liquid. James fell over lifelessly. I pushed myself up, opened my eyes, wiped blood from my face, and slid out from beneath the beheaded body of Morgan James.

Darius was standing next to me, staring numbly at his felled companion. Blood had hit the boy also, drenching his trousers. I stood. My legs were trembling. My head was filled with white noise. Blood congealed in my hair and dripped from my face. I wanted to be sick. But I knew what I must do. Hatred motivated me.

Snatching my knife back from Morgan James's lifeless hand, I pressed the blade to the flesh of Darius's throat and grabbed his hair with my free hand. I was snarling as I pressed down hard on the knife, neither human nor vampire. I'd become a savage animal set on taking a young boy's life.

CHAPTER NINETEEN

DEBBIE STOPPED me. "*No!*" she screamed, racing up behind me. There was such terror in her voice, that even in the midst of my bloodlust, I paused. She pulled up beside me, panting hard, eyes wide with horror. "No!" she wheezed, shaking her head desperately.

"Why not?" I snarled.

"He's a child!" she cried.

"No — he's Steve Leopard's son," I contradicted her. "A killer, like his father."

"He hasn't killed anyone," Debbie objected. "Morgan James killed Mr Tall. Now he's dead, you're even. You don't have to kill the boy too."

"I'll kill them all!" I screamed madly. It was like I'd become a different person, a bloodthirsty reaper. "Every vampaneze must die! Every vampet! Everyone who aids them!"

"Even the children?" Debbie asked sickly.

"Yes!" I roared. My headache was the worst it had ever been. It was like red-hot pins were being pushed through my skull from the inside out. Part of me knew this was wrong, but a larger part had seized on the hatred and urge to kill. That merciless part was screaming for revenge.

"Harkat," Debbie appealed to the Little Person. "Make him see sense!"

Harkat shook his neckless head. "I don't think I can stop him," he said, staring at me as if he didn't know me.

"You have to try!" Debbie shrieked.

"I don't know if I ... have the right," Harkat muttered.

Debbie turned to me again. She was crying. "You mustn't do this," she wept.

"It's my duty," I said stiffly.

She spat at my feet. "That's what I think of your *duty*! You'll become a monster if you kill that boy. You'll be no better than Steve."

I stopped. Her words had sparked a memory deep within me. I found myself thinking about Mr Crepsley and his last words to me before he died. He warned me not to devote my life to hatred. Kill Steve Leopard if the chance presented itself — but don't give myself over to some insane revenge quest.

What would he have done in my place? Kill the boy? Yes, if necessary. But *was* it? Did I want to kill Darius because I feared him and felt he had to be eliminated for the good of us all — or because I wanted to hurt Steve?

I gazed into the boy's eyes. They were fearful, but behind the fear there was ... sorrow. In Steve's eyes, evil lurked deep down. Not in Darius. He was more human than his father.

My knife was still pressed to his throat. It had sliced thinly into his flesh. Little rivulets of blood trickled down his neck.

"You'll destroy yourself," Debbie whispered hoarsely. "You'll be worse than Steve. *He* can't tell the difference between right and wrong. *You* can. He can live with his wickedness because he doesn't know any better, but it will eat you away. Don't do it, Darren. We don't wage war on children."

I stared at her, tears in my eyes. I knew she was right. I wanted to take the knife away. I couldn't believe I'd even tried to kill the boy. But still there was part of me that wanted to take his life. Something had awoken within me, a Darren Shan I'd never known existed, and he wasn't going to lie down without a fight. My fingers shook as they held the knife, but the furious angel of revenge inside me wouldn't let me lower them.

"Go ahead and kill me," Darius snarled suddenly. "It's what your kind does. You're murderers. I know all about you, so stop pretending you give a damn."

"What are you talking about?" I said. He only smiled sickly in reply.

"He's Steve's son," Debbie said softly. "He's been raised on lies. That's not his fault."

"My father doesn't lie!" Darius shouted.

Debbie moved around behind Darius so she could look me straight in the eye. "He doesn't know the truth. He's innocent, in spite of anything he's been tricked into doing. Don't kill an innocent, Darren. Don't become that which you despise."

I groaned deeply. More than ever I wanted to take the knife away, but still I wavered, fighting an inner battle which I didn't completely understand. "I don't know what to do!" I moaned.

"Then think of this," Harkat said. "We might need the boy to swap ... for Shancus. It makes sense not to kill him."

The fire within me died away. I lowered the knife, feeling a great weight lift from my heart. I smiled crookedly. "Thanks, Harkat."

"You shouldn't have needed that," Debbie said as I spun Darius around and tied his hands behind him with a strip of cloth which Harkat had ripped from his robes. "You should have spared him because it was the right thing to do — not because you might need him."

"Maybe," I agreed, ashamed of my reaction but not wanting to admit it. "But it doesn't matter. We can debate it later. First, let's find out what's happening with Shancus. Where's your phone?"

A minute later she was deep in conversation with Alice Burgess. They were still in pursuit of R.V. and Shancus. Vancha asked to speak to me. "We've a choice to make," he said. "I have R.V. in my sights. I can cut him down with a shuriken and rescue Shancus."

"Then why don't you?" I frowned.

"I think he's leading us to Steve Leonard," Vancha said.

I groaned softly and gripped the phone tightly. "What does Evra say?" I asked.

"This is our call, not his," Vancha responded with a whisper. "He's thinking only of his son. We have other concerns to consider."

"I'm not prepared to sacrifice Shancus to get to Steve," I said.

"I am," Vancha said quietly. "But I doubt it will come to that. I think we can retrieve the boy *and* get a shot at Leonard. But it's a risk. If you want me to play it safe and kill R.V. now, I will. But I believe we should chance it, let him lead us to Leonard, and take it from there."

"You're the senior Prince," I said. "You decide."

"No," Vancha retorted. "We're equals. Shancus means more to you than he does to me. I'll follow your lead in this one."

"Thanks," I said bitterly.

"Sorry," Vancha said, and even over the phone I could tell his regret was genuine. "I'd take responsibility if I could, but on this occasion I can't. Do I kill R.V. or follow?"

My eyes flicked to Darius. If I'd killed him, I'd have told Vancha to bring R.V. down and save Shancus — otherwise Steve would surely slaughter the snake-boy in revenge. But if I turned up with Darius captive, Steve would have to trade. Once we had Shancus back, we'd be free to pursue Steve later.

"OK," I said. "Let him run. Tell me where you are and we'll catch up."

A few minutes later we were on the move again, cutting across town, Debbie on the phone to Alice, taking directions. I could feel her eyes burning into my back — she didn't approve of the risk we were taking — but I didn't look around. As I ran, I kept reminding myself, "I'm a Prince. I have a duty to my people. The Lord of the Vampaneze takes priority over all." But it was a slim comfort, and I knew my sense of guilt and shame would be overwhelming if the gamble backfired.

CHAPTER TWENTY

WE WERE hurrying through the streets with Darius, taking back alleys to avoid the police patrols, when Harkat slowed, came to a stop and turned. He cocked his head sideways, raising one of the ears stitched beneath his grey skin.

"What is it?" I asked.

"Footsteps ... behind us. Can't you hear?"

"My ears are plugged up," I reminded him. "Are you certain?"

"Yes. I think it's just one person, but I ... could be wrong."

"We can't fight and hold on to Darius at the same time," Debbie said. "If we're to make a stand, we should either tie him up or let him go."

"I'm not letting him go anywhere," I muttered. "You two proceed. If R.V. leads the others to Steve, you need to be there with Darius, to trade for Shancus. I'll stay and deal with this. If I can, I'll catch you up."

"Don't be stupid," Debbie hissed. "We've got to stick together."

"Do what I say!" I snapped, harsher than necessary. I was very confused — hatred for Steve, fear that I might become the monstrous Lord of the Shadows, the pain of the purge — and in no mood to argue.

"Come on," Harkat said to Debbie. "We can't talk to him when he's ... like this. Besides, he's right. It makes more sense this way."

"But the danger—" Debbie began.

"He's a Vampire Prince," Harkat said. "He knows all about danger."

Harkat jerked Darius ahead, limping forward as quickly as he could. Debbie had no choice but to follow, though she looked back imploringly at me before turning a corner out of sight. I felt sorry for the way I'd snapped at her, and hoped I'd have a chance to apologize later.

I removed the cotton buds from my ears and nose and took a firm grip on my knife. By concentrating hard, I could dim the noise within my head and focus on the street sounds and scents. I heard footsteps approaching, soft, steady, coming straight towards me. I crouched low and readied myself for battle. Then a figure came into sight and I relaxed, stood and lowered my knife arm.

"Evanna," I greeted the witch.

"Darren," she replied calmly, stopping close by, studying me with an unreadable expression.

"Why aren't you with your father?" I asked.

"I will join him again presently," she said. "My place is here now, with you and your allies. Let us hurry after them, for fear we miss the confrontation."

"I'm going nowhere," I said, standing my ground. "Not until you give with some answers."

"Indeed?" Evanna purred archly. "I will need to hear some questions first."

"It's about the Lord of the Shadows."

"I don't think this is the time—"

"I don't care what you think!" I interrupted. "You told me years ago that the Lord of the Shadows would be either the Vampaneze Lord — Steve — or *me*. Mr Tall, before he died, said that the Lord of the Shadows would rise no matter who won the War of the Scars."

"Did he?" Evanna sounded surprised. "It was not like Hibernius to be so revealing. He was always the more secretive one."

"I want to know what it means," I pressed on, before she got sidetracked talking about her dead brother. "According to Mr Tall, the Lord of the Shadows will be a monster, and he'll kill Vancha."

"He told you that too?" Evanna was angry now. "He went too far. He should not have—"

"But he did," I stopped her, then took a step nearer. "He was wrong. He must have been. You too. I'm no monster. I would never harm Vancha, or any vampire."

"Don't be too sure of that," she said softly, then hesitated, choosing her next words carefully. "Usually, there are many paths between the present and future, dozens of options and outcomes. But sometimes there are only a few, or even just two. That is the case here. A Lord of the Shadows will come — this is definite. But he can be one of two people, you or Steve Leonard."

"But—" I began.

"Silence," she said commandingly. "Since we are so close to the time of choosing, I can reveal certain facts which before I could not. I wouldn't have spoken of this, but it seems my brother wished to inform you of your fate, perhaps to give you time to prepare for it. It is only right that I honour his final wishes.

"If you kill Steve Leonard, you *will* become a monster, the most despised and twisted the world has ever seen." My eyes bulged and I opened my mouth to protest, but she continued before I uttered a syllable. "Monsters are not born fully developed. They grow, they mature, they *become*.

"You are filling with hatred, Darren, hatred which will consume you. If you kill Steve, it will not be enough. You'll push on, driven by rages you cannot control. Because destiny has marked you out as a bearer of great power, you will create great havoc. You will destroy the vampaneze but that won't be enough. There will always be a new enemy to fight. During your quest, certain vampires will try to stop you. They too will die at your hands. Vancha will be one of them."

"No," I moaned. "I would never—"

"Not only vampires will obstruct you," Evanna went on, ignoring my protests. "Humans will interfere, leading you to turn against them. And, as the vampaneze and vampires fall at your hands, so will humanity. You will reduce this world to rubble and ash. And over the remains you will rule, all-powerful, all-controlling, all-hating, for the rest of your unnaturally long and evil life."

She stopped and smiled at me witheringly. "That is your future, where you taste success. In the other, you die at the hands of the alternate Lord of the Shadows, if not during the hunt for him, then later, when the rest of the clan has fallen. In many ways, that might be for the best. Now, have you any more questions?"

"I couldn't," I said numbly. "I wouldn't. There must be some way to avoid it."

"There is," Evanna said. She turned and pointed back the way she'd come. "Go. Walk away. Leave your friends. Hide. If you go now, you'll break the terms of your destiny. Steve will lead the vampaneze to victory over the vampires and become the Lord of the Shadows. You can lead a normal, peaceful life — until he brings the world crashing down around you, of course."

"But ... I can't do that," I said. "I can't turn my back on those who've put their trust in me. What about Vancha, Debbie, Shancus? I have to help them."

"Yes," Evanna said sadly. "I know. That is why you cannot escape. You have the power to run from your destiny, but your feelings for your friends won't allow you. You'll never retreat from a challenge. You can't. And so, even though you have the best will in the world, you'll see your destiny through to its bitter end — either death by Steve's hand, or a rise to infamy as the Lord of the Shadows."

"You're wrong," I said shakily. "I won't do that. I'm not evil. Now that I know, I won't let myself go down that road. If I kill Steve ... if we win ... I'll turn my back on my destiny then. I'll save the clan if I can, then slip away. I'll go where I can't do any harm."

"No," Evanna said simply. "You won't. Now," she went on before I could argue my case again, "let us hurry after your friends — this night is central to the future, and it would not do to miss a moment more of it." With that, she slid ahead of me and followed after the others, tracking them by means of her own, leaving me to trail behind, silent, dejected, bewildered — and terrified.

We caught up with Debbie, Harkat and Darius after several minutes. They were surprised to see Evanna, but she said nothing to them, just hung back and observed us silently. As we progressed, Debbie asked me if I'd been talking with Evanna. I shook my head, unwilling to repeat what I'd been told, still trying to make sense of it and convince myself that Evanna was wrong.

We regrouped with Vancha and Evra a quarter of an hour later. They'd tracked R.V. to a building and were waiting outside for us. "He went in a few minutes ago," Vancha said. "Alice has gone around the back, in case he tries to escape that way." He glanced at Evanna suspiciously. "Are you here to help or hinder, my Lady?"

"Neither, my Prince," she smiled. "I serve merely as a witness."

"Hurm!" he grunted.

I stared up at the building. It was tall and dark, with jagged grey stones and broken windows. There were nine steps leading up to the oversized front door. The steps were cracked and covered with moss. Apart from some more moss and broken windows, it hadn't changed much since my last visit.

"I know this place," I told Vancha, trying to forget about my conversation with Evanna and focus on the business at hand. "It's an old cinema theatre. This is where the Cirque Du Freak performed when Steve and I were kids. I should have guessed this was where he'd come. It brings everything full circle. Stuff like that is important to a maniac like Steve."

"You shut up about my dad!" Darius growled.

"You think Leonard's inside?" Vancha asked, cuffing Darius around the ear.

"I'm sure of it," I said, wiping streaks of Morgan James's blood from my forehead — there'd been no time to mop myself clean.

"What about Shancus?" Evra hissed. He was trembling with anxiety. "Will he harm my son?"

"Not as long as we hold *his* son captive," I said.

Evra stared at Darius, confused — he knew nothing about the boy — but my old friend trusted me, so he accepted my guarantee.

"How should we play this?" Debbie asked.

"Just march straight in," I said.

"Is that wise?" Vancha asked. "Perhaps we should try to sneak up on them from the back, or via the roof."

"Steve's prepared this for us," I said. "Anything we can think of, you can bet he's already considered. We can't out-guess him. We'd be fools to try. I say we go in, face him directly, and pray that the luck of the vampires is with us."

"The luck of the damned," Darius sneered. "You won't beat my father or any vampaneze. We're more than a match for the likes of you."

Vancha studied Darius curiously. He leant up close, sniffing like a dog. Then he made a small cut on the boy's right arm — Darius didn't even wince — dabbed a finger in the blood that oozed out, and tasted it. He pulled a face. "He's been blooded."

"By my father," Darius said proudly.

"He's a half-vampaneze?" I frowned, glancing at his fingertips — they were unmarked.

"The blood's weak within him," Vancha said. "But he's one of them. There's just enough blood in his system to ensure he can never regain his humanity."

"Did you volunteer for this, or did Steve force you?" I asked Darius.

"My father wouldn't force me to do anything!" Darius snorted. "Like every vampaneze, he believes in free choice — not like you lot."

Vancha looked at me questioningly. "Steve's fed him a load of rubbish about us," I explained. "He thinks we're evil, and his father's a noble crusader."

"He is!" Darius shouted. "He'll stop you from taking over the world! He won't let you kill freely! He'll keep the night safe from you vampire scum!"

Vancha cocked an amused eyebrow at me. "If we had time, I'd take great delight in setting this boy straight. But we haven't. Debbie — phone Alice and tell her to come here. We'll go in together — all for one and all that guff."

While Debbie was on the phone, Vancha pulled me aside and nodded at Evra, who was standing a few metres ahead of us, gazing at the entrance to the cinema, fingers twisted into desperate fists. "He's in a bad way," Vancha said.

"Of course," I muttered. "How would you expect him to react?"

"Are you clear on what we must do?" Vancha responded. I stared at him coldly. He grabbed my arms and squeezed tight. "Leonard *must* be killed. You and I are expendable. So are Debbie, Alice, Harkat, Evra — and Shancus."

"I want to save him," I said miserably.

"So do I," Vancha sighed. "And we will, if we can. But the Lord of the Vampaneze comes first. Remember what happens if we fail — the vampires will be destroyed. Would you trade the snake-boy's life for all those of our clan?"

"Of course not," I said, shaking myself free. "But I won't abandon him cheaply. If Steve's prepared to deal, I'll deal. We can fight him some other night."

"And if he won't deal?" Vancha pressed. "If he forces a showdown?"

"Then we'll fight, and we'll kill or we'll die — whatever the cost." I locked gazes with him so he could see I was telling the truth.

Vancha checked his shurikens and drew a few. Then we turned, gathered our allies around us — Debbie dragged Darius along — and advanced up the steps and into the old abandoned cinema theatre where, for me, all those years ago, the nightmares had begun.

CHAPTER TWENTY-ONE

IT WAS like stepping back into the past. The building was cooler and damper than before, and fresh graffiti had been scrawled across the walls, but otherwise it was no different. I led the way down the long corridor where Mr Tall had sneaked up on Steve and me, appearing out of the darkness with that incredible speed and silence which had been his trademark. A left turn at the end. I noted the spot where Mr Tall had taken and eaten our tickets. Back then, blue curtains had been draped across the entrance to the auditorium. There were no curtains tonight — the only change.

We entered the auditorium, two abreast, Vancha and Alice in front, Debbie and Evra next (Debbie pushing Darius in front of her), then Harkat and I. Evanna drifted along further back, detached from us by distance and attitude.

It was completely black inside the auditorium. I couldn't see anything. But I could hear deep, muffled breathing, coming from somewhere far ahead of us. "Vancha," I whispered.

"I know," he whispered back.

"Should we move towards it?" I asked.

"No," he replied. "It's too dark. Wait."

A minute passed. Two. Three. I could feel the tension rising, both in myself and those around me. But nobody broke rank or spoke. We stood in the darkness, waiting, leaving the first move to our foes.

Several minutes later, without warning, spotlights were switched on overhead. Everyone gasped and I cried out loud, hunching over, covering my extra-sensitive eyes with my hands. We were defenceless for a few vital seconds. That would have been the ideal time for an attack. I expected vampaneze and vampets to fall upon us, weapons flashing — but nothing happened.

"Are your eyes OK?" Debbie asked, crouching beside me.

"Not really," I groaned, slowly raising my eyelids a fraction, just enough to see out of. Even that was agony.

Holding a hand over my eyes, I squinted ahead and caught my breath. It was a good job we hadn't advanced. The entire floor of the auditorium had been torn out. In its place, spreading from one wall to the other, running from a few metres ahead of us all the way to the foot of the stage, was a giant pit, filled with sharpened stakes.

"Impressive, isn't it?" someone called from the stage. My eyes lifted. It was hard to see, because the lights were being trained on us from above the stage, but I gradually brought the scene into focus. Dozens of tall, thick logs dotted the stage, placed vertically, ideal cover. Sticking out from behind one log near the front was the grinning face of Steve Leopard.

When Vancha saw Steve, he drew a shuriken and threw it at him. But Steve had picked his spot carefully and the throwing star ended up buried in the wood of the log behind which he was standing.

"Bad luck, Sire," Steve laughed. "Care to make it the best throw out of three?"

"Maybe I can get him," Alice muttered, stepping up past Vancha. She raised her pistol and fired, but the bullet penetrated no deeper than the shuriken.

"Is that the preliminaries out of the way, or do you want to take a few more pot shots?" Steve called.

"I could possibly leap the pit," Vancha said dubiously, studying the rows of stakes between him and the stage.

"Don't be ridiculous," I grunted. Even vampires had their limits.

"I don't see anybody else," Debbie whispered, casting her eyes around the auditorium. The balcony above us — from where I'd spied on Steve and Mr Crepsley — could have been swarming with vampaneze and vampets, but I didn't think so — I could hear nothing overhead, not even a single heartbeat.

"Where's your army?" Vancha shouted at Steve.

"Around and about," Steve replied sweetly.

"Didn't you bring them with you?" Vancha challenged him.

"Not tonight," Steve said. "I don't need them. The only people sharing the stage with me are my fairy godfather —

a.k.a. Gannen Harst — a certain Righteous Vampaneze, and a very scared young snake-boy. What's his name again, R.V.?"

"Shancus," came the reply from behind a log to Steve's left.

"Shancus!" Evra roared. "Are you all right?"

There was no reply. My heart sank. Then R.V. pushed Shancus out from behind the log, and we saw that although his hands were tied behind his back, and he was gagged, he was still very much alive, and he looked unharmed.

"He's a spirited lad," Steve laughed. "A bit loud though, hence the gag. Some of the language he uses... Shocking! I don't know where kids today pick up such filthy words." Steve paused. "By the way, how's my own beloved flesh and blood doing? I can't see too well from here."

"I'm fine, Dad!" Darius shouted. "But they killed Morgan! The grey one cut off his head with an axe!"

"How grisly." Steve didn't sound the least bit upset. "I told you they were savages, son. No respect for life."

"It was revenge!" Harkat yelled. "He killed Mr Tall."

There was silence on the stage. Steve seemed lost for words. Then, from a log close by Steve, I heard Gannen Harst call out to R.V., "Is this true?"

"Yes," R.V. mumbled. "He shot him."

"How do you know he killed him?" Steve asked. "Tall might have simply been wounded."

"No," Evanna answered, her first word of the encounter. "He is dead. Morgan James murdered him."

"Is that you, Lady Evanna?" Steve asked uncertainly.

"Yes," she said.

"Not up to any mischief, I hope, like siding with the vampires?" He said it flippantly, but his anxiety was evident — he didn't fancy a clash with the Lady of the Wilds.

"I have never taken sides between the vampires and vampaneze, and have no intention of starting now," Evanna said coolly.

"That's OK then," Steve chuckled, confidence returning. "Interesting about Mr Tall. I always thought he couldn't be killed by ordinary weapons. I'd have gone after him a long time ago if I'd known he could be so easily bumped off."

"Gone after him for what?" I shouted.

"Harbouring criminals," Steve giggled.

"You're the only criminal here," I retorted.

Steve sighed theatrically. "See how they slander me, son? They soil this world with their murderous presence, then point the finger of blame elsewhere. That's always been the vampire way."

I started to respond, then decided I'd be wasting my time. "Let's cut the crap," I called instead. "You didn't lead us here for a war of words. Are you coming out from behind that log or not?"

"Not!" Steve cackled. "Do you think I'm insane? You'd cut me down dead!"

"Then why did you bring us here?" I looked around again, nervous. I couldn't believe he hadn't laid a trap, that there weren't dozens of vampaneze or vampets slithering up on us as we talked. Yet I didn't sense a threat. I could see Vancha was confused too.

"I want to chat, Darren," Steve said. "I'd like to discuss a peace treaty."

I had to laugh at that — it was such a ludicrous notion. "Maybe you want to become my blood-brother," I jeered.

"In a way, I already am," Steve said cryptically. Then his eyes narrowed slyly. "You missed Tommy's funeral while you were recovering."

I cursed fiercely but quietly. "Why kill Tommy?" I snarled. "Why drag him into your warped web of revenge? Did *he* 'betray' you too?"

"No," Steve said. "Tommy was my friend. Even while others were bad-mouthing me, he stuck by me. I had nothing against him. A great goalkeeper too."

"Then why have him killed?" I screamed.

"What are you talking about?" Darius cut in. "*You* killed Tom Jones. Morgan and R.V. tried to stop you, but... That's right, isn't it, Dad?" he asked, and I saw the first flickers of doubt stir in the boy's eyes.

"I told you, son," Steve replied, "you can't believe anything a vampire says. Pay no attention to him." Then, to me, he said, "Didn't you wonder how Tommy got his ticket to the Cirque Du Freak?"

"I just assumed..." I stopped. "You set him up!"

"Of course," Steve chuckled. "With *your* help. Remember the ticket you gave to Darius? He passed it on. Tommy was opening a sports store, signing autographs. Darius went along and 'swapped' his ticket for a signed football. We still have it lying around somewhere. Could be a collector's item soon."

"You're sick," I snarled. "Using a child to do your dirty work — disgusting."

"Not really," Steve disagreed. "It just shows how highly I value the young."

Now that I knew Steve had given Tommy the ticket, my mind raced ahead, putting the pieces of his plan together. "You couldn't have known for sure that Tommy would run into me at the show," I said.

"No, but I guessed he would. If he hadn't, I'd have worked out some other way to manoeuvre you together. I didn't need to, but I liked the idea. Him being here at the same time as us was providence. I'm just slightly miffed that Alan wasn't here too — that would have made for a complete reunion."

"What about my cup ticket? How did you find out about that?"

"I phoned Tommy that morning," Steve said. "He was astonished — first he bumps into his old pal Darren, then he hears from his old buddy Steve. What a coincidence! I faked astonishment too. I asked all about you. Learnt that you were coming to the match. He invited me as well, but I said I couldn't make it."

"Very clever," I complimented him icily.

"Not especially," Steve said with false modesty. "I simply used his innocence to ensnare you. Manipulating the innocent is child's play. I'm surprised you didn't see through it. You need to work on your paranoia, Darren. Suspect everyone, even those beyond suspicion — that's my motto."

Vancha edged up close to me. "If you keep him talking, maybe I can slip out back and attack him from the rear," he whispered.

I nodded my head a fraction and Vancha slid away slowly. "Tommy told me he'd been in contact with you in the past," I said loudly, hoping to mask the sound of Vancha's footsteps. "He said there was something about you that he had to tell me the next time we met, after the match."

"I can guess what that was," Steve purred.

"Care to share it with me?"

"Not yet," he said. Then, sharply, "If you take one more step towards that door, Mr March, the snake-boy dies." Vancha stopped and shot Steve a look of disgust.

"Leave my son alone!" Evra screamed. He'd been holding himself in check, but Steve's threat proved too much. "If you harm him, I'll kill you! I'll put you through so much agony, you'll pray for death!"

"My!" Steve cooed. "Such vindictiveness! You seem to have the knack of driving all your friends to violence, Darren. Or do you deliberately surround yourself with violent people?"

"Stuff it!" I grunted. Then, tiring of his verbal games, I said, "Are you going to fight or not?"

"I already answered that question," Steve said. "We'll fight soon, have no fear, but this is neither the time nor place. There's a rear tunnel — newly carved — which we'll leave by shortly. By the time you pick your way through the stakes, we'll be far out of reach."

"Then what are you waiting for?" I snarled. "Get the hell out!"

"Not yet," Steve said, and his voice was hard now. "There's the sacrifice to make first. In the old days, a sacrifice was always made before a large battle, to appease the gods. Now, it's true that the vampaneze don't have any official gods, but to be on the safe side..."

"*No!*" Evra screamed — it was as clear to him as to the rest of us what Steve meant to do.

"Don't!" I shouted.

"Gannen!" Vancha roared. "You can't allow this!"

"I have no say in it, brother," Gannen Harst responded from behind his log. He hadn't shown his face yet. I had the feeling he was ashamed to show it.

"Ready, R.V.?" Steve asked.

"I'm not sure about this, man," R.V. replied uneasily.

"Don't disobey me!" Steve growled. "I made you and I can break you. Now, you bearded, armless freak — are you ready?"

A short pause. Then R.V. answered softly, "Yes."

Vancha cursed and raced forward to force his way through the pit of stakes. Harkat lumbered after him. Alice and Debbie fired on the log protecting Steve, but their bullets couldn't pierce it. I stood, clutching my knife, thinking desperately.

Then a voice behind me called out shakily, "Dad?" Everybody paused. I looked back. Darius was trembling. "Dad?" he called again. "You're not really going to kill him, are you?"

"Be quiet!" Steve snapped. "You don't understand what's happening."

"But ... he's just a kid ... like me. You can't—"

"Shut up!" Steve roared. "I'll explain later! Just—"

"No," I interrupted, sliding up behind Darius. "There won't be any 'later'. If you kill Shancus, I'll kill Darius." For the second time that night I felt a dark spirit grow within me, and pressed the blade of my knife to the young boy's throat. Behind me, Evanna made a small cooing noise. I ignored her.

"You're bluffing," Steve jeered. "You couldn't kill a child."

"He could," Debbie answered for me. She stepped away. "Darren was going to kill him earlier. Harkat stopped him. He said we'd need the boy to trade for Shancus. Otherwise Darren would have killed him. Darius — is that the truth?"

"Yes," Darius moaned. He was weeping. Part of it was fear, but an equal part was horror. His father had raised him on lies and false heroics. Only now was he beginning to realize what sort of monster he'd aligned himself with.

I heard Steve mutter something. He peered out from around his log, studying us from the heights of the stage. I made no threatening moves. I didn't need to. My determination was clear.

"Very well," Steve snorted. "Throw away your weapons and we'll swap the two boys."

"You think we'll entrust ourselves to your untender mercies?" Vancha huffed. "Release Shancus and we'll turn your son over."

"Not until you shed your weapons," Steve insisted.

"And allow you to mow us down?" Vancha challenged him.

There was a short pause. Then Steve threw an arrow-gun away, far across the stage. "Gannen," he said, "am I carrying any other weapons?"

"A sword and two knives," Gannen Harst replied immediately.

"I don't mean those," Steve growled. "Do I have any long-range weapons?"

"No," Gannen said.

"What about you and R.V.?"

"We have none either."

"I know you don't believe a word I say," Steve shouted to Vancha, "but you trust your own brother, don't you? He's a pure vampaneze — he'd kill himself before he'd utter a lie."

"Aye," Vancha muttered unhappily.

"Then throw away your weapons," Steve said. "We won't attack if you don't."

Vancha looked to me for advice. "Do it," I said. "He's tied, just like we are. He won't risk his son's life."

Vancha was dubious, but he slipped off his belts of throwing stars and tossed them aside. Debbie threw her pistols away and so, reluctantly, did Alice. Harkat only had an axe, which he laid down on the floor beside him. I kept my knife to Darius's throat.

Steve stepped out from behind the log. He was grinning. I felt a great temptation to throw my knife at him — I might just have been able to strike him from this distance – but I didn't. As a Vampire Prince, and one of the hunters of the Vampaneze Lord, I should have. But I couldn't risk missing and enraging Steve. He'd kill Shancus if I did.

"Out you come, boys," Steve said. Gannen Harst and R.V. emerged from behind their logs, R.V. shoving the bound Shancus ahead of him. Gannen Harst was typically grim-faced, but R.V. was smiling. At first I thought it was a mocking smile, but then I realized it was a smile of relief — he was delighted he hadn't been called upon to kill the snake-boy. R.V. was a twisted, bitter, crazy man, but I saw then that he wasn't entirely evil — not like Steve.

"I'll take the reptile," Steve said, reaching for Shancus. "You go get the plank and extend it across the pit."

R.V. handed Shancus to Steve and retreated to the rear of the stage. He started dragging a long plank forward. It was awkward for him — he couldn't get a decent grip, because of the hooks Mr Tall had torn off. Gannen went to help him, keeping one eye on us. The pair began feeding the plank across the pit, letting it rest on blunt-tipped stakes, which I could now see had been placed there specifically for this purpose.

Steve watched us like a hawk while R.V. and Gannen were busy with the plank. He was holding Shancus in front of him, stroking the snake-boy's long green hair. I didn't like the way he was looking at us – I felt as though we were being X-rayed – but I said nothing, willing R.V. and Gannen to hurry up with the plank.

Steve's eyes lingered on Evra a long moment — he was smiling hopefully, hands half-reaching out to his son — then settled on me. He stopped stroking Shancus's hair and gently placed a hand on either side of his head. "Remember the games we played when we were children?" he asked craftily.

"What games?" I frowned. I had a terrible feeling — a sense of total doom — but I could do nothing but follow his lead.

"'Dare' games," Steve said, and something in his voice made R.V. and Gannen pause and look around. Steve's face was expressionless, but his eyes were alive with insane glee. "One of us would say, 'I dare you to do this,' and stick his hand in a fire or jab a pin in his leg. The other would have to copy him. Remember?"

"No!" I moaned. I knew what was coming. I knew I couldn't stop it. I knew I'd been a fool and made a fool's mistake — I'd assumed Steve was even the slightest bit human.

"I dare you to do this, Darren," Steve whispered dreadfully. Before I could reply — before anything else could happen — he seized Shancus's head tightly and twisted it sharply to the left, then the right. Shancus's neck snapped. Steve dropped him. Shancus fell to the floor. Steve had killed him.

CHAPTER TWENTY-TWO

STEVE'S ACT of pure, pointless evil caught everyone by gut-wrenching shock. For a long moment we just stared at him and the lifeless body by his feet. Even Steve looked stunned, as though he'd acted without thinking it through.

Then Evra went wild. "*Bastard!*" he screamed, hurling himself at the pit of stakes. If Harkat hadn't reacted and knocked him aside, Evra would have impaled himself on the stakes and died like his son.

"I can't believe..." Alice muttered, face whiter than usual. Then her features hardened and she ran for the pistol she'd discarded.

Debbie sank to her knees, weeping, unable to deal with such wickedness. As hardened as she'd become, nothing in her life had prepared her for this.

Harkat was struggling with Evra, pinning him down, protecting him from his rage. Evra was screaming hysterically and pounding Harkat's broad grey face with his scaly fists, but Harkat held firm.

Vancha was at the pit of stakes, lurching through them, clambering over the sharpened tips, driving towards the stage like a man possessed.

R.V. and Gannen Harst were staring at Steve, jaws slack.

Evanna was looking on silently. If the murder had shocked her, she was masking it incredibly well.

Darius was stiff with terror, holding his breath, eyes wide.

I was still behind Darius, my knife at his throat. I was the calmest of everyone there (except Evanna). Not because I was in any way unaffected by what had happened, but because I knew what I must do in retaliation. The fierce, hard, hating part within me had flared to life and taken over completely. I saw the world through different eyes. It was a dreadful, wicked place, where only the dreadful and wicked could prosper. To defeat an evil monster like Steve, I had to sink to his depths myself. Mr Crepsley had warned me not to, but he was wrong. What did it matter if I followed Steve down the road of total evil? Stopping him – getting revenge for all the people he'd killed – was the only thing I cared about now.

While I was thinking all this through, Gannen snapped to his senses and saw that Vancha was closing on them. He hurried to his Lord, grabbed Steve by the right arm and spun him towards the exit, cursing foully. R.V. rose shakily and stumbled after them. He stopped, vomited, then reeled ahead.

Alice found her pistol, brought it up and fired. But there were too many logs between her and the vampaneze. She didn't even get close to them.

Steve stopped by the tunnel entrance at the rear of the stage. Gannen tried to push him down it, but he shook his protector's hands away and turned to glare triumphantly — daringly — at me.

"Go on!" Steve screamed. "Show me you can do it! I dare you! I double dare you!"

In that moment, as if our minds were somehow joined, I understood Steve entirely. Part of him was appalled by his brutality. He was hanging dangerously on the edge of outright madness. As the monster within me had grown this night, so had the human within Steve. He needed me to match his evil deeds. If I killed Darius, Steve could justify his cruelty and continue. But if I didn't respond to his evil with an equally evil act of my own, it would drive home the truth about how far he'd fallen. He might even snap beneath the weight of full realization and go mad. I had the power to destroy him — with mercy.

But I couldn't find mercy within myself. The fires of fury in my heart and head demanded I kill Darius. Right or wrong, I had to avenge Shancus's death. An eye for an eye, a tooth for a tooth, a life for a life. Out of the corner of one eye I caught sight of Evanna. Her gaze was locked on me. There was no pity in her expression, merely the weariness of one who has seen all the evils of the world and must watch them repeat themselves over and over again.

"Dare accepted," I said, abandoning myself to my dark destiny, knowing in that moment that I was betraying all my moral beliefs. This was the start of the path to damnation. If I defeated Steve, I *would* become the Lord of the Shadows, and in the long, blood-red decades and centuries ahead, I'd be able to point back to this night and say, "That was where the monster was born."

I began to draw my knife across Darius's throat. This time Debbie didn't try to stop me — she sensed my damnation, and was powerless to save me. But then I paused. The throat was too impersonal a target. I wanted Steve to really *feel* this.

Lowering the knife, I cut away Darius's shirt, revealing his bare, pale chest. I positioned the tip of the knife over his heart and gazed at Steve, no longer blinking against the searing lights, my eyes dark, my lips tight over my teeth.

Steve's expression steadied. The beast within him had seen its mirror image in me, and was satisfied. He drew back from the madness, becoming his cold, crafty, calculating self again. He smiled.

I drew my arm back to its full extent, so I could strike swiftly with the knife. I meant to stab Darius with all my strength and kill him quickly. I might be a monster, but I wasn't an entirely heartless one. At least, not yet.

But Steve called out before I pierced his son's heart. "Be careful, Darren! You don't know who you're killing!"

I shouldn't have hesitated. I knew, if I did, that he'd derail me with some other twisted trick. Listening to demons was dangerous. Better to act in haste and shut your ears to them.

But I couldn't help myself. There was something darkly inviting about his tone. It was like when someone was about to tell a gruesome but hilarious joke. I could feel the awfulness of it, but also the humour. I had to hear him out.

"Darius," Steve chuckled, "tell Darren your mother's name." Darius gawped at his father, unable to respond. "Darius!" Steve roared. "He's about to drive a knife through your heart! Tell him your mother's name — *now!*"

"Ah-ah-ah-Annie," Darius wheezed, and I froze.

"And her surname?" Steve asked softly, relishing the moment.

"Shan," Darius whispered uncomprehendingly. "Annie Shan. What about it?"

"You see, Darren," Steve purred, winking at me before vanishing down the tunnel to freedom, "if you kill Darius, you won't just be slaughtering my son — you'll be murdering *your nephew!*"

TO BE CONCLUDED...

DARREN SHAN

SONS OF DESTINY

THE SAGA OF DARREN SHAN
BOOK 12

For:

Bas, Biddy and Liam – my three pillars

OBE's
(Order of the Bloody Entrails) to:

"Lucky" Aleta Moriarty

A and Bo – Bangkok's best banshees
Emily "Lilliputian" Chuang
Jennifer "Stacey" Abbots

Saga Editors:
Domenica De Rosa, Gillie Russell, Zoë Clarke and
Julia Bruce – you done good, girls!!!

Bloody Brilliant Buccaneers:
The Christopher Little Cutthroats

And an extra special thank you to all of my Shansters,
especially those who have kept me company on Shanville.
Even in death may you all be triumphant!

PROLOGUE

If my life was a fairy tale and I was writing a book about it, I'd start with, "Once upon a time there were two boys called Darren and Steve..." But my life's a horror story, so if I were to write about it, I'd have to begin with something like this instead:

Evil has a name — Steve Leopard.

He was born Steve Leonard, but to his friends (yes — he had friends once!) he was always Steve Leopard. He was never happy at home, didn't have a dad, didn't like his mum. He dreamt of power and glory. He yearned for strength and respect, and time in which to enjoy it. He wanted to be a vampire.

His chance came when he spotted a creature of the night, Larten Crepsley, performing in the wondrous magical show, the Cirque Du Freak. He asked Mr Crepsley to blood him. The vampire refused — he said Steve had bad blood. Steve hated him for that and vowed to track him down and kill him when he grew up.

Some years later, as Steve was preparing for his life as a vampire hunter, he learnt about the purple-skinned, red-eyed vampaneze. In legends, vampires are wicked killers who suck humans dry. That's hysterical rubbish — they only take small amounts of blood when they feed, causing no harm. But the vampaneze are different. They broke away from the vampire clan six hundred years ago. They live by laws of their own. They believe it's shameful to drink from a human without killing. They always murder when they feed. Steve's sort of people!

Steve went in search of the vampaneze, certain they'd accept him. He probably thought they were as twisted as he was. But he got it wrong. Although the vampaneze were killers, they weren't inherently evil. They didn't torture humans and they tried not to interfere with vampires. They went about their business quietly and calmly, keeping a lower-than-low profile.

I don't know this for sure, but I'm guessing the vampaneze rejected Steve, just like Mr Crepsley did. The vampaneze live by even stricter, more traditional rules than vampires. I can't see them accepting a human into their ranks if they knew he was going to turn out bad.

But Steve found a way in, thanks to that eternal agent of chaos — Desmond Tiny. Most just call him Mr Tiny, but if you shorten his first name and put it with his surname, you get Mr *Destiny*. He's the most powerful person in the world, immortal as far as anyone knows, a meddler of the highest order. He gave the vampaneze a present many centuries earlier, a coffin which filled with fire whenever a person lay within it, burning them to ash within seconds. But he said that one night someone would lie in the coffin and emerge unharmed. That person would be the Lord of the Vampaneze and had to be obeyed by every member of the clan. If they accepted this Lord, they'd gain more power than they'd ever imagined. Otherwise they'd be destroyed.

The promise of such power proved too much for Steve to ignore. He decided to take the test. He probably figured he had nothing to lose. He entered the coffin, the flames engulfed him, and a minute later he stepped out unburnt. Suddenly, everything changed. He had an army of vampaneze at his command, willing to give their lives for him and do anything he asked. He no longer had to settle for killing Mr Crepsley — he could wipe out the entire vampire clan!

But Mr Tiny didn't want the vampaneze to crush the vampires too easily. He thrives on suffering and conflict. A quick, assured victory wouldn't provide him with enough entertainment. So he gave the vampires a get-out clause. Three of them had the ability to kill the Vampaneze Lord before he came fully into his powers. They'd have four chances. If they were successful and killed him, the vampires would win the War of the Scars (that's what the battle between the vampires and vampaneze was known as). If they failed, two would die during the hunt, while the third would survive to witness the downfall of the clan.

Mr Crepsley was one of the hunters. A Vampire Prince, Vancha March, was another. The last was also a Prince, the youngest ever, a half-vampire called Darren Shan — and that's where *I* come in.

I was Steve's best friend when we were kids. We went to the Cirque Du Freak together, and through Steve I learnt of the existence of vampires and was sucked into their world. I was blooded by Mr Crepsley and served as his assistant. Under his guidance I studied the ways of vampires and travelled to Vampire Mountain. There I undertook my Trials of Initiation — and failed. Fearing death, I fled, but during my escape I uncovered a plot to destroy the clan. Later I exposed it, and as a reward I was not only accepted into the fold, but made a Vampire Prince.

After six years in Vampire Mountain, Mr Tiny set me on the trail of the Lord of the Vampaneze, along with Mr Crepsley and Vancha. One of Mr Tiny's Little People travelled with us. His name was Harkat Mulds. Little People are grey-skinned, stitched-together, short, with large green eyes, no nose, and ears sewn beneath the flesh of their heads. They're created from the remains of dead people. Harkat didn't know who he used to be, but we later found out he was Kurda Smahlt in his previous life — the vampire who'd betrayed the clan in the hope of preventing the War of the Scars.

Not knowing who the Vampaneze Lord was, we missed our first chance to kill him when Vancha let him escape, because he was under the protection of Vancha's vampaneze brother, Gannen Harst. Later, in the city of Mr Crepsley's youth, I ran into Steve again. He told me he was a vampaneze hunter and, fool that I was, I believed him. The others did too, although Mr Crepsley was suspicious. He sensed something wrong, but I convinced him to grant Steve the benefit of the doubt. I've made some terrible mistakes in my life, but that was certainly the worst.

When Steve revealed his true colours, we fought, and twice we had the power to kill him. The first time we let him live because we wanted to trade his life for Debbie Hemlock's — my human girlfriend. The second time, Mr Crepsley fought Steve, Gannen Harst and an impostor, who was pretending to be the Lord of the Vampaneze. Mr Crepsley killed the impostor, but then was knocked into a pit of stakes by Steve. He could have taken Steve down with him, but let him live so that Gannen and the other vampaneze would spare the lives of his friends. It was only afterwards that Steve revealed the truth about himself, and made the bitter loss of Mr Crepsley all the more unbearable.

There was a long gap between that and our next encounter. I went with Harkat to find out the truth about his past, to a waste world full of monsters and mutants, which we later discovered was Earth in the future. Upon my return I spent a couple of years travelling with the Cirque Du Freak, waiting for destiny (or Des Tiny) to pit Steve and me together again for one final clash.

Our paths finally crossed in our old home town. I'd returned with the Cirque Du Freak. It was strange revisiting the past, walking the streets of the town where I'd grown up. I saw my sister Annie, now a grown woman with a child of her own, and I ran into an old friend, Tommy Jones, who'd become a professional footballer. I went to watch Tommy play in an important cup game. His team won, but their celebrations were cut short when two of Steve's henchmen invaded the pitch and killed a lot of people, including Tommy.

I chased after the murderous pair, straight into a trap. I faced Steve again. He had a child called Darius with him — his son. Darius shot me. Steve could have finished me off, but didn't. It wasn't the destined time. My end (or his) would only come when I faced him with Vancha by my side.

Crawling through the streets, I was rescued by a pair of tramps. They'd been recruited by Debbie and an ex-police inspector, Alice Burgess, who were building a human army to help the vampires. Vancha March linked up with me while I was recovering. With the ladies and Harkat, we returned to the Cirque Du Freak. We discussed the future with Mr Tall, the owner of the circus. He told us that no matter who won the war, an evil dictator known as the Lord of the Shadows would rise to rule and destroy the world.

As we were trying to come to terms with the shocking news, two of Steve's crazed followers struck — R.V. and Morgan James, the pair who'd killed Tommy. With the help of Darius, they slaughtered Mr Tall and took a hostage — a young boy called Shancus. Half human, half snake, he was the son of one of my best friends, Evra Von.

As Mr Tall lay dying, Mr Tiny and a witch called Evanna mysteriously appeared out of nowhere. It turned out that Mr Tiny was Mr Tall's father, and Evanna his sister. Mr Tiny stayed to mourn the death of his son, while Evanna followed us as we chased after her brother's killers. We managed to kill Morgan James and capture Darius. As the others hurried after R.V. and Shancus, I stole a few words with Evanna. The witch had the ability to see into the future and she revealed that if I killed Steve, I would take his place as the dreaded Lord of the Shadows. I'd become a monster, murder Vancha and anybody else who got in my way, and destroy not just the vampaneze, but humanity as well.

As shocked as I was, there was no time to brood. With my allies, we tracked R.V. to the old cinema where Steve and I had first met Mr Crepsley. Steve was waiting for us, safe on the stage, separated from us by a pit which he'd had dug and filled with stakes. He mocked us for a while, then agreed to trade Shancus's life for Darius's. But he lied. Instead of releasing the snake-boy, he killed him brutally. I still had hold of Darius. In a blind, cold rage, I prepared to murder him for revenge. But just before I stabbed the boy, Steve stopped me with his cruellest revelation yet — Darius's mother was my sister, Annie. If I murdered Steve's son, I'd be killing my own nephew.

And with that he departed, cackling like the demon he was, leaving me to the madness of the blood-drenched night.

PART ONE

CHAPTER ONE

Sitting on the stage. Gazing around the theatre. Remembering the thrilling show I saw the first time I came. Comparing it to tonight's warped 'entertainment'. Feeling very small and lonely.

Vancha didn't lose his head, even when Steve played his trump card. He kept going, picked his way through the pit of stakes to the stage, then raced down the tunnel which Steve, Gannen and R.V. had fled by. It led to the streets at the rear of the theatre. No way of telling which way they'd gone. He returned, cursing with fury. When he saw Shancus, lying dead on the stage like a bird with a broken neck, he stopped and sank to his knees.

Evra was next across, following Vancha's route through the stakes, crying out Shancus's name, screaming for him not to die, even though he must have known it was too late, that his son was already dead. We should have held him back – he fell and pierced himself several times, and could easily have perished – but we were frozen with shock and horror.

Fortunately Evra made it to the stage without injuring himself too severely. Once there, he slumped beside Shancus, desperately checked for signs of life, then howled with loss. Sobbing and moaning with grief, he cradled the dead boy's head in his lap, tears dripping on to his son's motionless face. The rest of us watched from a distance. We were all crying bitterly, even the normally steel-faced Alice Burgess.

In time, Harkat also climbed through the stakes. There was a long plank on the stage. He and Vancha extended it over the pit, so that the rest of us could join them. I don't think anybody really wanted to go up there. For a long moment none of us moved. Then Debbie, sobbing with deep, wracking gulps, stumbled to the plank and hauled herself up.

Alice crossed the pit next. I brought up the rear. I was shaking uncontrollably. I wanted to turn and run. Earlier, I thought I knew how I'd feel if our gamble backfired and Steve killed Shancus. But I'd known nothing. I never truly expected Steve to murder the snake-boy. I'd let R.V. march the boy into Steve's den, certain no harm would come to my honorary godson.

Now that Steve had made a fool of me (yet again) and slaughtered Shancus, all I wanted was to be dead. I couldn't feel pain if I was dead. No shame. No guilt. I wouldn't have to look Evra in the eye, knowing I was responsible for his son's needless, shocking death.

We'd forgotten about Darius. I hadn't killed him — how

could I kill my own nephew? Following Steve's triumphant revelation, the hatred and anger which had filled me like a fire, drained away from me in an instant. I released Darius, having lost my murderous interest in him, and just left him on the far side of the pit.

Evanna was standing near the boy, idly picking at one of the ropes which encircled her body — she preferred ropes to ordinary clothes. It was clear from the witch's stance that she wouldn't interfere if Darius made a break for freedom. It would have been the simplest thing in the world for him to escape. But he didn't. He stood, sentry-like, trembling, waiting for us to summon him.

Finally Alice stumbled over to me, wiping tears from her face. "We should take them back to the Cirque Du Freak," she said, nodding at Evra and Shancus.

"In a while," I agreed, dreading the moment I'd have to face Evra. And what about Merla, Shancus's mother? Would *I* have to break the terrible news to her?

"No — now," Alice said firmly. "Harkat and Debbie can take them. We need to straighten some things out before we leave." She nodded at Darius, tiny and vulnerable under the glare of the lights.

"I don't want to talk about this," I groaned.

"I know," she said. "But we must. The boy might know where Steve is staying. If he does, this is the time to strike. They won't expect—"

"How can you even think about such things?" I hissed angrily. "Shancus is dead! Don't you care?"

She slapped my face. I blinked, stunned. "You're not a child, Darren, so don't act like one," she said coldly. "Of course I care. But we can't bring him back, and we'll achieve nothing by standing around, moping. We need to act. Only in swift revenge can we maybe find a small sliver of comfort."

She was right. Self-pity was a waste. Revenge was essential. As hard as it was, I dug myself out of my misery and set about sending Shancus's body home. Harkat didn't want to leave with Evra and Debbie. He wanted to stay and chase Steve with us. But somebody had to help carry Shancus. He accepted his task reluctantly, but made me promise we wouldn't face Steve without him. "I've come too far with you to ... miss out now. I want to be there when you ... cut the demon down."

Debbie threw her arms around me before leaving. "How could he do it?" she cried. "Even a monster couldn't ... wouldn't..."

"Steve's more than a monster," I replied numbly. I wanted to return her embrace, but my arms wouldn't work. Alice pried her away from me. She gave Debbie a handkerchief and whispered something to her. Debbie sniffed miserably, nodded, gave Alice a hug, then went to stand beside Evra.

I wanted to talk with Evra before he left, but I could think of nothing to say. If he'd confronted me, maybe I'd have responded, but he had eyes only for his lifeless son. Dead people often look like they're sleeping. Shancus didn't. He'd been a vibrant, buzzing, active child. All that vitality was lost now. Nobody could have looked upon him and thought he was anything but dead.

I remained standing until Evra, Debbie and Harkat had departed, Harkat carrying Shancus's body tenderly in his thick, grey arms. Then I slid to the floor and sat there for ages, staring around in a daze, thinking about the past and my first visit here, using the theatre and my memories as a barrier between me and my grief.

Eventually Vancha and Alice approached. I don't know how long the pair had been talking together, but when they came to stand before me they'd wiped their faces clean of tears and looked ready for business.

"Will I talk to the boy or do you want to?" Vancha asked gruffly.

"I don't care," I sighed. Then, glancing at Darius, who still stood alone with Evanna in the vastness of the auditorium, I said, "I'll do it."

"Darius," Alice called. His head rose immediately. "Come here."

Darius went straight to the plank, climbed up and walked across. He had an excellent sense of balance. I found myself thinking that was probably a by-product of his vampaneze blood — Steve had pumped some of his own blood into his son, turning him into a half-vampaneze. Thinking that, I began to hate the boy again. My fingers twitched in anticipation of grabbing him by the throat and...

But then I recalled his face when he'd learnt he was my nephew — shock, terror, confusion, pain, remorse — and my hatred for the boy died away.

Darius walked directly up to us. If he was afraid — and he must have been — he masked it bravely. Stopping, he stared at Vancha, then at Alice, finally at me. Now that I studied him closely, I saw a certain family resemblance. Thinking about that, I frowned.

"You're not the boy I saw before," I said. Darius looked at me uncertainly. "I went to my old home when we first came to town," I explained. "I watched from behind the fence. I saw Annie. She was bringing in laundry. Then you arrived and came out to help her. Except it wasn't *you*. It was a chubby boy with fair hair."

"Oggy Bas," Darius said after a second's thought. "My friend. I remember that day. He came home with me. I sent him out to help Mum while I was taking my shoes off. Oggy always does what I tell him." Then, licking his lips nervously, he looked around at all of us again and said, "I didn't know." It wasn't an apology, just a statement of fact. "Dad told me vampires were evil. He said you were the worst of the lot. Darren the cruel, Darren the mad, Darren the baby-killer.' But he never mentioned your surname."

Evanna had crossed the plank after Darius and was circling us, studying us as if we were chess pieces. I ignored her — there'd be time for the witch later.

"What did Steve tell you about the vampaneze?" I asked Darius.

"That they wanted to stop vampires killing humans. They broke away from the clan several hundred years ago and had battled to stop the slaughter of humans ever since. They drank only small amounts of blood when they fed, just enough to survive."

"You believed him?" Vancha snorted.

"He was my dad," Darius answered. "He was always kind to me. I never saw him like I saw him tonight. I'd no reason to doubt him."

"But you doubt him now," Alice noted wryly.

"Yes. He's evil." As soon as he said it, Darius burst into tears, his brave front collapsing. It can't have been easy for a child to admit his father was evil. Even in the midst of my grief and fury, I felt pity for the boy.

"What about Annie?" I asked when Darius had recovered enough to speak again. "Did Steve feed her the same sort of lies?"

"She doesn't know," Darius said. "They haven't spoken since before I was born. I never told her I was meeting him."

I breathed a small sigh of relief. I'd had a sudden, terrifying flash of Annie as Steve's consort, having grown up as bitter and twisted as him. It was good to know she wasn't part of this dark insanity.

"Do you want to tell him the truth about vampires and vampaneze, or will I?" Vancha asked.

"First things first," Alice interrupted. "Does he know where his father is?"

"No," Darius said sadly. "I always met him here. This is

where he was based. If he has another hideout, I don't know about it."

"Damn!" Alice snarled.

"No ideas at all?" I asked. Darius thought for a moment, then shook his head. I glanced at Vancha. "Will you set him straight?"

"Sure." Vancha quickly filled Darius in on the truth. He told him that the vampaneze were the ones who killed when they drank, though he was careful to describe their ways in detail — they kept part of a person's spirit alive within themselves when they drained a human dry, so they didn't look upon it as murder. They were noble. They never lied. They weren't deliberately evil.

"Then your father came along," Vancha said, and explained about the Lord of the Vampaneze, the War of the Scars, Mr Tiny's prediction and our part in it.

"I don't understand," Darius said at the end, forehead creased. "If the vampaneze don't lie, how come Dad lied all the time? And he taught me how to use an arrow-gun, but you said they can't use such weapons."

"They're not supposed to," Vancha said. "I haven't seen or heard of any others breaking those rules. But their Lord's above such laws. They worship him so much — or fear what will happen if they disobey him — that they don't care what he does, as long as he leads them to victory over the vampires."

Darius thought about that in silence for a long time. He was only ten years old, but he had the expression and manner of someone much older.

"I wouldn't have helped if I'd known," he said in the end. "I grew up thinking vampires were evil, like in the movies. When Dad came to me a few years ago and said he was on a mission to stop them, I thought it was a great adventure. I thought he was a hero. I was proud to be his son. I'd have done anything for him. I *did*..."

He looked like he was about to cry again. But then his jaw firmed and he stared at me. "But how did *you* get involved in this?" he asked. "Mum told me you died. She said you broke your neck."

"I faked my death," I said, and gave him a very brief rundown of my early life as a vampire's assistant, sacrificing everything I held dear to save Steve's life.

"But why does he hate you if you saved him?" Darius shouted. "That's crazy!"

"Steve sees things differently," I shrugged. "He believes it was his destiny to become a vampire. He thinks I stole his rightful place. He's determined to make me pay."

Darius shook his head, confused. "I can't understand that," he said.

"You're young." I smiled sadly. "You've a lot to learn about people and how they operate." I fell silent, thinking that those were some of the many things poor Shancus would never learn.

"So," Darius said a while later, breaking the silence. "What happens now?"

"Go home," I sighed. "Forget about this. Put it behind you."

"But what about the vampaneze?" Darius cried. "Dad's still out there. I want to help you find him."

"Really?" I looked at him icily. "You want to help us kill him? You'd lead us to your own father and watch while we cut his rotten heart out?"

Darius shifted uneasily. "He's evil," he whispered.

"Yes," I agreed. "But he's still your father. You're better off out of this."

"And Mum?" Darius asked. "What do I tell her?"

"Nothing," I said. "She thinks I'm dead. Let her go on thinking that. Say nothing of this. The world I live in isn't a fit world for children — and as a child who's lived in it, I should know! Take back your ordinary life. Try not to dwell on what's happened. In time you might be able to dismiss all this as a horrible dream." I placed my hands on his shoulders and smiled warmly. "Go home, Darius. Be good to Annie. Make her happy."

Darius wasn't pleased, but I could see him making up his mind to accept my advice. Then Vancha spoke. "It's not that easy."

"What?" I frowned.

"He's in. He can't opt out."

"Of course he can!" I snapped.

Vancha shook his head stubbornly. "He was blooded. The vampaneze blood is thin in him, but it will thicken. He won't age like normal children, and in a few decades the purge will strike and he'll become a full-vampaneze." Vancha sighed. "But his real problems will start long before then."

"What do you mean?" I croaked, though I sensed what he was getting at.

"*Feeding*," Vancha said. He turned his gaze on Darius. "You'll need to drink blood to survive."

Darius stiffened, then grinned shakily. "So I'll drink like you guys," he said. "A drop here, a drop there. I don't mind. It'll be kind of cool, in a way. Maybe I'll drink from my teachers and—"

"No," Vancha growled. "You can't drink like us. In the beginning, vampaneze were the same as vampires, except in their customs. But they've changed. The centuries have altered them physically. Now a vampaneze *must* kill when he feeds. They're driven to it. They have no choice or control. I was once a half-vampaneze, so I know what I'm speaking about."

Vancha drew himself up straight and spoke sadly but firmly. "In a few months the hunger will grow within you. You won't be able to resist. You'll drink blood because you have to, and when you drink, because you're a half-vampaneze — you'll *kill!*"

CHAPTER TWO

We marched in silence, in single file, Darius leading the way like Oliver Twist at the head of a funeral procession. Following the massacre at the stadium after the football match, a series of road blocks had been set in place around the town. But there weren't many in this area, so we made good time, having to take only a couple of short detours. I was at the back of the line, a few metres behind the others, worrying about the meeting to come. I'd agreed to it easily enough in the theatre, but now that we were getting closer, I was having second thoughts.

While I was running through my words, thinking of all the things I could and should say, Evanna slipped back to walk along beside me. "If it helps, the snake-boy's soul has flown straight to Paradise," she said.

"I never thought otherwise," I replied stiffly, glaring at her hatefully.

"Why such a dark look?" she asked, genuine surprise in her mismatched green and brown eyes.

"You knew it was coming," I growled. "You could have warned us and saved Shancus."

"No," she snapped, irritated. "Why do you people level the same accusations at me over and over? You know I have the power to see into the future, but not the power to directly influence it. I cannot act to change that which is to be. Nor could my brother."

"Why not?" I snarled. "You always say that terrible things will happen if you do, but what are they? What could be worse than letting an innocent child die at the hands of a monster?"

Evanna was quiet a moment, then spoke softly, so that only I could hear. "There are worse monsters than Steve Leonard, and worse even than the Lord of the Shadows — be he Steve or you. These other monsters wait in the timeless wings around the stage of the world, never seen by man, but always seeing, always hungering, always eager to break through.

"I am bound by laws older than mankind. So was my brother and so, to a large extent, is my father. If I took advantage of the present, and tried to change the course of a future I knew about, I'd break the laws of the universe. The monsters I speak of would then be free to cross into this world, and it would become a cauldron of endless, bloody savagery."

"It seems that way already," I said sourly.

"For you, perhaps," she agreed. "But for billions of others it is not. Would you have everyone suffer as you have — and worse?"

"Of course not," I muttered. "But you told me they were going to suffer anyway, that the Lord of the Shadows will destroy mankind."

"He will bring it to its knees," she said. "But he will not crush it entirely. Hope will remain. One day, far in the future, humans might rise again. If I interfered and unleashed the real monsters, hope would become a word without meaning."

I didn't know what to think about these other monsters of Evanna's — it was the first time she'd ever spoken of such creatures — so I brought the conversation back to centre on the monster I knew all too much about. "You're wrong when you say I can become the Lord of the Shadows," I said, trying to change my destiny by denying it. "I'm not a monster."

"You would have killed Darius if Steve hadn't said he was your nephew," Evanna reminded me.

I recalled the hateful fury which had flared to life inside me when I saw Shancus die. In that moment I became like Steve. I didn't care about right or wrong. I only wanted to hurt my enemy by killing his son. I'd seen a glimpse of my future then, the beast I could become, but I didn't want to believe it was real.

"That would have been in revenge for Shancus," I said bitterly, trying to hide from the truth. "It wouldn't have been the act of an out-of-control beast. I wouldn't become a monster just because of a single executioning."

"No?" Evanna challenged me. "There was a time when you thought differently. Do you remember when you killed your first vampaneze, in the caves of Vampire Mountain? You wept afterwards. You thought killing was wrong. You believed there were ways to resolve differences other than through violence."

"I still do," I said, but my words sounded hollow, even to me.

"You would not have tried to take the life of a child if you did," Evanna said, stroking the hairs of her beard. "You have changed, Darren. You're not evil like Steve, but you carry the seeds of evil within you. Your intentions are good, but time and circumstance will see you become that which you despise. This world will warp you and, despite your noble wishes, the monster within you will grow. Friends will become enemies. Truths will become lies. Beliefs will become sick jokes.

"The path of revenge is always lined with danger. By following the ways of those you hate, you risk turning into them. This is your destiny, Darren Shan. You cannot avoid it. Unless Steve kills you and he becomes the Lord of the Shadows instead."

"What about Vancha?" I hissed. "What if he kills Steve? Can't *he* become your bloody Lord of the Shadows?"

"No," she said calmly. "Vancha has the power to kill Steve and decide the fate of the War of the Scars. But moving beyond that, it's either you or Steve. There is no other. Death or monstrosity. Those are your options."

She moved ahead of me then, leaving me with my troubled, frantic thoughts. Was there truly no hope for me or the world? And if not, if I was trapped between death at the hands of Steve or replacing him as the Lord of the Shadows, which was preferable? Was it better to live and terrorize the world — or die now, while I was still halfway human?

I couldn't decide on an answer. There didn't seem to be one. And so I trudged along miserably and let my thoughts return to the more pressing issue — what to say to my grown-up sister who'd buried me as a child.

Twenty minutes later, Darius opened the back door and held it ajar. I paused, staring at the house, filled with a sense of foreboding. Vancha and Alice were behind me, and Evanna further behind them. I looked back at my friends pleadingly. "Do I really have to do this?" I croaked.

"Yes," Vancha said. "It would be wrong to risk his life without informing his mother first. She must decide."

"OK," I sighed. "You'll wait out here till I call?"

"Aye."

I gulped, then stepped over the threshold into the house where I'd lived as a boy. After eighteen long years of wandering, I'd finally come home.

Darius guided me to the living room, though I could have found my way blindfolded. Much had changed within the house — new wallpaper and carpets, furniture and light fittings — but it felt the same, warm and comfy, layered with memories of the distant past. It was like walking through a ghost house — except the house was real and I was the ghost.

Darius pushed the living-room door open. And there was Annie, her brown hair tied up in a bun, sitting in a chair in front of the TV, sipping hot chocolate, watching the news. "Decided to come home at last, did you?" she said to Darius, catching sight of him out of the corner of her eye. She laid the cup of hot chocolate down. "I was worried. Have you seen the news? There's—"

She saw me entering the room after Darius. "Is this one of your friends?" she asked. I could see her thinking I looked too old to be his friend. She was instantly suspicious of me.

"Hello, Annie," I said, smiling nervously, advancing into the light.

"Have we met before?" she asked, frowning, not recognizing me.

"In a way," I chuckled drily.

"Mum, it's—" Darius started to say.

"No," I interrupted. "Let her see for herself. Don't tell her."

"Tell me what?" Annie snapped. She was squinting at me now, uneasy.

"Look closer, Annie," I said softly, walking across the room, stopping less than a metre away from her. "Look at my eyes. They say the eyes never really change, even if everything else does."

"Your voice," she muttered. "There's something about..." She stood — she was the same height as me — and gazed steadily into my eyes. I smiled.

"You look like somebody I knew a long time ago," Annie said. "But I don't remember who..."

"You did know me a long time ago," I whispered. "Eighteen years ago."

"Nonsense!" Annie snorted. "You'd have only been a baby."

"No," I said. "I've aged slowly. I was slightly older than Darius when you last saw me."

"Is this a joke?" she half laughed.

"Look at him, Mum," Darius said intently. "Really *look* at him."

And she did. And this time I saw something in her expression and realized she'd known who I was the second she saw me — she just hadn't admitted it to herself yet.

"Listen to your instincts, Annie," I said. "You always had good instincts. If I'd had your nose for trouble, maybe I wouldn't have gotten into this mess. Maybe I'd have had more sense than to steal a poisonous spider..."

Annie's eyes widened. "No!" she gasped.

"Yes," I said.

"You can't be!"

"I am."

"But ... *No!*" she growled, firmly this time. "I don't know who put you up to this, or what you think you'll achieve by it, but if you don't get out quick, I'll—"

"I bet you never told anyone about Madam Octa," I cut her off. She trembled at mention of the spider's name. "I bet you kept that secret all these years. You must have guessed she had something to do with my 'death'. Maybe you asked Steve about it, since he was the one she bit, but I bet you never told Mum or—"

"*Darren?*" she wheezed, confused tears springing to her eyes.

"Hi, sis," I grinned. "Long time no see."

She stared at me, appalled, and then did something I thought only happened in corny old movies — her eyes rolled up, her legs gave way, and she fainted!

Annie sat in her chair, a fresh mug of hot chocolate cupped between her hands. I sat opposite her in a chair I'd dragged over from the other side of the room. Darius stood by the TV, which he'd turned off shortly after Annie fainted. Annie hadn't said much since recovering. Once she'd come to, she'd pressed back into her chair, gazed at me, torn between horror and hope, and simply gasped, "*How?*"

I'd spent the time since then filling her in. I spoke quietly and rapidly, starting with Mr Crepsley and Madam Octa, explaining the deal I'd struck to save Steve's life, giving her a quick rundown of the years since then; my existence as a vampire, the vampaneze, the War of the Scars, tracking the Vampaneze Lord. I didn't tell her Steve was the Lord or involved with the vampaneze — I wanted to see how she reacted to the rest of the story before hitting her with that one.

Her eyes didn't betray her feelings. It was impossible to guess what she was thinking. When I got to the part of the story involving Darius, her gaze slid from me to her son, and she leant forward slightly as I described how he'd been tricked into aiding the vampaneze, again being careful not to refer to Steve by name. I finished with my return to the old cinema theatre, Shancus's death, and the Vampaneze Lord's revelation that Darius was my nephew.

"Once Darius knew the truth, he was horrified," I said. "But I told him he mustn't blame himself. Lots of older and wiser people than him have been fooled by the Lord of the Vampaneze."

I stopped and awaited her reaction. It wasn't long coming.

"You're insane," she said coldly. "If you *are* my brother – and I'm not a hundred per cent convinced – then whatever disease stunted your growth also affected your brain. Vampires? Vampaneze? My son in league with a killer?" She sneered. "You're a madman."

"But it's true!" Darius exclaimed. "He can prove it! He's stronger and faster than any human. He can—"

"Be quiet!" Annie roared with such venom that Darius shut up instantly. She glared at me furiously. "Get out of my house," she snarled. "Stay away from my son. Don't ever come back."

"But—" I began.

"No!" she screamed. "You're not my brother! Even if you are, you're not! We buried Darren eighteen years ago. He's dead and that's the way I want him to stay. I don't care if you're him or not. I want you out of my life – *our lives* – immediately." She stood and pointed at the door. "*Go!*"

I didn't move. I wanted to. If it hadn't been for Darius, I would have slunk out like a kicked dog. But she had to know what her son had become. I couldn't leave without convincing her of the danger he was in.

While Annie stood, pointing at the door, hand trembling wildly, face twisted with rage, Darius stepped away from the TV. "Mum," he said quietly. "Don't you want to know how I fell in with the vampaneze and why I helped them?"

"There are no vampaneze!" she yelled. "This maniac has filled your imagination with lies and—"

"Steve Leonard's the Lord of the Vampaneze," Darius said, and Annie stopped dead. "He came to me a few years ago," Darius went on, edging slowly towards her. "At first we just went for walks together, he took me to the cinema and for meals, stuff like that. He told me not to say anything to you. He said you wouldn't like it, that you'd make him go away."

He stopped in front of her, reached up, took hold of her pointing hand and gently bent her arm down. She was staring at him wordlessly. "He's my dad," Darius said sadly. "I trusted him because I thought he loved me. That's why I believed him when he told me about vampires. He said he was telling me for my protection, that he was worried about me — and *you*. He wanted to protect us. That's where it began. Then I got more involved. He taught me how to use a knife, how to shoot, how to kill."

Annie sank back into her chair, unable to respond.

"It was Steve," Darius said. "Steve who got me into trouble, who killed the snake-boy, who made Darren come back to see you. Darren didn't want to — he knew he'd hurt you — but Steve left him with no choice. It's true, Mum, everything he said. You've got to believe us, because it was Steve, and I think he might come back — come after *you* — and if we aren't ready ... if you don't believe..."

He ground to a halt, running out of words. But he'd said enough. When Annie looked at me again, there was fear and doubt in her eyes, but no scorn. "*Steve?*" she moaned. I nodded unhappily and her face hardened. "What did I tell you about him?" she screamed at Darius, grabbing the boy and shaking him angrily. "I told you never to go near him! That if you ever saw him, you had to run and tell me! I said he was dangerous!"

"I didn't believe you!" Darius cried. "I thought you hated him just because he ran away, that you were lying! He was my dad!" He tore himself away from her and collapsed on the floor, weeping. "He was my dad," he sobbed again. "I loved him."

Annie stared at Darius crying. Then she stared at me. And then she also started to cry, and her sobs were even deeper and more painful than her son's.

I didn't cry. I was saving my tears. I knew the worst was yet to come.

CHAPTER THREE

Later. After the tears. Sitting around the living room. Annie had recovered from the worst of the shock. All three of us were drinking hot chocolate. I hadn't called the others in yet — I wanted some personal time with Annie before I dumped the full fallout from the War of the Scars upon her.

Annie made me tell her more about my life. She wanted to hear about the countries I'd visited, the people I'd met, the adventures I'd had. I told her some of the highlights, leaving out the darker aspects. She listened, dazed, touching me every few minutes to make sure I was real. When she heard I was a Prince, she laughed with delight. "Does that make me a princess?" she smiled.

"Afraid not," I chuckled.

In return, Annie told me what her life had been like. The hard months after I'd 'died'. Slowly returning to normal. She was young, so she recovered, but Mum and Dad never really got over it. She raised the question of whether or not they should be told I was alive. Then, before I could speak, she said, "No. They're happy now. It's too late to change the past. Best not to drag it up again."

I paid close attention when she spoke about Steve. "I was a teenager," she said angrily, "mixed-up and unsure of myself. I had some friends but not many. And no serious boyfriend. Then Steve came back. He was only a few years older than me, but he looked and acted grown-up. And he was interested in me. He wanted to talk to me. He treated me like an equal."

They spent a lot of time together. Steve put on a good act — kind, generous, loving. Annie thought he cared for her, that they had a future together. She fell in love with him, and gave her love to him. Then she found out she was expecting a baby.

"His face lit up when he heard," she said, shivering from the memory. Darius was by her side, solemn, silent, listening intently. "He made me believe he was delighted, that we'd get married and have lots of children together. He told me not to tell anyone — he wanted to keep it secret until we were husband and wife. He went away again. He said it was to earn money, to pay for our wedding and the baby's upkeep. He stayed away a long time. He returned late one night, while I was sleeping. Woke me up. Before I could say anything, he clamped a hand over my mouth and laughed. 'Too late to stop it now!' he mocked me. He said other things, horrible things. Then he left. I haven't heard from him since."

She had to tell Mum and Dad about the baby then. They were furious — not with her, but with Steve. Dad would have killed Steve if he'd found him. But nobody knew where Steve was. He'd vanished.

"Raising Darius was hard," she smiled, ruffling his hair, "but I wouldn't give up a day of it. Steve was wicked, but he gave me the most marvellous gift anyone could have ever given me."

"Soppy old cow," Darius grunted, fighting hard not to smile.

I was quiet a long time after that. I wondered if Steve had meant to use Darius against me even then. This was back before he met the vampaneze and learnt of his abominable destiny. But I bet he was already planning my downfall, one way or the other. Did he deliberately get Annie pregnant, so he could use his nephew or niece to hurt me? Knowing Steve as I did, I guessed those were his exact intentions.

Annie started telling me about her life with Darius, from how Mum and Dad helped rear him until they moved away, how the pair were managing now on their own. She worried about him not having a father, but her experience with Steve had made her wary of men, and she found it hard to trust anyone. I could have listened to Annie talk all night, telling tales about Mum, Dad and Darius. I was catching up on all those missed years. I felt like part of the family again. I didn't want it to stop.

But we were in the middle of a crisis. I'd delayed the moment of truth, but now I had to tell her about it. The night was drawing on, and I was keen to conclude the business I'd come about. I let her finish the story she was telling – about Darius's first week in school – then asked if I could introduce her to some of my friends.

Annie wasn't sure what to make of Vancha, Alice and Evanna. Alice dressed normally, but Vancha in his animal hides, with his straps of throwing stars and green hair, and the hirsute, deliriously ugly Evanna draped in ropes ... They would have stuck out like a couple of gargoyles anywhere!

But they were my friends (well, Vancha and Alice were, whatever about the witch), so Annie welcomed them — though I could tell she didn't entirely trust the trio. And I knew she sensed they weren't here just to make up the numbers. She guessed that something bad was coming.

We made small talk for a while. Alice told Annie about her years on the police force, Vancha described some of his Princely duties and Evanna gave her tips on how to breed frogs (not that Annie had any interest in that!). Then Darius yawned. Vancha looked at me meaningfully — it was time.

"Annie," I started hesitantly, "I told you Darius pledged himself to the vampaneze. But I didn't tell you what precisely that means."

"Go on," Annie said when I stalled.

"Steve blooded him," I said. "He transferred some of his vampaneze blood to Darius. The blood isn't very strong within him, but it will strengthen. The cells will multiply and take over."

"You're saying he'll become like you?" Annie's face was ashen. "He won't age normally? He'll need to drink blood to survive?"

"Yes." Her face crumpled — she thought that was the worst, the part I'd been holding back. I wished I could spare her the truth, but I couldn't. "There's more," I said, and she stiffened. "Vampires can control their feeding habits. It isn't easy — it requires training — but we can. Vampaneze can't. Their blood forces them to kill every time they feed."

"No!" Annie moaned. "Darius isn't a killer! He wouldn't!"

"He would," Vancha grunted. "He'd have no choice. Once a vampaneze gets the taste of blood, his urges consume him. He goes into a kind of trance and feeds until he's drained the source dry. He can't stop."

"But there must be some way to help him!" Annie insisted. "Doctors … surgery … medicine…"

"No," Vancha said. "This isn't a human disease. Your doctors could study him, and restrain him while he was feeding — but do you want your son to spend his life imprisoned?"

"Also," I said, "they couldn't stop him when he was older. As he comes into his full powers, he'll grow incredibly strong. They'd have to keep him comatose to control him."

"No!" Annie shouted, her face dark with stubborn rage. "I won't allow this! There must be a way to save him!"

"There is," I said, and she relaxed slightly. "But it's dangerous. And it won't restore his humanity — it will merely drive him towards a different corner of the night."

"Don't talk in riddles!" Annie snapped. "What does he have to do?"

"Become a vampire," I said.

Annie stared at me in disbelief.

"It's not as bad as it sounds," I went on quickly. "Yes, he'd age slowly, but that's something you and he could learn to cope with. And yes, he'd have to drink blood, but he wouldn't harm when he drank. We'd teach him to master his urges."

"No," Annie said. "There must be another way."

"There isn't," Vancha huffed. "And even this way isn't certain. Nor is it safe."

"I'll have to trade blood with him," I explained. "Pump my vampire cells into his body, and accept his vampaneze cells into mine. The vampire and vampaneze cells will attack each other. If all goes well, Darius will become a half-vampire and I'll carry on as before."

"But if it fails, you'll become a half-vampaneze and Darius won't change?" Annie guessed, trembling at the thought of such a horrible fate.

"No," I said. "It's worse that that. If it fails, I'll die — and so will Darius."

And then I sat back numbly and awaited her decision.

CHAPTER FOUR

Annie didn't like it — nobody did! — but we eventually convinced her that there was no other solution. She wanted to wait, think it over and discuss it with her doctor, but I told her it was now or never. "Vancha and I have a mission to complete," I reminded her. "We might not be able to come back later."

When we'd first discussed the transfusion, Vancha had volunteered. He didn't think it was safe for me to try. I was in the middle of the purge — my vampire cells were taking over, turning me into a full-vampire, and my body was in a state of flux. But when I pressed him, he admitted there was no real reason for thinking that the purge would have any affect on the procedure. It might even work in our favour — since my vampire cells were hyperactive, they might stand a better chance of destroying the vampaneze cells.

We'd tried to quiz Evanna about the dangers. She could look into the future and tell us whether it would succeed or not. But she refused to be drawn. "This has nothing to do with me," she'd said. "I will not comment on it."

"But it must be safe," I'd pressed, hoping for reassurance. "We're destined to meet Steve again. We can't do that if I die."

"Your final encounter with Steve Leonard is by no means set in stone," she'd replied. "If you die beforehand, he will become the Lord of the Shadows by default and the war will swing the way of the vampaneze. Do not think you are immune to danger because of your destiny, Darren — you *can* and perhaps *will* die if you attempt this."

But Darius was my nephew. Vancha didn't approve — he would have preferred to overlook Darius for the time being, and focus on Steve — but I couldn't leave the boy this way, with such a threat hanging over him. If I could save him, I must.

We could have handled the blood transfer with syringes, but Darius insisted on the traditional fingertips method. He was excited, despite the danger, and wanted to do it the old way. "If I'm going to be a vampire, I want to be a real one," he growled. "I don't want to hide my marks. It's all or nothing."

"But it'll be painful," I warned him.

"I don't care," he sniffed.

Annie's doubts remained, but in the end she agreed to the plan. She might not have if Darius had wavered, but he stuck to his guns with grim determination. I hated to admit it — and I didn't say it out loud — but he had his father's sense of commitment. Steve was insanely evil, but he always did what he set out to do, and nothing could change his mind once he'd made it up. Darius was the same.

"I can't believe this is happening," Annie sighed as I sat opposite Darius and prepared to drive my nails into the tips of his fingers. "Earlier tonight I was only thinking about doing the shopping tomorrow, and being here to let Darius in when he got home from school. Then my brother walks back into my life and tells me he's a vampire! And now, as I'm just getting used to that, I might lose him as swiftly as I found him — and my son too!"

She almost called it off then, but Alice stepped up behind her and said softly, "Would you rather lose him when he's human, or when he's a killer like his father?" It was a cruel thing to say, but it steadied Annie's nerves and reminded her of what was at stake. Trembling fiercely, weeping quietly, she stepped away and let me proceed.

Without any warning, I dug my nails into the soft flesh at the tips of Darius's fingers. He yelped painfully and jerked back in his chair. "Don't," I said as he raised his fingers to his mouth to suck them. "Let them bleed."

Darius lowered his hands. Gritting my teeth, I dug my right-hand nails into my left-hand fingertips, then did it the other way round. Blood welled up from ten fleshy springs. I pressed my fingers against Darius's and held them there while my blood flowed into his body, and his into mine.

We remained locked for twenty seconds ... thirty ... more. I could feel the vampaneze cells as soon as his blood entered my veins, itching, burning, sizzling. I ignored the pain. I could see that Darius was also aware of the change, and that it was hurting him more than me. I pressed closer against him, so it was impossible for him to break away.

Vancha stood guard, observing us, calculating. When he thought the time was right, he grabbed my arms and pulled my hands away. I gasped out loud, stood, half smiled, then fell to the floor, writhing in agony. I hadn't expected the cells to kick in so soon, and was unprepared for the brutal speed of the reaction.

During my convulsions, I saw Darius twisting sharply in his chair, eyes bulging, making choking noises, arms and legs thrashing wildly. Annie hurried towards him but Vancha knocked her aside. "Don't interfere!" he barked. "Nature must take its course. We can't get in its way."

For several minutes I jackknifed wildly on the floor. It felt like I was on fire inside my skin. I'd experienced blinding headaches and loads of discomfort during the purge, but this took me to new heights of pain. Pressure built at the back of my eyes, as though my brain was going to bulge out through my eye sockets. I dug the heels of my hands hard into my eyes, then into the sides of my head. I don't know if I was roaring or wheezing — I could hear nothing.

I vomited, then dry-heaved. I crashed into something hard — the TV. I rolled away from it and smashed into a wall. I dug my nails into the plaster and brick, trying to make the pain go away.

Finally the pressure subsided. My limbs relaxed. I stopped dry-heaving. Sight and sound returned, though my fierce headache remained. I looked around, dazed. Vancha was crouching over me, wiping my face clean, smiling. "You've come through it," he said. You'll be OK — with the luck of the vampires."

"Darius?" I gasped.

Vancha raised my head and pointed. Darius was lying on the couch, eyes closed, perfectly still, Annie and Alice kneeling beside him. Evanna sat in a corner, head bowed. For a horrifying moment I thought Darius was dead. Then I saw his chest lift softly and fall, and I knew he was just asleep.

"He'll be fine," Vancha said. "We'll have to keep a close eye on the two of you for a few nights. You'll probably have further fits, less severe than this one. But most who attempt this die of the first seizure. Having survived that, the odds are good for both of you."

I sat up wearily. Vancha took my fingers and spat on them, rubbing his spit in to help close the wounds.

"I feel awful," I moaned.

"You won't improve any time soon," Vancha said. "When I turned from vampanizm to vampirism it took my system a month to settle down, and almost a year to get back to normal. And you've got the purge to contend with too." He chuckled wryly. "You're in for some rough nights, Sire!"

Vancha helped me back to my chair. Alice asked if I'd like water or milk to drink. Vancha said blood would be better for me. Without blinking, Alice used a knife to cut herself and let me feed directly from the wound. Vancha closed the cut with his spit when I was finished. He beamed up at Alice. "You're some woman, Miss Burgess."

"The best," Alice replied dryly.

I leant back, eyes half closed. "I could sleep for a week," I sighed.

"Why don't you?" Vancha said. "You've only recently recovered from a life-threatening wound. You're in the middle of the purge. You've pulled off the most dangerous blood transfusion known to vampires. By the black blood of Harnon Oan, you've earned a rest!"

"But Steve..." I muttered.

"Leonard can wait," Vancha grunted. "We'll send Annie and Darius out of town — Alice will escort them — then get you settled in at the Cirque. A week in your hammock will do you the world of good."

"I guess," I said unhappily. I was thinking about Evra and Merla, and what I could find to say to them. There was Mr Tall to consider too — everyone at the Cirque Du Freak had loved him. Like Shancus, he was dead because of his association with me. Would the people there hate me because of that?

"Who do you think will take over from Mr Tall?" I asked.

"I've no idea," Vancha said. "I don't think anybody ever expected him to die, certainly not in such sudden circumstances."

"Maybe they'll break up," I mused. "Go their own ways, back to whatever they did before they joined. Some might have left the stadium already. I hope–"

"What was that about a stadium?" Annie interrupted. She was still tending to Darius — he was snoring lightly — but she'd overheard us talking.

"The Cirque Du Freak's camped in the old football stadium," I explained. "We're going back there when you leave, but I was saying to Vancha that—"

"The news," Annie interrupted again. "You didn't see tonight's news?"

"No."

"I was watching it when you came in," she said, eyes filling with fresh worry. "I didn't know that's where you were based, so I didn't connect it with you."

"Connect what?" I asked edgily.

"Police have surrounded the stadium," Annie said. "They say the people who killed Tom Jones and the others at the football match are there. I should have put it together earlier, when you were telling me about Tommy, but..." She shook her head angrily, then continued. "They're not letting anyone in or out. When I was watching the news, they hadn't moved in yet. But they said that when they did, they'd go in with full, lethal force. One of the reporters—" She stopped.

"Go on," I said hoarsely.

"He said he'd never seen so many armed police before. He..." She gulped and finished in a whisper. "He said they meant to go in as hard as they could. He said it looked like they planned to kill everyone inside."

CHAPTER FIVE

First things first — make sure Annie and Darius got away safely. I couldn't concentrate on helping my friends trapped inside the stadium if I was worrying about my sister and nephew. Once they were free of Steve's influence, safe somewhere he couldn't find them, I could focus on business entirely. Until that time I would only be a distracted liability.

Annie didn't want to go. This was her home and she wanted to fight to protect it. When, after telling her about some of the atrocities Steve had committed over the years, I convinced her they had to leave, she insisted I go with them. For years she'd believed I was dead. Now she knew otherwise, she didn't want to lose me again so quickly.

"I can't come," I sighed. "Not while my friends are in danger. Later, when it's over, I'll find you."

"Not if Steve kills you!" Annie cried. I had no answer for

that one. "What about Darius?" she pressed. "You said he needs training. What will he do without you?"

"Give us your mobile number," I said. "Alice will contact her people before we go to the stadium. In the worst case scenario, somebody will get in touch. A vampire will link up with you and instruct Darius, or guide him to Vampire Mountain, where Seba or Vanez can look after him."

"Who?" she asked.

"Old friends," I smiled. "They can teach him everything he'll ever need to know about being a vampire."

Annie kept trying to change my mind, telling me my place was with her and Darius, that I was her brother before I became a vampire and I should think of her first. But she was wrong. I left the human world behind when I became a Vampire Prince. I still cared for Annie and loved her, but my first loyalty was to the clan.

When she realized she couldn't win me round, Annie bundled Darius into the back of their car — he was still sound asleep — and tearfully went to gather some personal belongings. I told her to take as much as she could, and not to come back. If we defeated Steve, she and Darius could return. If not, somebody would fetch the rest of her stuff. The house would have to be sold, and they'd remain in hiding under the protection of the vampire clan, for as long as the clan was capable of looking after them. (I didn't say "Until the clan falls," but that's what I was thinking.) It wouldn't be an ideal life — but it would be better than winding up in the hands of Steve Leopard.

Annie hugged me with all her strength before getting into the car. "It's not fair," she wept. "There's so much you haven't told me, so much I want to know, so much I want to say."

"Me too," I said, blinking away tears. It was a weird feeling. Everything was happening at ten times the speed it should. It had only been a few hours since we returned to the Cirque Du Freak to chat with Mr Tall, but it felt like weeks had passed. His death, the chase, Morgan James's beheading, the theatre, Shancus being slaughtered by Steve, finding out about Darius, coming to see my sister … I wanted to put my foot down on the brake, take time out, make sense of all that was going on. But life makes its own rules and sets its own pace. Sometimes you can rein it in and slow it down — other times you can't.

"You really can't come with us?" Annie tried one last time.

"No," I said. "I want to … but no."

"Then I wish you all the luck in the world, Darren," she moaned. She kissed me, began to say something else, then broke down in tears. Hurling herself into the car, she checked on Darius, then started the engine and roared away, disappearing into the night, leaving me standing outside my old home — heartbroken.

"Are you all right?" Alice asked, creeping up behind me.

"I will be," I replied, wiping tears from my eyes. "I wish I'd been able to say goodbye to Darius."

"It's not goodbye," Alice said. "Just *au revoir*."

"Hopefully," I sighed, though I didn't really believe it. Win or lose, I had a sick feeling in my stomach that tonight was the last time I'd ever see Annie and Darius. I paused a moment to wish them a silent farewell, then turned around, put them from my thoughts, and let all my emotions and energies centre on the problems to hand and the dangers faced by my friends at the Cirque Du Freak.

Inside the house, we discussed our next move. Alice was for getting out of town as quickly as possible, abandoning our friends and allies. "Three of us can't make a difference if there are hordes of police stationed around the stadium," she argued. "Steve Leonard remains the priority. The others will have to fend for themselves."

"But they're our friends," I muttered. "We can't just abandon them."

"We must," she insisted. "It doesn't matter how much it hurts. We can't do anything for them now, not without placing our own lives in jeopardy."

"But Evra ... Harkat ... *Debbie.*"

"I know," she said, her eyes sad but hard. "But like I said, it doesn't matter how much it hurts. We have to leave them."

"I don't agree," I said. "I think..." I stopped, reluctant to voice my belief.

"Go on," Vancha encouraged me.

"I can't explain it," I said slowly, eyes flicking to Evanna, "but I think Steve's there. At the stadium. Waiting for us. He set the police on us before — when Alice was one of them — and I can't see him pulling the same trick twice. It would be boring the second time round. He craves originality and new thrills. I think the police outside are just for cover."

"He could have set a trap in the cinema theatre," Vancha mused, taking up my train of thought. "But that wouldn't have been as elaborate a setting as where we fought him before — in the Cavern of Retribution."

"Exactly," I said. "This is our big showdown. He'll want to go out on a high, with something outlandish. He's as much of a performer as anyone at the Cirque Du Freak. He loves theatrics. He'd relish the idea of a stadium setting. It would be like the ancient gladiator duels in the Colosseum."

"We're in trouble if you're wrong," Alice said uneasily.

"Nothing new about that," Vancha huffed. He cocked an eyebrow at Evanna. "Care to drop us a hint?"

To our astonishment, the witch nodded soberly. "Darren is right. You either go to the stadium now and face your destiny, or flee and hand victory to the vampaneze."

"I thought you couldn't tell us stuff like that," Vancha said, startled.

"The endgame has commenced," Evanna answered cryptically. "I can speak more openly about certain matters now, without altering the future."

"It'd alter it if we turned tail and ran like hell for the hills," Vancha grunted.

"No," Evanna smiled. "It wouldn't. As I said, that would simply mean the vampaneze win. Besides," she added, her smile widening, "you aren't going to run, are you?"

"Not in a million years!" Vancha said, spitting against the wall for added emphasis. "But we won't be fools about this either. I say we check out the stadium. If it looks like

Leonard's in residence, we'll force a way in and chop the fiend's head off. If not, we'll search elsewhere and the circus folk will have to make their own luck. No point risking our lives for them at this stage, aye, Darren?"

I thought of my freakish friends — Evra, Merla, Hans Hands and the rest. I thought of Harkat and Debbie, and what might happen to them. And then I thought of my people – the vampires – and what *would* happen to the clan if we threw our lives away trying to save our non-vampire allies.

"Aye," I said miserably, and though I knew I was doing the right thing, I felt like a traitor.

Alice and Vancha checked their weapons while I armed myself with some sharp kitchen knives. Alice made a few phone calls, arranging protection for Annie and Darius. Then, with Evanna in tow, we pulled out and I left my childhood home for the second time in my life, certain in my heart that I'd never again return.

CHAPTER SIX

The journey across town passed without incident. All the police seemed to have been sent or drawn to the stadium. We didn't run into any road blocks or foot patrols. In fact we met hardly anyone. It was eerily quiet. People were in their homes or in pubs, watching the siege on TV, waiting for the action to kick off. It was a silence I knew from the past, the silence that usually comes before battle and death.

Dozens of police cars and vans were parked in a ring around the stadium when we arrived, and armed guards stood watch at every possible entry or exit point. Barriers had been erected to keep back the public and media. Ultra-bright spotlights were trained on the walls of the stadium. My eyes watered from the glare of the lights, even from a long way off, and I had to stop to tie a strip of thick cloth around them.

"Are you sure you're up to this?" Alice asked, studying me doubtfully.

"I'll do what I have to," I growled, although I wasn't as convinced of my vow as I pretended to be. I was in rough shape, the roughest I'd been since my trip down the stream and through the stomach of Vampire Mountain when I'd failed my Trials of Initiation. The purge, my shoulder wound, overall exhaustion and the blood transfusion had sapped me of most of my energy. I wanted only to sleep, not face a fight to the death. But in life we don't usually get to choose the time of our defining moments. We just have to stand and face them when they come, no matter what sort of a state we're in.

A large crowd had gathered around the barriers. We mingled among them, unnoticed by the police in the darkness and crush of people — even the weirdly dressed Vancha and Evanna failed to draw attention. As we gradually pushed our way to the front, we saw thick clouds of smoke rising from within the stadium, and heard the occasional gun report.

"What's happening?" Alice asked the people nearest the barrier. "Have the police moved in?"

"Not yet," a burly man in a hunter's cap informed her. "But a small advance team went in an hour ago. Must be some new crack unit. Most of them had shaved heads and were dressed in brown shirts and black trousers."

"Their eyes were painted red!" a young boy gasped. "I think it was blood!"

"Don't be ridiculous," his mother laughed. "That was just paint, so the glare of the lights wouldn't blind them."

We withdrew, troubled by this new information. As we were leaving, I heard the boy say, "Mummy, one of those women was dressed in ropes!"

His mother responded with a sharp, "Stop making up stories!"

"Sounds like you were right," Alice said when we were at a safe distance. "The vampets are here, and they generally don't go anywhere without their masters."

"But why did the police let them in?" I asked. "They can't be working for the vampaneze — can they?"

We looked at each other uncertainly. Vampires and vampaneze had always kept their battles private, out of the gaze of humanity. Although both sides were in the process of putting together an army of select human helpers, they'd kept the war secret from humans in general. If the vampaneze had broken that age-old custom and were working with regular human forces, it signalled a worrying new twist in the War of the Scars.

"I can still pass for a police officer," Alice said. "Wait here. I'll try to find out more about this."

She slipped forward, through the crowd and past the barrier. She was immediately challenged by a policeman, but following a quick, hushed conversation, she was led away to talk to whoever was in command.

Vancha and I waited anxiously, Evanna standing calmly nearby. I took the time to analyse my situation. I was weak, dangerously so, and my senses were going haywire. My head was pounding and my limbs were trembling. I'd told Alice I was up for a fight, but in all honesty I couldn't say whether or not I'd be able to fend for myself. It would have been wiser to retreat and recover. But Steve had forced this battle. He was calling the shots. I'd have to struggle along as best I could and pray to the gods of the vampires for strength.

I started thinking about Evanna's prophecy again as I waited. If Vancha and I faced Steve this night, one of the three of us would die. If it was Vancha or me, Steve would become the Lord of the Shadows and the vampaneze would rule the night, as well as the world of mankind. But if Steve died, I'd become the Lord instead of him, turn on Vancha and destroy the world.

There must be some way to change that. But how? Try to make peace with Steve? Impossible! I wouldn't even if I could, not after what he'd done to Mr Crepsley, Tommy, Shancus and so many others. Peace wasn't an option.

But what other way was there? I couldn't accept the fact that the world was damned. I didn't care what Evanna said. There must be a way to stop the Lord of the Shadows from rising. There *must*. . .

Alice returned ten minutes later, her features dark. "They're dancing to a vampaneze tune," she said shortly. "I pretended I was an out-of-town chief inspector. I offered my assistance. The ranking officer said they had everything under control. I asked about the brown-shirted soldiers and he told me they were a special government force. He didn't say as much, but I got the feeling he's taking orders from them. I don't know if they've bribed or threatened him, but they're pulling his strings, no doubt about it."

"So you couldn't persuade him to let us in?" Vancha asked.

"I didn't have to," Alice said. "A way's already open. One rear entrance has been left unblocked. The approaching path is being kept clear. The police around that point aren't to interfere with anyone going in."

"He told you that?" I asked, surprised.

"He was under orders to tell anyone who asked," Alice said. She spat on the ground with disgust. "Traitor!"

Vancha looked at me with a thin smile. "Leonard's in there, isn't he?"

"No doubt about it," I nodded. "He wouldn't miss something like this."

Vancha cocked a thumb at the walls of the stadium. "He's laid this on for our benefit. We're the guests of honour. Be a shame to disappoint him."

"We probably won't come out of there alive if we go in," I noted.

"That's negative thinking," Vancha tutted.

"Then we're going to proceed?" Alice asked. "We're going to push on, even though we're outnumbered and outgunned?"

"Aye," Vancha said after a moment's thought. "I'm too long in the tooth to start bothering with wisdom now!"

I grinned at my fellow Prince. Alice shrugged. Evanna remained as blank-faced as ever. Then, without discussing it any further, we slipped around back to the unguarded entrance.

* * *

The lights weren't as bright at the rear of the stadium, and there weren't many people. Lots of police were about, but they deliberately ignored us, as they'd been told to. As we were about to advance through the gap in the ranks of police, Alice stopped us. "I've had an idea," she said hesitantly. "If we all go in, they can close the net around us and we won't be able to punch our way out. But if we attack from two fronts at once…"

She quickly outlined her plan. It made sense to Vancha and me, so we held back while she made several phone calls. Then we waited an impatient hour, taking it easy, preparing ourselves mentally and physically. As we watched, the smoke thickened from the fires inside the stadium, and the crowd around the barriers grew. Many of the newcomers were tramps and homeless people. They mixed with the others and slowly pushed forwards, where they waited close to the barriers, quiet, unnoticed.

When all was as it should be, Alice handed me a pistol and we bade her farewell. The three of us joined hands and wished each other luck. Then Vancha and I set our sights on the unguarded door. With Evanna following us like a ghost, we boldly walked past the ranks of armed police. They averted their eyes or turned their backs on us as we passed. Moments later we left the brightness outside for the darkness of the stadium tunnels and our date with destiny.

We had entered the leopard's den.

CHAPTER SEVEN

The tunnel twisted a lot, but ran directly under the stands to the open interior of the stadium. Vancha and I walked side by side in absolute silence. If Steve was waiting, and the night went against us, one of us would die within the next few hours. There wasn't much to say in a situation like that. Vancha was probably making his peace with the vampire gods. I was worrying about what would happen after the fight, fixed on the idea that there must be some way to stop the coming of the Lord of the Shadows.

There were no traps along the way and we saw nobody. When we left the confines of the tunnel, we stood by the exit for a minute, numbly absorbing the chaos which Steve's troops had created. Evanna moved away slightly to our left, and she studied the carnage too.

The big top of the Cirque Du Freak, along with most of the vans and tents, had been set ablaze — the source of the banks of smoke which clogged the air overhead. The performers and circus crew had been herded together about twenty metres ahead of the tunnel, clear of the stands. Harkat stood among them, near Evra and Merla. I'd never seen his grey face filled with such rage. They were surrounded by eight armed vampets, and spotlights which had been taken from inside the big top were trained upon them. Several dead bodies lay nearby. Most were backstage crew, but one was a long-serving star of the show — the skinny, supple, musical Alexander Ribs would never take to the stage again.

Ripping the piece of cloth away from my eyes, I let my sight adjust, then looked for Debbie among the survivors — there was no sign of her. In a panic, I examined the faces and forms of the corpses again, for fear she was lying among them — but I couldn't see her.

Several vampaneze and vampets patrolled the stadium, circling the burning tents and vans, controlling the flames. As I watched, Mr Tiny strolled out of the burning pyre of the big top, through a wall of fire, rubbing his hands together. He was wearing a red top hat and gloves — Mr Tall's. I understood instinctively that he'd left Mr Tall's body inside the tent, using it as a makeshift funeral pyre. Mr Tiny didn't look upset, but I could tell by his donning of the hat and gloves that, on some level, he'd been in some way affected by his son's death.

Between the burning tent and the surviving members of the Cirque Du Freak stood a new addition — a hastily constructed gallows. Several nooses hung from the crossbeam, but only one was filled — with the poor, thin neck of the snake-boy, Shancus Von.

I cried aloud when I spotted Shancus and made to rush towards him. Vancha gripped my left wrist and jerked me back. "We can't help him now," he growled.

"But—" I started to argue.

"Lower your gaze," he said quietly.

When I did, I saw that a band of vampaneze was grouped beneath the crossbeam and knotted ropes. All were armed with swords or battle-axes. Behind them, standing on something that raised him above them, and smirking evilly, stood their master, the Lord of the Vampaneze — Steve Leopard. He hadn't seen us yet.

"Easy," Vancha said as I stiffened. "No need to rush." His eyes were sliding slowly left and right. "How many vampaneze and vampets are here? Are there more hiding in the stands or behind the burning vans and tents? Let's work out exactly what we have to deal with before we go barging ahead."

Breathing deeply, I forced myself to think calmly, then studied the lie of the land. I counted fourteen vampaneze – nine grouped around Steve – and more than thirty vampets. I didn't see Gannen Harst, but guessed he would be close by Steve, hidden by the group of circus folk between us and the gallows.

"I make it a dozen-plus vampaneze and three times that amount of vampets, aye?" Vancha said.

"More or less," I agreed.

Vancha looked sideways at me and winked. "The odds are in our favour, Sire."

"You think so?"

"Most definitely," he said with fake enthusiasm — we both knew it didn't look good. We were vastly outnumbered by enemies with superior weapons. Our only ace card was that the vampaneze and vampets couldn't kill us. Mr Tiny had predicted doom for them if anybody other than their Lord murdered the hunters.

Without saying anything, we started forward at the exact same moment. I was carrying two knives, one in either hand. Vancha had drawn a couple of throwing stars but was otherwise unarmed — he believed in fighting with his bare hands at close quarters. Evanna moved when we did, shadowing our every footstep.

The vampets surrounding the imprisoned Cirque Du Freak troupe saw us coming but didn't react, except to close a little more tightly around the people they were guarding. They didn't even warn the others that we were here. Then I saw that they didn't need to — Steve and his cronies had already spotted us. Steve was standing on a box, or something, staring happily at us, while the vampaneze in front of him bunched defensively, weapons at the ready.

We had to pass the circus prisoners to get to Steve. I stopped as we drew level with Evra, Merla and Harkat. Evra and Merla's eyes were wet with tears. Harkat's green globes were shining with fury, and he'd pulled down his mask to bare his sharp grey teeth (he could survive up to half a day without the mask).

I gazed sorrowfully at Evra and Merla, then at the body of their son, dangling from the gallows further ahead. The vampets guarding my friends watched me cautiously but made no move against me.

"Come on," Vancha said, tugging at my elbow.

"I'm sorry," I croaked to Evra and Merla, unable to continue without saying something. "I wouldn't ... I didn't ... if I could..." I stopped, unable to think of anything else to say.

Evra and Merla said nothing for a moment. Then, with a screech, Merla smashed through the guards around her and threw herself at me. "I hate you!" she screamed, scratching my face, spitting with rage. "My son's dead because of you!"

I couldn't react. I felt sick with shame. Merla dragged me to the ground, yelling and crying, beating me with her fists. The vampets moved forward to pull her off, but Steve shouted, "No! Leave them alone! This is fun!"

We rolled away from the vampets, Merla driving me back. I didn't even raise my hands to defend myself as she called me every name under the moon. I just wanted the earth to open and swallow me whole.

And then, as Merla lowered her face as though to bite me, she whispered in my ear, "Steve has Debbie." I gawped at her. She roared more insults, then whispered again, "We didn't fight. They think we're gutless, but we were waiting for *you*. Harkat said you'd come and lead us."

Merla cuffed me about the head, then locked gazes with me. "It wasn't your fault," she said, smiling ever so slightly through her tears. "We don't hate you. Steve's the evil one — not you."

"But ... if I hadn't ... if I'd told Vancha to kill R.V..."

"Don't think that way," she snarled. "You're not to blame. Now help us kill the savages who *are*! Give us a signal when you're ready and we'll answer the call. We'll fight to the death, every last one of us."

She screamed at me again, grabbed me by the neck to strangle me, then fell off and punched the ground, sobbing pitifully. Evra pushed forward, collected his wife and led her back to the pack. He glanced at me once, fleetingly, and I saw the same thing in his expression that I'd seen in Merla's — sorrow for the loss of their son, hatred for Steve and his gang, but only pity for me.

I still felt at fault for what had happened to Shancus and the others. But Evra and Merla's sympathy gave me the strength to carry on. If they'd hated me, I doubt I could have continued. But now that they'd given me their backing, I not only felt able to push on — I felt that I had to. For their sakes, if not my own.

I got to my feet, acting shaken. As Vancha came to help me, I spoke quickly and quietly. "They're with us. They'll fight when we do."

He paused, then carried forward as though I hadn't spoken, checking my face where Merla had scratched me, loudly asking if she'd harmed me, if I was OK, if I wanted to rest a while.

"I'm fine," I grunted, pushing past him, showing my circus friends a stiff back, as if they'd insulted me. "Merla said Steve has Debbie," I hissed to Vancha out of the side of my mouth, barely moving my lips.

"We might not be able to save her," he whispered back.

"I know," I said stonily. "But we'll try?"

A short pause. Then, "Aye," he replied.

With that, we quickened our pace and made a beeline for the gallows and the grinning, demonic, half-vampaneze beast waiting underneath, face half hidden by the shadow of the dangling Shancus Von.

CHAPTER EIGHT

"Halt!" one of the nine vampaneze in front of Steve shouted when we were about five metres away. We stopped. This close, I saw that Steve was actually standing on the body of one of the circus crew — Pasta O'Malley, a man who used to sleepwalk and even sleep-read. I could also see Gannen Harst now, just to Steve's right, sword undrawn, watching us intently.

"Drop your throwing stars," the vampaneze said to Vancha. When he didn't respond, two of the vampaneze raised spears and pointed them at him. With a shrug, Vancha slid the shurikens back into their holders and lowered his hands.

I glanced up at Shancus, swinging in the light breeze. The crossbeam creaked. The sound was louder than normal for me because of the purge — like the squeal of a wild boar.

"Get him down," I snarled at Steve.

"I don't think so," Steve replied lightly. "I like the sight of him up there. Maybe I'll hang his parents beside him. His brother and sister too. Keep the whole family together. What do you think?"

"Why do you go along with this madman?" Vancha asked Gannen Harst. "I don't care what Des Tiny says about him — this lunatic can bring nothing but shame upon the vampaneze. You should have killed him years ago."

"He is of our blood," Gannen Harst replied quietly. "I don't agree with his ways – he knows that – but we don't kill our kin."

"You do if they break your laws," Vancha grunted. "Leonard lies and uses guns. Any normal vampaneze would be executed if they did that."

"But he isn't normal," Gannen said. "He is our Lord. Desmond Tiny said we would perish if we did not follow him and obey. Whether I like it or not, Steve has the power to bend our laws, or even ignore them completely. I'd rather he didn't, but it's not my place to chastise him when he does."

"You can't approve of his actions," Vancha pushed.

"No," Gannen admitted. "But he has been accepted by the clan, and I am only a servant of my people. History can judge Steve. I'm content to serve and protect, in line with the wishes of those who appointed me."

Vancha glared at his brother, trying to stare him down, but Gannen only gazed back blankly. Then Steve laughed. "Aren't family get-togethers a joy?" he said. "I was hoping you'd bring Annie and Darius along. Imagine the fun all six of us could have had!"

"They're far away from here by now," I said. I wanted to dive for him and rip his throat open with my bare hands and teeth, but his guards would have cut me down before I struck. I had to be patient and pray for a chance to present itself.

"How's my son?" Steve asked. "Did you kill him?"

"Of course not," I snorted. "I didn't have to. When he saw you murder Shancus he realized you were a monster. I filled him in on your past *glories*. Annie told him some old stories too. He'll never listen to you again. You've lost him. He's your son no more."

I hoped to wound Steve with my words but he just laughed them off. "Oh well, I was never that fond of him anyway. A scrawny, moody kid. No taste for blood. Although," he chuckled, "I guess he'll develop one soon!"

"I wouldn't be too sure of that," I retorted.

"I blooded him," Steve boasted. "He's half-vampaneze."

"No," I smiled. "He's a half-vampire. Like me."

Steve stared at me uncertainly. "You re-blooded him?"

"Yes. He's one of us now. He won't need to kill when he feeds. Like I said, he's no longer your son — in any way whatsoever."

Steve's features darkened. "You shouldn't have done that," he growled. "The boy was mine."

"He was never yours, not in spirit," I said. "You merely tricked him into believing he was."

Steve started to reply, then scowled and shook his head gruffly. "Never mind," he muttered. "The child's not important. I'll deal with him — and his mother — later. Let's get down to the good stuff. We all know the prophecy." He nodded at Mr Tiny, who was wandering around the burning tents and vans, paying no apparent interest to us. "Darren or Vancha will kill me, or I'll kill one of you, and that will decide the fate of the War of the Scars."

"If Tiny's right, or telling the truth, aye," Vancha sniffed.

"You don't believe him?" Steve frowned.

"Not entirely," Vancha said. "Tiny and his daughter—" He glared at Evanna —"have agendas of their own. I accept most of what they predict but I don't treat their predictions as absolute facts."

"Then why are you here?" Steve challenged him.

"In case they *are* correct."

Steve looked confused. "How can you not believe them? Desmond Tiny is the voice of destiny. He sees the future. He knows all that has been and will be."

"We make our own futures," Vancha said. "Regardless of what happens tonight, I believe my people will defeat yours. But I'll kill you anyway," he added with a wicked grin. "Just to be on the safe side."

"You're an ignorant fool," Steve said, shaking with outrage. Then his gaze settled on me. "I bet *you* believe the prophecy."

"Maybe," I replied.

"Of course you do," Steve smiled. "And you know it's you or me, don't you? Vancha's a red herring. You and I are the sons of destiny, the ruler and slave, the victor and vanquished. Leave Vancha behind, step up here alone, and I swear it will be a fair fight. You and me, man to man, one winner, one loser. A Vampaneze Lord to rule the night — or a Vampire Prince."

"How can I trust you?" I asked. "You're a liar. You'll spring a trap."

"No," Steve barked. "You have my word."

"Like that means anything," I jeered, but I could see an eagerness in Steve's expression. His offer was genuine. I glanced sideways at Vancha. "What do you think?"

"No," Vancha said. "We're in this together. We'll take him on as a team."

"But if he's prepared to fight me fairly…"

"That demon knows nothing about fairness," Vancha said. "He'd cheat — that's his nature. We'll do nothing the way he wants."

"Very well." I faced Steve again. "Stuff your offer. What next?"

I thought Steve was going to leap over the ranks of vampaneze and attack me. He gnashed his teeth, hands twisted together, shivering furiously. Gannen Harst saw it too, but to my surprise, rather than step in to calm Steve down, he took a half-step back. It was as if he wanted Steve to leap, like he'd had enough of his insane, evil Lord, and wanted this matter settled, one way or the other.

But just when it seemed as if the moment of final confrontation had come, Steve relaxed and his smile returned. "I do my best," he sighed. "I try to make it easy for everybody, but some people are determined not to play ball. Very well. Here's 'what next'."

Steve put his fingers to his lips and whistled sharply. From behind the gallows, R.V. stepped out. The bearded, ex-eco-warrior was holding a rope between three lonely-looking hooks (Mr Tall had snapped the other hooks off before he died). When he tugged on the rope, a bound woman shuffled out after him — Debbie.

I'd been expecting this, so I didn't panic. R.V. walked Debbie forwards a few paces, but stopped a long way short of Steve. The one-time campaigner for peace and the protection of mother nature didn't look very happy. He was twitchy, head jerking, eyes unfocused, nervously chewing at his lower lip, which was bleeding from where he'd bitten through the flesh. R.V. had been a proud, earnest, dedicated man when I first met him, fighting to save the world from pollution. Then he'd become a mad beast, intent only on gaining revenge for the loss of his hands. Now he was neither — just a ragged, sorry mess.

Steve didn't notice R.V.'s confusion. He had eyes only for Debbie. "Isn't she beautiful?" he mocked me. "Like an angel. More warrior-like than the last time we met, but all the lovelier because of it." He looked at me slyly. "Be a shame if I had to tell R.V. to gut her like a rabid dog."

"You can't use her against me," I said softly, gazing at Steve without blinking. "She knows who you are and what's at stake. I love her, but my first duty is to my clan. She understands that."

"You mean you'll stand there and let her die?" Steve shrieked.

"Yes!" Debbie shouted before I could reply.

"You people," Steve groaned. "You're determined to annoy me. I try to be fair, but you toss it back in my face and…" He hopped off of Pasta O'Malley's back and ranted and raved, striding up and down behind his guards. I kept a close watch on him. If he stepped out too far, I'd strike. But even in his rage he was careful not to expose himself.

All of a sudden Steve stopped. "So be it!" he snarled. "R.V. — kill her!"

R.V. didn't respond. He was gazing miserably down at the ground.

"R.V.!" Steve shouted. "Didn't you hear me? Kill her!"

"Don't want to," R.V. mumbled. His eyes came up and I saw pain and doubt in them. "You shouldn't have killed the kid, Steve. He did nothing to hurt us. It was wrong. Kids are the future, man."

"I did what I had to," Steve replied tightly. "Now you'll do the same."

"But she's not a vampire…"

"She works for them!" Steve shouted.

"I know," R.V. moaned. "But why do we have to kill her? Why did you kill the kid? It was Darren we were meant to kill. *He's* the enemy, man. He's the one who cost me my hands."

"Don't betray me now," Steve growled, stepping towards the bearded vampaneze. "You've killed people too, the innocent as well as the guilty. Don't get moralistic on me. It doesn't become you."

"But … but … but…"

"Stop stuttering and kill her!" Steve screamed. He took another step forward and moved clear of his guards without being aware of it. I steeled myself to make a dash at him, but Vancha was one move ahead of me.

"*Now!*" Vancha roared, leaping forward, drawing a shuriken and launching it at Steve. He would have killed him, except the guard at the end of the line saw the danger just in time and threw himself into the path of the deadly throwing star, sacrificing himself to save his Lord.

As the other guards surged sideways to block Vancha's path to their Lord, I sheathed my knives, drew the pistol I'd borrowed from Alice before entering the stadium, aimed it at the sky and pulled the trigger three times — the signal for all-out riot!

CHAPTER NINE

Even before the echoes of the report of my third shot faded, the air outside the stadium filled with answering gunfire, as Alice and her band of vampirites opened fire on the police standing guard. She'd summoned the homeless people before Vancha and I entered the tunnel, and positioned them around the barrier outside the stadium. After years of surviving on the scraps other people threw away, this was their time to rise. They had only a small amount of training and basic weapons, but they had passion and anger on their side, and the desire to prove themselves. So now, at my signal, they leapt the barriers around the stadium and attacked as a unified force, throwing themselves upon the startled police, sacrificing themselves where necessary, fighting and dying not just for their own lives, but for the lives of those who considered them trash.

We weren't sure of the intentions of the police. Steve might have told them to remain outside regardless of what happened within, in which case the attack by the vampirites would serve no purpose at all. But if they were there to support the vampaneze and vampets, to come to their aid if summoned, the vampirites could divert them and buy those of us inside the stadium a bit more space and time.

Most of the vampaneze guarding Steve moved to stop Vancha when he charged, but two lunged at me as I fired the pistol. They tackled me to the ground, knocking the gun from my hand. I struck out at them but they simply lay on top of me, pinning me down. They would have held me there, helpless, while their colleagues dealt with Vancha. Except...

The stars and crew of the Cirque Du Freak had also rallied to my signal. At the same time that the vampirites attacked the police, the prisoners inside the stadium turned on the vampets holding them captive. They attacked with their bare hands, driving the vampets back by sheer force of numbers. The vampets fired into the crowd and hacked wildly with their swords and axes. Several people fell, dead or wounded. But the group pushed on regardless, screaming, punching, kicking, biting — no force on Earth could hold them back.

While the bulk of the Cirque Du Freak troupe grappled with the vampets, Harkat led a small band towards the gallows. He'd grabbed an axe from a dead vampet and with one smooth swing he cut down a vampaneze who tried to intercept them, rushing past without breaking his stride.

Vancha was still locked in a struggle with Steve's guards, doing his best to break through to their Lord. He'd downed two of them but the others were standing firm. He was cut in many places, knife and spear wounds, but none fatal. Looking around, I saw Gannen Harst push Steve away from the threat. Steve was arguing with him — he wanted to take Vancha on.

Behind Steve and Gannen Harst, R.V. had let go of Debbie's rope and was backing away from her, shaking his head, hooks crossed behind his back, wanting no part of this. Debbie was tugging at her bonds, trying to wriggle free.

The two vampaneze holding me down saw Harkat and the others racing towards them. Cursing, they abandoned me and lashed out at their attackers. They were too swift for the ordinary circus folk — three died quickly — but Truska was part of the group, and she wasn't so easily despatched. She'd let her beard grow while she'd been waiting to fight — the unnatural blonde hair now trailed down past her feet. Standing back, she made the beard rise — she could control the hairs as though they were snakes — then directed the twisting strands towards one of the vampaneze. The beard parted into two prongs, then curled around the startled vampaneze's throat and tightened. He sliced at the hair and at Truska, but she had him too firmly in her grip. He fell to his knees, purple features darkening even further as he choked.

Harkat took on the other vampaneze, chopping at him with his axe. The Little Person lacked the speed of a vampaneze, but he was very powerful and his round green eyes were alert to his opponent's swift moves. He could fight as an equal, as he had many times in the past.

I circled around the vampaneze struggling with Vancha. I meant to go after Steve, but he and Gannen had linked up with three of the vampaneze who'd been roaming the grounds of the stadium. I didn't fancy the five-to-one odds, so I went to cut Debbie free instead.

"They surrounded the stadium shortly after Harkat and I arrived," she cried as I sliced through the ropes binding her arms. "I tried phoning, but it wouldn't work. It was Mr Tiny. He blocked my signal. I saw his watch glowing, and he was laughing."

"It's OK," I said. "We'd have come anyway. We had to."

"Is that Alice outside?" Debbie asked — the gunfire was deafening now.

"Yes," I said. "The vampirites seem to be enjoying their first taste of action."

Vancha lurched over to us, streaming blood. The vampaneze had given up on him and retreated, teaming up with the vampets and picking fights with the circus folk. "Where's Leonard?" Vancha bellowed.

I peered around the stadium but it was almost impossible to pick out any individuals in the press of bodies. "I had him in my sights a minute ago," I said. "He must be here somewhere."

"Not if Gannen flitted with him!" Vancha roared. He wiped blood clear of his eyes and looked for Steve and Gannen again.

"Are you badly wounded?" Debbie asked him.

"Scratches!" Vancha grunted. Then he shouted, "There! Behind the fat man!"

He rushed forward, bellowing madly. Squinting, I caught a glimpse of Steve. He was close to the enormous Rhamus Twobellies, warily backing away from him. Rhamus was literally falling on his opponents, squashing them lifeless.

Debbie darted away from me, picked the bodies of the dead vampaneze clean of their weapons, and returned with an array of knives and two swords. She gave one of the swords to me and hefted the other herself. It was too large for her, but she held it steady, face set. "You go get Steve," she said. "I'll help the others."

"Be—" I began, but she'd already raced out of earshot, "—careful," I finished softly. I shook my head, smiled briefly, then set off after Steve.

Around me the battle was raging. The circus folk were locked in bloody combat with the vampets and vampaneze, fighting clumsily but effectively, blind fury compensating for lack of military training. The gifted freaks were a huge help. Truska was causing havoc with her beard. Rhamus was an immovable foe. Gertha Teeth was biting off fingers, noses, sword tips. Hans Hands had tucked his legs behind his neck and was dodging between the enemy forces on his hands, too low for them to easily strike, tripping them up and dividing them.

Vancha had come to a halt, held up by the fighting. He started firing shurikens at those enemies ahead of him, to clear a path. Jekkus Flang stepped up beside him and added his throwing knives to Vancha's stars. A deadly, efficient combination. I couldn't help thinking what a great show they could have put on if we'd been playing to an audience tonight instead of fighting for our lives.

Mr Tiny was picking his way through the mass of warring bodies, beaming merrily, admiring the corpses of the dead, studying the dying with polite interest, applauding those locked in especially vicious duels. Evanna was edging towards her father, disinterested in the carnage, bare feet and lower ropes stained with blood.

Gannen and Steve were still backing away from the massive Rhamus Twobellies, using him as a shield — it was hard for anybody else to get at them with Rhamus in the way. I tracked them like a hound, closing in. I was almost at the mouth of the tunnel through which we'd entered the stadium when fresh bodies burst through it. My insides tightened — I thought the police had come to the aid of their companions, meaning almost certain defeat for us. But then, to my astonished delight, I realized it was Alice Burgess and a dozen or so vampirites. Declan and Little Kenny – the pair who'd rescued me from the street when Darius shot me – were among them.

"Still alive?" Alice shouted as her troops laid into the vampaneze and vampets, faces twisted with excitement and battle lust.

"How'd you get in?" I yelled in reply. The plan had been for her to cause a diversion outside the stadium, to hold up the police — not invade with a force of her own.

"We attacked at the front, as planned," she said. "The police rushed to that point, to battle *en masse* — they lack discipline. Most of my troops fled with the crowd after a few minutes — you should have seen the chaos! — but I slipped around the back with a few volunteers. The entrance to the tunnel is completely unguarded now. We—"

A vampet attacked her and she had to wheel aside to deal with him. I did a very quick head count. With the addition of the vampirites, we seriously outnumbered the vampaneze and vampets. Although the fighting was brutal and disorganized, we had the upper hand. Unless the police outside recovered swiftly and rushed in, we'd win this battle! But that would mean nothing if Steve escaped, so I put all thoughts of victory on hold and went in pursuit of him again.

I didn't get very far. R.V. had backed away from the fighting. He was heading for the tunnel, but I was standing almost directly in his path. When he saw me, he stopped. I wasn't sure what to do — fight or let him escape so that I could go after Steve? While I was making up my mind, Cormac Limbs stepped in between us.

"Come on, hairy!" he roared at R.V., slapping his face with his left hand, jabbing at him with a knife held in his right. "Let's be having you!"

"No!" R.V. moaned. "I don't want to fight."

"The devil you don't, you big, bearded, bug-eyed baboon!" Cormac shouted, slapping R.V. again. This time R.V. lashed out at Cormac's hand with his hooks. He cut two of the fingers off, but they immediately grew back. "You'll have to do better than that, stink-breath!" Cormac taunted him.

"Then I will!" R.V. shouted, losing his cool. Jumping forwards, he knocked Cormac over, knelt on his chest, and before I could do anything, he struck at Cormac's neck with his hooks. He didn't cut it clean off, but sliced about halfway through. Then, with a grunt, he hacked through the rest of it, and tossed Cormac's head aside like a ball.

"You shouldn't have messed with me, man!" R.V. groaned, rising shakily. I was about to attack him, to avenge Cormac's death, but then I saw that he was sobbing. "I didn't want to kill you!" R.V. howled. "I didn't want to kill anybody! I wanted to help people. I wanted to save the world. I..."

He ground to a halt, eyes widening with disbelief. Glancing down, I also came to a stunned stop. Where Cormac's head had been, two new heads were growing, shooting out on a pair of thin necks. They were slightly smaller than his old head, but otherwise identical. When they stopped growing, there was a short pause. Then Cormac's eyes fluttered open and he spat blood out of both mouths. His eyes came into focus. He looked at R.V. with one set and at me with the other. Then his heads turned and he stared at himself.

"So that's what happens when I cut my head off!" he exclaimed through both mouths at the same time. "I always wondered about that!"

"Madness!" R.V. screamed. "The world's gone mad! *Mad!*"

Spinning crazily, he rushed past Cormac, then past me, gibbering insanely, drooling and falling over. I could have killed him easily — but I chose not to. Standing aside, I let the wretch pass, and watched sadly as he staggered down the tunnel, out of sight. R.V. had never been right in the head since losing his hands, and now he'd lost his senses completely. I couldn't bring myself to punish this pathetic shadow of a man.

And now, at last — Steve. He and Gannen were part of a small band of vampaneze and vampets. They'd been forced towards the centre of the stadium by the freaks, circus helpers and vampirites. Lots of smaller fights were still being waged around the stadium, but this was their last big stand. If this unit fell, they were all doomed.

Vancha was closing in on the group. I joined him. There was no sign of Jekkus Flang — I didn't know whether he'd fallen to the enemy or run out of knives, and this wasn't the time to make enquiries. Vancha paused when he saw me. "Ready?" he asked.

"Ready," I said.

"I don't care which of us kills him," Vancha said, "but let me go first. If—" He stopped, face twisting with fear. "No!" he roared.

Following the direction of his eyes, I saw that Steve had tripped. Evra stood over him, a long knife held in both hands, determined to take the life of the man who'd killed his son. If he struck, the Lord of the Vampaneze would die by the hand of one who wasn't destined to kill him. If Mr Tiny's prophecy was true, that would have dire results for the vampire clan.

As we watched, unable to prevent it, Evra stopped abruptly. He shook his head, blinked dumbly — then stepped over Steve and left him lying on the ground, unharmed. Steve sat up, bleary-eyed, not sure what had happened. Gannen Harst stooped and helped him to his feet. The two men stood, alone in the crush, totally ignored by everyone around them.

"Over there," I whispered, touching Vancha's shoulder. Far off to our right, Mr Tiny stood, eyes on Steve and Gannen. He was holding his heart-shaped watch in his right hand. It was glowing redly. Evanna was standing beside him, her face illuminated by the glow of her father's watch.

I don't know if Steve and Gannen saw Mr Tiny and realized that he was protecting them. But they were alert enough to seize their chance and run for the freedom of the tunnel.

Mr Tiny watched the pair race free of danger. Then he looked at Vancha and me, and smiled. The glow of his watch faded and his lips moved softly. Even though we were a long way off, we heard him clearly, as if he was standing next to us. "It's time, boys!"

"Harkat!" I shouted, wanting him to come with us, to be there at the end, as he'd been by my side for so much of the hunt. But he didn't hear me. Nobody did. I glanced around the stadium at Harkat, Alice, Evra, Debbie. All of my friends were locked in battle with the vampaneze and vampets. None of them knew what was happening with Steve and Gannen Harst. They weren't part of this. It was just me and Vancha now.

"To the death, Sire?" Vancha murmured.

"To the death," I agreed miserably. I ran my eyes over the faces of my friends for what might be the final time, bidding silent farewells to the scaly Evra Von, the grey-skinned Harkat Mulds, the steely Alice Burgess and my beloved Debbie Hemlock, more beautiful than ever as she tore into her foes like an Amazonian warrior of old. Perhaps it was for the best that I couldn't bid them a proper farewell. There was so much to say, I don't know where I would have begun.

Then Vancha and I jogged after Steve and Gannen Harst, not rushing, sure that they wouldn't flit, not this time, not until we'd satisfied the terms of Mr Tiny's prophecy and Steve or one of us lay dead. Behind us, Mr Tiny and Evanna followed like ghosts. They alone would bear witness to the final battle, the death of one of the hunters or Steve — and the birth of the Lord of the Shadows, destroyer of the present and all-ruling monster of the future.

CHAPTER TEN

We followed Steve and Gannen down the hill at the rear of the stadium. They were fleeing towards the river, but they weren't racing at top speed. Either one of them was injured or, like ourselves, they'd simply accepted the fact that we had to fight, an evenly matched contest, to the bitter, bloody end.

As we jogged down the hill, leaving the stadium, lights and noises behind, my headache lessened. I would have been glad of that, except now that I was able to focus, I realized how physically drained I was. I'd been operating on reserve energy for a long time and had just about run dry. Even the simplest movement was a huge chore. All I could do was carry on as long as possible and hope I got an adrenaline burst when we caught up with our prey.

As we reached level ground at the bottom of the hill, I stumbled and almost fell. Luckily Vancha had been keeping an eye on me. He caught and steadied me. "Feel bad?" he asked.

"Awful," I groaned.

"Maybe you're not meant to go any further," he said. "Perhaps you should rest here and—"

"Save your breath," I stopped him. "I'm going on, even if I have to crawl."

Vancha laughed, then tilted my head back and examined my face, his small eyes unusually dark. "You'll make a fine vampire," he said. "I hope I'm around to celebrate your coming of age."

"You're not getting defeatist on me, are you?" I grunted.

"No." He smiled weakly. "We'll win. Of course we will. I just..."

He stopped, slapped my back and urged me on. Wearily, every step an effort, I threw myself after Steve and Gannen Harst again. I did my best to match Vancha's pace, swinging my legs as evenly as I could, keeping the rest of my body limp, relaxed, saving energy.

Steve and Gannen reached the river and turned right, jogging along the bank. As they came to the arch of a bridge spanning the river, they stopped. It looked like they were having an argument. Gannen was trying to pick Steve up — I assumed he meant to flit, with Steve on his back, as they'd escaped from us once before. Steve was having none of it. He slapped his protector's hands away, gesturing furiously. Then, as we closed upon them, Gannen's shoulders sagged and he nodded wearily. The pair turned away from the pass beneath the bridge, drew their weapons and stood waiting for us.

We slowed and walked the rest of the way. I could hear Mr Tiny and Evanna close behind — they'd caught up to us within the last few seconds — but I didn't turn to look back.

"You could use your shurikens," I whispered to Vancha as we came within range of Steve and Gannen Harst.

"That would be dishonourable," Vancha replied. "They've faced us openly, in expectation of a fair fight. We must confront them."

He was right. Killing mercilessly wasn't the vampire way. But I half wished he'd put his principles aside, for once, and fire his throwing stars at them until they dropped. It would be much simpler and surer that way.

We drew to a halt a couple of metres short of Steve and Gannen. Steve's eyes were alight with excitement and a slight shade of fear — he knew there were no guarantees now, no more opportunities for dirty tricks or games. It was a plain, fair fight to the death, and that was something he couldn't control.

"Greetings, brother," Gannen Harst said, bowing his head.

"Greetings," Vancha replied stiffly. "I'm glad you face us like true creatures of the night at last. Perhaps in death you can find again the honour which you abandoned during life."

"Honour will be shared by all here tonight," Gannen said, "both the living and the dead."

"They don't half go on a lot," Steve sighed. He squared up to me. "Ready to die, Shan?"

I stepped forward. "If that's what fate has in store for me — yes," I answered. "But I'm also ready to kill." With that I raised my sword and struck the first blow of the fight which would decide the outcome of the War of the Scars.

Steve stood his ground, brought his own sword up – it was shorter and easier to handle than mine – and turned my blow aside. Gannen Harst stabbed at me with his long, straight sword. Vancha slapped the blade wide of its target and pulled me out of immediate range of his brother.

Vancha only gave me a relatively gentle tug, but in my weakened state I staggered backwards and wound up in an untidy mess on the ground, close to Mr Tiny and Evanna. By the time I struggled to my feet, Vancha was locked in combat with Steve and Gannen Harst, hands a blur as he defended himself against their swords with his bare palms.

"He's a fierce creature, isn't he?" Mr Tiny remarked to his daughter. "Quite the beast of nature. I like him."

Evanna didn't reply. All her senses were focused on the battle, and there was worry and uncertainty in her eyes. I knew in that moment that she'd told the truth and really didn't know which way this would go.

I turned away from the onlookers and caught quick flashes of the fight which was unfolding at superhuman speed. Steve nicked Vancha's left arm near the top — Vancha kicked him in the chest in return. Gannen's sword scraped down Vancha's left side, slicing a thin gouge from breast to waist — Vancha replied by grabbing his brother's sword hand and wrenching it back, snapping the bones of his wrist. Gannen gasped with pain as he dropped the sword, then ducked for it and grabbed it with his left hand. As he came to his feet again, Vancha struck his head with his right knee. Gannen fell away with a heavy grunt.

Vancha spun round to deal with Steve, but Steve was already upon him, making short sweeps with his sword, keeping Vancha at bay. Vancha tried to grab the sword, but only succeeded in having the flesh of his palms cut open. I staggered up beside him. I wasn't of much use right then — I could barely raise my sword, and my legs dragged like dead weights — but at least it provided Steve with a double threat. If I could distract him, Vancha might be able to penetrate his defences and strike.

As I drew level with Vancha, panting and sweating, Gannen swung back into battle, dazed but determined, chopping angrily at Vancha, forcing him to retreat. I stabbed at Gannen, but Steve diverted my sword with his, then let go of the handle with one hand and punched me between the eyes. I dropped back, startled, and Steve drove the tip of his sword at my face.

If he'd had both hands on the sword, he'd have thrust it through me. But one-handed, he wasn't able to direct it as powerfully as he wished. I managed to knock it aside with my left arm. A deep cut opened up just below my elbow and I felt all the strength leave the fingers of that hand.

Steve stabbed at me again. I raised my sword to protect myself. Too late I realized he'd only feinted. Wheeling around, he threw himself into me, right shoulder first. He struck me heavily in the chest and I fell back, winded losing hold of my sword. There was a yell behind me and I crashed into Vancha. Both of us went down, Vancha taken by surprise, arms and legs entangled with mine.

It took Vancha no more than a second to free himself — but that second was all Gannen Harst required. Darting forward, almost too fast for me to see, he stuck the tip of his sword into the small of Vancha's back — then shoved it all the way through and out the front of Vancha's stomach!

Vancha's eyes and mouth shot wide open. Gannen stood behind him a moment. Then he stepped away and pulled his sword free. Blood gushed out of Vancha, both in front and behind, and he collapsed in agony, face twisted, limbs thrashing.

"May your gods forgive me, brother," Gannen whispered, his face haggard, eyes haunted. "Though I fear I'll never forgive myself."

I scrabbled away from the downed Prince, chasing my sword. Steve stood close by, laughing. With an effort, Gannen regained control and set about securing victory. Hurrying over to me, he stood on my sword so that I couldn't lift it, sheathed his own blade and grabbed my head with his good left hand. "Hurry!" he barked at Steve. "Kill him quick!"

"What's the rush?" Steve muttered.

"If Vancha dies of the wound I gave him, we'll have broken the rules of Mr Tiny's prophecy!" Gannen shouted.

Steve pulled a face. "Bloody prophecies," he grumbled. "Maybe I'll let him die and see what happens. Maybe I don't care about Tiny or..." He stopped and rolled his eyes. "Oh, how *silly* we are! The answer's obvious — *I'll* kill Vancha before he dies of your wound. That way we'll fulfil the requirements of the stupid prophecy *and* I'll get to hang on to Darren, so I can torture him later."

"Clever boy," I heard Mr Tiny murmur.

"Have it any way you wish!" Gannen roared. "But if you're going to kill him, kill him now, so that—"

"*No!*" someone screamed. Before anyone could react, a large shape shot out of the underpass beneath the bridge and hurled itself at Gannen, knocking him off me, almost toppling him into the river. Sitting up, I got a shocked fix on my most unlikely of rescuers — *R.V.!*

"Not gonna let you do it, man!" R.V. screamed, pounding Gannen Harst with his hooks. "You're evil!"

Gannen had been taken completely unawares, but he swiftly recovered, fumbled his sword free of its scabbard, and dug at R.V. with it. R.V. caught the sword with his gold right-handed hooks and smashed it against the ground, snapping it in two. With a roar of triumph, he slammed his silver left-handed hook into the side of Gannen's head. There was a crack and Gannen's eyes went blank. He slumped beneath R.V., unconscious. R.V. howled with joy, then drew both arms back to bring them down sharply and finish Gannen off.

Before R.V. could strike, Steve stepped up behind him and forced a knife up beneath his bushy beard, deep into his throat. R.V. shuddered and bowled Steve over. R.V. stood, spinning crazily, grabbing for the handle of the knife with his hooks. After missing it several times, he fell down, landing on his knees, head thrown back.

R.V. knelt there a moment, swaying sickeningly. Then his arms slowly rose. He gazed at the gold and silver hooks, his face glowing with wonder. "My hands," he said softly, and although his voice was gurgly with blood, his words were clear. "I can see them. My hands. They're back. Everything's OK now. I'm normal again, man." Then his arms dropped, his smile and pale red eyes froze in place, and his soul passed quietly on to the next world.

CHAPTER ELEVEN

I gazed at R.V.'s peaceful expression as he knelt in his death pose. He'd left his pain behind at last, for ever. I was glad for him. If he'd lived, he'd have had to carry around the memory of the evil he'd committed while in league with the vampaneze. Maybe he was better off this way.

"And now there's two — just me and you," Steve trilled, breaking my train of thought. I glanced up and saw him standing a few metres away from R.V., smiling. Gannen Harst was still out for the count, and although Vancha was alive, he was lying motionless, wheezing fitfully, unable to defend himself or attack.

"Yes," I agreed, standing and picking up my sword. My left hand wouldn't work and my system was maybe a minute or two away from complete shutdown. But I'd enough strength left for one last fight. First though — Vancha. I paused over him and studied at his wound. It was seeping blood and his face was creased with pain. He tried to speak but words wouldn't form.

As I hovered uncertainly by the side of my fellow Prince, unwilling to leave him like this, Evanna crossed to his side, knelt and examined him. Her eyes were grave when she looked up. "It is not fatal," she said softly. "He will live."

"Thank you," I muttered.

"Save your thanks," Mr Tiny said. He was standing directly behind me. "She didn't tell you to cheer you up, silly boy. It was a warning. Vancha won't die for the time being, but he's out of the fight. You're alone. The final hunter. Unless you turn tail and run, it's down to you and Steve now. If Steve doesn't die, death will come within the next few minutes for *you*."

I looked over my shoulder at the small man in the yellow suit and green wellington boots. His face was bright with bloodthirsty glee. "If death comes," I said shortly, "it will be a far more welcome companion than you."

Mr Tiny chuckled, then stepped away to my left. Rising, Evanna took up position on my right. Both waited for me to move, so that they could follow. I spared Vancha one final glance – he grinned painfully at me and winked – then faced Steve.

He backed away from me casually, entering the shadows beneath the bridge. I trailed after him, sword by my side, taking deep breaths, clearing my mind, focusing on the death-struggle to come. Although this could have been Vancha's battle, a part of me had known all along that it would come down to this. Steve and I were opposite sides of a coin, linked since childhood, first by friendship, then hatred. It was only fitting that the final confrontation should fall to the two of us.

I entered the cool darkness of the underpass. It took my eyes a few seconds to adjust. When they did, I saw Steve waiting, right eye twitching nervously. The river gurgled softly beside us, the only noise except for our panting and chattering teeth.

"There is where we settle matters, once and for all, in the dark," Steve said.

"As good a place as any," I replied.

Steve raised his left palm. I could vaguely make out the shape of the pink cross he'd carved into his flesh eighteen years before. "Remember when I did this?" he asked. "That night, I swore I'd kill you and Creepy Crepsley."

"You're halfway there," I noted dryly. "You must be delighted."

"Not really," he said. "To be honest, I miss old Creepy. The world's not the same without him. I'll miss you even more. You've been the driving force behind everything I've done since I was a child. Without you, I'm not sure I'll have much of an interest in life. If possible, I'd let you go. I enjoy our games — the hunt, the traps, the fights. I'd happily keep doing it, over and over, a new twist here, a fresh shock there."

"But life doesn't work like that," I said. "Everything has to end."

"Yes," Steve said sadly. "That's one thing I can't change." His mood passed and he regarded me with a sneer. "Here's where *you* end, Darren Shan. This is your grand finale. Have you made your peace with the vampire gods?"

"I'll do that later," I snarled, and swung my sword wide, moving forward so that on its return arc he'd be within range. But before it had completed its first arc, the tip of the sword smashed into the wall. It bounced off in a shower of sparks and a shock ran down my arm.

"Silly boy," Steve purred, mimicking Mr Tiny. He raised a knife. "No room here for swords."

Steve leapt forward and jabbed the knife at me. I pulled back and lobbed my sword at him, momentarily halting him. In that second, I drew one of the knives I'd brought from Annie's kitchen. When Steve advanced, I was ready. I caught his thrust with the hilt of my knife and turned his blade aside.

There was no room in the underpass to circle one another, so we had to jab and stab, ducking and weaving to avoid each other's blows. The conditions actually played into my favour — in the open I'd have had to be nimbler on my feet, spinning to keep up with Steve. That would have exhausted me. Here, since we were so cramped, I could stand still and direct my rapidly dwindling strength into my knife hand.

We fought silently, fast, sharp, impulsive. Steve nicked the flesh of my forearm — I nicked his. He opened shallow wounds on my stomach and chest — I repaid the compliment. He almost cut my nose off — I nearly severed his left ear.

Then Steve came at me from the left, taking advantage of my dead arm. He grabbed the material of my shirt and pulled me towards him, driving his knife hard at my belly with his other hand. I rolled with the force of his pull, throwing myself into him. His knife cut the wall of my stomach, a deep wound, but my momentum carried me forward despite the pain. I drove him down, landing awkwardly on him as he hit the path. His right hand flew out by his side, fingers snapping open. His knife shot free and struck the river with a splash, vanishing from sight in an instant.

Steve brought his empty right hand up, to push me off. I stabbed at it with my knife and hit home, spearing him through his forearm. He screamed. I freed my knife before he could knock it from my grip, raised it to shoulder height and redirected it, so the tip was pointing at Steve's throat. His eyes shot to the gleam of the blade and his breath caught. This was it. I had him. He'd been out-fought and he knew it. One quick thrust of the knife and—

Searing pain. A white flash inside my head. I thought Gannen had recovered and struck me from behind, but he hadn't. It was an aftershock from when I blooded Darius. Vancha had warned me about this. My limbs trembled. A roaring in my ears, drowning out all other sounds. I dry-heaved and fell off Steve, almost tumbling into the river. "No!" I tried to scream. "Not now!" But I couldn't form the words. I was in the grip of immense pain, and could do nothing against it.

Time seemed to collapse. Gripped by panic, I was dimly aware of Steve crawling on top of me. He wrestled my knife from my hand. There was a sharp stabbing sensation in my stomach, followed by another. Steve crowed, "Now I have you!

Now you're gonna die!" Something blurry passed in front of my eyes, then back again. Fighting the white light inside my head, I got my eyes to focus. It was the knife. Steve had pulled it out and was waving it in my face, teasing me, sure he'd won, prolonging the moment of triumph.

But Steve had miscalculated. The pain of the stabbing brought me back from the brink of all-out confusion. The agony in my gut worked against the pain in my head, and the world began to swim back into place around me. Steve was perched on top of me, laughing. But I wasn't afraid. Unknown to himself, he was helping me. I was able to think halfway straight now, able to plan, able to act.

My right hand stole to waist of my trousers as Steve continued to mock me. I gripped the handle of a second knife. I caught a glimpse of Mr Tiny peering over Steve's shoulder. He'd seen my hand moving and knew what was coming. He was nodding, though I'm not sure if he was encouraging me or merely bobbing his head up and down with excitement.

I lay still, gathering my very last dredges of energy together, letting Steve torment me with wild promises of what was to come. I was bleeding freely from the stab wounds in my stomach. I wasn't sure if I'd be alive come the dawn, but of one thing I was certain — Steve would die before me.

"—and when I finish with your toes and fingers, I'll move on to your nose and ears!" Steve yelled. "But first I'll cut your eyelids off, so you can see everything that I'm gonna do. After that I'll—"

"Steve," I wheezed, stopping him midflow. "Want to know the secret of winning a fight like this? Less talking — more stabbing."

I lunged at him, using the muscles of my stomach to force my body up. Steve wasn't prepared for it. I knocked him backwards. As he fell, I swung my legs around, then pushed with my knees and feet, so I drove him all the way back with the full weight of my body. He hit the pavement with a grunt, for the second time within the space of a few minutes. This time he managed to hold on to his knife, but that was no use to him. I wasn't going to make the same mistake twice.

No hesitation. No pausing to pick my point. No cynical, memorable last words. I put my trust in the gods of the vampires and blindly thrust my knife forward. I brought it around and down in a savage arc, and by luck or fate drove it into the centre of Steve's left breast — clean through his shrivelled forgery of a heart!

CHAPTER TWELVE

Steve's eyes and mouth popped wide with shock. His expression was comical, but I was in no mood to laugh. There was no recovery from a strike like that. Steve was finished. But he could take me with him if I wasn't careful. So instead of celebrating, I grabbed his left hand, holding it down tight by his side so he couldn't use his knife on me.

Steve's gaze slid to the handle of the knife sticking out of his chest. "Oh," he said tonelessly. Then blood trickled from the sides of his mouth. His chest heaved up and down, the handle rising and falling with it. I wanted to pull the knife out, to end matters — he could maybe go on like this for a minute or two, the knife stopping the gush of blood from his heart — but my left hand was useless and I didn't dare free my right.

Then — applause. My head lifted, and Steve's eyes rolled back in their sockets so that he could look behind him. Mr Tiny was clapping, bright red tears of joy dripping down his cheeks. "What passion!" he exclaimed. "What valour! What a never-say-die spirit! My money was always on you, Darren. It could have gone either way, but if I was a betting man, I'd have bet big on you. I said as much beforehand, didn't I, Evanna?"

"Yes, father," Evanna answered quietly. She was studying me sadly. Her lips moved silently, but even though she uttered no sounds, I was able to make out what she said. "To the victor, the spoils."

"Come, Darren," Mr Tiny said. "Pull out the knife and tend to your wounds. They're not immediately life-threatening, but you should have a doctor see to them. Your friends in the stadium are almost done with their foes. They'll be coming soon. They can take you to a hospital."

I shook my head. I only meant that I couldn't pull the knife out, but Mr Tiny must have thought I didn't want to kill Steve. "Don't be foolish," he snapped. "Steve is the enemy. He deserves no mercy. Finish him, then take your place as the rightful ruler of the night."

"You are the Lord of the Shadows now," Evanna said. "There is no room in your life for mercy. Do as my father bids. The sooner you accept your destiny, the easier it will be for you."

"And do you ... want me to ... kill Vancha now too?" I panted angrily.

"Not yet," Mr Tiny laughed. "That will come in its own time." His laughter faded and his expression hardened.

"Much will come in time. The vampaneze will fall, and so shall the humans. This world will be yours, Darren — rather, ours. Together we'll rule. Your hand at the tiller, my voice in your ear. I'll guide and advise you. Not openly – I haven't the power to directly steer you – but on the sly. I'll make suggestions, you'll heed them, and together we'll build a world of chaos and twisted beauty."

"What makes you ... think I'd have anything to do ... with a monster like you?" I snarled.

"He has a point, father," Evanna murmured. "We both know what lies in store for Darren. He will become a ruler of savage, unrelenting power. But he hates you. That hatred will increase over the centuries, not diminish. What makes you think you can rule with him?"

"I know more about the boy than you do," Mr Tiny said smugly. "He will accept me. He was born to." Mr Tiny squatted and looked straight down into Steve's eyes. Then he looked up into mine, his face no more than five or six centimetres away. "I have always been there for you. For both of you," he whispered. "When you competed with your friends for a ticket to the Cirque Du Freak," he said to me, "I whispered in your ear and told you when to grab for it."

My jaw dropped. I *had* heard a voice that day, but I'd thought it was only an inner voice, the voice of instinct.

"And when you," he said to Steve, "noticed something strange about Darren after your meeting with Larten Crepsley, who do you think kept you awake at night, filling your thoughts with doubt and suspicion?"

Mr Tiny pulled back half a metre. His smile had returned, and it now threatened to spread from his face and fill the tunnel. "*I* influenced Crepsley and inspired him to blood Darren. *I* urged Gannen Harst to suggest Steve try the Coffin of Fire. Both of you have enjoyed enormous slices of good fortune in life. You put it down to the luck of the vampires, or the survival instinct of the vampaneze. But it was neither. You owe your nine cat's lives — and quite a few more — to *me*."

"I don't understand," I said, confused and alarmed. "Why would you go to all that trouble? Why ruin our lives?"

"*Ruin?*" he barked. "With my help you became a Prince and Steve became a Lord. With my backing the two of you have led the creatures of the night to war, and one of you — *you*, Darren! — now stands poised to become the most powerful tyrant in the history of the world. I have *made* your lives, not ruined them!"

"But why us?" I pressed. "We were ordinary kids. Why pick on Steve and me?"

"You were never ordinary," Mr Tiny disagreed. "From birth — no, from conception you were both unique." He stood and looked at Evanna. She was staring at him uncertainly — this was news to her too. "For a long time I wondered what it would be like to father children," Mr Tiny said softly. "When, spurred on by a stubborn vampire, I finally decided to give parenthood a try, I created two offspring in my own mould, beings of magic and great power.

"Evanna and Hibernius fascinated me at first, but in time I grew tired of their limitations. Because they can see into the future, they – like me – are limited in what they can do in the present. All of us have to abide by laws not of our making. I can interfere in the affairs of mankind more than my children can, but not as much as I'd wish. In many ways my hands are tied. I can influence mortals, and I do, but they're contrary creatures and short-lived. It's difficult to manipulate large groups of humans over a long period of time — especially now that there are billions of them!

"What I longed for was a mortal I could channel my will through, a being not bound by the laws of the universe, nor shackled by the confines of humanity. My ally would have to start as a human, then become a vampire or vampaneze. With my help he would lead his clan to rule over all. Together we could govern the course of the world for hundreds of years to come, and through *his* children I could control it for thousands of years — maybe even the rest of time itself."

"You're mad," I growled. "I don't care if you did help me. I won't work with you or do what you want. I'm not going to link myself to your warped cause. I doubt that Steve would have either, if he'd won."

"But you *will* join me," Mr Tiny insisted, "just as Steve would have. You must. It's in your nature. Like sides with like." He paused, then said proudly and provocatively, "Son sides with sire."

"*What?*" Evanna exploded, leaping to an understanding sooner than I did.

"I required a less powerful heir," Mr Tiny said, his gaze fixed on me. "One who'd carry my genes and mirror my

504

desires, but who could act freely as a mortal. To weed out any weaknesses, I created a pair, then set them against each other. The weaker would perish and be forgotten. The stronger would go on to claim the world." He stuck his arms out, the gesture both mocking and strangely heartfelt. "Come and give your father a hug, Darren — *my son!*"

CHAPTER THIRTEEN

"You're mad!" I croaked. "I have a father, a real dad. It isn't you!"

"Dermot Shan was not your father," Mr Tiny replied. "You were a cuckoo's child. Steve too. I did my work quietly, unknown to your mothers. But trust me — you're both mine."

"This is outrageous!" Evanna screeched, her body expanding, becoming more that of a wolf than human, until she filled most of the tunnel. "It is forbidden! How dare you!"

"I acted within the confines of the universe's laws!" Mr Tiny snapped. "You'd know if I had not — all would be chaos. I stretched them a bit, but I didn't break them. I am allowed to breed, and my children – if they lack my magical powers – can act the same way as any normal mortal."

"But if Darren and Steve are your sons, then *you* have created the future where one of them becomes the Lord of the Shadows!" Evanna roared. "*You* have cast mankind into the abyss, and twisted the strands of the future to suit your own foul needs!"

"Yes," Mr Tiny chuckled, then pointed a finger at Evanna. "Do not cross me on this, daughter. I would not harm my own flesh and blood, but I could make life very unpleasant if you got on the wrong side of me."

Evanna glared at her father hatefully, then gradually resumed her regular shape and size. "This is unjust," she muttered. "The universe will punish you, perhaps not immediately, but eventually you'll pay a price for your arrogance."

"I doubt it," Mr Tiny smirked. "Mankind was heading towards an all-time boring low. Peace, prosperity, global communication, brotherly love — where's the fun in *that*? Yes, there were still plenty of wars and conflicts to enjoy, but I could see the people of the world moving ever closer together. I did my best, nudged nations along the path to battle, sowed seeds of discontent everywhere I could, even helped get a few tyrants wrongfully elected to some of the most powerful positions on Earth — I was sure those fine specimens would push the world to the brink!

"But no! No matter how tense things got, no matter how much meddling my minions did, I could see peace and understanding gradually winning through. It was time for drastic action, to take the world back to the good old days, when everyone was at everybody else's throat. I've simply restored the natural order of beautiful chaos. The universe won't punish me for that. If anything, I expect—"

"Shut up!" I screamed, surprising both Mr Tiny and Evanna. "It's bull, all of it! You're not my father! You're a monster!"

"And so are you," Mr Tiny beamed. "Or soon will be. But don't worry, son — monsters have all the fun!"

I stared at him, sickened, senses reeling, unable to take it all in. If this was true, everything in my life had been false. I was never the person I thought I was, only a pawn of Mr Tiny's, a time bomb waiting to explode. I'd been blooded simply to extend my life, so I could live longer and do more of Mr Tiny's work. My war with Steve had served only to get rid of the weaker of us, so that the stronger could emerge as a more powerful beast. I'd done nothing for the sake of the vampires or my family and friends — everything had been for Mr Tiny. And now that I'd proved myself worthy, I'd become a dictator and lay low anyone who opposed him. My wishes would count for nothing. It was my destiny.

"Fa-fa-fa..." Steve stammered, spitting blood from his mouth. With his free hand he reached out to Mr Tiny. "Father," he managed to croak. "Help ... me."

"Why?" Mr Tiny sniffed.

"I ... never ... had ... a ... Dad." Each word was a heart-churning effort, but Steve forced them out. "I ... want ... to ... know ... you. I'll ... serve ... you ... and ... love ... you."

"What on earth would I want with *love*?" Mr Tiny laughed. "Love is one of the most basic human emotions. I'm so pleased I was never cursed with it. Servitude, gratitude, fear, hatred, anger — these I like. Love ... you can take your love to the Lake of Souls when you die. Perhaps it will provide you with some comfort there."

"But … I'm … your … son," Steve cried weakly.

"You were," Mr Tiny sneered. "Now you're just a loser, and soon you'll be dead meat. I'll toss your carcass to my Little People to eat — that's how little I feel for you. This is a winner's world. Second place equals second rate. You're nothing to me. Darren's my only son now."

The pain in Steve's eyes was awful to behold. As a child, he'd been crushed when he thought I'd betrayed him. Now he'd been openly mocked and disowned by his father. It destroyed him. His heart had been full of hatred before this, but now that it was down to its last few beats, there was room only for despair.

But in Steve's anguish I found hope. Consumed by smugness, Mr Tiny had revealed too much, too soon. At the back of my brain an idea sparked into life. In a whirl I began to put various pieces together — Mr Tiny's revelation and Evanna's reaction. Evanna said Mr Tiny had created the future in which Steve or I was the Lord of the Shadows. He'd bent the laws he and she lived by, to twist things round and build a chaotic world which he and I could rule over. Evanna and Mr Tall had told me there was no escaping the Lord of the Shadows, that he was part of the world's future. But they were wrong. He was part of *Mr Tiny*'s future. Des Tiny might be the most powerful individual in the universe, but he was still only an individual. What one individual could build, another could destroy.

Mr Tiny's eyes were on Steve. He was laughing at him, enjoying Steve's dying misery. Evanna's head was bowed — she'd given in and accepted this. Not me. If I'd inherited Mr Tiny's evil, destructive streak, I'd also inherited his cunning. I'd stop at nothing to deny him his vision of a ruined future.

Slowly, everso slowly, I released Steve's left hand and moved my arm away. He had a free shot at my stomach now, in the perfect position to finish the job he'd started when he stabbed me earlier. But Steve didn't notice. He was wrapped up in his sorrow. I faked a cough and plucked at his left sleeve. If Mr Tiny had seen it, he could have stopped my plan there. But he thought he'd won, that it was all over. He couldn't even imagine the vaguest possibility of a threat.

Steve's gaze flickered down. He realized his hand was free. He saw his chance to kill me. His fingers stiffened on the handle of his knife ... then relaxed. For a terrible moment I thought he'd died, but then I saw that he was still alive. What made him pause was doubt. He'd spent most of his life hating me, but now he'd been told I was his brother. I could see his brain churning. I was a victim of Des Tiny, just as he was. He'd been wrong to hate me — I'd had no choice in what I'd done. In all the world, I was the person he should be closest to, and instead I was the person he'd hurt the most.

What Steve found in those last few moments was what I thought he'd lost for ever — his humanity. He saw the error of his ways, the evil he'd committed, the mistakes he'd made. There was possible salvation in that recognition. Now that he could see himself for what he truly was, perhaps, even at this late stage, he could repent.

But I couldn't afford humanity. Steve's salvation would be my undoing — and the world's. I needed him mad as hell, fire in his gut, filled with fury and hate. Only in that state could he find the power to maybe help me break Des Tiny's hold over the future.

"Steve," I said, forcing a wicked smile. "You were right. I *did* plot with Mr Crepsley to take your place as his assistant. We made a mug of you, and I'm glad. You're a nobody. A nothing. This is what you deserve. If Mr Crepsley was alive, he'd be laughing at you now, just like the rest of us are."

Mr Tiny howled with delight. "That's my boy!" he hooted. He thought I was getting one last dig in before Steve died. But he was wrong.

Steve's eyes refilled with hatred. The human within him vanished in an instant and he was Steve Leopard, vampire killer, again. In one fast, crazed movement he brought his left hand up and drove his knife deep into my stomach. Less than a second later he did it again, then again.

"Stop!" Mr Tiny yelled, seeing the danger too late. He lurched at us, to pull me off, but Evanna slid in front of him and blocked his way.

"No, father!" she snapped. "You cannot interfere in this!"

"Get out of my way!" he bellowed, struggling with her. "The fool's going to let Leonard kill him! We have to stop it!"

"Too late," I giggled, as Steve's blade slid in and sliced through my guts for a fifth time. Mr Tiny stopped and blinked dumbly, at a complete loss for what may well have been the first time in his long, ungodly life. "Destiny … rejected," I said with my final whole breath. Then I grabbed Steve tight as he lunged at me with his knife again, and rolled to my right, off the edge of the path, into the river.

We went into the water together, wrapped in each other's arms, and sank quickly. Steve tried stabbing me again, but it was too much for him. He went limp and fell away from me, his dead body dropping into the dark depths of the river, disappearing from sight within seconds.

I was barely conscious, hanging sluggishly, limbs being picked at and made to sway by the current of the river. Water rushed down my throat and flooded my lungs. Part of me wanted to strike for the surface, but I fought against it, not wanting to give Mr Tiny even the slightest opportunity to revive me.

I saw faces in the water, or in my thoughts — impossible to tell the difference. Sam Grest, Gavner Purl, Arra Sails, Mr Tall, Shancus, R.V., Mr Crepsley. The dead, come to welcome me.

I stretched my arms out to them, but our fingers didn't touch. I imagined Mr Crepsley waving, and a sad expression crossed his face. Then everything faded. I stopped struggling. The world, the water, the faces faded from sight, then from memory. A roaring which was silence. A darkness which was light. A chill which burnt. One final flutter of my eyelids, barely a movement, impossibly tiring. And then, in the lonely, watery darkness of the river, as all must do when the Grim Reaper calls — I died.

INTERLUDE

✶

Timelessness. Eternal gloom. Drifting in slow, never-ending circles. Surrounded but alone. Aware of other souls, trapped like me, but unable to contact them. No sense of sight, hearing, taste, smell, touch. Only the crushing boredom of the present and painful memories of the past.

✶

I know this place. It's the Lake of Souls, a zone where spirits go when they can't leave Earth's pull. Some people's souls don't move on when they die. They remain trapped in the waters of this putrid lake, condemned to swirl silently in the depths for all eternity.

I'm sad I ended up here, but not surprised. I tried to live a good life, and I sacrificed myself at the end in an effort to save others, so in those respects I was maybe deserving of Paradise. But I was also a killer. Whatever my reasons, I took lives and created unhappiness. I don't know if some higher power has passed judgement on me, or if I'm imprisoned by my own guilt. It doesn't really matter, I guess. I'm here and there's no getting out. This is my lot. For ever.

✶

No sense of time. No days, nights, hours, minutes — not even seconds. Have I been here a week, a year, a century? Can't tell. Does the War of the Scars still rage? Have the vampires or vampaneze fallen? Has another taken my place as the Lord of the Shadows? Did I die for no reason? I don't know. I probably never will. That's part of my sentence. Part of my curse.

✱

If the souls of the dead could speak, they'd scream for release. Not just release from the Lake, but from their memories. Memories gnaw away at me relentlessly. I remember so much of my past, all the times where I failed or could have done better. With nothing else to do, I'm forced to review my life, over and over. Even my most minor errors become supreme lapses of judgement. They torment me worse than Steve ever did.

I try to hide from the pain of the memories by retreating further into my past. I remember the young Darren Shan, human, happy, normal, innocent. I spend years, decades — or is it just minutes? — reliving the simple, carefree times. I piece together my entire early life. I recall even the smallest details — the colours of toy cars, homework assignments, throwaway conversations. I go through everyday chat a hundred times, until every word is correct. The longer I think about it, the deeper into those years I sink, losing myself, human again, almost able to believe that the memories are reality, and my death and the Lake of Souls nothing but an unpleasant dream.

✱

But eternity can't be dodged for ever. My later memories are always hovering, picking away at the boundaries of the limited reality which I've built. Every so often I flash ahead to a face or event. Then I lose control and find myself thrust into the darker, nightmarish world of my life as a half-vampire. I relive the mistakes, the wrong choices, the bloodshed.

So many friends lost, so many enemies killed. I feel responsible for all of them. I believed in peace when I first went to Vampire Mountain. Even though Kurda Smahlt betrayed his people, I felt sorry for him. I knew he did it in an effort to avoid war. I couldn't understand why it had come to this. If only the vampires and vampaneze had sat down and talked through their differences, war could have been avoided.

When I first became a Prince, I dreamt of being a peace-monger, taking up where Kurda left off, bringing the vampaneze back into the clan. I lost those dreams somewhere during the six years I spent living within Vampire Mountain. Surviving as a vampire, learning their ways, training with weapons, sending friends out to fight and die ... It all rubbed off on me, and when I finally returned to the world beyond the mountain, I'd changed. I was a warrior, fierce, unmoved by death, intent on killing rather than talking.

I wasn't evil. Sometimes it's necessary to fight. There are occasions when you have to cast aside your nobler ideals and get your hands dirty. But you should always strive for peace, and search to find the peaceful solution to even the most bloody of conflicts. I didn't do that. I embraced the war and went along with the general opinion — that if we killed the Vampaneze Lord, all our problems would be solved and life would be hunky-dory.

We were wrong. The death of one man never solved anything. Steve was just the start. Once you set off down the road of murder, it's hard to take a detour. We couldn't have stopped. The death of one foe wouldn't have been enough. We'd have set about annihilating the vampaneze after Steve, then humanity. We'd have established ourselves as the rulers of the world, crushing all in our path, and I'd have gone along with it. No, more than that — I'd have led, not just followed.

That guilt, not just of what I've done but of what I would have done, eats away at me like a million ravenous rats. It doesn't matter that I'm the son of Desmond Tiny, that wickedness was in my genes. I had the power to break away from the dark designs of my father. I proved that at the end, by letting myself die. But why didn't I do it sooner, before so many people were killed?

I don't know if I could have stopped the war, but I could have said, "No, I don't want any part of this." I could have argued for peace, not fought for it. If I'd failed, at least I maybe wouldn't have wound up here, weighed down by the chains of so many grisly deaths.

✷

Time passes. Faces swim in and out of my thoughts. Memories form, are forgotten, form again. I blank out large parts of my life, recover them, blank them out again. I succumb to madness and forget who I was. But the madness doesn't last. I reluctantly return to my senses.

I think about my friends a lot, especially those who were alive when I died. Did any of them perish in the stadium? If they survived that, what came next? Since Steve and I both died, what happened with the War of the Scars? Could

Mr Tiny replace us with new leaders, men with the same powers as Steve and me? Hard to see how, unless he fathered another couple of children.

Was Harkat alive now, pushing for peace between the vampires and vampaneze, like he had when he was Kurda Smahlt? Had Alice Burgess led her vampirites against the vampets and crushed them? Did Debbie mourn for me? Not knowing was an agony. I'd have sold my soul to the Devil for a few minutes in the world of the living, where I could find answers to my questions. But not even the Devil disturbed the waters of the Lake of Souls. This was the exclusive resting place of the dead and the damned.

∗

Drifting, ghostly, resigned. I fixate on my death, remembering Steve's face as he stabbed me, his hatred, his fear. I count the number of seconds it took me to die, the drops of blood I spilt on the riverbank where he killed me. I feel myself topple into the water of the river a dozen times ... a hundred ... a thousand.

That water was so much more alive than the water of the Lake of Souls. Currents. Fish swam in it. Air bubbles. Cold. The water here is dead, as lifeless as the souls it contains. No fish explore its depths, no insects skim its surface. I'm not sure how I'm aware of these facts, but I am. I sense the awful emptiness of the Lake. It exists solely to hold the spirits of the miserable dead.

I long for the river. I'd meet any asking price if I could go back and experience the rush of flowing water again, the chill as I fell in, the pain as I bled to death. Anything's better than this limbo world. Even a minute of dying is preferable to an eternity of nothingness

✶

One small measure of comfort — as bad as this is for me, it must be much worse for Steve. My guilt is nothing compared to his. I was sucked into Mr Tiny's evil games, but Steve threw himself heart and soul into them. His crimes far outweigh mine, so his suffering must be that much more.

Unless he doesn't accept his guilt. Perhaps eternity means nothing to him. Maybe he's just sore that I beat him. It could be that he doesn't worry about what he did, or realize just how much of a monster he was. He might be content here, reflecting with fondness on all that he achieved.

But I doubt it. I suspect Mr Tiny's admission destroyed a large part of Steve's mad defences. Knowing that he was my brother, and that we were both puppets in our father's hands, must have shaken him up. I think, given the time to reflect — and that's all one can do here — he'll weep for what he did. He'll see himself for what he truly was, and hate himself for it.

I shouldn't take pleasure in that. There, but for the grace of the gods ... But I still despise Steve. I can understand why he acted that way, and I'm sorry for him. But I can't forgive him. I can't stretch that far. Perhaps that's another reason why I'm here.

✶

I'm retreating from the painful memories again. Withdrawing from the vampire world, pretending it never happened. I imagine myself as a child, living the same days over and over, refusing to go beyond the afternoon when I won a ticket to the Cirque Du Freak. I build a perfect, sealed-off, comfortable reality. I'm Darren Shan, loving son and brother, not the best behaved boy in the world, but far from the worst. I do chores for Mum and Dad, struggle with homework, watch TV, hang out with my friends. One moment I'm six or seven years old, the next ten or eleven. Continually twisting back upon myself, living the past, ignoring all that I don't want to think about. Steve's my best friend. We read comics, watch horror movies, tell jokes to each other. Annie's a child, always a child — I never think of her as a woman with a son of her own. Vampires are monsters of myth, like werewolves, zombies, mummies, not to be taken seriously.

It's my aim to become the Darren of my memories, to lose myself completely in the past. I don't want to deal with the guilt any more. I've gone mad before and recovered. I want to go mad again, but this time let madness swallow me whole.

I struggle to vanish into the past. Remembering everything, painting the details more precisely every time I revisit a moment. I start to forget about the souls, the Lake, the vampires and vampaneze. I still get occasional flashes of reality, but I clamp down on them quickly. Thinking as a child, remembering as a child, becoming a child.

I'm almost there. The madness waits, arms spread wide, welcoming me. I'll be living a lie, but it will be a peaceful, soothing lie. I long for it. I work hard to make it real. And I'm getting there. I feel myself sliding closer towards it. I reach for the lie with the tendrils of my mind. I feel around it, explore it, start to slip inside it, when all of a sudden — a new sensation...

Pain! Heaviness. Rising. The madness is left behind. The water of the Lake closes around me. Searing pain! Thrashing, coughing, gasping. *But with what?* I have no arms to thrash, no mouth to cough, no lungs to gasp. Is this part of the madness? Am I...

And suddenly my head — an actual, real *head!* — breaks the surface. I'm breathing air. Sunlight blinds me. I spit water out. My arms come clear of the Lake. I'm surrounded, but not by the souls of the dead — by nets! People pulling on them. Coming out of the Lake. Screaming with pain and confusion — but no sounds. Body forming, incredibly heavy after all this weightless time. I land on hard, warm earth. My feet drag out of the water. Amazed, I try to stand. I make it to my knees, then fall. I hit the ground hard. Pain again, fresh and frightening. I curl up into a ball, shivering like a baby. I shut my eyes against the light and dig my fingers into the earth to reassure myself that it's real. And then I sob feebly as the incredible, bewildering, impossible realization sinks in — *I'm alive!*

PART TWO

CHAPTER FOURTEEN

The sun hammered down fiercely upon me but I couldn't stop shivering. Someone threw a blanket around me, hairy and thick. It itched like mad, but the sensation was delicious. Any sensation would have been welcome after the numbness of the Lake of Souls.

The person who'd draped the blanket over me knelt by my side and tilted my head back. I blinked water from my eyes and focused. It took a few seconds, but finally I fixed on my rescuer. It was a Little Person. At first I thought it was Harkat. I opened my mouth to shout his name happily. Then I did a double take and realized this wasn't my old friend, just one of his grey, scarred, green-eyed kind.

The Little Person examined me silently, prodding and poking. Then he stood and stepped aside, leaving me. I wrapped the blanket tighter around myself, trying to stop the shivers. After a while I worked up the strength to look around. I was lying by the rim of the Lake of Souls. The earth around me was hard and dry, like desert. Several Little People stood nearby. A couple were hanging up nets to dry — the nets they'd fished me out with. The others simply stared off into space or at the Lake.

There was a screeching sound high overhead. Looking up, I saw a huge winged beast circling the Lake. From my previous trip here, I knew it was a dragon. My insides clenched with fear. Then I noticed a second dragon. A third. A fourth. Jaw dropping, I realized the sky was full of them, dozens, maybe hundreds. If they caught sight of me...

I started to scrabble weakly for safety, then paused and glanced at the Little People. They knew the dragons were there, but they weren't bothered by the giant flying reptiles. They might have dragged me out of the Lake to feed me to the dragons, but I didn't think so. And even if they had, in my feeble state I could do nothing about it. I couldn't flee or fight, and there was nowhere to hide. So I just lay where I was and waited for events to run their course.

For several minutes the dragons circled and the Little People stood motionless. I was still filled with a great chill, but I wasn't shivering quite as much as when I first came out of the Lake. I was gathering what small amounts of energy I could call on, to try and walk over to the Little People and quiz them about what was going on, when somebody spoke behind me.

"Sorry I'm late."

I looked over my shoulder, expecting Mr Tiny, but it was his daughter, (my half-sister!) Evanna, striding towards me.

She looked no different from how I remembered her, though there was a sparkle in her green and brown eyes which had been absent when last we met.

"Whuh!" I croaked, the only sound I was able to make.

"Easy," Evanna said, reaching me and bending to squeeze my shoulder warmly. "Don't try to speak. It will take a few hours for the effects of the Lake to wear off. I'll build a fire and cook some broth for you. That's why I wasn't here when you were fished out — I was looking for firewood." She pointed to a mound of logs and branches.

I wanted to besiege her with questions, but there was no point taxing my throat when it wasn't ready to work. So I said nothing as she picked me up and carried me to the pile of wood like a baby, then set me down and turned her attention to the kindling.

When the fire was burning nicely, Evanna took a flat circular object out from beneath the ropes she was wearing. I recognized it immediately — a collapsible pot, the same sort that Mr Crepsley had once used. She pressed it in the middle, causing it to pop outwards and assume its natural shape, then filled it with water (not from the Lake, but from a bucket) and some grass and herbs, and hung it from a stick over the flames.

The broth was weak and tasteless, but its warmth was like the fire of the gods to me. I drank deeply, one bowl, another, a third. Evanna smiled as I slurped, then sipped slowly from a bowl of her own. The dragons screeched at regular intervals overhead, the sun burnt brightly, and the scent of the smoke was magical. I felt strangely relaxed, as if this was a lazy summer Sunday afternoon.

I was halfway through my fourth bowl before my stomach growled at me to say, "Enough!" Sighing happily, I laid the bowl down and sat, smiling lightly, thinking only of the good feelings inside. But I couldn't sit silently for ever, so eventually I raised my gaze, looked at Evanna and tested my vocal chords. "Urch," I creaked — I'd meant to say "Thanks."

"It's been a long time since you spoke," Evanna said. "Start simply. Try the alphabet. I will hunt for more wood, to sustain the fire. We won't be staying here much longer, but we may as well have warmth while we are. Practise while I am gone, and we can maybe talk when I return."

I did as the witch advised. At first I struggled to produce sounds anything like they should be, but I stuck with it and gradually my As started to sound like As, my Bs like Bs, and so on. When I'd run through the alphabet several times without making a mistake, I moved on to words, simple stuff to begin with — cat, dog, Mum, Dad, sky, me. I tried names after that, longer words, and finally sentences. It hurt to speak, and I slurred some words, but when Evanna eventually came back, clutching an armful of pitiful twigs, I was able to greet her in a gravelly but semi-normal voice. "Thanks for the broth."

"You're welcome." She threw some of the twigs on to the fire, then sat beside me. "How do you feel?"

"Rough as rust."

"Do you remember your name?"

I squinted at her oddly. "Why shouldn't I?"

"The Lake twists the minds of people," she said. "It can destroy memories. Many of the souls forget who they are. They go mad and lose track of their pasts. You were in there a long time. I feared the worst."

"I came close," I admitted, hunching up closer to the fire, recalling my attempts to go mad and escape the weight of my memories. "It was horrible. Easier to be crazy in there than sane."

"So what is it?" Evanna asked. When I blinked dumbly, she laughed. "Your name?"

"Oh." I smiled. "Darren. Darren Shan. I'm a half-vampire. I remember it all, the War of the Scars, Mr Crepsley, Steve." My features darkened. "I remember my death, and what Mr Tiny said just before it."

"Quite the one for surprises, isn't he — our father?"

She looked at me sideways to see what I'd say about that, but I couldn't think of anything — how do you respond to the news that Des Tiny is your dad, and a centuries-old witch is your half-sister? To avoid the subject, I studied the land around me. "This place looks different," I said. "It was green when I came with Harkat, lots of grass and fresh earth."

"This is further into the future," Evanna explained. "Before, you travelled a mere two hundred or so years ahead of the present. This time you have come hundreds of thousands of years, maybe more. I'm not entirely certain. This is the first time our father has ever allowed me to come here."

"Hundreds of…" My head spun.

"This is the age of dragons," Evanna said. "The age after mankind."

My breath caught in my throat, and I had to clear it twice before I could respond. "You mean humanity has died out?"

"Died out or moved on to other worlds or spheres." Evanna shrugged. "I cannot say for sure. I know only that the world belongs to dragons now. They control it as humans once did, and dinosaurs before them."

"And the War of the Scars?" I asked nervously. "Who won that?"

Evanna was silent a moment. Then she said, "We have much to speak about. Let's not rush." She pointed at the dragons high above us. "Call one of them down."

"What?" I frowned.

"Call them, the way you used to call Madam Octa. You can control dragons like you controlled your pet spider."

"How?" I asked, bewildered.

"I will show you. But first — call." She smiled. "They will not harm us. You have my word."

I wasn't too sure about that, but how cool would it be to control a dragon! Looking up, I studied the creatures in the sky, then fixed on one slightly smaller than the others. (I didn't want to bring a large one down, in case Evanna was wrong and it attacked.) I tracked it with my eyes for a few seconds, then stretched out a hand towards it and whispered, "Come to me. Come down. Come, my beauty."

The dragon executed a backwards somersault, then dropped swiftly. I thought it was going to blast us into a thousand pieces. I panicked and tried to run. Evanna hauled me back into place. "Calmly," she said. "You cannot control it if you break contact, and now that it knows we are here, it would be dangerous to let it have its own way."

I didn't want to play this game, but it was too late to back out now. With my heart beating fiercely, I fixed on the swooping dragon and spoke to it again. "Easy. Pull up. I don't want to hurt you — and I don't want you to hurt us! Just hover above us a bit and..."

The dragon pulled out of its fall and came to a halt several metres overhead. It flapped its leathery wings powerfully. I could hear nothing over the sound, and the force of the air knocked me backwards. As I struggled to right myself, the dragon came to land close beside me. It tucked its wings in, thrust its head down as though it meant to gobble me up, then stopped and just stared.

The beast was much like those I'd seen before. Its wings were a light green colour, it was about six metres long, scaled like a snake, with a bulging chest and thin tail. The scales on its stomach were a dull red and gold colour, while those on top were green with red flecks. It had two long forelegs near the front of its body, and two small hindlegs about a quarter of the way from the rear. Lots of sharp claws. A head like an alligator, long and flat, with bulging yellow eyes and small pointed ears. Its face was dark purple. It also had a long forked tongue and, if it was like the other dragons, it could blow fire.

"It's incredible," Evanna said. "This is the first time I have seen one up so close. Our father excelled himself with this creation."

"Mr Tiny made the dragons?"

Evanna nodded. "He helped human scientists create them. Actually, one of your friends was a key member of the team — Alan Morris. With our father's aid he made a breakthrough which allowed them to be cloned from a combination of dinosaur cells."

"*Alan?*" I snorted. "You're telling me Alan Morris made dragons? That's total and utter..." I stopped short. Tommy had told me Alan was a scientist, and that he'd specialized in cloning. It was hard to believe the foolish boy I'd known had grown up to become a creator of dinosaurs — but then again, it was hard to believe Steve had become the Vampaneze Lord, or myself a Vampire Prince. I suppose all influential men and women must start out as normal, unremarkable children.

"For many centuries, the rulers of this world will keep the dragons in check," Evanna said. "They'll control them. Later, when they lose their hold on power – as all rulers must – the dragons will fly free and multiply, becoming a real menace. In the end they'll outlive or outlast all the humans, vampires and vampaneze, and rule the world in their turn. I'm not sure what comes after them. I've never looked that far ahead."

"Why doesn't it kill us?" I asked, eyeing the dragon uneasily. "Is it tame?"

"Hardly!" Evanna laughed. "Normally the dragons would tear us apart. Our father masks this area from them — they can't see the Lake of Souls or anyone around it."

"This one sees us," I noted.

"Yes, but you're controlling it, so we are safe."

"The last time I was here, I was almost roasted alive by dragons," I said. "How can I control them now when I couldn't before?"

"But you could," Evanna replied. "You had the power — you just didn't know it. The dragons would have obeyed you then, as they do now."

"Why?" I frowned. "What's so special about me?"

"You're Desmond Tiny's son," Evanna reminded me. "Even though he did not pass on his magical powers to you, traces of his influence remain. That is why you were skilled at controlling animals such as spiders and wolves. But there is more to it than that."

Evanna reached out, her hand extending far beyond its natural length, and touched the dragon's head. Its skull glowed beneath the witch's touch. Its purple skin faded, then became translucent, so I could see inside to its brain. The oval, stone-like shape was instantly familiar, though it took me a few seconds to recall what it reminded me of. Then it clicked.

"The Stone of Blood!" I exclaimed. While this was much smaller than the one in the Hall of Princes, it was unmistakably the same type. The Stone of Blood had been a gift to the vampires from Mr Tiny. For seven hundred years the members of the clan had fed their blood to it, and used it to keep track of and communicate with each other. It was an invaluable tool, but dangerous — if it had fallen into the hands of the vampaneze, they could have tracked down and killed almost every living vampire.

"Our father took the brain of a dragon into the past and gave it to the vampires," Evanna said. "He often does that — travels into the past and makes small changes which influence the present and future. Through the Stone of Blood he bound the vampires more tightly to his will. If the vampires win the War of the Scars, they will use the Stone to control the dragons, and through them the skies. I don't think the vampaneze will use it if they win.. They never trusted this gift of Desmond Tiny's — it was one of the reasons they broke away from the rest of the vampire clan. I'm not sure what their relationship with the dragons would be like. Perhaps our father will provide them with some other way of controlling the beasts — or maybe it will please him to let them be enemies."

"The Stone of Blood was supposed to be the clan's last hope," I muttered, unable to take my eyes off the dragon's glowing brain. "There was a legend — if we lost the war with the vampaneze, the Stone of Blood might some night help us rise again."

Evanna nodded and removed her hand from the dragon's head. It stopped glowing and resumed its normal appearance. The dragon didn't seem to have noticed any change. It continued staring at me, awaiting my command.

"Above all else, our father craves chaos," Evanna said. "Stability bores him. He has no interest in seeing any race rule for ever. For a time it pleased him to let humans rule this planet, since they were violent, always at war with one another. But when he saw them heading the way of peace during the latter half of the twentieth century – or thought he did; to be honest, I don't agree with his assessment – he set about overthrowing them. He will do the same with their successors.

"If the vampaneze win the War of the Scars and wipe out the vampires, he'll use the Stone in the future. He will lead humans to it and teach them to extract the blood cells and build a new army of cloned vampires. But they won't be vampires as you know them. Desmond will control the cloning process and meddle with the cells, twisting and re-shaping them. The new creatures will be more savage than the original vampires, with less developed brains, slaves to the whim of our father." Evanna smiled twistedly. "So yes, our father told the truth when he said the Stone of Blood could help the vampires rise again — but he kept a few of the less savoury facts to himself."

"Then neither side can truly win," I said. "He's just setting the victors up for a later fall."

"That has always been Desmond's way," Evanna said. "What he helps create, he later destroys. Many empires – Egyptian, Persian, British – have already learnt that to their cost."

"Egyptian?" I blinked.

"Our father is a great fan of empires," Evanna said. "Cavemen hitting each other with sticks and bones were of very limited interest to him. He prefers to see people killing each other with more effective weapons, and in greater numbers. But for mankind to advance barbarically, it also had to advance in other ways. It had to grow socially, culturally, spiritually, technologically, medically. Only a nation which was great in all aspects could wage war greatly.

"Our father has had his hand in most of the notable architectural, technical or medical breakthroughs of mankind. He could never openly lead, but he influenced slyly. The only area where he had no real power was that of literature. Desmond is not a fictional dreamer. Reality is everything to him. He has no interest in the wonderful stories of mankind. Writers have always been alien to him — he does not read works of fiction, or take any notice of them."

"Never mind that," I grunted, not giving a hoot about Mr Tiny's choice of reading material. "Tell me more about his meddling with mankind, and time-travelling. You say Mr Tiny goes into the past to change the present and future. But what about the time paradox?" I'd seen lots of science fiction movies and TV shows. I knew all about the problems associated with the theory of time travel.

"There is no paradox," Evanna said. "The universe keeps natural order. The key events of the past cannot be changed — only the people involved."

"Huh?" I said.

"Once something important happens in the present – the universe, to give the higher force a name, decides what is important or not – it can never be changed," Evanna explained. "But you can alter the people involved. For instance, now that it has happened, you cannot travel to the past and prevent World War Two — but you *could* go back and kill Adolf Hitler. The universe would immediately create another person to fill his shoes. That person would be born like any normal person, grow up, then do what Hitler did, with precisely the same results. The name would change, but nothing else."

"But Hitler was a monster," I said. "He murdered millions of people. Do you mean, if Mr Tiny went back and killed him, some innocent guy would take his place? All those people would still die?"

"Yes," Evanna said.

"But then that person wouldn't have chosen their fate," I frowned. "They wouldn't be responsible for their actions."

Evanna sniffed. "The universe would have to create a child with the potential for wickedness — a good man cannot be forced to do evil — but once it did, yes, that person would become a victim of destiny. It does not happen often. Our father only occasionally replaces important figures of the past. Most people have free will. But there *are* a few who don't."

"Am I one of them?" I asked quietly, fearing the answer.

"Most definitely not," Evanna smiled. "Your time is the present time, and you are an original creation. Though you were manipulated by our father since birth, the path you trod had not been laid down by anyone before you."

Evanna thought for a few seconds, then tried to explain the situation in a way which I could more easily understand.

"Although our father cannot change the events of the past, he can make minor alterations," she said. "If something happens in the present which is not to his liking, he can return to the past and create a train of events designed to lead to a solution to whatever is troubling him. That's how vampires came to be so numerous and powerful."

"Mr Tiny created vampires?" I shouted — there was a myth that he'd made us, but I'd never believed it.

"No," Evanna said. "Vampires came into being by themselves. But there were never many of them. They were weak and disorganized. Then, in the middle of the twentieth century, our father decided mankind was taking a path towards peace and unity. Disliking it, he travelled to the past and spent a couple of decades trying different approaches to undermine humanity. In the end he settled on vampires. He gave them extra strength and speed, the power to flit and share their thoughts — all the supernatural abilities which you know about. He also provided them with leaders who would knock them into shape and turn them into an army.

"As powerful as the clan became, our father ensured they couldn't be a threat to humans. Originally vampires were able to come out by day — Desmond Tiny made them prisoners of the night, and robbed them of the gift of childbirth. Carefully shackled and maintained this way, the vampires had to live separately to the world of man and remain in the shadows. Since they didn't change anything important in the human history, the universe let them exist, and they eventually become part of the present — which is when our father was free to use them however he wished."

"And the present was my time?" I asked.

"Yes," Evanna said. "Time passes at the same rate, whether our father is in the past, present or future. So, since he spent almost twenty years stuck in the past, trying to find a way to topple humanity, it was late in the twentieth century when he returned to the present."

"And because vampires were now part of that present," I said, my brain hurting as I tried to keep up with all this mind-boggling information, "they were free to influence the future?"

"Correct," Evanna said. "But our father then saw that the clan wouldn't launch an attack on humanity if left to their own devices — they were content to stay out of the affairs of men. So he went back again — just for a few months this time — and engineered the vampaneze breakaway. By then planting the legend of the Lord of the Vampaneze, he edged them towards conflict with the vampires."

"And that led to the War of the Scars, and eventually the downfall of humanity," I growled, sick at the thought of the little man's terrible slyness.

"Well," Evanna smiled, "that was the plan."

"Do you mean—" I began to say excitedly, sensing hope in her smile.

"Hush," Evanna stopped me. "I will reveal all shortly. But now it is time for us to move on." She pointed to where the sun was setting on the horizon. "The nights are colder in this time than in yours. We will be safer underground. Besides," she said, rising, "we have an appointment to keep."

"With who?" I asked.

She looked at me steadily. "Our father."

CHAPTER FIFTEEN

Mr Tiny was the last person in the world – in all of time! – that I wanted to see. I argued with Evanna hotly, wanting to know why I should present myself to him, or what it could achieve. I hated and feared the meddler more than ever now that I knew so much about him.

"I want to be on the opposite side of the world to wherever he is!" I cried. "Or in another universe, if possible!"

"I understand," Evanna said, "but we must go to him regardless."

"Is he forcing you to do this?" I asked. "Is he the one who ordered me fished out of the Lake? Is he making you take me to him, so that he can mess my life up all over again?"

"You will find out when you meet him," Evanna said coolly, and since I didn't really have any option but to follow her lead – she could have had me tossed back into the Lake if I disobeyed – eventually, and with much angry muttering, I reluctantly followed after her as she set off into the arid wilderness.

As we left the warmth of the fire, the dragon flapped its wings and took to the skies. I watched it join the throng of dragons far above me, then lost track of it. When I looked back at Evanna, I saw that she was still staring up at the sky. "I wish we could have gone for a flight," she said, sounding curiously sad.

"On the dragon?" I asked.

"Yes. It has always been a wish of mine to fly on a dragon."

"I could call it back," I suggested.

She shook her head quickly. "This isn't the time for it," she said. "And there are too many of them. The others would see us on its back and attack. I don't think you would be able to control so many, not without more practice. And while I can mask us from them downhere, I couldn't up there."

As we continued to walk, I looked around and backwards, and my gaze settled on the Little People standing motionless by the Lake. "Why are that lot here?" I asked.

"This is the age in which our father fishes for the souls of the dead to create his Little People," Evanna said, without looking back or slowing. "He could take them from any time, but it's easier this way, when there is nobody to interfere. He leaves a small band of his helpers here, to fish when he gives the order." She glanced at me. "He could have rescued you much earlier. In the present, only two years have passed. He had the power to remove you from the Lake then, but he wanted to punish you. Your sacrifice threw his plans into disarray. He hates you for that, even though you are his son. That's why he sent me forward to this point in time to help you. In this future, your soul has suffered for countless generations. He wanted you to feel the pain of near-eternal imprisonment, and perhaps even go mad from it, so that you couldn't be saved."

"Nice," I grunted sarcastically. Then my eyes narrowed. "If that's the way he feels, why rescue me at all?"

"That will soon become clear," Evanna said.

We walked a long way from the Lake. The air was turning cold around us as the sun dipped. Evanna was looking for a specific spot, pausing every few seconds to examine the ground, then moving on. Finally she found what she was searching for. She came to a halt, knelt and breathed softly on the dusty earth. There was a rumbling sound, then the ground split at our feet and the mouth of a tunnel opened up. I could only see a few metres down it, but I sensed danger.

"Don't tell me we have to go down there," I muttered.

"This is the way to our father's stronghold," she said.

"It's dark," I stalled.

"I will provide light," she promised, and I saw that both her hands were glowing softly, casting a dim white light a few metres ahead of her. She looked at me seriously. "Stay by my side down there. Don't stray."

"Will Mr Tiny get me if I do?" I asked.

"Believe it or not, there are worse monsters than our father," she said. "We will be passing some of them. If they get their hands on you, your millennia of torment in the

Lake of Souls will seem like a pleasant hour spent on a beach."

I doubted that, but the threat was strong enough to ensure I kept within a hair's breadth of the witch as she started down the tunnel. It sloped at a fairly constant thirty-degree angle. The floor and walls were smooth and made of what looked like solid rock. But there were shapes moving within the rock, twisted, inhuman, elongated shapes, all shadows, claws, teeth and tendrils. The walls bulged outwards as we passed — the *things* trapped within were reaching for us. But none could break through.

"What are they?" I croaked, sweating from fear as much as the dry heat of the tunnel.

"Creatures of universal chaos," Evanna answered. "I told you about them before — they're the monsters I spoke of. They are kin to our father, though he is not as powerful as them. They are imprisoned by a series of temporal and spatial laws — the laws of the universe which our father and I live by. If we ever break the laws, these creatures will be freed. They will turn the universe into a hell of their own making. All will fall beneath them. They'll invade every time zone and torture every mortal being ever born — for ever."

"That's why you were angry when you found out I was Mr Tiny's son," I said. "You thought he'd broken the laws."

"Yes. I was wrong, but it was a close-run thing. I doubt if even he was sure of his plan's success. When he gave birth to Hibernius and me, we knew of the laws, and we obeyed them.

If he was wrong about you — if he'd given you more power than he meant to — you could have unknowingly broken the laws and brought about the ruin of everything we know and love." She looked back at me and grinned. "I bet you never guessed you were that important to the world!"

"No," I said sickly. "And I never wanted to be."

"Don't worry," she said, her smile softening. "You took yourself out of the firing line when you let Steve kill you. You did what Hibernius and I never thought possible — you changed what seemed an inevitable future."

"You mean I prevented the coming of the Lord of the Shadows?" I asked eagerly. "That's why I let him kill me. It was the only way I could see to stop it. I didn't want to be a monster. I couldn't bear the thought of destroying the world. Mr Tiny said one of us had to be the Lord of the Shadows. But I thought, if both of us were dead..."

"You thought right," Evanna said. "Our father had edged the world to a point where there were only two futures. When you killed Steve *and* sacrificed yourself, it opened up dozens of possible futures again. I could not have done it — I would have broken the laws if I'd interfered — but as a human, you were able to."

"So what's happened since I died?" I asked. "You said two years have passed. Did the vampires defeat the vampaneze and win the War of the Scars?"

"No," Evanna said, pursing her lips. "The war still rages. But an end is within sight — an end very much not to our father's liking. Persuasive leaders are pushing for peace, Vancha and Harkat Mulds on the side of the vampires, Gannen Harst for the vampaneze. They are debating a treaty, discussing the guidelines by which both sides can live as one. Others fight against them – there are many in both clans who do not wish for peace – but the voices of reason are winning out."

"Then it worked!" I gasped. "If the vampires and vampaneze make peace, the world will be saved!"

"Perhaps," Evanna hummed. "It's not as clear-cut as that. Under Steve, the vampaneze made contact with human political and military leaders. They promised them long lives and power in exchange for their help. They wanted to create nuclear and chemical warfare, with the aim of bringing the world and its survivors under their direct control. That could still happen."

"Then we've got to stop it!" I shouted. "We can't let—"

"Easy," Evanna hushed me. "We are trying to prevent it. That's why I am here. I cannot meddle too deeply in the affairs of mankind, but I can do more now than before, and your actions have convinced me that I *should* interfere. Hibernius and I always stayed neutral. We did not get involved in the affairs of mortals. Hibernius wished to, but I argued against it, afraid we might break the laws and free the monsters." She sighed. "I was wrong. It's necessary to take risks every now and then. Our father took a risk in his attempt to wreak havoc — and I must now take one in an attempt to secure peace."

"What are you talking about?" I frowned.

"Mankind has been evolving," she said. "It has a destiny of its own, a growth towards something wonderful, which our father is intent on ruining. He used the vampires and vampaneze to throw mankind off course, to reduce the cities of the world to rubble, to drag humans back into the dark ages, so that he could control them again. But his plan failed. The clans of the night now seek to reunite and live separately from mankind, hidden, doing no harm, as they did in the past.

"Because the vampires and vampaneze have become part of the present, our father cannot unmake them. He could return to the past and create another race to combat them, but that would be difficult and time-consuming. Time, for once, is against him. If he cannot divide the clans within the next year or so, it is unlikely that he will be able to bring about the downfall of mankind which he craved. He might — and no doubt will — plot afresh in the future, and seek some other way to break them, but for the time being the world will be safe."

Evanna paused. Her hands were directed towards her face, illuminating her features. I'd never seen her look so thoughtful. "Do you remember the story of how I was created?" she asked.

"Of course," I said. "A vampire — Corza Jarn — wanted vampires to be able to have children. He pursued Mr Tiny until he agreed to grant him his wish, and by mixing Corza Jarn's blood with a pregnant she-wolf, and using his magic on her, he fathered you and Mr Tall."

"That was not his only reason for creating us," Evanna said, "but it was an important one. I can bear a vampire or a vampaneze's children, and they in turn could have children of their own. But any children of mine will be different from their fathers. They will have some of my powers — not all — and they'll be able to live by day. Sunlight won't kill them."

She looked at me intently. "A new breed of creature, an advanced race of vampire or vampaneze. If I gave birth to such children now, it would drive the clans apart. The war-mongers of both sides would use the children to stir up new visions and violence. For instance, if I had a child by a vampire father, those vampires opposed to peace would hail the child as a saviour, and say he was sent to help them wipe out the vampaneze. Even if the wiser vampires prevailed, and talked down the troublemakers, the vampaneze would be afraid of the child and suspicious of the vampire clan's long-term plans. How could they discuss peace terms, knowing they were now inferior to vampires, for ever at risk?

"The War of the Scars promises to end because both sides see that it might go on for ever. When the Lord of the Vampaneze and the vampire hunters were active, everybody knew the war would have a destined end. Now that Steve and you are dead, it might never finish, and neither vampires nor vampaneze want that. So they're willing to talk about peace.

"But my children could change everything. With the renewed promise of victory — either for the vampires or vampaneze, depending on which I chose to be the fathers of my young — the war would continue. As my children grew — and they'd grow quickly, since they'd be creatures of a certain amount of magic — they'd be raised on hatred and fear. In time they'd become warriors and lead their clan to victory over the other — and our father's plan would fall back into place, a little later than anticipated, but otherwise intact."

"Then you mustn't have them!" I exclaimed. "Mr Tiny can't make you, can he?"

"Not directly," she said. "He has threatened and bribed me ever since the night you and Steve died. But he does not have the power to force me to give birth."

"Then it's OK." I smiled weakly. "You won't have any children, and that will be that."

"Oh, but I will," Evanna said, and lowered her hands so that they shone on her stomach. "In fact, I'm pregnant already."

"*What?*" I exploded. "But you just said—"

"I know."

"But if you—"

"I know."

"But—"

"Darren!" she snapped. "I. Know."

"Then why do it?" I cried.

Evanna stopped to explain. As soon as she paused, the shapes in the walls began to press closer towards us, hissing and snarling, claws and tendrils extending, stretching the fabric of the rock. Evanna spotted this and strode forward again, speaking as she walked.

"I asked Desmond to free your spirit. Guilt drove you to the Lake of Souls, and would have kept you there eternally — there is no natural escape from that Lake of the damned. But rescue is possible. Souls can be fished out. Knowing that you were my half-brother, I felt honour-bound to free you."

"What about Steve?" I asked. "He was your half-brother too."

"Steve deserves his imprisonment." Her eyes were hard. "I feel pity for him, since he was to some extent a victim of our father's meddling. But Steve's evil was primarily of his own making. He chose his path and now must suffer the consequences. But you tried to do good. It wasn't fair that you should rot in the Lake of Souls, so I pleaded with our father to help." She chuckled. "Needless to say, he refused.

"He came to me a few months ago," she continued. "He realized his plans were unravelling and he saw me as his only solution. He'd spent most of the time since your death trying to convince me to have children, with no more success than I'd had trying to get him to free you. But this time he took a fresh approach. He said we could help each other. If I had a child, he'd free your soul."

"You agreed to that?" I roared. "You sold out the world just to help me?"

"Of course not," she grunted.

"But you said you were pregnant."

"I am." She looked back at me and smiled shyly. "My first thought was to reject our father's offer. But then I saw a way to use it to our advantage. There is still no guarantee of a peaceful settlement between the vampires and vampaneze. It looks promising but is by no means certain. If talks break down, the war could continue, and that would play into our father's hands. He would have time to go back to the past and create a new leader, one who could pick up where Steve left off.

"I was thinking of this when Desmond put his suggestion to me. I recalled the way you tricked him, and wondered what you would do in my situation. Then, in a flash, I saw it.

"I accepted his proposal but told him I wasn't sure whether I wanted a vampire's child or a vampaneze's. He said it didn't matter. I asked if I could choose. He said yes. So I spent some time with Gannen Harst, then with Vancha March. When I returned to our father, I told him I had chosen and was pregnant. He was so delighted, he didn't even complain when I refused to reveal who the father was — he just quickly arranged to send me here to free you, so that we could move forward without any further distractions."

She stopped talking and rubbed her stomach with her hands. She was still smiling that strange shy smile.

"So whose is it?" I asked. I didn't see what difference it made but I was curious to know the answer.

"Both," she said. "I am having twins — one by Vancha, one by Gannen."

"A vampire child *and* a vampaneze child!" I cried, excited.

"More than that," Evanna said. "I have allowed the three blood lines to mix. Each child is one third vampire, one third vampaneze, and one third me. That's how I've tricked him.

He thought any baby of mine would divide the clans, but instead they will pull them closer together. My children, when they are ready, will breed with other vampires and vampaneze, to give birth to a new, multi-race clan. All divisions will be erased and finally forgotten.

"We're going to create peace, Darren, in spite of our father. That's what you taught me — we don't have to accept destiny, or Des Tiny. We can create our own future, all of us. We have the power to rule our lives — we just have to make the choice to use it. You chose when you sacrificed your life. Now I've chosen too — by giving life. Only time will tell what our choices lead to, but I'm sure that whatever future we help usher in, it has to be better than the one our father planned."

"Amen to that!" I muttered, then followed her silently down the tunnel, thinking of the future and all the surprises and twists it might hold. My head was buzzing with thoughts and ideas. I was having to take on board so much, so quickly, that I felt overwhelmed by it all, not sure what to make of everything. But there was one thing I was absolutely sure of — when Mr Tiny found out about Evanna's babies, he'd all but explode with anger!

Thinking of that, and the nasty little meddler's face when he heard the news, I burst out laughing. Evanna laughed too, and the laughter stayed with us for ages, following us down the tunnel like a flock of chuckling birds, acting almost like a protective spell against the banks of walled-in, ever-moving, ever-reaching monsters.

CHAPTER SIXTEEN

About an hour later the tunnel ended and we entered the home of Desmond Tiny. I'd never really thought of him having a home. I just assumed he wandered the world, always on the move, in search of bloodshed and chaos. But, now that I considered it, I realized every monster needs a den to call its own, and Mr Tiny's had to be the strangest of them all.

It was a huge — and I mean HUGE — cave, maybe a couple of miles or so wide, and stretching as far ahead as I could make out. Much of the cave was natural, stalagmites and stalactites, waterfalls, beautifully weird rock colours and formations. But much more of it was incredibly *un*natural.

There were grand old cars from what I guessed must be the 1920s or 1930s floating in the air overhead. At first I thought they were attached to the ceiling by wires, but they were in constant motion, circling, crossing paths, even looping around like planes, and not a wire in sight.

There were mannequins all over the place, dressed in costumes from every century and continent, from a primitive loincloth to the most outrageous modern fashion accessories. Their blank eyes unsettled me — I got the feeling that they were watching me, ready to spring to life at Mr Tiny's command and leap upon me.

There were works of art and sculpture, some so famous that even an art cretin like me recognized them — the *Mona Lisa*, *The Thinker*, *The Last Supper*. Mixed in with them, displayed like art exhibits, were dozens of brains preserved in glass cases. I read a few of the labels — Beethoven, Mozart, Wagner, Mahler. (That one gave me a jump — I'd gone to a school named after Mahler!)

"Our father loves music," Evanna whispered. "Where humans collect sheet music or gramophone records–" She obviously hadn't heard about CDs yet! "–he collects brains of composers. By touching them, he can listen to all the tunes they ever composed, along with many they never completed or shared with the world."

"But where does he get them from?" I asked.

"He travels to the past when they have just died and robs their graves," she said, as though it was the most casual thing in the world. I thought about questioning the right and wrong of something like that, but there were weightier issues to deal with, so I let it slide.

"He likes art too, I take it," I said, nodding at a flowery Van Gogh.

"Immensely," Evanna said. "These are all originals of course — he doesn't bother with copies."

"Nonsense!" I snorted. "These can't be real. I've seen some of the real paintings. Mum and Dad—" I still thought of my human Dad as my real father, and always would. " —took me to see the *Mona Lisa* in the Loo once."

"The Louvre," Evanna corrected me. "That is a copy. Some of our father's Little People are created from the souls of artists. They make perfect copies of pieces he especially admires. Then he slips back to the past and swaps the copy for the original. In most cases even the actual artist cannot tell the difference."

"You're telling me the *Mona Lisa* in Paris is a fake?" I asked sceptically.

"Yes." Evanna laughed at my expression. "Our father is a selfish man. He always keeps the best for himself. What he wants, he takes — and he normally wants the best of everything. Except books." Her voice became pointed, as it had earlier when she'd been talking about his attitude towards books. "Desmond never reads works of fiction. He doesn't collect books or pay any attention to authors. Homer, Chaucer, Shakespeare, Dickens, Tolstoy, Twain — all have passed him by unmarked. He doesn't care what they have to say. He has nothing to do with the world of literature. It's as if it exists in a separate universe from his."

Once again I didn't see her point in telling me this, so I let my interest wander. I'd never been a big art fan, but even I was impressed by this display. It was the ultimate collection, capturing a slice of pretty much all the artistic wonder and imagination mankind had ever conjured into being.

There was far too much for any one person to take in. Weapons, jewellery, toys, tools, albums of stamps, bottles of vintage wine, Fabergé eggs, grandfather clocks, suites of furniture, thrones of kings and queens. A lot of it was precious, but there were plenty of worthless items too, stuff which had simply caught Mr Tiny's fancy, such as bottle tops, oddly shaped balloons, digital watches, a collection of empty ice-cream tubs, thousands of whistles, hundreds of thousands of coins (old ones mixed in with brand new ones), and so on. The treasure cave in *Aladdin* seemed like a bargain bin in comparison.

Even though the cave was packed with all manner of wonders and oddities, it didn't feel cluttered. There was plenty of space to walk about and explore. We wound our way through the various collections and artefacts, Evanna pausing occasionally to point out a particularly interesting piece — the charred stake on which Joan Of Arc was burnt, the pistol which had been used to shoot Lincoln, the very first wheel.

"Historians would go crazy in this place," I noted. "Does Mr Tiny ever bring anybody here?"

"Almost never," Evanna said. "This is his private sanctuary. I've only been here a handful of times myself. The exceptions are those he pulls out of the Lake of Souls. He has to bring them here to turn them into Little People."

I stopped when she said that. I'd had a sudden premonition. "Evanna..." I began, but she shook her head.

"Ask no more questions," she said. "Desmond will explain the rest to you. It won't be long now."

Minutes later we reached what felt like the centre of the cave. There was a small pool of green liquid, a pile of blue robes and, standing beside them, Mr Tiny. He was staring at me sourly through the lenses of his thick glasses.

"Well, well," he drawled, hooking his thumbs behind his braces. "If it isn't the young martyr himself. Meet anyone interesting in the Lake of Souls?"

"Ignore him," Evanna said out of the side of her mouth.

Mr Tiny waddled forward and stopped a few metres shy of me. His eyes seemed to dance with fire this close up. "If I'd known what a nuisance you were going to be, I'd never have spawned you," he hissed.

"Too late now," I jeered.

"No it isn't," he said. "I could go back and erase you from the past, make it so you never lived. The universe would replace you. Somebody else would become the youngest ever Vampire Prince, hunt for the Vampaneze Lord, etc. — but *you* would never have existed. Your soul wouldn't just be destroyed — it would be unmade completely."

"Father," Evanna said warningly, "you know you aren't going to do that."

"But I could!" Mr Tiny insisted.

"Yes," she tutted, "but you won't. We have an agreement. I've upheld my end. Now it's your turn."

Mr Tiny muttered something unpleasant, then forced a fake smile. "Very well. I'm a man of my word. Let's get on with it. Darren, my woebegotten boy, get rid of that blanket and hop into the pool." He nodded at the green liquid.

"Why?" I asked stiffly.

"It's time to recast you."

A few minutes earlier, I wouldn't have known what he was talking about. But Evanna's hint had prepared me for this. "You want to turn me into a Little Person, don't you?" I said.

Mr Tiny's lips twitched. He glared at Evanna, but she shrugged innocently. "A right little know-it-all, aren't you?" he huffed, disgusted that I'd ruined his big surprise.

"How does it work?" I asked.

Mr Tiny crossed to the pool and crouched beside it. "This is the soup of creation," he said, running a finger through the thick green liquid. "It will become your blood, the fuel on which your new body runs. Your bones will be stripped bare when you step in. Your flesh, brain, organs and soul will dissolve. I shall mix the lot up and build a new body out of the mess." He grinned. "Those who've been through it tell me it's a most frightfully painful procedure, the worst they've ever known."

"What makes you think I'm going to do it?" I asked tightly. "I've seen how your Little People live, mindless, speechless, unable to remember their original identities, slaves to your whims, eating the flesh of dead animals — even humans! Why should I place myself under your spell like that?"

"No deal with my daughter if you don't," Mr Tiny said simply.

I shook my head stubbornly. I knew Evanna was trying to out-fox Mr Tiny, but I didn't see why this was necessary. How could I help bring about peace between the vampires and vampaneze by going through a load of pain and becoming a Little Person? It didn't make sense.

As if reading my thoughts, Evanna said softly, "This is for *you*, Darren. It has nothing to do with what is happening in the present, or the War of the Scars. This is your only hope of escaping the pull of the Lake of Souls and going to Paradise. You can live a full life as you are, in this waste world, and return to the Lake when you die. Or you can trust us and place yourself in our father's hands."

"I trust *you*," I said to Evanna, shooting an arch look at Mr Tiny.

"Oh, my boy, if you only knew how much that hurts," Mr Tiny said miserably, then laughed. "Enough of the dawdling. You either do this or you don't. But take heed, daughter — by making the offer, I've fulfilled my end of the bargain. If the boy refuses to accept your advice, on his head be it. I'll expect you to keep your word."

Evanna looked at me questioningly, not placing any pressure on me. I thought about it at length. I hated the idea of becoming a Little Person. It wasn't so much the pain as letting Mr Tiny become my master. And what if Evanna was lying? I'd said I trusted the witch, but thinking back, I realized there was precious little reason to trust her. She'd never betrayed her father before, or worked for the good of any individual. Why start now? What if this was a twisted scheme to ensnare me, and she was in league with Mr Tiny, or had been tricked into doing his bidding? The whole thing stank of a trap.

But what other option had I? Give Evanna the cold shoulder, refuse to enter the pool, walk away? Even assuming Mr Tiny let me leave, and the monsters in the tunnel didn't catch me, what would I have to look forward to? A life lived in a world full of dragons, followed by eternity in the Lake of Souls, wasn't my idea of a good time! In the end I decided it was better to gamble and hope for the best.

"OK," I said reluctantly. "But there's one condition."

"You're in no position to set conditions," Mr Tiny growled.

"Maybe not," I agreed, "but I'm setting one anyway. I'll only do it if you guarantee me a free memory. I don't want to wind up like Harkat, not knowing who I was, obeying your orders because I've no free will of my own. I'm not sure what you have planned for me once I become a Little Person, but if it involves serving as one of your fog-brained slaves…"

"It doesn't," Mr Tiny interrupted. "I admit I quite like the idea of having you toady to me for a few million years or so, but my daughter was very precise when it came to the terms of our agreement. You won't be able to talk but that's the only restriction."

"Why won't I be able to talk?" I frowned.

"Because I'm sick of listening to you!" Mr Tiny barked. "Besides, you won't need to speak. Most of my Little People don't. Muteness hasn't harmed any of the others, and it won't harm you."

"OK," I muttered. I didn't like it, but I could see there was no point arguing. Stepping up to the edge of the pool, I shrugged off the blanket which the Little People had draped around me shortly after I emerged from the Lake of Souls. I stared into the dark green liquid. I couldn't see my reflection in it. "What—" I started to ask.

"No time for questions!" Mr Tiny barked and nudged me hard with an elbow. I teetered on the edge of the pool a moment, arms flailing, then splashed heavily into what felt like the sizzling fires of hell.

CHAPTER SEVENTEEN

Instant agony and burning. My flesh bubbled, then boiled away. I tried to scream but my lips and tongue had already come undone. My eyes and ears melted. No sensation except pain.

The liquid stripped my flesh from my bones, then set to work on the marrow within the bones. Next it burnt through to my inner organs, then ate me up from the inside out. Inside my head my brain sizzled like a knob of butter in a heated frying pan, and melted down just as quickly. My left arm — just bone now — tore loose from my body and floated away. It was soon followed by my lower right leg. Then I came apart completely, limbs, charred organs, tiny strips of flesh, bare pieces of bone. All that stayed constant was the pain, which hadn't lessened in the slightest.

In the midst of my suffering came a moment of spiritual calm. With whatever remained of my brain, I became aware of a separation. There was another presence in the pool with me. At first I was confused, but then I realized it was the flicker of Sam Grest's soul which I'd carried within me since drinking his blood at the time of his death. Sam had passed on to Paradise many years ago, and now this final shard of his spirit was departing this world too. In my mind's eye a face formed in the liquid, young and carefree, smiling in spite of the torment, popping a pickled onion into his mouth. Sam winked at me. A ghostly hand saluted. Then he was gone and I was finally, totally alone.

Eventually the pain ceased. I'd dissolved completely. There were no pain sensors left to transmit feelings, and no brain cells to respond to them. A weird peace descended. I'd become one with the pool. My atoms had mixed with the liquid and the two were now one. I *was* the green liquid. I could sense the hollow bones from my body drifting to the bottom of the pool, where they settled.

Some time later hands — Mr Tiny's — were dunked in the liquid. He wiggled his fingers and a shiver ran up the memory of my spine. He picked up the bones from the floor — being careful to scrape up every single piece — and dumped them on the ground of the cave. The bones were covered in molecules of the liquid — molecules of *me* — and through them I felt Mr Tiny putting the bones together, snapping them into small pieces, melting some down, bending or twisting others, creating a frame entirely different to my previous form.

Mr Tiny worked on the body for hours. When he had all the bones in place, he packed them full with organs — brain, heart, liver, kidneys — then covered them with clammy grey flesh, which he stitched together to hold the organs and bones in place. I'm not sure where the organs and flesh came from. Perhaps he grew them himself, but I think it more likely that he harvested them from other creatures — probably dead humans.

Mr Tiny finished with the eyes. I could feel him connecting the orbs up to my brain, fingers working at lightning-fast speed, with all the precision of the world's greatest surgeon. It was an incredibly artistic undertaking, one which even Dr Frankenstein would have struggled to match.

Once he'd finished with the body, he stuck his fingers back into the liquid of the pool. The fingers were cold this time, and grew colder by the second. The liquid began to condense, becoming thicker. There was no pain. It was just strange, like I was squeezing in upon myself.

Then, when the liquid was a fraction of the size it had been, with the texture of a thick milk shake, Mr Tiny removed his hands and tubes were inserted. There was a brief pause, then suction from the tubes, and I felt myself flowing through them, out of the pool and into ... what? ... not tubes like those which had been stuck into the pool, but similar...

Of course — *veins!* Mr Tiny had told me the liquid would serve as my fuel — my blood. I was leaving the confines of the pool for the fleshy limits of my new body.

I felt myself fill the gaps, forcing my way through the network of veins and arteries, making slow but sure progress.

When the liquid hit the brain and gradually seeped into it, absorbed by the cold grey cells, my bodily senses awoke. I became aware of my heartbeat first, slower and heavier than before. A tingle ran through my hands and feet, then up my newly crafted spine. I twitched my fingers and toes. Moved an arm slightly. Shook a leg softly. The limbs didn't respond as quickly as my old limbs had, but maybe that was just because I wasn't used to them yet.

Sound came next, a harsh roaring noise at first, which gradually died away to allow normal sounds through. But the sounds weren't as sharp as before —like all the Little People, my ears had been stitched within the skin of my head. Hearing was soon followed by a dim sense of vision — but no smell or sense or taste, since – again, in common with all of Mr Tiny's creations – I'd been created without a nose.

My vision improved as more and more blood was transferred to my new brain. The world looked different through these eyes. I had a wider field of view than before, since my eyes were rounder and bigger. I could see more, but through a slightly green haze, as though staring through a filter.

The first sight I fixed on was Mr Tiny, still working on my body, monitoring the tubes, applying a few final stitches, testing my reflexes. He had the look of a loving, devoted parent.

Next I saw Evanna, keeping a close eye on her father, making sure he didn't pull any tricks. She handed him needles and string from time to time, like a nurse. Her expression was a mixture of suspicion and pride. Evanna knew all of Mr Tiny's shortcomings, but she was still his daughter, and I could see now that despite her misgivings she loved him — in a way.

Eventually the transfer was complete. Mr Tiny removed the tubes — they'd been stuck in all over, my arms, legs, torso, head — and sealed the holes, stitching them shut. He gave me a final once-over, fixed a spot where I was leaking, did some fine-tuning at the corners of my eyes, checked my heartbeat. Then he stepped back and grunted. "Another perfect creation, even if I do say so myself."

"Sit up, Darren," Evanna said. "But slowly. Don't rush."

I did as she said. A wave of dizziness swept over me when I raised my head, but it soon passed. I pushed up gradually, pausing every time I felt dizzy or sick. Finally I was sitting upright. I was able to study my body from here, its broad hands and feet, thick limbs, dull grey skin. I noted that, like Harkat, I was neither fully male nor female, but something in between. If I could have blushed, I would have!

"Stand," Mr Tiny said, spitting on his hands and rubbing them together, using his spit to wash himself. "Walk about. Test yourself. It won't take you long to get used to your new shape. I design my Little People to go into immediate action."

With Evanna's help I stood. I weaved unsteadily on my feet, but soon found my balance. I was much stouter and heavier than before. As I'd noticed when lying down, my limbs didn't react as quickly as they once did. I had to focus hard to make my fingers curl or to edge a foot forward.

"Easy," Evanna said as I tried to turn and almost fell back into the now empty pool. She caught and held me until I was steady again. "Slowly, one bit at a time. It won't take long — just five or ten minutes." I tried to ask a question but no sound came out. "You cannot speak," Evanna reminded me. "You do not have a tongue."

I slowly raised a chunky grey arm and pointed a finger at my head. I stared at Evanna with my large green eyes, trying to transmit my question mentally. "You want to know if we can communicate telepathically," Evanna said. I nodded my neck-less head. "No. You have not been designed with that ability."

"You're a basic model," Mr Tiny chipped in. "You won't be around very long, so it would have been pointless to kit you out with a bunch of unnecessary features. You can think and move, which is all you need to do."

I spent the next several minutes getting to know my new body. There were no mirrors nearby, but I spotted a large silver tray in which I could study my reflection. Hobbling over to it, I ran a critical green eye over myself. I was maybe four and a half feet tall and three feet wide. My stitches weren't as neat as Harkat's, and my eyes weren't exactly level, but otherwise we didn't look too different. When I opened my mouth I saw that not only did I lack a tongue, but teeth too. I turned carefully and looked at Evanna, pointing to my gums.

"You will not have to eat," she said.

"You won't be alive long enough to bother with food," Mr Tiny added.

My new stomach clenched when he said that. I'd been tricked! It *had* been a trap, and I'd fallen for it! If I could have spoken, I'd have cursed myself for being such a fool.

But then, as I looked for a decent weapon to defend myself with, Evanna smiled positively. "Remember why we did this, Darren — to free your soul. We could have given you a new, full life as a Little Person, but that would have complicated matters. It's easier this way. You have to trust us."

I didn't feel very trusting, but the deed was done. And Evanna didn't look like somebody who'd been tricked, or who was gloating from having tricked me. Putting fears of betrayal and thoughts of fighting aside, I decided to stay calm and see what the pair planned next for me.

Evanna picked up the pile of blue robes which had been lying near to the pool and came over with them. "I prepared these for you earlier," she said. "Let me help you put them on." I was going to signal that I could dress myself, but Evanna flashed me a look which made me stop. Her back was to Mr Tiny, who was examining the remains of the pool. While his attention was diverted, she slipped the robes on over my head and arms. I realized there were several objects inside the robes, stitched into the lining.

Evanna locked gazes with me and a secret understanding passed between us — she was telling me to act as if the objects weren't there. She was up to something which she didn't want Mr Tiny to know about. I'd no idea what she might have hidden in the robes, but it must be important. Once the robes were on I kept my arms out by my sides and tried not to think about the secret packages I was carrying, in case I accidentally tipped off Mr Tiny.

Evanna gave me a final once-over, then called out, "He is ready, father."

Mr Tiny waddled across. He looked me up and down, sniffed snootily, then thrust a small mask at me. "You'd better put that on," he said. "You probably won't need it, but we might as well be safe as sorry."

As I strapped on the mask, Mr Tiny bent and drew a line in the earth of the cave floor. He stepped back from it and clutched his heart-shaped watch. The timepiece began to glow, and soon his hand and face were glowing too. Moments later a doorway grew out of the line in the ground, sliding upwards to its full height. It was an open doorway. The space between the jambs was a grey sheen. I'd been through a portal like this before, when Mr Tiny had sent Harkat and me into what would have been the future (what still might be, if Evanna's plan failed).

When the doorway was complete, Mr Tiny nodded his head at it. "Time to go."

My eyes flicked to Evanna — was she coming with me? "No," she said in answer to my unasked question. "I will return to the present through a separate door. This one goes further back." She stooped so we were at the same height. "This is goodbye, Darren. I don't imagine I'll ever make the journey to Paradise — I don't think it's intended for the likes of me — so we'll probably never see each other again."

"Maybe he won't go to Paradise either," Mr Tiny sneered. "Perhaps his soul is meant for the great fires beneath."

Evanna smiled. "We don't know all the secrets of the beyond, but we've never seen any evidence of a hell. The Lake of Souls seems to be the only place where the damned end up, and if our plan works, you won't go back there. Don't worry — your soul will fly free."

"Come on," Mr Tiny snapped. "I'm bored with him. Time to kick him out of our lives, once and for all." He pushed Evanna aside, grabbed the shoulder of my robes and hauled me to the doorway. "Don't get any smart ideas back there," he growled. "You can't change the past, so don't go trying. Just do what you have to — tough luck if you can't work out what that is — and let the universe take care of the rest."

I turned my face towards him, not sure what he meant, wanting more answers. But Mr Tiny ignored me, raised a wellington-clad foot, then — without a word of farewell, as though I was a stranger who meant nothing to him — booted me clean through the door and back to a date with history.

CHAPTER EIGHTEEN

"Ladies and gentlemen, welcome to the Cirque Du Freak, home of the world's most remarkable human beings."

I had no eyelids, so I couldn't blink, but beneath my mask my jaw dropped a hundred miles. I was in the wings of a large theatre, staring out at a stage and the unmistakable figure of the dead Hibernius Tall. Except he wasn't dead. He was very much alive, and in the middle of introducing one of the fabled Cirque Du Freak performances.

"We present acts both frightening and bizarre, acts you can find nowhere else in the world. Those who are easily scared should leave now. I'm sure there are people who..."

Two beautiful women stepped up next to me and prepared to go on. They were tugging at their glittering costumes, making sure they fit right. I recognized the women — Davina and Shirley. They'd been part of the Cirque Du Freak when I first joined, but had left after a few years to get jobs in the ordinary world. The life of a travelling performer wasn't for everyone.

". . . is unique. And none are harmless," Mr Tall finished, then walked off. Davina and Shirley moved forward and I saw where they were heading — the Wolf Man's cage, which stood uncovered in the middle of the stage. As they left, a Little Person took his place by my side. His face was hidden beneath the hood of his blue robes, but his head turned in my direction. There was a moment's pause, then he reached up and pulled my hood further over my face, so that my features were hidden too.

Mr Tall appeared by our side with the speed and silence for which he was once renowned. Without a word he handed each of us a needle and lots of orange string. The other Little Person stuck the needle and string inside his robes, so I did the same, not wanting to appear out of place.

Davina and Shirley had released the Wolf Man from his cage and were walking through the audience with him, letting people stroke the hairy man-beast. I studied the theatre more closely while they paraded the Wolf Man around. This was the old abandoned cinema theatre in my home town, where Steve had murdered Shancus, and where — many years earlier — I had first crossed paths with Mr Crepsley.

I was wondering why I'd been sent back here — I had a pretty good hunch — when there was a loud explosion. The Wolf Man went wild, as he often did at the start of an act — what looked like a mad outburst was actually carefully staged. Leaping upon a screaming woman, he bit one of her hands off. In a flash, Mr Tall had left our side and reappeared next to the Wolf Man. He pulled him off the screaming woman, subdued him, then led him back to his cage, while Davina and Shirley did their best to calm down the crowd.

Mr Tall returned to the screaming woman, picked up her severed hand and whistled loudly. That was the signal for my fellow Little Person and me to advance. We ran over to Mr Tall, careful not to reveal our faces. Mr Tall sat the woman up and whispered to her. When she was quiet he sprinkled a sparkly pink powder on to her bleeding wrist and stuck the hand against it. He nodded to my companion and me. We pulled out our needles and string and started to stitch the hand back on to the wrist.

I felt light-headed while I stitched. This was the greatest sense of déjà vu I'd ever experienced! I knew what was coming next, every second of it. I'd been sent back into my past, to a night which had been etched unforgettably into my memory. All the times I'd prayed for the chance to come back and change the course of my future. And now, in the most unexpected of circumstances, here it was.

We finished stitching and returned backstage. I wanted to stand in the shadows again and watch the show — if I remembered correctly, Alexander Ribs would come on next, followed by Rhamus Twobellies — but my fellow Little Person was having none of it. He nudged me ahead of him, to the rear of the theatre, where a young Jekkus Flang was waiting. In later years Jekkus would become an accomplished knife-thrower, and even take part in the shows. But in this time he'd only recently joined the circus, and was in charge of preparing the interval gift trays.

Jekkus handed each of us a tray packed with items such as rubber dolls of Alexander Ribs, clippings of the Wolf Man's hair, and chocolate nuts and bolts. He also gave us price tags for each item. He didn't speak to us — this was back in the time before Harkat Mulds, when everyone thought Little People were mute, mindless robots.

When Rhamus Twobellies stomped offstage, Jekkus sent us out into the audience to sell the gifts. We moved among the crowd, letting people study our wares and buy if they wished. My fellow Little Person took charge of the rear areas of the theatre, leaving me to handle the front rows. And so, a few minutes later, as I'd come to suspect I would, I came face to face with two young boys, the only children in the entire theatre. One was a wild child, the sort of kid who stole money from his mother and collected horror comics, who dreamt of being a vampire when he grew up. The other was a quiet, but in his own way equally mischievous boy, the kind who wouldn't think twice about stealing a vampire's spider.

"How much is the glass statue?" the impossibly young and innocent Steve Leopard asked, pointing to a statue on my tray which you could eat. Shakily, fighting to keep my hand steady, I showed him the price tag. "I can't read," Steve said. "Will you tell me how much it costs?"

I noted the look of surprise on Darren's — Charna's guts! — on *my* face. Steve had guessed straightaway that there was something strange about the Little People, but I hadn't been so sharp. The young me had no idea why Steve was lying.

I shook my head quickly and moved on, leaving Steve to explain to my younger self why he'd pretended he couldn't read. If I'd been feeling light-headed earlier, I felt positively empty-headed now. It's a remarkable, earth-shattering thing to look into the eyes of a youthful you, to see yourself as you once were, young, foolish, gullible. I don't think anyone ever remembers what they were really like as kids. Adults think they do, but they don't. Photos and videos don't capture the real you, or bring back to life the person you used to be. You have to return to the past to do that.

We finished selling our wares and headed backstage to collect fresh trays full of new items, based on the next set of performers — Truska, Hans Hands, and then, appearing like a phantom out of the shadows of the night, Mr Crepsley and his performing tarantula, Madam Octa.

I couldn't miss Mr Crepsley's act. When Jekkus wasn't looking I crept forward and watched from the wings. My heart leapt into my mouth when my old friend and mentor walked on to the stage, startling in his red cloak with his white skin, orange crop of hair and trademark scar. Seeing him again, I wanted to rush out and throw my arms around him, tell him how much I missed him and how much he'd meant to me. I wanted to say that I loved him, that he'd been a second father to me. I wanted to joke with him about his stiff manner, his stunted sense of humour, his overly precious pride. I wanted to tell him how Steve had tricked him, and gently wind him up for being taken in by the pretence and dying for no reason. I was sure he'd see the funny side of it once he stopped steaming!

But there could be no communication between us. Even if I'd had a tongue, Mr Crepsley wouldn't have known who I was. On this night he hadn't yet met the boy named Darren Shan. I was nobody to him.

So I stood where I was and watched. One final turn from the vampire who'd altered my life in so many ways. One last performance to savour, as he put Madam Octa through her paces and thrilled the crowd. I shivered when he first spoke – I'd forgotten how deep his voice was – then hung on his every word. The minutes passed slowly, but not slowly enough for me — I wanted it to last an age.

A Little Person led a goat on stage for Madam Octa to kill. It wasn't the Little Person who'd been with me in the audience — there were more than two of us here. Madam Octa killed the goat, then performed a series of tricks with Mr Crepsley, crawled over his body and face, pulsed in and out of his mouth, played with tiny cups and saucers. In the crowd, the young Darren Shan was falling in love with the spider — he thought she was amazing. In the wings, the older Darren regarded her sadly. I used to hate Madam Octa – I could trace all my troubles back to the eight-legged beast – but not any longer. None of it was her fault. It was destiny. All along, from the first moment of my being, it had been Des Tiny.

Mr Crepsley concluded his act and left the stage. He had to pass me to get off. As he approached, I thought again about trying to communicate with him. I wasn't able to speak, but I could write. If I grabbed him and took him aside, scribbled a message, warned him to leave immediately, to get out now...

He passed.

I did nothing.

This wasn't the way. Mr Crepsley had no reason to trust me, and explaining the situation would have taken too much time — he was illiterate, so I'd have had to get somebody to read the note for him. It might also have been dangerous. If I'd told him about the Vampaneze Lord and all the rest, he might have tried to change the course of the future, to prevent the War of the Scars. Evanna had said it was impossible to change the past, but if Mr Crepsley — prompted by my warning — somehow managed to do so, he might free those terrible monsters which even Mr Tiny was afraid of. I couldn't take that risk.

"What are you doing here?" someone snapped behind me. It was Jekkus Flang. He poked me hard with a finger and pointed to my tray. "Get out there quick!" he growled.

I did as Jekkus ordered. I wanted to follow the same route as before, so that I could study myself and Steve again, but this time the other Little Person got there before me, so I had to trudge to the rear of the theatre and do the rounds there.

At the end of the interval Gertha Teeth took to the stage, to be followed by Sive and Seersa (the Twisting Twins) and finally Evra and his snake. I retreated to the rear of the theatre, not keen on the idea of seeing Evra again. Although the snake-boy was one of my best friends, I couldn't forget the pain I'd put him through. It would have hurt too much to watch him perform, thinking about the agony and loss he was to later endure.

While the final trio of acts brought the show to a close, I turned my attention to the objects stitched into the lining of my robes. Time to find out what Evanna had sent me back with. Reaching underneath the heavy blue cloth, I found the first of the rectangular items and ripped it loose. When I saw what it was, I broke out into a wide toothless smile.

The sly old witch! I recalled what she'd told me on the way from the Lake of Souls to Mr Tiny's cave — although the past couldn't be changed, the people involved in major events could be replaced. Sending me back to this period in time was enough to free my soul, but Evanna had gone one step further, and made sure I was able to free my old self too. Mr Tiny knew about that. He didn't like it, but he'd accepted it.

However, working on the sly, unknown to her father, Evanna had presented me with something even more precious than personal freedom — something that would drive Des Tiny absolutely cuckoo when he found out how he'd been swindled!

I pulled all the other objects out, set them in order, then checked the most recent addition. I didn't find what I expected, but as I scanned through it, I saw what Evanna had done. I was tempted to flick to the rear and read the last few words, but then decided I'd be better off not knowing.

I heard screams from within the theatre — Evra's snake must have made its first appearance of the night. I didn't have much time left. I slipped away before Jekkus Flang sought me out and burdened me with another tray. Exiting by the back door, I sneaked around and re-entered the cinema at the front. I walked down the long corridor to where an open door led to a staircase — the way up to the balcony.

I climbed a few steps, then set Evanna's gift down and waited. I thought about what to do with the objects — the *weapons*. Give them to the boy directly? No. If I did, he might use them to try to change the future. That wasn't allowed. But there must be a way to get them to him later, so that he could use them at the right time. Evanna wouldn't have given them to me if there wasn't.

It didn't take me long to figure it out. I was happier when I knew what to do with the gift, because it also meant I knew exactly what to do with young Darren.

The show ended and the audience members poured out of the theatre, eagerly discussing the show and marvelling aloud. Since the boys had been sitting near the front, they were two of the last to leave. I waited in silence, safe in the knowledge of what was to come.

Finally, a frightened young Darren opened the door to the stairway, slipped through, closed it behind him, and stood in the darkness, breathing heavily, heart pounding, waiting for everyone to file out of the theatre. I could see him in spite of the gloom – my large green eyes were almost as strong as a half-vampire's – but he had no idea I was there.

When the last sounds had faded, the boy came sloping up the stairs. He was heading for the balcony, to keep an eye on his friend Steve and see that he came to no harm. If he made it up there, his fate would be sealed and he'd have to live the tormented life of a half-vampire. I had the power to change that. This, in addition to freedom from the Lake of Souls, was Evanna's gift to me — and the last part of the gift as far as Mr Tiny was aware.

As young Darren drew close, I launched myself at him, picked him up before he knew what was happening, and ran with him down the stairs. I burst through the door into the light of the corridor, then dumped him roughly on the floor. His face was a mask of terror.

"D-d-d-don't kill me!" he squealed, scrabbling backwards.

In answer I tore my hood back, then ripped off my mask, revealing my round, grey, stitched together face and huge gaping maw of a mouth. I thrust my head forward, leered and spread my arms. Darren screamed, lurched to his feet and stumbled for the exit. I pounded after him, making lots of noise, scraping the wall with my fingers. He flew out of the theatre when he got to the door, rolled down the steps, then picked himself up and ran for his life.

I stood on the front door step, watching my younger self flee for safety. I was smiling softly. I'd stand guard here to be certain, but I was sure he wouldn't return. He'd run straight home, leap beneath the bed covers and shiver himself to sleep. In the morning, not having seen what Steve got up to, he'd phone to find out if his friend was OK. Not knowing who Mr Crepsley was, he'd have no reason to fear Steve, and Steve would have no reason to be suspicious of Darren. Their friendship would resume its natural course and, although I was sure they'd talk often about their trip to the Cirque Du Freak, Darren wouldn't go back to steal the spider, and Steve would never reveal the truth about Mr Crepsley.

I retreated from the entrance and climbed the steps up to the balcony. There, I watched as Steve had his showdown with Mr Crepsley. He asked to be the vampire's assistant. Mr Crepsley tested his blood, then rejected him on the grounds that he was evil. Steve left in a rage, swearing revenge on the vampire.

Would Steve still seek out that revenge now that his main nemesis — me — had been removed from the equation? When he grew up, would his path still take him away from normal life and towards the vampaneze? Was he destined to live his life as he had the first time round, only with a different enemy instead of Darren Shan? Or would the universe replace Steve, like me, with somebody else?

I had no way of knowing. Only time would tell, and I wouldn't be around long enough to see the story through to its end. I'd had my innings, and they were just about over. It was time for me to step back, draw a line under my life, and make my final farewell.

But first — one last cunning attempt to wreck the plans of Desmond Tiny!

CHAPTER NINETEEN

The key events of the past can't be changed, but the people in it can. Evanna had told me that if she went back and killed Adolf Hitler, the universe would replace him with somebody else. The major events of World War II would unfold exactly as they were meant to, only with a different figurehead at the helm. This would obviously create a number of temporal discrepancies, but nothing the higher force of the universe couldn't set right.

While I couldn't alter the course of my history, I *could* remove myself from it. Which was what I'd done by scaring off young Darren. The events of my life would unravel the same way they had before. A child would be blooded, travel to Vampire Mountain, unmask Kurda Smahlt, become a Vampire Prince, then hunt for the Vampaneze Lord. But it wouldn't be the boy I'd frightened off tonight. Somebody else — some other child — would have to fill the shoes of Darren Shan.

I felt bad about putting another kid through the tough trials of my life, but at least I knew that in the end – in death – he would be triumphant. The person who replaced me would follow in my footsteps, kill the Vampaneze Lord and die in the battle, and out of that death peace would hopefully grow. Since the child wouldn't be responsible for his actions, his soul should go straight to Paradise when he died — the universe, I hoped, was harsh but fair.

And maybe it wouldn't even be a boy. Perhaps I'd be replaced by a girl! The new Darren Shan didn't have to be an exact replica of the old one. He or she could come from any background or country. All the child needed was a strong sense of curiosity and a slightly disobedient streak. Anyone with the nerve to sneak out late at night and go see the Cirque Du Freak had the potential to take my place as Mr Crepsley's assistant.

Since my part would change, the parts of others could change too. Maybe another girl – or boy – would fill Debbie's role, and somebody else could be Sam Grest. Perhaps Gavner Purl wouldn't be the vampire who was killed by Kurda, and even Steve could be replaced by another. Maybe Mr Crepsley wouldn't be the one to die in the Cavern of Retribution, and would live to be a vampire of ancient years and wisdom, like his mentor, Seba Nile. Many of the parts in the story – the saga – of my life might be up for grabs now that the central character had been changed.

But that was all wild speculation. What I did know for certain was that the boy I'd once been would now lead a normal life. He'd go to school, grow up like anybody else, get a job, maybe raise a family of his own one day. All the things the original Darren Shan had missed out on, the new Darren would enjoy. I'd given him his freedom — his humanity. I could only pray to the gods of the vampires that he made the most of it.

The objects stitched into the lining of my robes were my diaries. I'd kept a diary just about as long as I could remember. I'd recorded everything in it — my trip to the Cirque Du Freak, becoming Mr Crepsley's assistant, my time in Vampire Mountain, the War of the Scars and hunt for the Vampaneze Lord, right up to that final night when I'd had my fatal last run-in with Steve. It was all there, everything important from my life, along with lots of trivial stuff too.

Evanna had brought the diary up to date. She must have taken it from the house where Debbie and Alice were based, then described all that had happened on that blood-drenched night, the showdown with Steve and my death. She'd then briefly outlined my long years of mental suffering in the Lake of Souls, followed by a more detailed account of my rescue and rebirth as a Little Person. She'd even gone beyond that, and told what happened next, my return, the way I'd scared the original Darren away, and...

I don't know what she wrote in the last few pages. I didn't read that far. I'd rather find out for myself what my final actions and thoughts are — not read about them in a book!

After Steve left and Mr Crepsley retired to the cellar where his coffin was stored, I went in search of Mr Tall. I found him in his van, going over the night's receipts. He used to do that regularly. I think he enjoyed the normality of the simple task. I knocked on the door and waited for him to answer.

"What do you want?" he asked suspiciously when he saw me. Mr Tall wasn't used to being surprised, certainly not by a Little Person.

I held the diaries out to him. He looked at them warily, not touching them.

"Is this a message from Desmond?" he asked. I shook my neck-less head. "Then what...?" His eyes widened. "No!" he gasped. "It can't be!" He pushed my hood back — I'd replaced it after I'd scared off the young me — and studied my features fiercely.

After a while Mr Tall's look of concern was replaced by a smile. "Is this my sister's work?" he enquired. I nodded my chunky head a fraction. "I never thought she'd get involved," he murmured. "I imagine there's more to it than just freeing your soul, but I won't press you for information — better for all concerned if I don't know."

I raised the diaries, wanting him to take them, but Mr Tall still didn't touch them. "I'm not sure I understand," he said.

I pointed to the name — Darren Shan — scrawled across the front of the top copy, then to myself. Opening it, I let him see the date and the first few lines, then flicked forward to where it described my visit to the Cirque Du Freak and what had happened. When he'd read the part where I told about watching Steve from the balcony, I pointed up and shook my head hard.

"Oh," Mr Tall chuckled. "I see. Evanna not only saved your soul — she gave the old you his normal life back."

I smiled, pleased he finally understood. I closed the diary, tapped the cover, then offered the books to him again. This time he took them.

"Your plan is clear to me now," he said softly. "You want the world to know of this, but not yet. You are right — to reveal it now would be to risk unleashing the hounds of chaos. But if it's released later, around the time when you died, it could affect only the present and the future."

Mr Tall's hands moved very swiftly and the diaries disappeared. "I will keep them safe until the time is right," he said. "Then I will send them to ... who? An author? A publisher? The person you have become?"

I nodded quickly when he said that.

"Very well," he said. "I cannot say what he will do with these — he might consider them a hoax, or not understand what you want of him — but I'll do as you request." He started to close the door, then paused. "In this time, of course, I do not know you, and now that you have removed yourself from your original timeline, I never shall. But I sense we were friends." He put out a hand and we shook. Mr Tall only very rarely shook hands. "Good luck to you, friend," he whispered. "Good luck to us all." Then he quickly broke contact and closed the door, leaving me to retire, find a nice quiet spot where I could be alone — and die.

I now know why Evanna commented on Mr Tiny not being a reader. He has nothing to do with books. He doesn't pay attention to novels or other works of fiction. If, many years from now, an adult Darren Shan comes along and publishes a series of books about vampires, Mr Tiny won't know about it. His attention will be focused elsewhere. The books will come out and be read, and even though vampires aren't avid readers, word will surely trickle back to them.

As the War of the Scars comes to a wary pause and leaders on both sides try to forge a new era of peace, my diaries will — with the luck of the vampires — hit book shops around the world. Vampires and vampaneze will be able to read my story (or have it read to them if they're illiterate). They'll discover more about Mr Tiny than they ever imagined. They'll see precisely how much of a meddler he really is, and learn of his plans for a desolate future world. Armed with that knowledge, and united by the birth of Evanna's children, I'm certain they'll band together and do all they can to stop him.

Mr Tall will send my diaries to the grown Darren Shan. I don't imagine he'll add any notes or instructions of his own — he dare not meddle with the past in that way. It's possible the adult me will dismiss the diaries, write them off as a bizarre con job, and do nothing with them. But knowing me the way I do (now *that* sounds weird!), I think, once he's read them, he'll take them at face value. I like to believe I always had an open mind.

If the adult me reads the diaries all the way to the end, and believes they're real, he'll know what to do. Rewrite them, fiddle with the names so as not to draw unwelcome attention to the real people involved, rework the facts into a story, cut out the duller entries, fictionalize it a bit, create an action-packed adventure. And then, when he's done all that — sell it! Find an agent and publisher. Pretend it's a work of fantasy. Get it published. Promote it hard. Sell it to as many countries as he can, to spread the word and increase the chances of the story capturing the attention of vampires and vampaneze.

Am I being realistic? There's a big difference between a diary and a novel. Will the human Darren Shan have the ability to draw readers in and spin a tale which keeps them hooked? Will he be able to write a series of novels strong enough to attract the attention of the children of the night? I don't know. I was pretty good at writing stories when I was younger, but there's no way of knowing what I'll be like when I grow up. Maybe I won't read any more. Maybe I won't want to or be able to write.

But I've got to hope for the best. Freed from his dark destiny, I've got to hope the young me keeps on reading and writing. If the luck of the vampires is really with me (with *us*) maybe that Darren will become a writer even before Mr Tall sends the package to him. That would be perfect, if he was already an author. He could put the story of my life out as just another of his imaginative works, then get on with writing his own stuff, and nobody — except those actually involved in the War of the Scars — would ever know the difference.

Maybe I'm just dreaming. But it *could* happen. I'm proof that stranger things have taken place. So I say: Go for it, Darren! Follow your dreams. Take your ideas and run with them. Work hard. Learn to write well. I'll be waiting for you up ahead if you do, with the weirdest, twistiest story you've ever heard. Words have the power to alter the future and change the world. I think, together, we can find the right words. I can even, now that I think about it, suggest a first line for the book, to start you out on the long and winding road, perhaps something along the lines of, "I've always been fascinated by spiders..."

CHAPTER TWENTY

I'm on the roof of the old cinema, lying on my back, studying the beautiful sky. Dawn is close. Thin clouds drift slowly across the lightening horizon. I can feel myself coming undone. It won't be much longer now.

I'm not one hundred per cent sure how Mr Tiny's resurrection process works, but I think I understand enough of it to know what's going on. Harkat was created from the remains of Kurda Smahlt. Mr Tiny took Kurda's corpse and used it to create a Little Person. He then returned Harkat to the past. Harkat and Kurda shouldn't have been able to exist simultaneously. A soul can't normally share two bodies at the same time. One should have given way for the other. As the original, Kurda had the automatic right to life, so Harkat's body should have started to unravel, as it did when Kurda was fished out of the Lake of Souls all those years later.

But it didn't. Harkat survived for several years in the same time zone as Kurda. That makes me assume that Mr Tiny has the power to protect his Little People, at least for a while, even if he sends them back to a time when their original forms are still alive.

But he didn't bother to protect *me* when he sent me back. So one of the bodies has to go — this one. But I'm not moaning. I'm OK with my brief spell as a Little Person. In fact, the shortness of this life is the whole point! It's how Evanna has freed me.

When Kurda was facing death for the second time, Mr Tiny told him that his spirit wouldn't return to the Lake — it would depart this realm. By dying now, my soul – like Kurda's – will fly immediately to Paradise. I suppose it's a bit like not passing "Go" on a Monopoly board and going straight to jail, except in this case "Go" is the Lake of Souls and "jail" is the afterlife.

I feel exceptionally light, as though I weigh almost nothing. The sensation is increasing by the moment. My body's fading away, dissolving. But not like in the green pool of liquid in Mr Tiny's cave. This is a gentle, painless dissolve, as though some great force is unstitching me, using a pair of magical knitting needles to pick my flesh and bones apart, strand by strand, knot by knot.

What will Paradise be like? I can't answer that one. I can't even hazard a guess. I imagine it's a timeless place, where the dead souls of every age mingle as one, renewing old friendships and making new acquaintances. Space doesn't exist, not even bodies, just thoughts and imagination. But I have no proof of that. It's just what I picture it to be.

I summon what little energy I have left and raise a hand. I can see through the grey flesh now, through the muscles and bones, to the twinkle of the stars beyond. I smile and the corners of my lips continue stretching, off my face, becoming a limitless, endless smile.

My robes sag as the body beneath loses the ability to support them. Atoms rise from me like steam, thin tendrils at first, then a steady stream of shafts which are all the colours of the rainbow, my soul departing from every area of my body at once. The tendrils wrap around one another and shoot upwards, bound for the stars and realms beyond.

There's almost nothing left of me now. The robes collapse in on themselves completely. The last traces of my spirit hover above the robes and the roof. I think of my family, Debbie, Mr Crepsley, Steve, Mr Tiny, all those I've known, loved, feared and hated. My last thought, oddly, is of Madam Octa — I wonder if they have spiders in Paradise?

And now it's over. I'm finished with this world. My final few atoms rise at a speed faster than light, leaving the roof, the theatre, the town, the world, far, far behind. I'm heading for a new universe, new adventures, a new way of being. Farewell world! Goodbye Darren Shan! So long old friends and allies! This is it! The stars draw me towards them. Explosions of space and time. Breaking through the barriers of the old reality. Coming apart, coming together, moving on. A breath on the lips of the universe. All things, all worlds, all lives. Everything at once and never. Mr Crepsley waiting. Laughter in the great beyond. I'm going … I'm … going … I'm … gone.

THE END

THE SAGA OF DARREN SHAN
MAY 8TH 1997 – MAY 19TH 2004